PENGUIN BO

A Party in San Niccolò

Christobel Kent was born in London in 1962 and now lives in Cambridge with her husband and four children; in between she has lived in Modena, in northern Italy, and in Florence. *A Party in San Niccolò* is her first book.

A Party in San Niccolò

CHRISTOBEL KENT

PENGUIN BOOKS

PENGUIN BOOKS

Published by the Penguin Group
Penguin Books Ltd, 80 Strand, London WC2R ORL, England
Penguin Putnam Inc., 375 Hudson Street, New York, New York 10014, USA
Penguin Books Australia Ltd, 250 Camberwell Road,
Camberwell, Victoria 3124, Australia
Penguin Books Canada Ltd, 10 Alcorn Avenue, Toronto, Ontario, Canada M4V 3B2
Penguin Books India (P) Ltd, 11, Community Centre,
Panchsheel Park, New Delhi – 110 017, India
Penguin Books (NZ) Ltd, Cnr Rosedale and Airborne Roads,
Albany, Auckland, New Zealand
Penguin Books (South Africa) (Pty) Ltd, 24 Sturdee Avenue,
Rosebank 2196, South Africa

Penguin Books Ltd, Registered Offices: 80 Strand, London WC2R ORL, England

www.penguin.com

First published 2003

1

Copyright © Christobel Kent, 2003
Map copyright © Andrew Farmer, 2003
All rights reserved

The moral right of the author has been asserted

Set in 11/13 pt Monotype Dante
Typeset by Rowland Phototypesetting Ltd, Bury St Edmunds, Suffolk
Printed in England by Clays Ltd, St Ives plc

To my father

Acknowledgements

I would like to thank my agent, Laura Morris, my editor, Harriet Evans, my friends Richard Beswick and Ilsa Yardley and my husband, for their criticism, their patient encouragement and their kindness.

For their unfailing friendship and hospitality I must also thank those Florentines, native and adoptive, who shared their beautiful city with me: Camilla Baines, Rossella Concistoro, Helen and Pasquale Glave and Leonardo Ferrali.

Author's Note

In writing *A Party in San Niccolò* I have tried, as far as possible, to be true to the geography of Florence. The street names and locations in the city that I have described are, therefore, for the most part real, the only significant exception being the Vicolo degli Innocenti, which does not exist. The characters, however, are entirely fictional, and therefore bear no relation to the actual inhabitants of the addresses I have given them in this novel. Any resemblance to real persons, living or dead, is entirely coincidental.

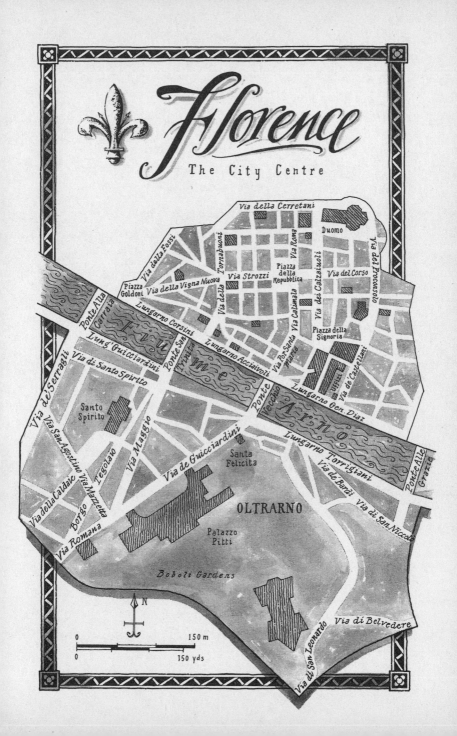

Monday

I

As the S223, fast, narrow and dangerous, curves south out of Siena and down towards the sea, it leaves the rounded, painterly contours of Chianti behind, for something altogether darker and more mountainous. The neon-lit bar of a truck stop carved out of the red earth marks the transition, then the road dips. Velvety black hills, densely forested with holm-oak, juniper and myrtle, rise up to enclose it and almost all signs of human habitation disappear; there are none of the stone villas surrounded by cypresses that colonize the landscape between Siena and Florence; no terraces of olives nor carefully tended vineyards. Here begins the part of southern Tuscany known as the Maremma: barely inhabited, uncultivated, shunned for its malarial swamps since the departure of the Romans and threaded through with pungent, sulphurous springs.

The road climbs, then, as a huge valley opens up ahead, becomes a bridge, two miles long and hundreds of feet above the valley floor. The river winds through stripped cork trees, willow and hazel thickets, and only occasionally the roof of a dilapidated farm building can be glimpsed through the vegetation. As the bridge is reunited with the valley's steep far side, it widens to include one of the lay-bys to be found every couple of miles between Siena and Grosseto. This May morning, at about seven o'clock, there is still dew on the scrubby grass and stunted wild flowers bordering the lay-by, and on the miscellaneous debris scattered on the gravel: crumpled cans, condoms, cigarette butts, a piece of newspaper smeared with dirt. The lay-by is enclosed by a thick, tangled hedge; behind the hedge the mountainside falls back steeply down to the

3

river. Set near the hedge, midway along the lay-by, facing out towards the road, is what appears to be a carefully composed tableau: a small, collapsible stool and, resting against it, a large, opened golf umbrella, alternating pink and purple. In front of the stool, on the ground, is one teetering, cork-soled, plastic-strapped platform sandal, and behind the stool, at the mouth of a low tunnel through the undergrowth, is the other, on its side as though its owner had just stumbled out of it.

In a dark Florentine backstreet just before dawn the insistent metallic judder of an alarm starts up. A not-unfamiliar addition to the city's street noise, it seems at first to go unheeded, although at this hour it rings strident in the silent, apparently empty streets. But then a man appears at the top of a dark, carpeted stairway above the endlessly ringing bell and descends towards the source of the sound.

The stairway ends in a long narrow room, windowed at either end, one window barred by an expanding metal shutter, the other, which is smaller and apparently had no such protection, has been smashed, a jagged hole about four feet in diameter gaping in it at waist height. The man moves towards it through the room, which in the dim grey light harbours all manner of strange shapes. Quickening his pace he passes a carved throne, a marble nymph, her hands in her hair; the spread wings of a stuffed bird of prey, its feathers furred with dust, loom over him out of the darkness. In front of the broken window stands a little yellow silk divan, and there he stops, the sound of the alarm bell vibrating in the room around him, and looks down.

The girl is spreadeagled on her back in a shower of broken glass, her arms flung back over her head; one hand, dangling from the divan and still just perceptibly in motion, almost touches the floor. A crumpled silk camisole is pulled up to expose the girl's flat belly, its navel torn and bleeding where a

4

stud has been torn out by some violent struggle, and the first signs of massive bruising are beginning to appear on the vulnerable flesh. Her long slender arm is pale, but her neck is livid with the signs of profound trauma, her face bluish in the uncertain light and her open eyes pools of black. He kneels at her head and places his ear to her mouth, then jerks it back as though burnt when his skin comes into contact with her own, which is very cold, and as her pale face comes out of the shadow cast by his head, he sees that the whites of her eyes are suffused with blood from tiny haemorrhages. He moves back from her towards a switch on the wall beside an old-fashioned desk. Abruptly the alarm stops, no more than five minutes after it had begun, and in the sudden, resounding silence that follows, the ghost of a laugh, a distant skittering of footsteps on the flagstones echo from somewhere down the labyrinth of darkened streets. He reaches for the phone.

Frances Richardson opened her eyes and thought, as she had thought on waking for the thirteen years since her husband's death, *Still here*. She turned her head to the side, looking at the photograph in a tarnished silver frame that rested on a small oak table by the bed, and felt the small, secret pang of irritation she always felt on considering Roland; alive, he had presented her with many and varied reasons to be angry with him, and now he annoyed her only by the obstinate, unchanging definiteness of his absence. Frances looked up at the faded garlands and roses of the fresco on the vaulted ceiling of her tiny bedroom and through its door into her dark drawing room, where sunlight filtered through the slits in the three tall sets of arched shutters, laid her head back on her pillow, closed her eyes and smiled.

Outside, in the narrow street, *motorini* buzzed past, their high-pitched whines amplified by the height of the stone *palazzi* lining the Via delle Caldaie. Frances could hear Liliana setting up crates outside her shop, chiding her husband, Gianni, as he unloaded his tiny three-wheeled van. Slowly, carefully – *How did I get so* old *suddenly*, she thought – Frances stood up and went to the window, opening the peeling shutters wide. Hearing the creak and clang, Liliana looked up and smiled. *Buon compleanno, Signora Frances*, she called. *Happy birthday*. Frances made a rueful face, and shrugged. Still here, after all. She turned to look inwards, into the dark room, the sun warming her back, and contemplated with satisfaction the prospect of a day spent engaged in the final organization of her party.

Frances's birthday party was an event of some significance in the Florentine social calendar. Although she was not rich, she owned her apartment, which was large by the city's standards, and she lived fairly quietly for most of the year. She ate out only modestly and infrequently, and, when she needed to escape the intense, suffocating heat of July and August, would take the train down to stay with friends in Cortona, high above the Val di Chiana, where occasionally a breeze would blow some freshness through the narrow streets, and where there were friendly swimming pools to be borrowed on the outskirts of the old town.

She rarely stayed for more than a day or two, unwilling to surrender her independence and disciplined in her determination not to outstay her welcome, but in this way the income she received from Roland's pension, combined with the rent from the English house, kept her quite happily and permitted her, every year, to throw her party. It was keenly anticipated and much discussed by Frances's guests, an assortment of new and old friends, exiles, expatriates and hangers-on, always with the addition of a small number of people she did not know at all but who happened to have drifted into town at the right time and in the right person's wake.

Three doors along, one floor down and on the opposite,

and less desirable, side of the Via delle Caldaie, a man stood at his own open window, his square, blunt-nailed hands resting on the windowsill and a thoughtful frown on his broad face as he listened to the exchange between Liliana and Frances, Lady Richardson. Frank Sutton leant a little way out of his window, far enough to see Frances's back and her neat, silvery-white head gleaming in the sun while still remaining concealed by shadow himself. In his hands he held an invitation, printed in black on heavy cream card, to Frances's party, which, according to the heavy script, was to be held the following Friday at the Casa Ferrali.

In previous years Frances's parties had been held in her apartment on the Via delle Caldaie, an opportunity for the Florentines and the expatriate community alike to inhale the atmosphere of English bohemia at its most civilized: old velvet, the faded lustre of Georgian silver and glass, the mingling scents of Moroccan patchouli, musk-roses and gardenia, Frances's bookshelves declaring her foreignness in shabby old editions of Yeats and Blake, Aphra Behn and George Eliot. But this year, it seemed, things were going to be different; this year Frances would be celebrating at the heart of the Italian city, in the gardens and on the *piano nobile* of a great house that had for 400 years been in the hands of the same Florentine family and was now inhabited by Frances's old friend Nino Ferrali and his wife, Lucienne.

Frank Sutton had been a regular guest at Frances's birthday parties since his first year in Florence, ten years ago; her radar had managed to pick him up only three months after his arrival. He had been only a stringer then, interviewing poets and architects more in hope than expectation of ever being published, it seemed, and covering the occasional beatification in Rome. Had he been ambitious he would have gone to live down there, and there were plenty of Frances's friends who wondered why she bothered to go on inviting him, a failure, or at least an oddity, still marooned in this backwater after ten years.

He turned back inside and stood as if in contemplation of the crowded interior of his own flat. On the bed a small, battered, old-fashioned suitcase sat open, either in the process of being packed or unpacked, probably, on balance the latter as most of its contents seemed crushed and grubby. Towers of books and papers climbed precariously up the walls, crates of wine and water occupied the space beneath his desk, yesterday's clothes and a dressing-gown lay in the doorway, books lay open on the floor and a round metal tray from the bar below with a sticky espresso cup, crumbs and a twist of paper napkin sat at the foot of his bed. The only calm and ordered space was occupied by his work table, next to the far window, a laptop computer open and already humming on its surface. Frank looked thoughtfully at the computer for a moment or two, then picked his way through the debris towards a darkened hallway.

A few moments later Sutton appeared in the street below, emerging from the massive, studded front door to his building. He threaded his way through the market stalls to the newspaper stand in the Piazza Santo Spirito to collect a fat bundle of Italian papers, returned to the Via delle Caldaie, and turned into the Caffè Medici. Although, technically, Frank Sutton's flat had a kitchen (consisting, as Frances had witnessed, of an ancient fridge which administered an electric kick like a cattle prod if the occasional visitor made the mistake of touching it and the tap at the same time, and a single ring of the kind usually supplied in camper vans), he had never been known to use it; and he was generally to be observed in the Medici around mealtimes, chewing thoughtfully on a brioche or a dried-up *tramezzino*, apparently as unconcerned about his diet as he was about his appearance.

2

The sandals lying beside the busy road belong to Evelina; they are only three weeks old, and are two sizes too big for her, but she doesn't need them any more. Evelina is caught between two rocks several hundred feet below her sandals, bent in half at the waist like a doll. Her head is down; she has been dead for several hours now and her body is stiffening into this awkward position. It is not immediately apparent what killed Evelina, although there is plenty of evidence of injury. It could have been the fall; her face looks caved in above the left eye where it rests against the rock, partly hidden by the stiff sheaf of her hair, gleaming with hairspray and coarse from straightening. Her head is tilted oddly sideways as though her neck might be broken; the one visible eye is barely closed, and a sliver of white gleams dully below the heavy dark lid, and, while in her left ear the gleam of a big gold hoop is visible, the right is unadorned, its pierced hole ripped and crusted with blood. Her gleaming dark legs, long in proportion to her child's body and fully exposed by her tiny shorts, are scratched and grazed all along their length, and there is a deep laceration over her instep. Her toenails are painted with glitter polish, and the soles of her feet are cut and bloody.

Evelina is wearing her favourite purple halter top; the girls often fight over the bin bags of clothes, seconds from the market, that Betty brings for them to wear, and Evelina was pleased to get this one – Glory wanted it, but Betty, who always had the last word, let Evelina have it in the end, because she was the youngest. It is hard to say when her body will be found; there is no one to register her as missing, unless you count Betty, or the man Betty sent to collect the girls, neither of whom, all things considered, is much of a prospect, and she isn't near any of the paths through the Maremma's dark scrub – known as *macchia*, which means 'stain' – used by those who intermittently tend the land. Evelina is fourteen, which is young to die, even for a girl from Nigeria, where, had she remained in her village, she could have expected to live for another thirty-seven years.

Three doors down from Frank Sutton's flat, the Caffè Medici was a good local; it was Frances's, too. It was not ostentatious, but was a step up from basic, having a couple of tables and some booths, such as the one Frank was occupying, for extra discretion, and regulars who took tables were charged only bar prices rather than the hefty surcharge generally levied on tourists for the privilege. From the beginning of May, three or four tables and some potted jasmine would be squeezed between the pavement and the traffic and you could sit outside, if you didn't mind the noise and the fumes and the delivery vans edging past. The Via delle Caldaie was little more than an alley, mostly used by locals cutting through from the Via Romana to Santo Spirito, at the outer edge of the tourist centre of Florence. The Medici was handy for the Annalena Gate – the back entrance to the Boboli Gardens – and was just visible to anyone emerging from the lovely, austere façade of Santo Spirito, Brunelleschi's last, unfinished church, so the place managed to catch a bit of tourist trade.

Although the Medici was just a little backstreet café, its bar was marble, the mirrors were polished and you could buy five different single malts, as well as the usual Italian *digestivi*: Unicum, Cynara and Vecchia Romagna. Massi, senior barman and the owner's son, could quote from Dante and Boccaccio, collected fresh brioches from the *pasticceria* every morning and always wore a clean, ironed shirt, in summer changing into a fresh one after lunch, his sleeves carefully rolled to just below the elbow. He knew how to mix Negronis, Manhattans and a dry Martini, and you could even get a glass of champagne, though Frances didn't know how much you'd have to pay for it.

Frances was well aware that in England no such place was available to her; pubs were not for elderly ladies with cut-glass vowels, however open-minded or outgoing those ladies might be. The easy intimacy of her place at the marble bar of the Medici, exchanging a few friendly words with Massi or with her neighbours, having a cappuccino on her way to market or an aperitif as the sun left the piazza, suited her so perfectly that every day she gave thanks for its unassuming presence in her life, so far from the oppressive, maudlin misogyny, the flashing lights and aggressive adolescent clientele of the village pub, or the toe-curling gentility and lace-curtained fug of a provincial tearoom. This was why Frances loved living abroad; she fitted into no class here, she was treated with courtesy because of her age and not her social position and she was permitted to chat gravely at the bar with whoever might be standing next to her, without fear of being thought condescending.

This morning the bar was almost empty; by the time Frances walked in it was long past the eight-thirty rush-hour, when most of the southern suburbs seemed to be in there, Piaggios and Vespas triple-parked outside while their owners swallowed cappuccino and pastries in five minutes flat on their way to work. Frances leant happily on the polished marble and smiled at Massi as he acknowledged her arrival with a friendly nod. She looked around the small, brightly lit room and could see the back of Frank Sutton's head as he sat at a table in the corner, bent in concentration over a newspaper. He was often in here; what had always seemed to her a rather pleasantly undemanding part of the foreign correspondent's job was a morning spent examining the Italian newspapers in search of titbits of interest to the British public. Not for the first time she wondered about Frank, so determinedly solitary, it seemed, and she decided not to disturb him. Massi set Frances's little cup of coffee down on the bar in front of her and she reached down the shining length of the marble counter for the sugar dispenser.

At the far end of the bar, drinking orangeade, was a tall black girl she vaguely recognized – Betty? – usually in here in the evenings, when the clientele could get a lot rougher; Frances herself rarely came in after seven or eight, only occasionally in search of bottled water, or wine to take to dinner. Betty's nose was pierced, with a tiny gold ring through one nostril, and her face was scarred. She wore orange pedal-pushers, tight over her round, muscular bottom, thrust up and out by the pitch of her fraying raffia-soled platforms. She turned to look at Frances scornfully, and Frances looked back unafraid, smiling in admiration at the fierceness in her gaze. She sipped her coffee. The girl turned back to Massi.

'So you don't know where Evelina's got to?' he was asking her.

Betty shook her head angrily. 'Just disappeared. Left my shoes behind, though. The driver, he shouted for her but she didn't come, so he went. She'll turn up, one way or another.' Massi nodded without much conviction, and Betty looked back at him without expression. She shrugged, and turned to look out at the street.

The girl's Italian was good, though overlaid with a thick African accent, and Frances, listening, thought she had probably been in the city for some time. The Nigerian immigrants to Florence in particular and Italy in general were mostly illegal; many of them, it was obvious even to Frances, trafficked in prostitution, or, in the case of the men, were lured across the Mediterranean to sell the knock-off handbags they hauled about the main tourist sites in grubby tablecloths, always ready to gather them up and trudge away when the *carabinieri* approached. The prostitutes and street hawkers lived in obscure, ill-lit and badly policed parts of town, squeezed into dangerously converted, overcrowded and windowless flats, controlled by some mysterious and sinister power and largely distrusted and ostracized by the locals. Some lived here, in the shabbier parts of the Oltrarno, perhaps for easy access to the tourist roads to the south, perhaps because it had its own particular atmosphere, Frances thought, of lazy tolerance, although that might have been her benign imagination.

'Seen Stefano, then?' Massi said to Betty, as she turned away from him. Out of the corner of her eye Frances saw Frank's head straighten as he looked up from his paper. The girl turned back, suddenly alert.

'Why?'

Massi shrugged. 'He was looking for you last night. Owe him money, do you?'

'Owe him money? No way; I don't buy what he's selling. He owes me, more like, I gave him stuff to sell a month ago. I'll smash his face in when I see him.' She sniffed, and drained her glass of sticky orange dregs.

Massi shook his head, and exchanged a glance with Frances. Both of them knew the man – everyone knew Stefano. The girl's attempt at bravado sounded hollow and neither of them were convinced, Frances felt.

The first time Frances had seen Stefano, years ago now, he was sitting on his bench in the Piazza Santo Spirito, probably, although she couldn't have said how soon after her arrival in Florence he had found a place on her map of the city's inhabitants. She had been struck then by how handsome he was. Tall, for an Italian, something over six foot, she thought (instinctively measuring him, as she tended to measure men, against Roland in his prime). Stefano had thick white hair almost to his shoulders, smooth dark skin and the profile and bearing of a Roman emperor, or perhaps a Cherokee. There was something noble about him, hawklike, and his eyes were deep-set and a surprising clear light blue.

Stefano wasn't flashy – his clothes were good, but old – and he never seemed aggressive; on the contrary, he had a mild, gentle manner that somehow gave him more presence as he sat like any other itinerant on his bench, nodding and smiling and speaking softly to the assortment of derelicts and drop-outs and the addicts, twitching with nervous anticipation, who would gather around him. So when Frances eventually learnt, somehow – through Frank? – that Stefano was not a kind of gutter saint but was a dealer and a career criminal it disturbed her, that her instincts could have betrayed her. It was an early and instructive example to her of her romantic foreigner's tendency – a tendency she refused quite to surrender – to assume that the natural physical ease and good taste she so often observed among the Italian people were signs of moral worth, rather than lovely habits learnt over centuries, accidents of birth.

Frances wondered, now, what Stefano was doing with the Nigerian girls. There seemed to be few kinds of criminal activity in the city he wasn't somehow engaged in, and she had always had a feeling that he had some involvement with prostitution. She had seen him with an Eastern European girl, whom she'd initially thought might have been a girlfriend but who turned out to be something else; a dark-eyed girl with her head bowed, Stefano's hand clamped too tightly on her wrist. But not an African girl; the Nigerians seemed to keep themselves to themselves. Most likely Betty owed him some money, presumably for drugs, and he was getting it back in the usual way.

With one last look at Betty, who was leaning forward with her backside thrust out, elbows on the bar, her chin cupped in her hands and frowning in concentration, Frances pushed a pile of coins over to Massi to pay for her coffee, picked up her shopping and turned to the door.

Frances had come to live in the Oltrarno, the part of Florence that lies south of the river, after Roland's death. A largely working-class district, tucked in between the Arno and the city's thick mediaeval walls, it was quite unlike the cool luxury and seething tourist boulevards north of the river, where everything seemed to converge on the great dome of the cathedral and the tide of visitors surged and eddied around the huge green-and-white edifice.

Crossing the river to the south, over the mediaeval clutter of the Ponte Vecchio or the graceful span of the Ponte Santo Trínita, the atmosphere of the city relaxed. Warm, noisy and dirty, the narrow streets were full of workshops: upholsterers, ironmongers, people making leather boxes, or faking 'antique' gold frames for the foreigners. *Contadini* – peasant farmers whose patiently tended smallholdings and crumbling farmhouses still co-existed with apartment blocks in the Florentine suburbs – brought irises and heaps of bitter salad leaves from their gardens to the market in the Piazza Santo Spirito, and loud arguments spilt out of kitchen windows in the evenings. And, although Frances had never before lived in a working-class district anywhere, to her the Oltrarno felt like home. She was treated with friendly generosity and accorded respect; and even though she was embedded safely in the city, if she looked down to the south she could see hills, and straggling, neglected terraces of arthritic old olive trees, all that remained of the ancient estates of Arcetri and Galluzzo. Slanting across the horizon and visible from almost every corner of the Oltrarno was the great cypress avenue that formed the broad spine of the Boboli, backlit on summer evenings by the crackle and flare of thunderstorms.

After those two months in the cottage waiting for Roland

to die, trapped in the damp and the rain, Roland getting out of bed later every day until finally he would only move from the bed to his chair by the smoky little fire at teatime then not at all, Frances had taken him back to London. She would not bury him in the local church – Norman, rather pretty and the reason they had ended up in the village, Roland's father being buried there – but in a crowded churchyard in Soho, where bodies were probably stacked on bodies. She liked to think of him there, where he had been happy, his laughing handsome face at Muriel's, at the French House, drinking ouzo at Jimmy's. It would have infuriated her to think of him out in the sticks, in the village now clustered around with 'executive homes', the little shop selling stale salami and Happy Shopper washing powder, with its 'Do not ask for credit, as a refusal may offend' propped on the shelf behind the till.

Alone and bereft, huddled in the gloom beneath the cottage's low ceiling, as rain dripped from the eaves in the wettest spring since records began, Frances had felt herself on the verge of despair, something she had never before felt in her life. She didn't want visitors any more, stopped wanting to get out of bed in the morning or, in fact, to wake up at all. She spent three weeks looking from Roland's chair to her sodden garden, and finally she understood that she would have to leave.

She had put the house up for rent and decided to go, just for a week or two, to Florence. She had first visited the city as a sixteen-year-old in the summer of 1938, sent by her parents to learn about Leonardo, the Sienese masters, Galileo and the Renaissance. She had been a paying guest at the Casa Ferrali in the part of the Oltrarno known as San Niccolò, which was named after the pretty church that stood at its centre. The Casa Ferrali was one of the patrician houses that stood at the tail-end of the Via de' Bardi, a broad street of decaying palaces built by the great families of Florence who followed the Medici when they acquired the Pitti Palace and moved south of the river.

More than forty-five years on, after the funeral, Frances telephoned Nino Ferrali, the family's only son and her companion and chaperone for that long-ago summer. Frances's friendship with Nino had survived largely unaltered since their first meeting, in part because Nino and Roland had, against all predictions, immediately found each other amusing and sympathetic, but also because Nino had married Lucienne, Frances's best friend. Frances had known Lucienne since 1949, two years after her marriage to Roland, when they had been posted to Paris. She had been studying fine art, and subsidising herself by making intricate, miniature sculptures out of wire and copper scrap and selling them in Montmartre. Frances loved Lucienne, and here in Florence she particularly relished Lucienne's eccentricity, which far outclassed anything a mere Englishwoman could manage. Roland had introduced Nino to Lucienne, rather reluctantly, never imagining that the rather serious and impoverished son of the Florentine nobility would worship her on sight and spend the rest of his life following her admiringly, as she strode ahead, gesturing, pointing the world out to him. Now Lucienne and Nino, the odd couple, lived in peaceable companionship in the old house by the Arno in the winter, in Cortona in the summer, and they still made some money by permitting weddings in the grand first-floor apartments and the gardens, orchestrated by Lucienne. It had taken Frances less than a week with them, a week of listening to their constant gentle bickering as she rested in the sun on the wide balcony of the *piano nobile*, tendrils of wisteria curling at her feet, to decide that she didn't have to go back.

Frances loved her flat; it had been a piece of luck finding it, or so she had been assured by Nino, as good-sized apartments in Florence were a rarity now that the Italian birth rate was in dramatic decline and the average family could fit into a space half the size of Frances's. It had five long, arched windows in all looking on to the Via delle Caldaie; one was at the end of the long, narrow kitchen, three in the huge *salone*, and the fifth in the little bedroom, almost like a monk's cell had it not been for the extravagantly painted ceiling, leading off the *salone*. Frances's kitchen was primitive, with a couple of electric rings, a cracked sink and a small fridge, but the sun flooded it every morning, and to sit, bathed in light and warmth at her table in the window, observing the activity of the street below and occasionally also the apartment opposite, was one of the first of many daily reminders of how happy she was to be here, and not back in England. The bathroom had been installed in the thirties and remained untouched since, covered with chipped, pale-green tiling, a rusty bath and only a tiny curtained window looking on a narrow internal lightwell, but Frances couldn't have cared less. To begin with she had thought she would have liked a balcony of her own to bask on, but after a year or two of more sun than she knew what to do with she came, like the Florentines, to prize the dim cool of her drawing room, and the sensation that came with it that she was no longer a tourist, but was becoming a native.

At the small wooden table – room for only two chairs – in her kitchen, pushed right up against the window which, today, was open, Frances piled the fruit she'd bought at the market into a green bowl. She sat down to drink the second – the first, for social reasons, always taken in the Medici – of the two large cups of milky coffee she drank every day for break-fast, even though her doctor had advised her that the human digestive system is unable to digest cow's milk once the human in question is more than three years old. She did not believe him, but she did, firmly, believe in living one's life by certain rituals, and her daily two cups of coffee constituted the first of these.

Today, her seventy-fifth birthday, Frances would have lunch

with Lucienne and Nino. As she leant from her window, Frances could see them, slowly making their way up from the Via Maggio where, she knew, they would have been window-shopping among the gilded Renaissance mirrors and salon chairs. Tiny, tanned and wrinkled, like a little jewelled monkey, Lucienne was wearing an emerald-green tiered silk skirt with a silver mesh belt, a silk singlet, ballet slippers and her wire-rimmed glasses; in her mouth, without even a hint of affectation, was clenched a small clay pipe, like Popeye's. Courtly and amiable, Nino walked a pace or two behind her, dressed in an ancient but perfectly preserved linen suit and carrying Lucienne's bags. Frances smiled as she watched them approach, and thought how lucky she was to have old friends near her, friends to whom her entire history – her girlhood, her marriage, her widowhood – was transparent, to whom she did not need to explain herself, to whom she was the same as she had been nearly fifty years before. And they to her.

3

At four-thirty in South London a clammy grey dawn was breaking. Gina lay at the edge of the extra-large double bed, her eyes suddenly wide open. She didn't know what had woken her; perhaps Stella, lying diagonally across the bed between them, like the central bar of a capital N, had kicked, or muttered, or perhaps it was the same thing that so often woke her in the middle of the night. Gina was afraid of something; anxiety, they'd call it, but she didn't feel anxious, exactly, as she started awake – she felt like something was after her, adrenaline pumping through her as though she'd been running. She craned her neck to look past Stella at

Stephen, his head tilted back, mouth slightly open, and resting on his chest another, smaller head. Not Dan, too. All her fault, though: when they crept in she'd comfort them, soothed by their knack of instant relaxation once in her arms, unwound by the scent of their tangled hair in her nostrils. It would be later, forced into a corner, her head at an awkward angle and her arm gone dead from the weight of the head resting on it, that she would wake up with her heart pounding. Gina looked around at the room's familiarity emerging from the dark, the pale, smooth outlines of a chair, her dressing table, the folds of the undrawn curtains sharpening as the dawn light grew stronger.

There were, of course, the usual things to be afraid of: that her children would find their way into the attic and fall from the cobwebbed window, the only one in the house without a lock; that the bruises on their legs would turn out to be leukaemia; that she would lose sight of Dan or Stella at the swimming pool while they slipped beneath the thrashing legs, trapped on the bottom; that one day she would give in and let Jim go to the rec on his own and a greasy-haired paedophile would talk him into the back of a stinking van. That she would die before the children grew up. And at the back of her mind she stored the unfading memory of everything she had ever done wrong, for which these things might be a punishment. She had always known, you could not escape being told, that motherhood held its terrors; what she had not suspected was that they would be so extreme and so uncontrollable.

Outside the long window she could see the outline of the horse-chestnut emerge as the night faded, a great cumulo-nimbus of a tree with its roots curling through the foundations of a dozen houses in the terrace, its waxy candles of blossom gleaming white. The birdsong had just begun, almost deafening, and with it came some dim echo of childhood awakening, just at the moment when spring tips over into early summer.

At least it was getting light. And today, she remembered belatedly, there was some good in waking up at four-thirty, with the alarm set for five and a plane to catch. She rolled carefully away from Stella and eased herself off the bed.

Downstairs, at the kitchen table in her dressing-gown, Gina laid out cereal bowls, tracked down school bags and swimming things, then went to the back door to sip her tea. The sun was just coming up, and she felt some warmth from it, and caught the scent of the honeysuckle coming over next door's wall, and the musky sweetness of her own, sprawling roses. Even at five she could hear the roar of London's traffic starting up, and she thought of the children's school, deserted now. The other mothers in the school playground never seemed to falter. Talking loudly about soft-play centres, violin lessons, their wedding anniversaries, boasting, as discreetly as they were able, of their children's talents, and coolly appraising other people's. She would stand, patiently – what else could she do? – as Dan kicked her on the ankles and screamed when she told him again that, no, he couldn't go to Jake's house, he hadn't been invited; she could feel their eyes on her and looked straight ahead, unwilling to receive their sympathetic smiles. *Something wrong with that child*, they were thinking, *ADD, autism, dyspraxia, wickedness*; and at the thought that they might be right, her stomach contracted.

Gina Donovan had not had any programme in mind when she had children; she had thought that love would be enough. Actually, while pregnant with Jim, her first child, now ten, she had been afraid that she would not be able to love him when he arrived, not knowing him then; it was only when he was there before her eyes, his slick purple body and swollen red face, wrinkled and folded like a pug's, that her fear unravelled in a miraculous instant and she felt her life begin again. Suddenly brave, she rushed ahead, pregnant with Dan before she stopped to think, then Stella three years after that, building a family around her. She lay beside them as babies, breathing them in, nuzzling them, intoxicated, until they stirred awake. As they grew, however, it seemed that love was not quite all they needed; or perhaps she didn't know how to marshal her love in the right way. Tough love was not what she was good at. She didn't want to say no to them, to order their lives, choose their schools, take them to music group or tumbletots or send them off for French and violin after school. Nonetheless she knuckled under, and wearily forced them to eat their vegetables, did not allow them a second ice-cream, and begged them to turn off the television, but she felt her clearness of purpose diluted by the hundreds of tiny tasks required of her. She felt she had become as severe as her own mother, frowning, always denying them something, mouthing rules. She watched them shrug off her love, saw it washed away in the stream, their lives rushing past her. Even Stella struggled now, when Gina lay down beside her, and she barely saw Jim, rushing off to play war games or Nintendo with his friends after school, asking to be allowed to go out alone on his bike, giving in awkwardly to a kiss goodnight.

Stephen appeared in the kitchen door, and saw her expression.

'Don't look like that.' She could see him subduing his impatience. 'We'll be fine. They'll be at school for most of it; they'll hardly notice the difference.'

I don't suppose they will, thought Gina, but it didn't make her feel any better. *Stop being such a miserable cow*.

'Actually, I'm beginning to look forward to it,' she said with a little effort. 'It's just the flight and everything – you know I always dread the journey, rooting about for my passport at the last minute and that kind of stuff. And I'm a bit nervous about seeing Jane again after all this time. Do you really think she's mellowed? No, no, it'll be lovely, not worrying about them all the time. Are they still asleep?'

'Stella was stirring a bit,' Stephen said. 'They can go to the airport in their pyjamas, can't they? I'll have time to get them dressed when we get back. We don't need to wake them yet.'

But she heard footsteps on the stairs; Jim first, clumping down, beautiful, black-eyed and smooth-skinned, scowling, followed by Dan and Stella, Dan howling as Stella elbowed him, Stella screeching furiously at him to get out of the way.

'No, no, no! *I* want Mummy; she's *my* Mummy; I want her first.'

Gina sighed.

The drive to the airport took less than an hour. At first, as they wound their way through south London, Sydenham Hill, Crystal Palace, South Norwood, rows and rows of peaceful redbrick Edwardian villas behind gaudy cherry trees coming into bloom and limes unfurling their bright, perfect leaves, the children whispered and pointed, sleepily excited under their blankets. Gina wondered how she could leave them. Then, around about Croydon, Stella began on her hymns. After what seemed like a hundred tuneless repetitions of 'Give me oil in my lamp, keep me burning', Jim switched from hissing furiously at her to shut up, to bellowing, and finally resorted to pinching her until she squealed.

'Am I coming on the aeroplane with you?' Dan asked, apparently oblivious to Jim and Stella wrestling beside him. Gina's heart sank.

'No, darling, you know I'm going on a little holiday, all on my own. We told you. I'll be back on Saturday and you're coming to fetch me from the airport.'

Dan clenched his teeth, then howled. 'But I want to go on the aeroplane with you.' He arched his back and drummed his heels furiously on the back of her seat. Stephen exhaled impatiently. Gina looked back between the seats at her writhing, screaming children, each one in the throes of uninhibited protest against her going, and thought, *Soon I will be on the aeroplane. Out of here.*

'*Chose extraordinaire!*' Lucienne exclaimed when Frances opened the heavy door to her apartment to let them in. 'Do you know what we saw in the Via Maggio? Outside Pierluigi's shop, a black van and they were taking out a corpse from the shop!' She kissed Frances three times, distractedly, from one cheek to the other and back. 'Happy birthday, my darling,' she added.

'You don't know it was a corpse, *cara*,' said Nino, mildly.

'Of course it was, in a bag, with a zip, like a suit bag from the dry-cleaner's, actually – black with a gold zip, but on a stretcher. Don't you think that must have been a body?'

'Well,' said Frances, 'it does sound like it'. She remembered the undertakers coming for Roland, trying to get the stretcher round the tight turn in the staircase, and people walking past in the street outside, a woman she saw every day walking past with her dog, not even mildly curious as this worst possible thing was happening to her, Roland underneath the zippered black nylon. Evidently, people were more curious here.

'Did you see anyone? Did you see Pierluigi?' she asked. She was very fond of Pierluigi, and, although he had always seemed very robustly healthy, he did spend four hours of every day eating and drinking with his syndicate in a restaurant called the Quattro Leoni, around the corner from his shop – the very restaurant, in fact, in which she celebrated her birthday with Lucienne and Nino every year. She ushered them into the drawing room and they all sat, Frances on a wooden chair at the oak refectory table running the length of the wall, Lucienne and Nino side by side on her worn velvet sofa, its scarlet cushions faded to pale coral and gilded arms chipped.

'Yes, yes, he was there, talking to a policeman,' said Lucienne. 'It wasn't him, in the bag, and actually even if he had not been there, much smaller than him, the shape, I am sure. But perhaps a murder, do you think, with the police there?'

The thought of a murder committed in Pierluigi's shop struck Frances as very improbable. He was so lazy, so amiable, and the contents of his shop so innocuous; the most conventional kind of antiques. Overstuffed brocade armchairs, dusty chandeliers, dull engravings. But appearances were frequently deceptive and conducting business in Italy, she had learnt, was never straightforward.

Frances loved the Via Maggio, the showpiece for this particular business. Pierluigi's shop could be found at the far end of it, near to the Ponte Santo Trínita. Ancient, straight, broad and elegant, with comfortably wide pavements, it led from the tiny Piazza San Felice to the Ponte Santo Trínita, forming part of the main route into the city from the Porta Romana. As the midday sun shone down its length, you could walk in the shade cast by the great projecting eaves of the sombre *palazzi* that led down to the river; one of these, its shuttered windows overlooking the Piazza San Felice, was the Casa Guidi, where the Brownings and their son had lived. Another, its soft, dark-brown stucco façade intricately decorated with swirls and curlicues in powdery white sgraffito, had been built for the Venetian mistress of one of the Medicis and spoke of the Via Maggio's particular charm; the irresistible, careless beauty of the greatly beloved.

The ground floor of almost every one of these noble buildings, the English church being one of the few exceptions, was a showroom for antiques or reproductions, built or restored in the small workshops in the narrow streets and alleys leading off the Via Maggio. Some specialized in Florentine mirrors, some in chandeliers, or ornate, spindly salon furniture; the grander shops recreated whole stage sets in their windows, Renaissance drawing rooms complete with frescoes and birdcages and classical statuary; others were stuffed with junk.

Frances had never once seen a customer in any of these shops, although occasionally a van with German plates could be seen at a cant on the kerb, the traffic backing up behind it as far as the city walls as it was loaded with a roomful of portraits and busts to be taken back to Frankfurt or Hamburg. But generally the Via Maggio's atmosphere was one of lazy affluence and good taste, unsullied by commercial activity, and its inhabitants benign, gracious and indolent.

Pierluigi himself seemed to spend most of his time at the back of his shop, where he could look out at the church of Santo Spirito, lounging on one of his sofas, drinking coffee with one or other of his competitors and gossiping. He was a handsome man, with thick greying hair and a bushy moustache, and always beautifully dressed; he had at least one girlfriend, as Frances had observed from her window, and perhaps several. As the weather grew warmer, he would often arrive at nine, put a sign in the window indicating that he was working away from the shop, and, Frances suspected, would drive to the coast for the day. Not today, though.

4

High above Frances's apartment, and closer to the Via Maggio, sitting under the tiny, exquisite *loggia* that surmounted her three-storey apartment, Jane Manzini, née Stamp, was also considering the prospect of Frances's party. She sipped her coffee, looking down on the rear window of Frances's kitchen and, looming ahead of her, the prison bulk of the Palazzo Pitti, barely softened by the dusty grey-green terraces and avenues of its gardens. Would Gina want to go to the party? She'd been a party girl once, after all. One couldn't really leave her behind. She wondered about Gina; what was really the matter with her? Stephen had been pretty cool about the whole thing on the phone to Jane. Just stress, he thought; she'd burst into tears at the supermarket checkout and she needed to get away from the children for a short while. But Jane felt there must be something he wasn't telling her; she could not understand how three children – two of them at school, for heaven's sake – could be that stressful. Not like running a business. She'd never had any trouble with Nicky's two, her stepdaughters; they weren't exactly matey with her, but then they were teenagers, and their mother probably didn't encourage them to like her. But she managed them pretty easily; it was just a question of being firm, letting them know the rules. Children like rules. Come to think of it, when did Beatrice get in last night, with that friend of hers? She could always send Gina down to the country house; Nicky would hardly be there this week. Nobody would want her at the party if she was depressed; although Frances herself probably wouldn't mind. Gina couldn't be in that bad a state, anyway. Wait and see.

Two floors down, Jane could hear Inés preparing for the day, the clatter of plates through the open kitchen windows. Sixteen on the course this week: £16,000, less tax and a couple of thousand for their accommodation; she supposed it was worth it, when she looked at it like that. She was getting just a little bit tired of the cookery school now, though; twelve years of bossy women from the Home Counties coming out, relieved only by the occasional male (always something rather odd about the men, never her type), telling her they already *knew* how to make pumpkin tortelloni, and they were hoping for something a little more advanced. Occasionally there came a client who took it all seriously, who wanted to learn, for whom the preparation of food seemed to have a profound spiritual significance, and there had been a time when Jane might have been seduced by that, too. Now, though, they annoyed her, with their earnestness and their naivety – their faith, for God's sake.

These days Jane prided herself on staying very professional, polite and helpful at all times. And if the clients got too pushy, she would just discreetly let them know the extent of her local knowledge, contacts with the vineyards and the oil producers and the butchers, wood-fired brick pizza oven built by a local crafstman, and all that, just to put them in their place and give them some names to drop when they got home. Though God knows, they all seemed to have their own wood-fired pizza ovens in Gloucestershire these days.

Jane breathed deeply, trying to ignore the noise Inés was making, and looked out to the south, to the hills and olive trees. Nicky was clever to have got this little *palazzo* so early on; the views really couldn't be better. Shame about the Pitti Palace, that great grim prison-house façade, but there was always the Boboli and the hills out to Bellosguardo, then managing to get next door to house the students had been a coup. She rubbed some expensive high-factor sun lotion on to her face and neck, then applied a thick layer to her upper chest; she particularly disliked that leathery look, the trashy mahogany expat tan and wrinkled cleavage, and unless one was very careful this climate would always catch up with one's skin, sooner or later. And of course there was cancer. She closed her eyes, then heard the door open behind her and felt her husband's hands rest lightly on her shoulders. He smelt delicious, of lime and basil, the cologne he had mixed in London and sent out in tissue-lined boxes.

'Darling. When did you get back? I must have been asleep. Did you have an awful drive?'

'Mmm, yes. I left Rome at about midnight. I thought the motorway would be clear, but it never is, is it. I didn't want to wake you, so I slept downstairs.' Niccolò Manzini's voice was very soft, carefully modulated even when he was furious; it had been almost the first thing Jane had noticed when she met him, and to her it denoted delicacy, refinement, feminine sympathy. At forty-five Niccolò was seven years older than Jane but more handsome now even than he had been when he married her, slender, his dark hair very short, grey at the temples, and his eyes the brindled grey-green supposed to be characteristically Florentine, as was his name, although in fact his father had been from Milan and his mother was English. He sat down opposite her at the nineteenth-century wooden garden table and chairs, found by Jane in a little antique shop in Buonconvento. The shop was owned by an Englishwoman, and the chairs had been rather expensive, but they were very pretty.

Jane smiled. She suppressed without difficulty the thought that she wouldn't have actually minded being woken. 'You are sweet. So lovely to have you back; last week seemed to go so-o slowly. Ghastly lot of students this time. So, how was it? Did you manage to sort everything out with the *questura?*'

Niccolò regarded his wife with an expression that might have been amusement, or perhaps indulgence.

'I think so. It might have been just a bit of trouble-making. The *carabinieri* like to throw their weight around; they were just reminding me that they can stop the building work any time they want, it doesn't matter how big the project is. They said the *guardia di finanza* might want to look at our books, but I think if they really meant it they'd have already been in touch. And Giuseppe knows better than to use illegal labour.'

Jane didn't think it at all unlikely that Giuseppe, Nicky's foreman in Rome, was employing illegal immigrants – after all, everyone else did – but Nicky obviously didn't want to talk about it. He was often secretive, inscrutable, and Jane knew that he hated to be observed in certain activities. He had been particularly vague about this summons from the *carabinieri*, although it was true that they often just issued incomprehensible demands to comply with this or that ancient regulation; she had certainly had enough of them over the cookery school.

Niccolò had never invited her interest in his architectural practice, although in the early days of their marriage she had tried to learn. He always responded carefully if she asked a question, but she could tell that it irritated him to explain himself, so soon enough she decided not to ask too much or too often. They worked together on some things, after all: on the house in the country, and the converting of this *palazzo* into the cookery school, and on their own huge flat on the floors above and subsequently on turning the *palazzo* next door into the school's accommodation. She had liked acting as client to the famous architect, explaining her needs to him and having them translated into the perfect spaces. Jane found Niccolò's sure grasp of his buildings' dimensions and possibilities very seductive, and she learnt a great deal about his taste – if she failed to do so, she soon realized, their marriage would not last long. She watched him as he looked distractedly down into the street, and wondered what was bothering him. She spoke again.

'Have you seen your little angel Beatrice this morning? I told them not to be back late, but of course they were – they weren't back when I came up to bed. She went out with Natasha – do you think that girl takes drugs? She's horribly pale. And thin.'

Jane didn't see why she had to be the one keeping tabs on her stepdaughter, Beatrice, and the company she kept; if it was obvious to Jane that Beatrice's close triangular relationship with Natasha Julius and Ned Duncan was unhealthy, then surely Niccolò should take it on board too? Jane had a niggling little soft spot for Ned Duncan that she tried to suppress; perhaps, she thought, it was because he so closely resembled the young men she had been attracted to herself as a girl, an attraction she had always known she should stifle before it was born, for soft and beguiling and poetic boys with wild tendencies. The wrong kind of boys.

Ned Duncan, very sweet and charming though he was, was back living off his mother, close to being disinherited by his father by all accounts and, all things considered, not much of a prospect as a boyfriend for Beatrice, Jane thought, particularly as he never seemed to want to spend much time with her unless Natasha came along too. And Natasha Julius was very beautiful, Jane grudgingly admitted, but she was out of control. Jane could picture her, her oval face, huge dark eyes that seemed all pupil, milky-skinned, dainty as a cat, stroking Beatrice's hair while the younger girl smiled, stretched out on Jane's velvet sofa and eyeing her narrowly through her slanting eyes as though she knew something Jane didn't.

What was Natasha doing out here again, staying with the Duncans? Beatrice at least was here legitimately, on her gap year, an authorized absence. They had mumbled something, when Jane had asked Natasha sharply why she wasn't in London, about recuperating after an illness. Jane guessed that she had probably dropped out of university, not for the first time, either; the girl's idiot mother, not a brain left in her head after all the drugs she must have taken in the seventies, obviously assumed a few months spent in Florence was a good substitute for education.

It seemed to be a common assumption. The old city was full of teenagers with no one keeping much of an eye on them, from gangs of disgruntled, muscle-bound American college boys on their 'culture' module, to London trust-fund girls drifting about wearing terrible ethnic clothes and disappearing off to carry out dreary New Age ceremonies in the hills. There wasn't much in the way of night-life for them in the city – a few cheap-looking nightclubs and the odd Internet café were about all Florence had to offer. There were plenty of drugs about, though; that awful collection of hippies hanging about in Piazza Santo Spirito was what stopped prices in the Oltrarno really taking off. And she couldn't understand what possessed Beatrice and Natasha Julius, that they should want to get in with that crowd; she had seen them there often enough, slumming it under the Palazzo Guadagni with a lot of unwashed, dope-smoking vagrants. The thought sharpened Jane's resentment of her sullen stepdaughter and her lazy, directionless friends.

Niccolò looked away, up to the tower of Bellosguardo, already bleached by the brightness of the day.

'Really, I've hardly exchanged a word with Natasha; they all look the same to me, those girls. And Beatrice was having a shower when I was making my coffee, so she did get in – though I think you might have waited up for them.'

Jane restrained the response she felt Beatrice deserved, and instead asked, 'You know Gina Donovan's arriving this afternoon? I did tell you, didn't I?'

'Yes, yes, you did.' Niccolò looked annoyed, all the same. 'God, how do you get roped into this kind of thing, just because you knew each other however many years ago. Will she need looking after? I'm going back to Rome tomorrow evening, you know, and I probably won't be back until Friday.'

'But you will come back then, in time for Frances's party, won't you?'

Niccolò sighed. 'Yes, don't worry. But please, let's not stay too late. Now, look, I've got to go.' He lifted his jacket from the back of his chair and headed for the door.

Absently Jane acknowledged his departure, her mind already ahead of her, focusing on Friday. Although Nicky expressed his impatience with them every year, she knew that he enjoyed Frances's parties, where he was fêted by everyone, the engineer of pale, perfect empty spaces, in impeccable counterpoint to Florence's complicated and decadent architectural history. Frances's flat – or at least her *salone* – was perfect for entertaining, its proportions marvellous, and she had some nice pieces of furniture; and curiously, although none of it was exactly to Niccolò's taste, being rather baroque and elaborate as well as in very poor repair, he seemed to find it easy to relax there, absolved of any critical obligation. The Casa Ferrali would be fun, for a change, though, with that extraordinary garden – and with a restaurant providing the food, Jane wouldn't be sweating over a Sardinian suckling-pig roast in chef's whites this year. She might be able to dress up and mingle, for once, and there was that rather lovely sculptor she never seemed to get around to talking to.

Jane smiled to herself, and began to contemplate her wardrobe.

The social habits of the English residents were profoundly mysterious to many of the long-term residents of Florence, and in particular of the Oltrarno, where a village atmosphere prevailed, offering many more opportunities for gossip and snooping than could be found in the north of the city, where there was a higher turnover of tourists and a faster pace of life. Although the English interacted cheerfully and generously, for the most part, with the indigenous population, among themselves things were quite different.

The *inglesi* tended to make formal arrangements to see each other, such as dinner parties or soirées, they operated a complex and apparently clandestine class system, ranking each other on a very precise social scale with arcane – to the average Italian, who perhaps didn't recognize that his own social scale was just as happily obscure to the foreigner – rules of exclusion and involvement. They greeted each other in the street guardedly, often appearing quite bad-tempered and uncomfortable at being caught off-guard, out of their personal territory and in a public, shared space, keen to get away, to get back home.

An Italian, by contrast, would enjoy a leisurely conversation, even with a perfect stranger, in the street, always as happy there as entertaining at home, perhaps happier. Strangest of all to the locals were the rifts that seemed to spring up between the *inglesi*; one would have thought that, far from home as they were, they would be keen to associate with each other, to overlook differences, to embrace their common nationality, to talk with nostalgic fondness of home. But instead some seemed to go out of their way to avoid each other.

Take, for example, the behaviour of Niccolò Manzini, a moment after saying goodbye to his wife. He let himself out into the street below and stood for a moment swinging his jacket from a finger, as if considering which way to turn, failing even to acknowledge the presence, no more than three feet away from him across the road, of Frank Sutton, who in turn ignored Niccolò. The San Fredianini, the local residents, put such behaviour down to English eccentricity, to some obscure foreign rule of public conduct. Had they known that Frank Sutton and Niccolò Manzini had been at school together for some years, they might have shaken their heads in sorrowful disbelief. Considering the English – and, despite his name, they considered Niccolò Manzini to be as English as Frank Sutton – to be disciplined, highly civilized and unemotional, with Northern European reticence where matters of passion and honour were concerned, it would not have occurred to a casual observer that the men's actions could stem from anything as primitive and familiar as hatred.

Frank passed Niccolò heading south down the Borgo Tegolaio, sauntering slowly into the sun with a roll of newspapers under his arm, and after a moment or two Niccolò turned in the opposite direction, north, towards the Arno and the city. At no point did either man turn back to look at the other, although they were unobserved and the street quite empty, and slowly the distance between them grew until they reached opposing ends of the same street and disappeared into the crowds of the main thoroughfare.

So few trains called at Pisa *aeroporto* that weeds grew up through the tracks, and the train waiting at the deserted platform when Gina walked out of the airport was almost empty, as there was still an hour to go before it was due to depart for Florence. Gina climbed up into the hot, dusty interior of the train and chose a window seat. She folded her coat and put it, with her suitcase, on the overhead rack, then laid her newspaper on the seat beside her and her paper cup of espresso and bottle of water on the table. The journey hadn't been too bad. At check-in she had felt unsettled, unable to believe it could be as simple as this. She could walk without hindrance, with just one small suitcase, no pushchair, no child clamouring to get out and be carried, no one squabbling, spilling her coffee or smearing slimy trails around her neck and at the hem of her skirt. She had sat and read her newspaper at the boarding gate, but had been nagged by the sense that something was missing, that she had left something behind.

Gina had not even begun to hope that the train would remain empty when, as she tipped her head back to swallow the thimbleful of espresso, she felt someone walk past her. A tall boy sat down across the table, followed by another, and another, one crowding up against the back of the next and suddenly filling all the seats around her. A fourth appeared and looked at Gina, sitting in the seat he had obviously expected to fill. Seeing her, he obediently sat down across the aisle and was soon joined by another, older man. The boys – they could not, she thought, be more than sixteen or seventeen, although they were all very tall, hollow-chested and spindly, like plants grown too fast, their legs awkwardly filling up the space between the seats – were Swedish, or perhaps Norwegian, she thought. They wore stiff, shiny jeans, hanging low on their hips, trainers and Adidas shirts. The one sitting opposite her wore a baseball cap and had crooked teeth; next to him sat one with a stubbly head and a pierced lower lip, the stud set with a red stone. The boy across the aisle had soft white-blond hair with a floppy fringe, and very pale-blue eyes, but along his jawline spread a rash of angry purple spots. They all began talking, jeering and laughing at each other in loud, hoarse voices. Already self-conscious, without the familiar buffer of her children, squalling for her attention and keeping her occupied, Gina began to feel exposed, uncomfortably aware of the inch of pale knee she was exposing and the shadowy bulge of an incipient varicose vein.

Eventually the train jolted and began to move, and Gina started to read her newspaper. She found it difficult to concentrate, and, with her elbows drawn in in response to the expansion of the boy next to her, she felt hemmed in, oppressed by the boys' size and dominance over their shared space. They fidgeted and yawned; one removed his trainers, to guffaws of disgust, and another stretched a leg lazily into the aisle. They sang snatches of song lyrics in exaggerated American accents. Gina gave up and stuffed her paper down by her side, and immediately the boys got out a pack of cards and began to lay them out on the table. Gina realized that her self-consciousness was ridiculous, as they were barely aware she was there. It occurred to her that, only a couple of years before, they would have been children, smaller than her, and now they dwarfed her. Would Jim look like this in six years' time? She looked at them surreptitiously, experiencing a kind of awe at their raucous ugliness, so entirely a passing product of their adolescence, and she felt, suddenly, the relief of no longer being young.

She started to wonder why the boys were here. She imagined their days spent complaining as they were forced around one cloister or another, and their evenings wandering the old city's streets in search of excitement, and it occurred to her that this was a habit she had almost lost since having children, the habit of curiosity about passing strangers. Generally there would have been too many other things to occupy her on a journey such as this, and she began to enjoy the luxury of being able to observe at leisure, not flustered, nor anxious, nor indignant in anticipation of other passengers' complaints, without having to pause to feed a child or dig around in her bag for felt-pens and colouring books.

The train had left the plains around Pisa and was moving through the Appenines to the west of Florence, steep, wooded hills, villages, the Arno winding through them, crossing the path of the train and then back, choked with reeds here and there and gradually widening as they approached Florence. They passed pretty towns perched on steep green hills, then the hills flattened out and the vista was blurred by a mesh of pylons, light industrial estates, shanty towns clinging to the river's banks. Then finally in the far distance, the great terracotta dome of the cathedral appeared, like a mirage shimmering in the heat haze above all the shabby accretions of the city. Despite herself, Gina felt a bubble of excitement rising in her, and she stood to get her bag down, slipping out of the huddle of card-playing boys. They closed over the space smoothly, as though she had never been there.

Gina left the carriage and stood by the door. At eye-level on the window frame was a strip of metal stamped with the stern admonition *E pericoloso sporgersi* and she smiled at the tongue-twisting, rococo foreignness of the words. *It is dangerous to lean out.* Gina watched the grubby outskirts of Florence slide slowly past. She liked the domesticity revealed by the washing-lines and broken bicycles littering the little balconies of suburban apartment blocks; the components of her own life, rearranged under a hot sun or in the shadow of a stuccoed high-rise. She felt poised, ready, tightening her grip on the suitcase, and she checked her watch; three-thirty. Jane had said she'd be in all afternoon.

Pierluigi, the antique dealer from whose shop Lucienne and Nino had seen a body bag stretchered out a few hours earlier, was at his usual table at the Quattro Leoni when Frances walked in with them at one o'clock; he was a little pale and, unless it was Frances's imagination, wearing a more sober suit and tie than usual.

'*Signora*, your birthday again already?' Franco, the restaurant's manager, came out from behind his reservations book and embraced her carefully. 'We have laid a table for you outside, but if you think it is a little cool then we can also put you inside, at your favourite table by the window.'

Frances began to protest that it was at least thirty degrees outside, but stopped, curiosity overcoming her.

'Well, perhaps it is a little early still to be outside. I feel the cold more than I used to.'

Franco smiled approvingly and sympathetically at this sign, at last, of sensible attention to the elements from the English *signora*, and showed the three to the window seats, which happened to offer an excellent opportunity to eavesdrop on whatever conversation might be carried on at Pierluigi's table in the corner. They ordered white wine, pasta and veal.

Pierluigi, head sunk in his hands, was being interrogated by three of his syndicate: Giannino, who sold mostly armour and heavy jewellery, right down near the bridge; Leo, who specialized in updated antiques, upholstered in modern fabrics, or stripped back to the bare wood; and Roberta, a specialist in *trompe-l'œil* murals. Pierluigi looked inexpressibly sad and Frances felt a sudden access of warmth for the antique dealer; she wondered, not for the first time, why the Italians were always depicted as incorrigibly light-hearted. It was the English, after all, who considered the proper response to death to be laughter, and none of Frances's compatriots would, she thought, have access to such inner reserves of melancholy as were being displayed here.

They were, of course, asking about the police presence at the shop that morning.

'Was she trying to steal something, do you think?' asked Roberta. *She?* thought Frances.

'No, no, she had been pushed through the window. She was half in the shop, half still out in the street. I don't know why they didn't collect her from round the back; it was the back window she fell through. They spent forever "collecting evidence" from the shop, though the only evidence I could see was blood on my little *divano*. Whoever did it really made a mess of her. She . . .' He stopped, and shook his head. 'It was as though she was staring at me. Her eyes were full of blood. Even the *carabinieri* were shocked. It seems she could have died from any one of four or five injuries. Internal bleeding . . .' The antique dealer, as a rule so suave and imperturbable, put a hand to his forehead and bowed his head, his voice tailing off. The others stared at him, and Pierluigi looked up, his brow drawn together as though it pained him to remember what he had seen. 'I think she was attacked in the street outside the shop. One of those foreign kids, English, German, I don't know, she wasn't Italian, I'd swear it.' Pierluigi was quite animated, but hangdog at the same time, as if he needed to find a reason for it being his shop window she'd been pushed through.

Frances looked at Lucienne and Nino. They weren't even pretending not to eavesdrop, and their veal was congealing on their plates. She shook her head at them.

'We shouldn't be doing this. None of our business. Come on now, shall we go over to the house after lunch and walk in the gardens? Lucienne, you can tell me what you think of my ideas. I want to hang little Chinese paper lanterns in the trees, and we must have a look at the top terrace, under the walls, to see whether we can all eat there.'

Lucienne shook herself visibly, and her Indian earrings tinkled.

'Of course, of course, darling. So morbid of us.'

By now the four antique dealers had begun to complain about the *carabinieri*, their arrogance, their rudeness, their southern brutality and their lack of respect for private property – namely Pierluigi's stock. The three foreigners managed to tune out without difficulty, as a conversation like this could be overheard at one table or another at any given lunchtime, and they moved on to wild strawberries, a little pot of coffee between them, and discussion of the safety standards of Chinese paper lanterns.

5

Hot and confused, the suitcase that had seemed so compact at home now heavy and cumbersome, its reinforced corners bumping painfully at her calves on the walk from the station south through the humid city, Gina made a decision: she would go into the next bar she passed and just ask. The heat of the stone pavements burnt through the soles of her shoes and she felt deafened and half-suffocated by the clamorous afternoon traffic, building towards its six o'clock peak. She had walked up and down the Borgo Tegolaio looking for number 36, but the numbers, confusingly, did not follow one after the other, and she had passed two number 36s, one numbered in red, one in blue. Jane's directions had been minimal, but it hadn't occurred to Gina that she would need to know the colour of the door number she was looking for. She was shocked by how dirty Florence was, too, particularly here on the south side, after half an hour spent winding through its narrow alleys. Above first-floor level, the buildings seemed in good repair, painted, shuttered and neat, and higher up the carved eaves overhung the street elegantly deeply, but at street level the stucco was stained, peeling and scrawled with graffiti, the narrow, uneven pavements (how grateful she was to be without a child in a buggy) booby-trapped with dog shit, and blue plastic dumpsters, overflowing with rubbish, were shoved up against shabby front doors. With weary gratitude, Gina turned into the cool marble interior of the Caffè Medici.

'*Signora?*'

Gina gazed wanly at the barman, who seemed to be smiling at her in a friendly sort of way, and asked for a glass of water in her halting, rusty Italian. She felt quite hopeless; unpractised at managing alone, it seemed almost beyond her to formulate the right question. She took a deep breath.

'*Cerco la scuola di cucina della Signora Stamp, una signora inglese, Borgo Tegolaio numero 36.*'

At the sound of Jane's name, a man looked up at her from the copy of *La Nazione* he was scrutinizing in the corner booth. Self-conscious – about her accent, the lack of make-up that marked her out, she was sure, as a dowdy Englishwoman, her light-blue T-shirt, faded and crumpled – she passed her hands over her unruly hair and tried not to return his gaze. He seemed to be looking at her quite hard.

'I can show you where Jane Stamp lives, if you like,' he said. Gina felt there was something unsettling about the intensity of his examination, but his face was in shadow, his back to the brightness at the door.

'Could you? You know her, then?' She couldn't disguise her relief. 'I feel very stupid; I can't seem to work out how the numbers go.'

The man's face emerged from the shadow as he stood slowly and walked over to her, a bundle of newsprint under his arm. His was a square, open face, serious but not unfriendly. His eyes were a clear, light colour, somewhere between grey and green. Awkwardly he held out his hand.

'I'm Frank Sutton. It's red for business numbers, blue for residential. But sometimes the distinction is rather blurred. Are you a student? I thought the courses began on a Sunday.'

Gina watched as her rescuer gave the barman a 10,000-lire note and was rewarded with a raised eyebrow, and she felt a stir of curiosity as Sutton frowned at him. She wondered how it appeared to the barman, her walking out with a near stranger, and what he might know about this man. They walked out into the street.

'No, no.' She laughed. 'I was at university with Jane; we're friends, sort of – though I haven't seen her in years. I'm staying with her for a bit, getting away from my children; it's a bit cheeky after such a long time, but I couldn't really face the thought of being in a hotel on my own. I'm out of practice at being on my own, but perhaps that's obvious.' She flushed, aware of perhaps having given more information than had been asked for.

They walked back to the Borgo Tegolaio, and Frank Sutton led her to Jane's building, the entrance a graceful arched pair of wooden doors set in grey stone, its stucco painted a soft yellowish-ochre. They stopped, awkward suddenly.

'You didn't tell me how you know Jane,' Gina said.

'Oh, we all know Jane. And Niccolò.' He pressed the bell, and the door clicked open. Sutton hesitated, then followed Gina into the dark hallway, his broad back blocking out the light behind her completely, before he leant past her and pressed a light switch.

On the first floor a plain brass plate advertised 'Jane Stamp Scuola di Cucina'; as they walked past it Gina heard the sound of heavy deadlocks sliding back and a door being opened on the floor above.

'Gina, darling, is that you?'

At the sound of Jane's voice, clear, bright and authoritative, Gina's stomach gave a little flip, and any sense of her own authority that ten years of professional life and another ten as a mother might have conferred on her fled as though it had never been. As she turned the last flight of stairs Gina saw her. The last time they had been this close to each other had been at Jane's wedding, some thirteen years before, Jane sweeping down an Adam staircase in Manchester Square in white satin with an expression of high excitement and profound satisfaction on her face, turning to toss her bouquet over her head, to be caught by Gina.

She seemed barely to have aged at all, at least from the distance of ten feet that remained between them. Her hair was a pale creamy-blonde – Jane remembered it as darker – and her skin startlingly fair for someone who had spent so long this far south. She was wearing loose, dark-grey linen trousers and a white shirt, and the hand she stretched out towards Gina was smooth, with silvery, manicured fingernails. She looked very expensive. Gina remembered the dinner parties in Jane's college rooms, cut glass and napkins, networking even then. And while the rest of them had had to recycle the same party dress time after time, Jane always came up with something new, and shoes and handbags and cashmere throws. Gina suddenly felt keenly aware of her own creased clothes, her legs sturdy in Birkenstock sandals; she felt like a large, slow-moving animal steaming in the heat.

'Let me look at you. You're exhausted. I am sorry there's no lift; it's the price you pay for the lovely staircase.' She held out her arms, and Gina put down her bags and allowed herself to be embraced. Jane's cheek felt cool and smooth, and she smelt of flowers.

'Hello, Jane,' she said. 'I hope this is all right, just dumping myself on you like this. Am I interrupting a class? Oh!' remembering that her guide was still there, she turned, apologetic, 'This is . . . I . . .'

'Frank Sutton,' said Jane, with a hint of impatience she hardly bothered to conceal. Then she seemed to reconsider. 'Thank you, Frank. Sweet of you to help. You obviously haven't introduced yourselves. This is Gina Donovan, an old friend from university. Now, are you busy this evening? You could come to dinner, make up the numbers?'

Frank returned Jane's smile warily, as though trying to read her change of tack. 'Well, I have got a piece to write tonight.' He looked at Gina, and she had the distinct impression that she was a factor in his decision, an impression she attempted to dismiss immediately it had occurred to her. 'But maybe . . . I can probably finish it off by about eight-thirty.' He looked as though he'd been taken by surprise, and opened his mouth as though to take the words back, but Jane was too quick for him.

'That's settled, then.' She smiled with satisfaction. 'See you at eight-thirty. Now, come in, Gina, I'm sure you'd like a shower and a rest. Are you missing the children yet?' And she ushered Gina smoothly inside and left Frank on the landing to contemplate her elegant front door.

Gina put her suitcase down gingerly and looked around. The tiny lobby opened out into a huge white room, its walls soft and chalky, its ceilings vaulted and here and there decorated with a fragment of ancient fresco. Beneath the long windows was an arrangement of pale grey-green velvet sofas and on the furthest of them a girl was slouching, her long legs, in dark, skin-tight jeans, stretching into the middle of the room and her body almost flat, head pressed into the back of the sofa. There was bad temper in every angle of her body.

'Say hello, Beatrice. This is Gina, a friend of mine from a long time ago.'

Gina took a step towards Beatrice, who raised herself on her elbows and half turned towards her. Her dark hair, parted severely in the middle and as straight as if it had been ironed, hung almost to her waist.

'Hi,' she said, after a while. 'An old friend, huh. Didn't know you had any old friends, Janey.' And she stared at Gina curiously for a minute or two before looking narrowly at Jane.

Gina shifted uncomfortably, reminded of how little there was between her and Jane, and how long ago. She looked at Jane, but her smooth pale face revealed nothing.

'So I can go out now, yeah? I'm supposed to meet Tash at six. We're going up to the villa to eat.'

Jane sighed exaggeratedly. 'I suppose so. I've given up expecting you to eat with us. How are you going to get back?'

'Ned'll give me a lift, I should think. Or someone else. I'm not a kid.'

'Teenagers! Just you wait. Yours are still small enough to be lovable, aren't they?' Gina could see Beatrice scowling at Jane behind her back as she levered herself upright from the sofa and loped towards the door, flicking her hair back over her shoulders in a practised motion. Gina felt rather envious, thinking of how naive she had been as a teenager. Though having Jane as a stepmother might be a bit of a trial.

'Mmm. Yes, still very lovable,' she said wistfully.

Jane took Gina up brick stairs worn soft and smooth leading to a bedroom in the eaves, French windows the full height of the room opening on to a bright balcony.

'Have a shower and a rest and then just come down when you feel ready, darling. It's only five or so, plenty of time before dinner, and Nicky will be home soon. He's dying to see you again. You will change, won't you?'

Gina felt Jane eyeing her crumpled appearance with consternation. She nodded, wondering what outfit there might be in her suitcase that Jane would approve of. Jane gave a little wave and floated back downstairs.

Alone, Gina looked around more carefully. The room was spotlessly clean, large and plain except for the bed, which had a huge carved headboard and was covered with an old white lace bedspread, flanked by two gilt wall sconces. The floor was terracotta and the ceiling ribbed with chestnut beams. Under the roof it felt warm, and fragrant with the scent of old wood and clean linen, luxuriously foreign. Gina lay back on the bed and breathed deeply, feeling as though she had entered another life, and the one she had left, redolent of chicken nuggets and cauliflower and yogurt-stained loose covers and Thomas the Tank Engine, was fast receding into the distance. Through the heavy wooden door in the corner of the room she glimpsed the aquamarine gleam of a bathroom, and a stack of white towels carefully balanced on a delicate wooden chaise. *A shower*, she thought. *Mmm.*

As Jane walked through her drawing room, smoothing the sofa that still held the impression of Beatrice's obdurate, hunched figure, in a rare moment of self-examination she was wondering about the wisdom of having invited Frank Sutton to dinner. Jane was well aware that Niccolò loathed him, although she wasn't sure why, except that it had something to do with school and, she suspected, something to do with a girl. It piqued her interest suddenly. *Still*, she thought, *plenty of people hate people they went to school with*; she could think of a few herself. Old schoolfriends – and she didn't count Gina among hers, being a university friend – had an irritating habit, like one's parents, of reminding one of one's immature years, bringing up embarrassing and irrelevant details of temper tantrums and old crushes. Boys were more mysterious, though, at least to Jane; she tried, and failed, to imagine what kind of musty adolescent conflict could still make itself felt at thirty years' distance.

Perhaps it had just been curiosity that had led her to issue the invitation, and then again perhaps part of her motivation had been an obscure desire to annoy Niccolò after last night. Actually, she could see that Frank had taken to Gina, and that would help her out, if Gina was going to be as socially hopeless as she looked and clam up at the dinner table. And it was always useful to have a journalist on your side, wasn't it? But certainly she wouldn't mind seeing how Niccolò would react; after all, as he'd never seen fit to enlighten her on the subject of Frank Sutton, she wasn't to know, was she? That settled, Jane drifted down the cool grey corridor to her dressing room, to change for dinner.

As Frank Sutton walked away from Jane Manzini's front door his face had an expression of frustrated anger, as though he had made a mistake and was regretting it. He breathed out heavily, a short, impatient breath, then shook his head and walked on, towards the Piazza Santo Spirito.

The piazza was warm and the early evening atmosphere sleepy. Florence was short on friendly squares; those north of the river were either gloomy, Victorian and dominated by traffic, or ruled by chic and expensive bars, their white-jacketed, perma-tanned waiters twirling and bobbing with silver trays and keeping the *hoi polloi* at bay. The delicate beauty of Santa Croce was obscured since it had been designated a kind of gladiatorial arena for tourists, hosting spectacle after spectacle, from rock concert to mediaeval joust. Only Santo Spirito was more or less dedicated to the poor, the great church at one end offering its sprawling steps as sanctuary to dreadlocked travellers and beggars, their bedding stacked like sandbags at its base. The stone benches around the scummy central fountain, shaded by acacias and elms stirring gently in the warm spring wind, drew the low-budget tourists with their backpacks and their sandwiches, and the chipped and spattered stone ledge around the foot of the Palazzo Guadagni, a building as beautiful as any in Florence, was home to the southern city's drug-addicted population and their dealers.

Tonight, around five, they were beginning to gather in the evening heat, as the city was stirring itself back to life for the evening's shopping and the *passeggiata*. By midnight they'd all be there, twenty-five or so slumped against the wall, mumbling and smiling and smoking, but now there was only a handful, gathered around a man like a leather-jacketed Native American with his lined brown skin, beaked nose and thick white hair. Stefano. There were a couple of bikers, and a girl in a wheelchair, and beside her a dark-eyed girl – a woman, perhaps only thirty-five but she looked older – wearing flashy gilt earrings and a low-cut dress that showed the bones of her chest. She glanced over at Stefano now and again as she smoked, the ash almost down to the butt when she raised it to her lips. It might not have been obvious to the casual observer, but you wouldn't have to look too closely to understand – as Frances had understood when, on her way home one evening, she had watched Stefano circle this tired woman's wrist with his pincered fingers in an unmistakable gesture – that Stefano controlled her, even though she was seated at some distance from him and he never once looked in her direction.

Stefano's heavy-lidded eyes were surveying the resident drunk as he lurched and spun beneath the statue of Verdi, singing and kissing his fingers to the tourists, smiling beatifically with his eyes closed. A young man with long hair walked fast out of a side-street and crossed the Via Mazzetta without looking, folding something up and wadding it into the palm of his hand before slapping it into Stefano's hand. Stefano in turn put his arm around the younger man's shoulders and smiled broadly, revealing very good teeth. As Frank Sutton walked past, Stefano looked up at him sideways through the crowd, and nodded.

Frances was standing at the bar of the Medici wearing a long purple velvet coat, her hair swept back, drinking a martini. She saw Massi nod and turned to see Frank Sutton in the doorway.

'Darling Frank, it's been too long. You've been away, haven't you? Getting too warm for you in the city?'

He looked taken aback. 'Yes, yes, I've been away. You do keep your eyes open, don't you, Frances? Research trip, on the New Grand Tour. How the latest lot of bright young things spend their time. *Waste* their time, from what I've seen.'

'So where did you go, looking for bright young things?' Frances asked. Frank shrugged.

'Naples first, then Rome; I'm keeping Florence till last. There were quite a lot of school trips, Americans and English, some university groups, mostly art and architecture students. Quite a few backpackers camping in the national parks, actually. Discovering the alternative Italy. But really I don't think they come here any more, not of their own accord, they think it's like a museum. They'd rather go to India.'

Frank looked uncomfortable talking about his work, Frances thought. Perhaps he was embarrassed by his subject matter; it wasn't the kind of commission that was likely to win him any accolades.

'Do have a drink with me,' she said, soothingly. 'I'm just hiding out here for a bit; Lucienne and Nino were getting a little bit much, do you know?'

Frank nodded with some warmth, and Frances remembered that Lucienne and Nino had cornered him at her last party for at least an hour, by the end of which he had looked as though he were drowning. Much as she loved them, Frances did see that the pleasant drone of their ceaseless, singsong argument might seem rather suffocating, particularly to someone like Frank. As far as Frances could tell, Frank had not yet found himself tempted to share more than the least significant areas of his life with another human being, and he would inevitably be bemused by them, a couple grown so old together they were almost fused.

'Thanks, Frances,' he said slowly, and she wondered why he smiled so rarely. 'I just came in for a coffee. I've got to write for a bit; I'm invited to dinner at Jane's, and I've got to finish this off first.'

Frances raised her eyebrows. It wasn't exactly that Frances found the suspicion that Frank might have a social life rather surprising; it was more that she wondered what Jane was up to. If Frances, on the basis of a fairly slender insight into Frank's past, had managed to pick up an unspoken but electric mutual hostility between Frank and Niccolò, then surely Jane, as Niccolò's wife, must know they loathed each other. Or perhaps not. For an astute woman, Jane did have some startling gaps in her human understanding.

'An honour, invited to Jane's, well.' Frances was fishing. 'I wonder whether she does the cooking herself, these days? She was so good, when she started, I do remember. And she has always been very sweet about cooking for my parties. I hope she's not offended I'm using caterers this year. But, but, but, will the great man be there, Niccolò? Or am I being obtuse? Not just you two?'

Frank almost blushed, protesting, before apparently realizing that Frances was being mischievous.

'Not just the two of us. I suppose Niccolò will be there. I've been told to write a piece about his great project in Rome, so this ought to be a good opportunity.' He didn't look particularly happy at the prospect. 'Jane has got an old girlfriend staying; she – the girlfriend, Gina – came in here trying to find the school and I took her there, and Jane roped me in to make up the numbers. That's what she said.' He was frowning as though he suspected he had been tricked.

Frances smiled at him kindly.

'Well, it will be fun, won't it? Or at least interesting; I shall look forward to hearing about it at the party. You are coming, aren't you? I do love to have you there, you know.'

The truth was, Frances liked to have Frank, and others of his generation, at her party to represent the family she had failed to generate; it seemed to her to be necessary to have representatives of several generations to give a party balance and a sense of movement, to stop it stagnating.

Frances and Roland had no children, nor had they ever discussed the lack. She suspected they would not have been able to find the words, and she knew without ever having to open the subject that they could not have submitted to any of the primitive investigative procedures then available to the infertile. Frances was aware, now, that there were many things she would not have been able to do had she had children, and she accepted the shape her life had taken, but she did feel a residual longing that always ended up being reinforced rather than appeased by the presence of other people's children at her parties.

'You know I wouldn't miss it. And I'm looking forward to seeing inside the Casa Ferrali; it has a bit of a reputation, doesn't it?'

Frances grimaced. 'Don't say that to Nino; it's a rather touchy subject. I think some terrible things happened there in the war. There were some Germans there, used it as a brothel, mostly, so the story goes. Of course, the Ferralis had been kicked out to the country house, but it was pretty awful when they got back. I never saw it like that, you know; by the time I moved here they'd restored the house and you would never have guessed.'

Frances wasn't sure whether she believed what she was saying; so much of what had happened in Florence over the centuries seemed imprinted on the architecture, all those great brutal palaces. And the Casa Ferrali did have an atmosphere; although the great rooms were beautiful, hung with silk, sweet with wax polish and lavender, the house harboured pockets of cool air in the ground-floor rooms, and a dark, musty little boxroom where a patch of plaster had been lifted with the damp to reveal signs and markings, graffiti that spoke of ancient violence. Sutton looked away suddenly, out into the street, then back at his empty coffee cup. He kissed Frances as he said goodbye.

'I'll let you know what happens this evening, Frances. Happy birthday.'

He stopped in the doorway. 'Frances,' he said, and turned back to catch her eye, as she was laughing with Massi at the bar, and she came and stood at his shoulder, following his gaze into the Via delle Caldaie.

On the other side of the narrow street a couple were walking slowly past, the girl with her face buried in the collar of the boy's jacket, his arm around her shoulder talking softly and intently to her. Her long hair hung down like a curtain across her face until she suddenly shook it back and it was revealed, a mask pale with shock, her mouth turned downwards and eyes wide and dark.

'Isn't that Manzini's daughter? Jane's stepdaughter? The younger one?'

Frances frowned. 'Yes. What can have happened to her? That's Ned Duncan with her.'

Ned Duncan looked round, perhaps at the sound of his name. They were no more than a few yards from the Medici and he was clearly recognizable as the same young man whom half an hour earlier had been sitting with Stefano's arm around his shoulders, and Frank looked at him now intently. His face pale and anxious, Ned Duncan turned quickly back to the girl. Frank and Frances watched them walk slowly and awkwardly away from him down the narrow street, the girl's face still turned into the boy's jacket, her shoulders hunched. It didn't look to Frances as though he was taking her home.

They walked on, Ned and Beatrice, away from the lights of the piazza and the illuminated sign that shone out on to the pavement outside the Medici, away from Frances and Frank Sutton. Because of the difference in height, Beatrice was pressed into Ned's side, her head at his shoulder, and they had to walk slowly for Ned to match his stride to her shorter one, his arm still tight around her shoulders.

'It's all right, it's all right, Bea,' Ned said gently. 'It's – you're safe, now. You're OK.'

She looked at him without comprehension.

'Who would do that, Ned? She never hurt anyone, did she? I mean, she – they didn't take anything from her, did they? Are there people who just do that? Kind of, random? Or do you think it's – us? Do they hate us?' Her gesture took in the street, the city, the activity behind them in the bright piazza. He squeezed her more tightly, his head bowed, his dark hair hanging over his face, and shook his head.

'I don't know, I don't know.' There was something like despair in his voice. 'She was –' his voice broke. 'She wasn't careful, was she? She didn't think about the consequences, you know, like when she went to that after-hours place, making friends with those guys.' Now he jerked his head back towards the piazza. 'She'd talk to anyone, wouldn't she?' His voice was pleading, now. 'She took a lot of risks–'

'But –' Beatrice stopped, frowning. Ned started again.

'That doesn't mean – I didn't mean – she didn't have it coming, no, no. She was, just, well you know, Bea, you know. I guess it must have been random. She walked down the wrong street or – something. Said the wrong thing to the wrong guy.'

Beatrice hung her head. 'If only you'd walked her home,

instead of me. Taken her back with you.' He shook his head. 'Bea, baby girl, that wouldn't have worked, would it? She didn't want to be walked home, ever.' Slowly they began walking again, through the narrow streets and towards the edge of town.

6

To Gina, used to a bath stained with rust and cluttered with boats and ducks and unidentifiable pieces of broken plastic, Jane's guest bathroom appeared like a place of almost holy purity and order. The room was lined with pale, luminously blue mosaic tile, like an Arab casket or the inside of a swimming pool, and Gina found herself unable to avoid the sight of her naked self reflected in a huge mirror almost covering one wall. She frowned.

Gina hadn't thought much about her body for years; not, in fact, since Jim was born. At first, she had felt herself rise gloriously above it, buoyed up, after all those gloomy months of pregnancy, by the euphoria of a new baby, but later she had deliberately pushed the thought away. Perhaps it was looking at herself against the glowing, film-set perfection of this bathroom rather than in the speckled, grubby glass of her dressing-table mirror at home, but she felt faintly alarmed by how unfamiliar her body seemed to have become. She peered at herself, perplexed. Not fat, exactly, but softened up, worn if not yet quite worn out, thicker in the waist, her skin puckered here and there, solid rather than graceful around the hips. It was Jane, so groomed and polished and ironed, she thought suddenly, she'd always had this effect. Gina reminded herself that she was on holiday, and looked again into the mirror, thinking, *Could be worse*, and stepped into the shower.

On opening her suitcase and surveying its contents, Gina's heart sank. She'd put in a few of the things she used to wear to work, but when she tried on the linen suit she found it was too tight at the waist, and stuffed it back into her case. She put on a plain blue cotton dress because she liked the colour and that looked all right; at least she didn't feel trussed up in it. She used to love buying clothes; what happened to that? She'd lost all confidence, somehow; she didn't know what suited her, what was fashionable or appropriate, and jeans seemed fine for the playground even if her changed body shape meant that they were tight where they had once been loose and vice versa.

Through the open window she heard the pleasant chink and clatter of a table being laid, and thought about Jane's comment to Frank about making up the numbers. She wondered whether this was to be a dinner party and whether she would be able to think of anything to say. They'd tried to have dinner parties after Jim was born, although she always felt desperately in need of sleep even before the guests had arrived; they'd given up when one evening, humiliatingly, she had come down after disappearing from the table for the third time to comfort the crying Jim to find that everyone had gone home. Then she had cried, too, looking at the debris of her apple crumble and vichysoisse and all the washing up.

Gina walked out on to the little terrace, and found herself high above the street, almost blinded by the setting sun. It was wonderfully, exotically warm, and suddenly four or five swallows hurtled past at eye-level, banking like a squadron of jet fighters then wheeling in front of her and whistling off down the narrow canyon of the street. Gina felt like laughing with exhilaration at the sight of them, their perfect, breathtaking speed. She suddenly felt very cheerful.

Downstairs, Jane was setting a number of small, fat candles

along a dining table of some smooth, dark wood, already laid with napkins and silver and heavy wine glasses. At the table's centre stood an arrangement of dark peonies. She turned, saw Gina and smiled; perhaps she has mellowed, thought Gina, the smile seemed genuine enough.

'Come and sit down. Let's have a drink, I think we're allowed.'

There was a tray of shallow champagne glasses and a bottle of wine, beaded with moisture in the humid evening air, resting on a low carved Indian table between the silvery velvet sofas. Gina settled gratefully into the deep soft cushions below a window, and accepted a glass of wine. Jane had changed too, she saw, into a long dark dress and little soft embroidered slippers, a heavy silver bracelet on her long, white-skinned arm. Not for the first time, Gina wondered how she managed to look like that. Jane arranged herself carefully opposite Gina and leant forward.

'How are you, really, darling? Stephen told me you'd been rather down lately. Some kind of depression?' She sipped her wine and tilted her head to one side, expectantly.

Gina wondered what Stephen had said to Jane. She felt irrationally annoyed at the thought of the two of them shaking their heads sorrowfully over her; she knew after all that Stephen must have said something to Jane about her *difficulties* when he asked if she could come and stay. Suddenly it dawned on her, as she looked at Jane, that she and Stephen had slept together, all those years ago. Jane had specialized in micro-relationships in her first year at college, Gina remembered, lining up partners in quick succession with an economy of effort that was almost admirable; if they didn't measure up to her social requirements, and most of them didn't, they didn't get a second chance. Perhaps because of this businesslike approach, she had never been thought of as promiscuous. It had never occurred to Gina before that she'd slept with Stephen, though. It would explain why Stephen had been so quick to phone her and ask for help, after that episode in the supermarket, when he'd had to leave work to come and get her. She ground her teeth.

'Actually, I think I'm fine,' she said, and she could almost believe she was, sitting here, feeling the first sip of wine coursing recklessly through her veins. But Jane went on looking at her, inquiringly, so she tried to explain anyway.

'Oh, you know, it can be horribly monotonous at home with small children, and you do sometimes feel as though you're going mad. It's hard to get out anywhere, to do anything; to begin with you keep starting things and not being able to finish them and then, after a while, you don't bother even to start –' She broke off, feeling how pointless it was to try to explain this to Jane, who would never, to judge by her expression, have allowed herself to get into such a position of powerlessness.

'I do understand,' said Jane, who didn't. 'Of course,' she continued, 'I've had to bring up Nicky's daughters, more or less.'

How awful, thought Gina, *how like hell*, wondering whether it might be possible to love someone else's children enough to get through all the flak of early childhood without murdering them. Jane seemed very composed about it.

'How old were the girls when you married Niccolò?' Gina found it hard to imagine Jane negotiating with a food-spattered toddler, and she certainly didn't have that worn-out, demoralized look, the look of those who live under an occupying power, that dealing with that stage of a child's development seemed to leave imprinted on a parent's features.

'Oh, Juliet was about seven, I think, and Beatrice, she was just three or four. Very young.' Jane stopped. 'Melissa was furious,' she finished, flatly. 'She didn't actually let Niccolò see them for several years after that; they were at boarding school by the time they began visiting.'

Gina was taken aback, doing horrified calculations. He'd left his wife with two young children. Worse, Jane and Niccolò's affair had gone on way before they married – the first wife must have got pregnant with Beatrice during that time. She felt faintly disgusted; had she known this when she went to Jane's wedding? Surely not. Jane looked at her, absorbing her expression with a hint of impatience.

'But you know, she was quite . . . unreasonable. She was a very unstable woman, quite impossible to live with. Sometimes we have to accept that there are certain circumstances under which a relationship – even if there are children involved – under which it is better for all concerned if a relationship is abandoned.' She sat back in the cushions of the sofa with an air of resting her case. Gina felt rather naive, and remained silent for a few moments before trying to start again on a more positive note.

'Did you never,' she began cautiously, 'you and Nicky, did you think about –' she stopped, realizing that perhaps this was not a question she should ask.

'Children? Oh no,' Jane laughed, a pretty, light-hearted laugh. 'No, Nicky's got his two, he really didn't want any more. And with the cookery school, and the girls being out here most holidays after a while, I just thought that our relationship was quite perfect as it was. You know,' she leant forward, confiding, 'so few people have that kind of relationship and I really didn't want to spoil it.'

Gina – whose own father, she suspected, had not wanted children, to judge by the distance he had always managed to place between them – felt her heart harden against Niccolò. She wondered, briefly, whether she and Stephen would still be together, if they hadn't had the children. She couldn't imagine it at all. The telephone rang in the corner of the room, and Jane got up to answer it.

Left to herself, Gina sipped her wine, savouring the aromatic bubbles, trying to master her incomprehension of Jane's world, in which people moved freely through their lives, exchanging partners and allowing other people – the people they had been betrayed by – to look after their children. It seemed to require skills quite unlike those she had so painfully acquired in what she thought of as her 'ordinary' marriage.

She looked out of the window where dusk had fallen; a soft, warm dark evening, not quite night yet. She saw a sudden movement outside, then, as her eyes adjusted, realized that there was a circle of bats; quite distinct from the swallows she had seen earlier, they didn't describe long, smooth arcs, but jerked and fluttered, making little sharp turns and drops after the night insects in the air. She hadn't seen bats since her childhood, and they made the city seem more ancient and sinister, its great rooftops inhabited by these tiny living gargoyles. Then something in Jane's voice, a note of muted panic, of pleading, as she talked into the receiver in the far corner of the room, made her turn and listen.

'No, no, darling, I didn't mean . . .' Jane broke off and Gina could hear the angry crackle of a response, then, 'No, no, you must stay, of course, no, it's fine. When do you think –' Again she was interrupted furiously. 'Darling, darling, no, you must just come when you can. I'll see you later. Lovely.' She smiled woodenly, a hostess's placatory smile, into the receiver before replacing it. She stood there a moment longer then turned back to Gina, the smile still in place.

'So silly, darling, bloody Nicky's going to be late. Still, we'll manage very well without him, won't we?'

7

Frances was alone in the gardens of the Casa Ferrali, gazing up at the moon. It hung, low and golden, just above the mediaeval wall of the city, which towered over the house and bestowed upon the garden its extraordinary shape and atmosphere. Frances had been rather afraid to go out into the garden as a girl; she would certainly have never dared go there at night, moonlit or not.

When she had arrived in Florence almost sixty years earlier, Frances had been a pale, tentative girl. Her parents were always, on the outside at least, a golden couple; Frances still had a photograph of them arm in arm stepping off some great Cunard liner, her father looking quizzically from beneath a rakish fedora, her mother in floor-length ocelot and red lipstick and smiling for the camera. Frances's father had been made rich by the inheritance of a rubber plantation and glamorous by his daring as a First World War pilot; her mother was the luminously beautiful third daughter of a baronet, and her great, swimming blue eyes had been commemorated in a Broadway lyric before Frances was even born. But her parents were not happy; or, rather, they were not happy together.

Frances was their only child, and, although on and off through her childhood she was aware of the possibility that she should expect a brother or sister, none arrived. Instead, at her parents' frequent parties – that tendency at least, she thought fondly, she had inherited from them – her mother's friends would lean down towards her with a gust of powder and rosewater, stroke her cheek and murmur well-meaning, consolatory nothings about her poor mother's difficulties in producing another child.

As she grew, Frances understood that, whatever physical

problems her mother may or may not have had in conceiving, there were other obstacles to the family's growth. Her father's mistresses, for example, some of whom were transparent even to Frances; the long periods he spent away from home, looking for investment opportunities in South America, visiting the plantation, or just socializing in Cap d'Antibes or Long Island, while Frances's mother grew increasingly fragile and clung to him with ever greater desperation when he did return to their draughty redbrick mansion in Cadogan Square. And, as a result, Frances grew up anxious, often frowning with the effort of understanding her parents' unhappiness, while they paid her only intermittent and distracted attention. They were fond but profoundly incompetent parents by modern standards, Frances often reflected, distracted when they were there and, increasingly, absent altogether from their daughter's life.

The young Frances, her own lovely eyes and good cheekbones always overshadowed by her mother's (in later life she was quite grateful for this, as it had the useful effect of curing her of vanity), was surrendered, at first to her governesses. She was educated at home by a succession of women of late middle-age, little means and varying abilities, but she found her education soothing; there was endless Tennyson, Browning and algebra, and geography lessons quite marvellously surreal in their irrelevance to her confinement in Belgravia. She liked learning, somehow all the more when what she was learning had no practical application; and at sixteen she could almost imagine becoming a governess herself, slipping into a pleasant half-life spent intoning poetry in a dim schoolroom. But then her parents decided they should send her to Florence.

Like a plant stunted and pale for want of light suddenly placed in a southern sun, Frances found her proper environment, and she bloomed. Even on the train down through Europe, heading south, she sat up straighter in her seat, she gazed out of the window, she pressed her cheek against the glass, looked up at the electric blue of the sky and into the sun. At the station of Santa Maria Novella – the old station – Frances walked out into the press of people, of foreign bodies, and she took a deep, delirious breath of freedom. And now, nearly sixty years later, looking up at the golden moon and thinking, suddenly, that her parents might, after all, have decided to send her to Switzerland instead, Frances felt that she had been a very lucky woman indeed. It was here, in this very place, that her life began, and it was here that she would celebrate it, at her party.

In front of Frances as she stood in the moonlight, the ground sloped steeply back and upwards from the house; at its foot it was warm and sheltered, a tiny Renaissance garden carved out of the hill, with a grotto, a fountain and a statue encircled with roses. This, the lower third of the garden, was enclosed by the warm russet stucco of the house and overhung by the bright leaves and drooping blossom of the glorious, sixty-foot wisteria, its twisted grey trunk thicker than Frances's waist, that wound its way up through the balconies to the roof. This was where she, Nino and Lucienne would sit companionably on warm evenings, listening to the rustle of birds and insects in the trees, and this was where Frances planned to greet her guests, a trestle laid with white damask and champagne beneath the golden leaves.

Frances thought of Frank now, remembering being in her forties herself, and living with Roland in Budapest, the age of no return, the hope of children waning, closer to death than birth. But to her Frank seemed so young, still, far too young to have given up hope, to have become irrevocably lonely. She thought to be young and to live alone for so long did have an insidious effect on the character; one developed strange tics and quirks of behaviour, and peculiar eating habits. She knew Frank had had the occasional, transitory girlfriend; there'd been a rather serious PhD student from the university, and somebody's empty-headed daughter, studying painting and restoration at the institute instead of finishing school. They all seemed to be just passing through the city, and she did think that might have been why he chose them, although of course many people in Florence were on their way somewhere else. Only the lazy, the under-achievers, those in hiding or at the end of their active lives seemed to settle here. Dear Frank. Perhaps at the party . . . But she had thought this every year since they had first met, and he was yet to arrive or leave with a woman. She was beginning to wonder whether there were things about him she didn't know; perhaps he had flaws she had not yet encountered.

The central part of the garden of the Casa Ferrali was the section that had frightened Frances as a sixteen-year-old, and to tell the truth she still found it a little gloomy. Three little rustic stone steps led up against the wall away from the grotto and the fountain, and entered a miniature, dark wood, as though from a fairy tale; it even concealed a small, deep well, built of stone. The trees were mostly holm-oaks, stumpy evergreens, their leaves almost black and forming a heavy canopy which blocked out almost all sun, even at midday. In the dense shade dusty paths wound through the bare trunks and over their knotted roots, up the steep hillside. The only way out, at the top of the hill, was almost completely hidden, set to one side, oblique, and so allowed little light in. Although the trees extended for only forty feet or so up the hill, what was no more than a copse would seem to expand as the young Frances entered and the darkness closed around her, and it was easy to imagine flickering, clandestine movements behind the slender trunks and in the pockets of deeper shade. And now, at night, the full moon overhead only seemed to emphasize the velvety darkness at the mouth of the wood, and Frances did not feel inclined to enter.

She and Lucienne had wandered through the trees after

lunch, as it was here that Frances planned to suspend painted paper lanterns from the branches; these, she thought, would transform it with their coloured light, lemon-yellow, pink and violet and green, into a benignly magical cave or a fairy colony. Lucienne had shivered as they walked, though, tripping over the roots, knobbed and protruding like bones, and when they walked past the little well, so cunningly hidden that it seemed more like a trap or the entrance to an animal's set, and giving off a dank, cold smell, she had made a little sound, of fear or disgust. She had gone gamely on, giving deliberate and careful consideration to Frances's ideas, and perhaps, after all, it had just been the unexpected cool of the shade as they came in out of the afternoon's unseasonal warmth that had unsettled her. Nonetheless, both women had been glad to emerge at the top, under the golden stone of the city wall, and Frances had pressed her chilled hands against its warm flank, and felt her age.

A broad, grassy path at the foot of the wall, perhaps fifteen feet wide, planted on both sides with fig, pear and almond trees; this was the part of Nino's garden Frances loved the most, and it was here, if the weather held, that she planned to have long tables laid for supper. The stones of the high wall, facing southwest, held the day's heat and, because this was the topmost part of the garden, as though held up to the sun, the light lingered here longest. The delicate, fragrant leaves of the fruit trees leant together prettily overhead to form a green tunnel, dappled with sunlight. Whenever she came up here, escaping now, as then, from the oppression of indoors, and the endless, fussy inquisition of the Ferrali family, Frances felt as though she were a girl again, barefoot with her face in the short-cropped, velvety grass and breathing in its country smell, looking up through the almond blossom at the sun and the brilliant sky, dreaming about love and wishing she did not ever have to go back to Cadogan Square.

Now, though, Frances turned her back on the wall and the

moon and the dark trees and looked up at the house, where Nino stood on the balcony, wringing his hands at her recklessness for going out into the cold evening without a shawl, and calling her in for supper. Behind him the drawing room glowed with light and colour; below, the arched entrance to the stone passage leading under the house to the Via de' Bardi was quite dark. Frances smiled up at Nino, and walked back inside.

The number Frank had been summoned to make up turned out to be six, although Niccolò's absence reduced it again to five. An expatriate American art historian called James Mackie and his companion, a striking, dark-haired woman called Olympia who looked like a Spanish princess or a prima ballerina but who turned out, no less glamorously, to be a painter, arrived promptly at eight. Olympia, at thirty-odd, was at least twenty-five years James's junior, although Gina thought maybe it was rather provincial of her to even notice. They seemed very pleasant; friendly and charming and full of admiration for her escape from her family and advice on what she should do while in Florence.

'Whatever you do, don't go near the Duomo – the cathedral – or the Uffizi or any of the big churches, unless you want to spend days just queueing,' Olympia declared, looking defiantly at James. They were all sitting on the sofas below the windows, the night outside quite dark now, and had started on a second bottle of champagne, brought by Inés, as Jane had murmured something about supervising the ravioli and drifted off to the kitchen. James and Olympia seemed very much at home, stretched elegantly on the velvet cushions as though they were regular guests.

James didn't seem too put out by Olympia's prohibition; he merely responded peaceably that perhaps an early visit to the Uffizi would be rewarding, or a little walk up to San Miniato. 'It's surprisingly empty, even at this time of year; it's rather a long walk uphill and I think maybe the pacemaker brigade don't reckon they'll make it.'

'Mmm, maybe,' Olympia conceded. 'But the Boboli is so lovely early in the morning.' Turning to Gina: 'You know, the Boboli Gardens? It's a bit like a maze, lots of high hedges, so it never feels too crowded. And you may be allowed into the orangery, which is glorious. And you must go shopping, of course, that's the best bit. Come with me, we can buy party dresses for Friday.'

James rolled his eyes at this. Gina, secretly thrilled and alarmed at the thought of a shopping trip with the very polished and exquisitely dressed Olympia, and confused by the implication that there was a party to attend, opened her mouth to respond but was interrupted by the muted scream of the doorbell.

After half an hour or so with James and Olympia, Gina was enjoying herself. When the doorbell sounded announcing Frank's arrival, Jane called to Inés from the kitchen that her hands were floury from rolling pasta. Gina found herself thinking, in a way that reminded her uncomfortably of her mother, that it might have been more practical to buy someone else's home-made pasta, as it seemed a messy business that kept Jane from her guests. Jane did look pretty, though, wiping her hands on a long white apron that outlined the enviable curve of her hips as she emerged from the kitchen to press her cool cheek against Frank's in faintly reluctant greeting as he stood awkwardly in the doorway. He did not seem much impressed by the tableau of domestic perfection Jane represented, however, smiling only slightly and offering her a bunch of long-stemmed, waxy lilies before turning to look over at the dinner table. Gina was suddenly aware of the flush in her cheeks from the wine, and the strap of her dress slipping from her shoulder. Jane pushed Frank towards them.

'Frank, could you bear to manage without an aperitif? We

really should sit down straight away, or the ravioli will be overdone. Inés has laid the antipasto out already.'

'I – no, of course. No aperitif.' Frank raised his hands in front of him in a gesture almost of surrender, and Jane smiled at him graciously, unwound her apron, and carefully smoothed her dress.

As the group shuffled around the impeccable dining table, waiting for Jane to direct them to their seats, Frank spoke again.

'Jane, I saw your stepdaughter this evening, with Ned Duncan, apparently – Frances recognized him. Is she all right? She seemed rather upset about something.'

Jane raised her eyes to heaven and tutted impatiently.

'God, I don't want to hear it. She's been such a pain, ever since she came out here. I expect he's chucked her. Nicky'll be pleased, he can't stand Ned Duncan, Honourable or not. Personally, I'm beginning to think she could do a lot worse, particularly with her attitude problem. And at least he's got some charisma. It's so typical that she's managed to screw it up.'

Sutton frowned, as though he was about to take issue, but then seemed to reconsider. He shrugged and sat down, as instructed, next to Gina.

At the centre of the table was a long white platter of tiny green figs, cut to expose their rosy flesh, and different kinds of cured meat, beautifully arranged and decorated with fig leaves. A place laid for Niccolò remained empty at the head of the table. They all fell briefly silent, except for the occasional murmured compliment, and Gina ate hungrily, this being her first meal since the indeterminate sludge they'd been served on the aeroplane, and with her appetite given an edge by the wine. Finally she slowed, then sat back and looked discreetly at Frank, on her left. He was still eating, slowly and deliberately, his eyes on his food. He was dressed quite informally, almost shabbily, although he was clean-shaven and she thought he was wearing a clean shirt, albeit frayed at the cuff she could see emerging from the elderly tweed jacket. She noticed that he had broad hands, his thumbs wide and curved, and held his knife and fork a little clumsily. He looked old-fashioned to her, his ageing clothes and air of slight dishevelment suggesting a poet or an intellectual from the 1950s, Albert Camus or Louis MacNeice, raffish and clever and unworldly. She smiled and he looked up, as though she had made a sound.

'I'm sorry, I was looking at your cuffs,' she said, incomprehensibly, then laughed at herself. She wondered if she was drunk, and drank some water from a heavy tumbler she assumed was hers. *Water glasses, how sophisticated*, she thought dreamily.

Frank looked at her, curious, she thought, but not irritated. She made an effort.

'They're a bit frayed.'

'Oh, yes.' He sounded relieved. 'Yes. I'm no good at shopping, or mending, so most of my shirts look a bit like this.'

She decided not to say anything about a woman's touch, and instead just smiled again. The others were talking about the restoration of some frescoes by Masaccio somewhere in the city; James thought the restoration catastrophic, and Olympia was agreeing as she lit up a cigarette and blew the smoke elegantly towards the open window. Jane was frowning at her all the same, almost visibly restraining herself from waving her hand under her nose. Gina sat and listened, quite unable to join in the conversation but not in the least unhappy.

Inés came in to clear away the small plates, and Jane leapt up.

'I'll get the ravioli. Pasta really has to be eaten *straight away*.' And she shot a warning glance at Olympia before sweeping into the kitchen. Olympia made a little moue of indifference before stubbing out her cigarette recklessly in her side plate. She caught Gina's eye wickedly, and Gina struggled unsuccessfully not to smile.

'How are your family managing without you?' Frank asked. 'Have you phoned home yet?' Gina felt a twinge of panic, and wondered what time it was. She hadn't thought of them in hours. She had planned to phone before they went to bed.

'No,' she said, and just as she was wondering, uneasily, what Jane would say if she asked to leave the table, the hostess emerged from the kitchen, white apron back on, carrying a great heap of delicate ravioli gleaming buttery yellow in a deep bowl and enveloped in a cloud of fragrant steam. As she leant across them to place the dish on the table, the door clicked open at the far end of the room and Niccolò walked in.

Gina suddenly felt quite sober. There was something about him that made you feel in need of sharpening up. She realized that she had expected him to come in angry, as Stephen would have if he'd been delayed at work by the kind of unnecessary bureaucracy Jane had implied, but he seemed very cheerful, smiling as he walked steadily towards them. He was handsome. Gina had remembered that much from the wedding; also that he had designed everything himself, from Jane's wedding dress (bad luck, someone had muttered at the time) to the floral arrangements (wildflowers from a Rothschild garden, a lot of dark ivy). His face was dark and narrow, his eyes quicksilver green. Inés stood at his elbow and took his long, soft leather jacket as he removed it; he seemed very warmly dressed for a late spring evening, a dark suit beneath the coat. First he stopped by Olympia, bending to kiss her. Gina noticed that his fingers were very long and slender. She looked up and saw that Jane was looking at them, too, as they rested lightly at the nape of Olympia's neck.

Niccolò straightened. 'Sorry I had to be late, darling.' He turned and kissed Jane on the cheek, pausing to brush a speck of flour from the dark wool of his sleeve. 'Just in time; it looks wonderful.' Then he came over to Gina and clasped her hand lightly between his; feeling rather uncomfortable, she half turned, awkwardly, to look up at him.

'How lovely to see you again,' he said, as though their wedding had been yesterday rather than thirteen years earlier. 'I can't believe you haven't been out before. I'm sorry to be late on your first evening; it was a planning meeting I just couldn't get out of. Perhaps you've heard about Italian bureaucracy?'

He released her hand slowly and took his place at the head of the table. It was only then that he seemed to notice Frank Sutton at the far end of the group, and nodded stiffly in his direction. Gina saw Olympia look down into her lap as though to disguise a smile of discomfiture; the uneasy formality between the men was lost on none of the guests.

Frank cleared his throat. 'Niccolò. Nice to see you.' His voice was level and calm, and he went on. 'Have you been in Rome? My editor's very keen for me to write about your new project down there. Perhaps I should make an appointment to visit?' At this Jane brightened visibly, Gina could see; perhaps this was why she'd invited Frank Sutton.

'It's a cemetery,' said Niccolò flatly, a hint of suspicion in the glance he levelled at Frank. It was such a surprising thought that Gina forgot her unease and spoke up. 'Do they need architects for cemeteries?' Niccolò turned towards her.

'It's a whole complex, a place of worship, burial plots, and a structure to contain cremated remains. Actually it's more a piece of sculpture than a building, though it does house bodies, here and there.' He laughed lightly. 'And there will be private commissions for *mausolea*.'

'Poor Nicky,' Jane said. 'It's going to be so perfect, very like that lovely Scarpa, you know, organic minimalism, and the moment it's finished they'll plaster it with those awful tacky photos of their loved ones, and plastic carnations. Ugh.' She grimaced.

Niccolò shrugged and turned towards the window, distracted momentarily by a noise that echoed up from the street below, a shriek, followed by the sound of loud and vehement argument in Italian. Olympia sprang up and ran to look out, followed by Frank. Looking down from the bright window the street seemed very dark, but he could see the gleam of a *carabiniere*'s peaked cap and his dark uniform, almost black in the moonlight. He saw the flailing of white fists, a young girl's, her wrists held firmly by the policeman as she tried to beat on his chest. The man reached out an arm towards the doorbell, and in the next moment the bell rang loudly in the Manzinis' apartment.

Beatrice, escorted firmly through the door by the young policeman, caught sight of her father and burst into tears, and obviously not for the first time that evening. She no longer looked enviably sophisticated, but much younger than her seventeen years, her face swollen and distorted with misery, strands of damp hair plastered to her cheek. She pushed the *carabiniere* away and ran to her father, sobbing and hiccuping incoherently, and he put his arm gently around her shoulders. His face very pale and his voice ominously soft, he addressed the policeman.

'What is this?'

Gina caught sight of Jane's face. She looked furious.

The policeman tried to reply, but before he could Beatrice let out a long wail, clutching at her father's lapels. 'It's Tash, Daddy, Tash, someone – she's dead, someone killed her, they killed her!' She gasped for breath and the pitch of her voice rose until it was a terrified, desperate child's, like Dorothy crying for Toto in *The Wizard of Oz*.

'*Signore*, we must talk to your daughter. She was with the young woman Natasha Julius last night, perhaps very shortly before she was murdered. Tomorrow you must come with her to the police station.'

8

In the square, the evening was beginning to take off. The bars and restaurants lining the eastern side were full, with more customers waiting, and the huge wooden doors to the Palazzo Guadagni had been closed, denying the addicts entry to the cavernous, dimly lit hallway that served their limited purpose so well. The dark blue-and-red police van that was stationed there from early morning in an effort to deter drug users and travellers from turning the place into their own fiefdom had disappeared for the night, and around the fountain the socially excluded had come out to play.

On one bench sat a couple of Spanish bikers, long black hair in ponytails, rolling cigarettes and chatting to the girl, Cinzia, in the wheelchair. She wore a studded leather jacket and a tight, low-cut T-shirt that exposed a tattoo over one breast, and she was very animated, her eyes shining. A group of young backpackers lay on the ground, heads resting on their packs and legs crossed languidly at the ankles as they drank beer from bottles; not hardened travellers, by the look of their soft cheeks and new rucksacks, just dossing for a night or two, waiting for space to open up at the hostel around the corner. Those with no place to go were already stretched out around the base of the church, drinking wine; their skin was burnished and coppery, their dreadlocks glinting golden from the sun and their sleeping bags torn and filthy. They stashed their few valuables under their clothing and squatted between the cars when the cafés barred them from using the toilet.

Some were already motionless, trying to sleep, while others twisted and turned in their efforts to find comfort on the unforgiving stone pavement. But it was quiet here, and the light dimmer, and further on, where the piazza dwindled into a delta of forked and narrow streets, one of them the alley where the rear window to Pierluigi's shop was to be found, now boarded against intruders, it was darker still. The city's mediaeval alleys were ill-lit, partly as a result of endless local squabbles about defacing the ancient buildings with the glare of sodium lighting; for the same reason there were, of course, no surveillance cameras, and this worked to the advantage of those who conducted their business out of doors but nevertheless appreciated a little privacy.

One alley followed the curve of the church sharply to the left and into almost complete darkness; inside the curve, beneath the overhang of a precariously extended tenement, stood Stefano and Mila, the dark-eyed woman Frances had seen him with now and then in the piazza, the woman who had been there, smoking, that evening as Frank walked to the Medici. She looked slight next to Stefano, and her head was bowed as he spoke to her.

'I don't care,' he was saying. 'Twenty-four hours off is enough. Generous. You've taken the tablets, it should have cleared up by now.'

Mila raised her head. 'He said two days, that doctor. At least.' Stefano snorted. 'It's not his money, though, is it. Sitting there eating food I've paid for. Smoking my fags. And I don't like you hanging round me, either.'

Mila shrugged unhappily.

'I'm not a charity. You'll be back out there tomorrow morning, like it or not.'

Stefano turned and walked into the light, his eyes down and

his expression unreadable, leaving Mila standing there, her arms stiffly hanging by her side, clenching and unclenching her hands. *Bastard*, she thought. *You bastard*.

Nearly a mile away, across the great dark hump of the Boboli Gardens, Stefano walked fast down the Via de' Bardi towards the Porta San Miniato, the nearest gate out of the city. He kept close to the wall, averting his face from the yellow glow of the lamps that were strung on wires between the roof-tops high overhead. He slipped beneath the gate like a ghost, and ducked between the little houses that clustered outside it, the rustic brightness of their geraniums and painted shutters in marked contrast to the sepulchral gloom within the city walls he had passed through a moment earlier. There he climbed into a dark, expensive-looking car; almost silently it moved away from the kerb and in less than a minute all that remained to be seen were the car's taillights, disappearing off up to the Via Senese, the main road out of Florence, heading south.

When Frances finally said goodnight to Nino at the great wooden door, it was after midnight and the street was empty and silent, curving away from her down towards the lights of the Ponte Vecchio and the last, straggling tourists wandering home from dinner. Warmed by the wine and the pleasant, idle conversation, Frances walked slowly, and as she walked, in an uncharacteristically reflective mood, she found herself wondering what use her life might be said to have been.

She had had a long and happy, if not obviously productive, marriage. She had enjoyed the luxury of living in several beautiful places: Paris, Lisbon, Budapest, Rome and now here, her lovely resting place. She had tried painting, sculpture, gardening and pottery; and although none of these experiments had produced any great work of art, it had never occurred to her that they might not, all the same, have been worth undertaking. She had no children; her genes were now nowhere but in her own ageing body, but she was not unhappy. If she could be said to have a gift, it was for happiness – more a piece of luck than a talent, certainly, but nevertheless she could at least be satisfied that she had nurtured and not squandered it. *My parties*, she thought, *my parties are my storehouse of pleasure and contentment; they are the earth in which I bury my talents and see them multiply.*

Frances passed into the lee of an ancient, cracking wall supporting an old, untended raised garden. All along its top, pale irises were growing wild; papery, lilac-coloured iris *fiorentina* tumbling down with their long-bladed leaves and opulent blooms clinging to the cracks in the wall like a weed. She could smell something on the wind, sweet and elusive; lime blossom, perhaps, or magnolia, some breath of spring blown down from the gardens on the hill above, and she imagined her party, again, everyone gathered together under the trees, drinking and eating and laughing and glittering, perfumed, dressed carefully, extravagantly, ridiculously, talking, talking, talking. She longed for it, that moment at a party when a new sound, a kind of music, starts up, when everyone seems to be engaged in happy conversation with someone, every face is leaning in to look at another, smiling. Frances drew her long velvet coat around her and thought, finally, *This may be my last party.*

The Piazza Pitti was not quite empty still; a few restaurants had tables outside and the couples sitting at them didn't seem to feel the cold. *Honeymooners*, thought Frances, remembering her own. Frances didn't believe in God, or spirits, or reincarnation or any kind of hereafter, but she did think, sometimes, *It will be nice to see Roland again.* She couldn't quite shake the thought that he would be there, wherever there was. She slipped down an alley barely wider than a man, and turned into the Borgo Tegolaio, where she saw James Mackie and Olympia Driver emerge from number 36 and turn north, deep in conversation. As she stood and watched them go, Frank came out, and she remembered his dinner invitation. He was frowning as though he had something on his mind, then he looked up and saw her.

'May I?' she smiled, and linked her arm in his.

Gina lay awake in the unaccustomed luxury of a double bed all to herself. The room, at the top of the house, had held on to the day's heat and so she had left the long windows open on the inside, closing only the external shutters. The moonlight filtered through the slats and lay in stripes on the brick floor, and Gina could still hear what seemed to her to be a great deal going on outside.

A large group of American teenagers, laughing hysterically, had just passed, there were still cars and motorbikes, and it seemed that many of the Manzinis' neighbours were still awake, to judge by the clattering of plates, scraping of chairs and strident conversation echoing in the lightwell behind her room, audible through the bathroom's open window. Unable to sleep, Gina welcomed the sounds. Her suburban terrace in London would by now be profoundly, unnaturally quiet, any sound swiftly stifled; here she felt as though she was surrounded by life noisily, heedlessly shared. At home she would be lying stiff with suppressed panic, listening for wheezing in the night, the padding of feet in the corridor; tonight she was going over the evening's extraordinary events in her mind with a sense of guilty exhilaration.

The policeman had left almost as suddenly as he had arrived, merely repeating his injunction to Niccolò, as Beatrice's legal parent – she remembered him looking pointedly at Jane, who had responded by looking even more furious – to accompany the girl to the police station the following morning. 'Because of her age, *signore*, you understand; she must be accompanied.'

Beatrice had collapsed on to the sofa, sobbing defeatedly,

once he had gone, and had refused comfort from anyone but her father. He had muttered something fiercely to Jane, who had disappeared to her bathroom, returning with half a Valium, and together they persuaded Beatrice to take it, and to have a drink.

Through all of this Gina had sat quite quietly on the sofa, rigid with an overpowering sense of her own helplessness and the inappropriateness of her being present at all. At last Jane, perhaps out of duty as a hostess, sat down beside her, and Gina whispered to her through dry lips, 'Who is she? Natasha?'

Jane sighed. 'Beatrice's best friend. The girl she was going to meet when you arrived. She's . . . she was always around. Her parents – separated – they let her come over whenever she wanted. To stay with the Duncans, this time; sometimes she stayed here. Not recently, though. I don't think she liked me very much.' And she shrugged, her eyes veiled, her thoughts apparently turning to something she didn't want to share with Gina.

Beatrice had calmed down enough to give them some details about Natasha's death. She had been murdered, late the previous night or, more likely, in the early hours, beaten around the head in one of the alleys behind the church, asphyxiated, ended up pushed, or thrown, through a window.

'We came back into town, we'd been down in the country, swimming in the river. We were just sitting in the piazza, you know, chilling out.' She stopped, sobbing. 'She seemed so happy, she just kept finding everything hysterically funny, you know. It was pretty late when we left; Ned walked me back here. But there were still loads of people around, she should have been safe. It's always safe.'

That evening, Beatrice said, she had been with Ned; he had taken her to his parents' villa in the southern hills and he had told her what he had heard on the grapevine in the Piazza Santo Spirito, that Natasha was dead.

Ned hadn't known the details, he was adamant, although she thought he might have been sparing her. It had been down to the policeman to tell her, somewhat unwillingly, how her friend had died, when he had arrived at the villa, looking for Ned.

'I wanted to know where it happened.' She was crying hard now. 'Why is that? Why do people always want to know where? And when I knew, I couldn't get it out of my head, the thought of her lying there, all smashed up. Many injuries, that's what they said. Not Tash any more. Get her up, I wanted to tell them, I'll have her, give her to me, I'll tell her to get up and come with me, stop lying there.'

She had stared around at them, her eyes vacant with grief, as though they might be able to explain how someone died like that, how someone did all that growing and developing, turned from a baby into a woman then only to stop short, extinguished, in a backstreet a long way from home.

Finally she had been persuaded into bed, limp and red-eyed with exhaustion, leaving the adults alone with the news.

Niccolò had remained largely silent; he was still pale, and looked older, rubbing his forehead slowly with one hand, his eyes downcast. Jane didn't seem so inhibited by what they had heard.

'Well, I did think – didn't I just say this morning, Nicky – that I thought Natasha might be the wrong sort of girl for Beatrice to be hanging out with? I mean –' she realized, perhaps, that she wasn't sounding very compassionate – 'I mean, it did look as if Natasha was getting involved with drugs, at least to me.'

'For God's sake, Jane, the girl's dead,' said Niccolò.

'But drugs, I mean, they don't seem terribly violent, the guys in Santo Spirito. More like comatose, most of the time,' said Olympia. 'But I suppose you never know.'

Frank, looking thoughtful, said he didn't think there was

much drug-related violence in the area, only theft, a few break-ins, but not even much mugging to speak of, at least not compared to what went on in bigger cities.

'I did look into it a bit, when they launched the clean-up campaign a couple of years ago. They seemed to be more worried about how bad it looked to the tourists, the dealing on the streets.'

Gina, stiff with horror, had remained silent. Natasha had been nineteen, Jane had said when Gina asked, taking time out from her university course, for some health reasons Jane dismissed as nonsense – forgetting the circumstances enough to return to her usual scathing self – some stress-related viral illness, exhaustion or a glandular infection. Gina wondered who had given Jane this explanation; perhaps the girl – Natasha – perhaps Natasha had other reasons for leaving, for following her friends across Europe.

Gina couldn't help wondering, with a kind of nascent, sympathetic terror, where Natasha's parents were now, and whether they had other children. She thought of them pacing about in an airport lounge, unable to speak to each other without recrimination. By now they must have seen the police, been told what had happened; they must be in a hotel somewhere, making arrangements. Perhaps they couldn't bury her yet, if the police needed the body. Had Natasha Julius's parents, like Gina with her own children, spent their daughter's childhood afraid that some danger might appear from which they would find themselves unable to protect her? Had they shivered in sympathy whenever a child's disappearance was reported in the newspapers, had to turn off the television rather than witness a parent's grief at some terrible press conference or other? Had they thought, now that their daughter was almost an adult, that the dangers were past?

In the darkness, Gina felt herself tense with the thought of all the freedoms she would have to grant her children as they grew; so far, they weren't even allowed to walk to school alone. Boys on bikes would come to the door, asking if Jim could come out to the recreation ground, and she always said no. She couldn't imagine the day when she would let him leave the country on his own. She hadn't phoned home, she thought suddenly. Not that she'd promised, and she felt strangely reluctant, knowing in advance the note of poorly disguised exasperation she would detect in Stephen's voice, the clamouring and shouting of the children, the peculiarly unsatisfying exchanges she would have with each of them. With Jim, monosyllabic, Stella, pleading for some complicated favour, and Dan, who would shout and shout at her and then cry piteously. Maybe tomorrow.

Gina wondered how someone could be murdered in a place like Florence. She thought of the sleepy square she had walked through on her way to Jane's that afternoon. Perhaps some of those laid-back locals harboured a secret hatred of the foreigners who treated their beautiful city as though it was their own. Maybe the girl had a jealous boyfriend – didn't they always say you're most likely to be killed by someone you know? Maybe it was drugs. Maybe that was why she had left university. Their lives, the lives, of these children – like Beatrice, whom she had thought so sophisticated – at home in all the drawing rooms of Europe, fluent in three or four languages, casually borrowing the second and third homes of each other's parents, no longer seemed to her to be glamorous and carefree. She thought instead of how little there was to tether these children, or to comfort them if they needed comfort.

The others had left quite quickly, once Beatrice had gone, Frank looking at Gina oddly, she thought, as though he felt rather sorry for her as he kissed her goodnight, Olympia squeezing her arm meaningfully and whispering that she would call tomorrow. As the door closed behind their guests,

Niccolò and Jane had sprung subtly but perceptibly apart; ignoring each other and for that matter, Gina. Jane had gone into her kitchen to prepare for the following day and Niccolò passed her in the corridor, presumably to bed.

What had struck Gina was the silence between the two of them, and the space. They didn't touch each other, not even a hand on the shoulder to express the end of the day's stresses, no going over the day's events, momentous though they had been. After a while Gina had ventured a few steps after them to say goodnight, then stopped. She could see Jane in her blindingly white kitchen, walking slowly around a vast table beneath chrome downlighters, straightening a wooden spoon here, a bowl there, all laid out for the following day's classes. Down the corridor, to Gina's left, Niccolò emerged noiselessly from the bedroom where Beatrice had been put to sleep. Uncomfortably aware that she must be in the way, Gina had retreated up the narrow staircase to her own bedroom, but as she went up she could hear the unmistakable hiss of a furious but muted argument starting up behind her, the kind of heated whispers that are intended to conceal a row from the children, or the guests, but never do.

Gina found herself curious about Jane and Nicky's marriage, and Beatrice in the middle. Where she and Stephen were knotted together by their children, bound by thousands of tiny threads, their shared guilt, irritation, exhaustion and love, Beatrice seemed as a wedge driven cleanly between Jane and Niccolò. Gina wondered how the marriage could function under such circumstances; perhaps there were mysterious forces at work she had no experience of, forces of attraction less wholesome than those she was used to.

She yawned. It was quieter now. Every now and then voices could be heard in the street below, but they were less animated than before; people on their way home, winding down, and the periods of silence expanded between them. *Tomorrow*, she

81

thought, *a walk in the park, a café, wandering through the shops with Olympia. No murder, no mayhem, no traumatized children.* And she slept.

Frank and Frances, arm in arm on the short, leisurely walk home to the Via delle Caldaie, had had an interesting conversation.

'Frank. So how was Niccolò Manzini?' Frances was feeling mischievous.

Frank looked at her sharply. 'Fine. Well, until his daughter arrived he seemed fine. She was brought home by a *carabiniere*; apparently her best friend was murdered on Sunday night.'

'No! What best friend? Murdered where?' Frances did not immediately connect what Frank was saying with what Lucienne and Nino had seen on the Via Maggio; her first thought was that the girl had been murdered in London, where Beatrice lived. But when Frank continued, it became clear that it had been Natasha Julius the police had carried out of Pierluigi's shop in a body bag.

'Oh, no.' Frances felt irrationally distressed, now that she knew something about the dead child. She didn't want to be able to visualize such a violent act perpetrated almost on her own doorstep. 'No, no. When did you get back last night? Did you see anything? I can't bear to think of it.'

'They found her body early this morning, apparently, but Beatrice didn't find out until this evening, when she went out. She was supposed to be meeting the girl. Ned Duncan told her. In fact, that must have been what was happening when we saw them outside the Medici. I suppose the police came to talk to him at the Villa Duncan, then brought her home.'

He stopped, frowning as though considering something. 'Frances, do you know anything about the boyfriend? Beatrice's boyfriend, Ned? You know everybody.' He sounded casual, but Frances could tell he wasn't.

'Well, I knew his grandfather a bit, George Duncan. Earl Duncan. He was five years older than me, or so. He bought the villa, you know, just after the war; it can hardly have cost him anything. Not a Medici villa, but pretty grand, in very poor repair, but quite lovely, or at least it was, until Ned's mother got hold of it. He wasn't a very nice man, though, the grandfather, actually quite horrible. He hated Ned's mother, called her a tart to her face and all over the papers, quite often, but that didn't stop the son – Ned's father – marrying her. Perhaps that's *why* he married her, to spite his father.'

Frank nodded absently. 'I think I've seen Ned Duncan in the gossip columns, hanging around with models at openings, that kind of stuff,' he said. 'I didn't realize he spent so much time out here, though. What are the parents like?'

'Well,' said Frances, reluctantly, not quite sure where Frank was heading, 'I've seen them at Nino's, for dinner, once or twice, and I generally invite them to my parties, because I don't have a good enough reason not to – I'm surprised you haven't come across them. Anyway, lately I think they've – what's the phrase? – grown apart. She spends most of her time out here, and he's only interested in the estate. The great heritage, some horrible pile in the Midlands stuffed with hideous paintings. He's always developing some new sideline to keep the place going, the fishing lake and the stables and the clay pigeons. I have the feeling –' she broke off, frowning – 'I think he has turned against Ned, rather. There was something . . . there was some gossip about Ned and some model, what was it? And George turned into his own father, quite brutal. Refused to have anything to do with Ned.' She sighed.

'So he lives with his mother?'

'A lot of the time, yes, I think so. Poor boy. I don't really like her much, to tell the absolute truth; she is rather . . . rather vicious, actually, is the word. A nasty gossip – not that I'd like to side with George. She's very polished, these days, very gracious but not kind. A snob, with terrible taste.'

Frances grimaced. 'Oh, listen to me, how awful I sound. But Ned, well, he's spent most of his life at school so it's rather hard to tell whether he's inherited it or not. The viciousness, I mean. He's always very polite when I've seen him here, actually rather sweet. I feel rather sorry for him, and I thought his friendship with little Beatrice . . . I thought that reflected rather well on him. She's a girl who's considerably nicer than her parents, so I don't see why he can't be.'

'So he spends a lot of time out here. And Beatrice, and the dead girl did, too. It's interesting, isn't it, considering how little there is in Florence for them to do?'

Frances paused to consider the question. It was true that Ned Duncan, Natasha Julius and Beatrice Manzini were off-season visitors to Florence; in Frances's experience the sons and daughters of the English aristocracy who had yet to sell off their Tuscan villas generally arrived later in the year, when their expensive private schools and universities were out, and spent a lot of time in the country, Florence in August being roasting, humid and deserted. And if they did stay in the city, they weren't usually to be found this side of the river, more with the American crowd around Santa Croce, or shopping in the Via de' Tornabuoni if they had enough money. The attractions of the Oltrarno were, in order of importance to a bored teenager, drugs, the alternative lifestyle and, optimistic-ally, the bohemian tendency, the workshops and the warmth of the working-class inhabitants.

'Well,' Frances mused, 'yes, I do see him around. Do you know, he isn't an ordinary young man. But that might not be a bad thing, that he's here when no one else seems to be. Perhaps he just loves the atmosphere; certainly you and I do, don't we?' Frank nodded, but she couldn't see what he was thinking. She changed tack. 'When I heard about the . . . the murder, do you know it didn't occur to me it might be one of them, Natasha Julius, one of the rich girls. From what Pierluigi said . . . He said he thought it was one of the travellers, if that's what they call themselves. Perhaps she got herself into something dangerous.'

They stopped, outside Frances's front door. Frances put her arms around Frank and embraced him more warmly than usual; and, feeling the elastic smoothness of his cheek, sensing that his mind was moving away from her in a different direction entirely, it occurred to her that she was getting old. Sutton held the door open while Frances found the switch to the hall's feeble light, then let it slowly swing shut as she disappeared into the gloom and he stood in the street, his face in shadow, looking back down the street to the Piazza Santo Spirito and beyond, to the dark alley where Natasha Julius's body had so recently lain.

At the back door to his shop, not fifty yards from where Stefano's conversation with Mila had taken place an hour or so earlier, Pierluigi was busy moving out some old stock; six or seven packing cases, nailed shut, stood on the pavement outside the boarded-up window, and more, not yet filled, lids leaning against them, could be glimpsed inside the shop through the glass door. Giannino was helping him load the full cases on to a trolley, two or three at a time, wheeling them down the road to a lock-up they sometimes used, the four of them. The lock-up – a *fondo*, or ground-floor storage area, usually used as a garage – didn't offer particularly good conditions for storing antiques, being damp, poorly ventilated and cluttered with *motorini* in various states of repair, but the advantage of it was that it was good for keeping the odd antique piece of dubious provenance out of the way.

They worked in silence for a while, then Giannino straightened up.

'Look, this is nothing to do with us. It was random. How could it be a warning? A couple of Kalashnikovs and a wrecking ball, that's what I call a warning.' And he snorted indignantly.

Tight-lipped, Pierluigi kept working, as if he wouldn't dignify Giannino with a response, but then he stopped, unable to let it pass.

'Better safe than sorry. We might have sold a dodgy piece to the wrong guy, somewhere along the line. Let's just get on with it, eh?'

Giannino didn't seem to want to let it rest. 'Couldn't be Giulietta, could it, getting jealous?' Giulietta was the most prominent among Pierluigi's girlfriends, and well aware of her position. Giannino barked with laughter. 'Come to think of it, Kalashnikovs and a wrecking ball would be more her style, too.'

Pierluigi ignored him. Giannino went on.

'No, take it from me, it's nothing to do with our little deals here and there. We barely even break the law, not by some people's standards. I'd like to know who it was, all the same. Barbaric; she was just a kid. I'll bet it wasn't an Italian, that's for sure. Albanian, they're savages. A gypsy, maybe.'

But Pierluigi just shook his head at these musings, and for the next half-hour they worked steadily, in silence. The packing cases all sealed up and shipped around the corner, together they hauled the *fondo*'s steel shutter down to the ground and padlocked it shut with a decisive flourish, as though drawing a line under the events of the previous twenty-four hours. The night was cool but both men were sweating. Pierluigi clapped Giannino on the shoulder, and they walked their separate routes home through the night, Pierluigi a hundred yards or so to his penthouse over the Via Maggio, Giannino further downmarket, to an artisan's cottage in San Frediano. At last the city seemed completely still, her streets quite empty, guarded by the great brooding buildings that had, after all, borne witness to greater atrocities than the quick death of a girl.

Tuesday

9

Jane was woken by the sound of a buzzer below. She lay waiting, but as it didn't ring again she didn't move, or even open her eyes. She was calculating. It was just too tricky having Gina around just now; although actually, Jane reflected, she didn't seem too bad, not the neurotic she'd expected at all. Reserved, but then she always had been, still pretty, in a faded sort of way, Jane grudgingly admitted, and something under the surface, something resolute, something that put up resistance. Still, with all this police business going on, and Nicky very unpredictable, a house guest – any house guest, really – was too much.

Jane decided she would suggest that Gina might like to go down to the country house in the Maremma tomorrow, just for a day or two. Florence would, after all, be horribly crowded and the weather forecast, for unseasonably high temperatures, meant that the only sensible option would be to go out to the hills. Nicky could give her a lift on his way down to Rome, or – she had a suspicion she wouldn't be able to rely on Nicky's co-operation – maybe Frank. There was always something a journalist could go down to Rome for, and he'd mentioned the possibility of visiting Nicky's site down there. She suppressed the ghost of a doubt at the good sense of putting Gina, set free from her domestic circumstances, in a car with a reasonably good-looking journalist for a couple of hours, unchaperoned. And Gina could always come back for Frances's party, at the end of the week. Jane reached a hand to the side to ask Niccolò what he thought, then remembered, furious, that he had gone to his dressing room; these days he didn't even feel he needed an excuse.

If she was going to talk Gina into going, she'd better make sure everything was sorted out down there. She opened her eyes to the golden light flooding her bedroom and reached for the phone.

Seventy miles south, the telephone rang in the front room of Barbara Venturi's tiny, impeccably clean stone cottage in the village of Leccio, a few modest dwellings and a rustic pizzeria strung along on a ridge above the river Ombrone. Barbara spoke to the English *signora* for no more than five minutes; the instructions she received were familiar. She replaced the receiver and immediately dialled her niece, who helped her, since her arthritis had got worse, with the cleaning work she carried out for Signora Manzini and a handful of other foreigners with holiday homes in the area. Within fifteen minutes her niece and her boyfriend had arrived on their Vespa; Barbara mounted her own, more elderly version, and they set off for Il Rondinaio, the Manzinis' country house.

On the way, the Venturi convoy stopped at Giorgio's house; Giorgio tended the garden at Il Rondinaio, watering the coarse lawn in the summer drought, cleaning out the swimming pool, pruning, weeding the vegetable plot and doing any heavy work for Barbara in the house. At night the orange light above Giorgio's porch at his own smallholding – two hectares of olives and one of vines, unproductive and overgrown – was visible to the girls working the road below, the notorious S223; indeed, if the little group of workers had moved right to the edge of the narrow, winding road they were now buzzing along briskly, and had leant over – not advisable, as the bare, rocky hillside dropped away precipitously at that side – to look down at the river, they might have seen Evelina's body, far below. They wouldn't have thought much of it, even if they'd seen her; the woods and scrub, though apparently silent and empty, often held rough sleepers, most of them German, lighting fires and setting up camp illegally under the cover of the forest. This was a volcanic region, and the hot springs that were to be found, often quite unexploited, here and there along the river's course, seemed to be a magnet for a certain kind of unkempt foreigner, tolerated with surprising good humour by the older generation of locals, who made use of the reeking sulphurous water's healing properties.

But Barbara and her growing entourage weren't looking down, and they didn't see the body; nor did they see Stefano, in the dirty brown Opel he used for this purpose, drawing up to deposit Mila at the head of a dirt-track off the busy road, no more than half a mile north from the lay-by where Evelina's sandals still lay. Barbara had better things to do than to stare at prostitutes, and they headed on up to the top of the ridge, much admired for its breathtaking views across the dark, empty hills, where Il Rondinaio loomed, shuttered and silent, above them.

Stefano wanted rid of Mila but she didn't like sitting in uneasy silence in the dusty car any more than he did; perhaps, she thought, he didn't think it was worth driving all this way with just one girl. There had been a time, a couple of years back, when there'd been three or four of them. Anna got sick – AIDS, though no one bothered to say it, even, but there came a time, you could see the signs. She had a sister, Mara, and she ran off, disappeared anyway, and the last one, a young girl, no more than sixteen, she overdosed only a month or so after she'd arrived from Romania. And then there was one.

'Go on, get out, we're late. Got your mobile? I don't know what you're wearing that for, you look like my grandmother. I'll be back at nine.'

Stefano wore a suit, and his shirt collar was digging into his neck. He was sweating; the old Opel didn't have air-conditioning, and it was already in the eighties. He pulled

Mila's door shut, and the car's sagging rear end accelerated off the gravel of the lay-by, kicking up white dust behind it.

Mila wondered what had got into him, and looked down at her dress; it was brown, but it was like silk, not real of course, but still. He just didn't like her; he was disgusted that his girl didn't pull in the same kind of customers as the others, the African girls, Evelina and Glory and the rest, in their hotpants and halter tops, and anyway her legs weren't good enough; pale, with thread veins flowering on her thighs, and her knees gone soft and dimpled. She shrugged, unfolded her chair in the dusty shade and thrust her bag out of sight in the bushes.

The road was still quiet, though further back down the road towards Grosseto she could hear the workmen they'd passed, chainsaws and strimmers buzzing as they hacked back the foliage on the verges. Mila walked out into the middle of the road and craned her neck to see around the corner. Evelina's pitch was empty. They were lazy, those girls, just liked lying in bed eating sweets. Mila was surprised they got away with it. Still, maybe she hadn't got back till late. Then she saw Evelina's umbrella, open at the back of the lay-by, and she frowned. She could hear a car and ran back to the verge. When it had passed, a family in it going down to the sea with the mother in the passenger seat, staring at her curiously, she ran up the road towards the umbrella.

It didn't take her more than a minute, she'd have said, barefoot on the hot tarmac, to arrive at Evelina's pitch. Panting in the heat, she looked behind her as she ran across the gravel to the back of the lay-by. She stopped. *Maybe Evelina's already here*, she thought without conviction, *but where?* She'd never leave her umbrella out like that; she always stashed it somewhere, if she had a customer. Betty had bought it for her; she loved that umbrella, hung on to it like it was a teddy bear, not to mention the kind of dark threats she'd get if she lost it, a voodoo curse or a beating for her mother back home. Somehow it didn't feel like she'd just gone off to the shop or something, and if she was with a customer, where was his car?

Something about it didn't look right, either. It was resting against Evelina's stool, and a thin plastic carrier stuffed with rubbish had been dumped down next to it, the ripped and faded cover from a child's car seat and a crushed plastic water bottle; as though Evelina's possessions had stopped being hers, and had become random garbage. If Evelina had set up here, no one would have dumped rubbish right beside her, and if they had – sometimes people could be evil, it was true – Evelina would have moved it away. What it looked like was that Evelina's stuff had been here for a while, maybe all yesterday. Mila tried to think. Sunday night. Had she looked out, to see if the Nigerian girl was still there, when Stefano drove her back up to the city on Sunday night?

The reassuring buzz of the road-clearing crew seemed a long way away up here, though Mila could still hear it, distantly. Otherwise it was almost silent, a perfect clear early morning, even some birds singing in the trees above her. A car hadn't passed in a while now. Tentatively Mila touched the umbrella, and then she saw Evelina's sandal and felt a pounding in her throat. She should run. But she couldn't go until she knew for sure, so she looked around once, then on she went, around the stool to the entrance to the tunnel in the underbrush. She saw the other sandal, on its side, and squatted down for a closer look. Still just the whirr of the strimmers in the distance. The sandal's strap was broken, and stained with something dark. Mila didn't want to go down, into the tunnel through the undergrowth. It was where Evelina did some of her customers, cramped and stinking, brackish, urine and something worse, and it was dark.

Reluctantly, Mila half crouched and shuffled in. The path beneath her feet was uneven and littered with condoms, stones, twigs – she didn't want to look down. It sloped sharply away, out of sight, and slowly she edged forward. It wasn't so quiet in here; she could hear tiny noises, rustling, the snapping of a twig, and her own breathing. Suddenly she couldn't bear to be in there, and with a violent heave backed out, into the light. She stood, blinking in the sun, and behind her she felt the passage of a succession of cars, a gust of displaced air whipping her skirt around her legs, and heard the grind of changing gears, sensed the drivers staring, though she couldn't see them.

In the sudden silence that followed Mila stared down at Evelina's things – the umbrella, the stool, the shoes – and, although she could feel the heat of the sun on her back, the hairs rose on her bare arms; she shivered. She turned quickly and looked at the hills to either side of the road, at the dense carpet of trees, the wild acacias, the myrtle and cork trees that might conceal Evelina, sleeping, or hiding, or hurt, or dead. Mila wondered who could be in there now, watching her, and she began to run, her sandals in her hand, back down the road towards the sound of the road-clearing crew and a lorry with a queue of cars behind it, its engine straining as it climbed the hill at the approach to the bridge from the south.

The buzzer that had failed to interrupt Jane's calculations had not, as she had assumed, been answered by Inés, but by Gina. Unable by force of habit to sleep later than five-thirty – which, rather cheeringly, turned out to be six-thirty in Italy – after five minutes' contemplation of the etiquette of early rising, Gina had tiptoed downstairs in the dark, the need for a cup of tea overcoming everything else.

The drawing room was dim, though the grey light of early morning was beginning to brighten it through the slats of the shutters. To Gina's surprise, she could see a light on in the kitchen, and as she approached it Niccolò Manzini appeared in the doorway. She jumped back slightly and he looked up.

His chin was dark with stubble, and his narrow face looked tired and drawn. He held a cup of coffee between his hands, and smiled at her as if to reassure her.

'Coffee?' he asked cheerfully. 'No, tea. Am I right?'

Gina smiled. 'Thanks. So sad to be so predictably English.'

As she watched him fill the kettle Gina wondered what he was doing up so early. Perhaps because she had an over-active imagination, or because she was unused to men with his kind of charisma, she had found him unsettling at dinner, something unreadably, alarmingly intense about the relationships he had with his wife, his daughter, even with Frank Sutton; she had found his reaction to the murder quite other than she would have expected. Stephen, for example, would have puzzled over it with the rest of them, but Niccolò Manzini had remained almost silent. Had he been angry? Disturbed? Afraid? She didn't have experience of a wide variety of male reactions, so perhaps his response fell within the normal range. Certainly now he was in front of her, handing her a cup of tea, he seemed like an ordinary man, disarmingly tired and anxious.

Gina made herself relax; she should have stayed in a hotel, she told herself. She hated being a guest, having to creep about, unsure of what she could and couldn't do, where was out of bounds. Still, it was hardly Bluebeard's castle, she told herself; the minimalist apartment couldn't have been less Gothic. Although it appeared to have any number of hidden cupboards and oubliettes, if the kitchen was anything to go by – she had just watched Niccolò press what looked like a simple panel of pale wood but turned out to be a door, which sprang open to reveal ranked rows of tea and coffee. She sat down gingerly at the wooden slab of table and sipped her tea, which was very hot and faintly scented.

'Not a good start to your holiday. Sorry,' said Niccolò after a pause.

Gina didn't know what to say. She shrugged a little. 'I hope it's all cleared up soon,' she said. 'It must be awful for your daughter. Did you know the girl – the murdered . . . Natasha very well? Jane said she used to stay here sometimes.'

Niccolò looked at her, frowning slightly. 'Well, not really. Beatrice's best friend; she was always here. But you know what teenage girls are like. Not mature conversationalists. And the kids would only come out in the summer, holiday time, that kind of thing. Longer this time, because Bea's got her year out, so no commitments. Though I'd be happier if she found something useful to do instead of just . . . Maybe this wouldn't have happened, if they – ' He broke off, and smiled rather stiffly; perhaps it was her imagination again, but he seemed cooler, less friendly suddenly. She tried to change the subject.

'It's a lovely flat. Dinner was wonderful, well, it was, until . . . Your friends are very nice.'

Niccolò nodded slowly. He was very good-looking, she thought once again, beautiful eyes. Perhaps he had killed Natasha, she suddenly found herself thinking, and her mind ran on ahead of her. Perhaps she knew something about him, she was blackmailing him . . . And all the while Gina looked at him quite calmly, and wondered what it was about him that put such thoughts in her head. Too slight, perhaps; men who probably weighed less than her made Gina uncomfortable. And she had the unmistakable feeling that she was in his way.

'Yes,' he said. 'Olympia and James are interesting people. And Frank Sutton, of course, though I can't help being wary of journalists. Questionable motives, don't you think?' He smiled at her, a candid, open smile, and Gina felt wrong-footed.

'Didn't you – isn't he an old friend of yours?' She tried to make it sound a neutral question. But then the buzzer sounded and without thinking she went to the intercom.

'Is Beatrice there?' It was a young man's voice, soft, pleading.

She turned back to Niccolò and held the intercom out to him. 'Beatrice?' she said. He took it, his smile gone, and listened while the young man's voice spoke urgently into the speaker in the street below.

'No, you can't. Do you know what the time is?' Manzini was angry. 'You know what kind of state she was in yesterday. She's asleep, and when she wakes up she's got to talk to the police –' He was interrupted, but talked over the voice. 'Leave her alone, Ned.' His voice was low, and his tone wasn't friendly.

Gina backed into the kitchen and gently placed her cup in the sink, then she slipped back past Niccolò with an apologetic wave. As she passed he nodded to her, still holding the intercom and smiling a little stiffly. She took the stairs two at a time up to her room.

Plenty of people wondered why Frank Sutton had ended up in Florence and not New York, or London, or Rome at the very least. It was such a backwater, in journalistic terms, nothing newsworthy had happened in Florence, bar the occasional act of God or Red Brigade outrage, in 500 years. It was a tourist place, full of history, most of it ancient, and anyone who gave in to the temptation to settle in here turned into history, sooner rather than later.

Sutton put it down, when asked, to laziness; the psychiatrists, both amateur and professional, among his acquaintance put it down to his mother. When he was thirteen and away at school – in fact, at the same experimental boarding school attended at the time by Niccolò Manzini – Frank's mother had killed herself, in their old estate car, in the garage adjoining their house. There had been some surprise that Frank's father had continued to send him to the boarding school for some years after his mother's death, but perhaps he had been at a loss as to how to care for the boy at home.

It was impossible to deny that later on, while at university, Frank Sutton had undergone a change: from being a brilliant undergraduate he became a reluctant, procrastinating PhD student, and then an increasingly peripatetic journalist, turning down the big stuff he was offered on the strength of his reputation at Oxford in favour of interviews with obscure novelists. Most people's idea of a journalist was the investigative kind, a news journalist, but Frank Sutton seemed to prefer his reality mitigated, by art, or ritual, or history, and all of them were well catered for here. And he would say, when pushed, that he preferred the freedom of an ancient provincial city to the gruesome alternatives of spare man on the London dinner-party circuit or under the strip-lighting of an open-plan office in Canary Wharf. But Frances, for one, and Olympia, with whom he had had a brief affair shortly after his arrival in Florence, for another, were beginning to worry about his growing distaste for the mainstream, both professionally and personally.

It was particularly unusual, therefore, for Frank Sutton to be scrolling through cuttings in the early-morning gloom of his still-shuttered flat, engaged in what was, undeniably, the investigation of a piece of genuine news, namely the murder of Natasha Julius.

Frank was using his laptop to search the Internet for references to the murdered girl. It came up with a lot on her father, a fairly well-known if not very widely read novelist – a magical realist – who lived in Hamburg, divorced from her mother, an English ex-model, sixties vintage. Natasha had lived mostly with the mother, it seemed. The computer's search of newspaper archives tracked down a few diary pieces in which she was pictured, sometimes with her mother, mostly in London, as well as one season's worth of fashion shots – obviously she had worked for a spell as a catwalk model. She had been a startlingly beautiful girl; her black hair cropped like a boy's, her face a pale oval out of which gazed great dark eyes, her expression dreamily serene. Then Sutton drew up a picture of Natasha at the inauguration of a new gallery, a fantastically sleek structure of sandstone and glass recognizable as the work of Niccolò Manzini. Natasha was standing between Beatrice and Niccolò, her arm around her best friend's shoulders, looking up, awestruck, at the building's towering atrium. Manzini was looking at Natasha's exquisite profile, smiling slightly, and his hand rested lightly on her hip. Sutton sat back in his chair, looking at the image for some time before saving the page.

Now Frank brought up cuttings relating to Ned Duncan. Although Duncan was still only twenty-two, he already had quite a file – mostly from gossip columns, though there was one tiny news item referring to a suspended sentence for possession of cannabis three years previously. The quantity of cannabis reportedly found in Duncan's possession was quite considerable, and anyone familiar with drugs law would have assumed that it was only because of the boy's age, or thanks to a very good lawyer, that he had escaped the more severe penalty for which he would have been liable had he been charged with dealing. The school Duncan was attending at the time was a very expensive boot camp for the problem children of the moneyed classes, and it had a reputation as a last resort. Duncan was subsequently expelled.

Not much of his chequered past could have been deduced from the other cuttings Frank found, though. The few photographs he came upon showed the young man chatting politely with minor royals, a notoriously badly behaved conceptual artist, PR men and B-list fashion celebrities at a selection of parties – a private view, a film première, the opening of a Bond Street couture palace and at a catwalk show in New York. He was generally described as an entrepreneur, though there was a six-month stint as an A & R man for a record company; there was usually some reference to his father's fortune. There seemed to be one constant: the girl. Not Beatrice Manzini. Catherine Morley – Cat Morley – was her name. She was a model, too, with extraordinary almond eyes; tiny and pale, not one of the tall, golden-skinned kind. She never seemed to be smiling. She had died, in a hotel in New York, of an overdose, around about the time that the cuttings referring to Ned Duncan abruptly stopped, halfway through the previous year.

Frank Sutton instructed his computer to print out all of the cuttings he had downloaded from the Internet. Then, after a moment's hesitation, instead of logging off, he typed in Niccolò Manzini's name, something intent and hurried about his stance, like an addict ashamed of satisfying a craving, and clicked on 'search'.

Jane's proposal met surprisingly little resistance from Gina: within five minutes of her arrival at the breakfast table under the little loggia, she had agreed that a few days in the quiet of the countryside would be very welcome. Perhaps it was the temperature; at eight-thirty in the morning and after a cool shower, Jane could already feel the heat prickling her skin.

Jane drank her black coffee in satisfied silence; all that remained was to break the news to Nicky, and she had just begun to wonder why he was taking so long in the shower when he appeared at the door, looking pale and tired.

'I've got to go. Beatrice is waiting downstairs. I don't know when we'll be back.' He turned as if to go straight down.

'Yes – wait, darling; I thought it would be nice for Gina to go down to the country tomorrow, just for a day or two, as everything's so awful here at the moment.' She looked at him, waiting.

'What?' Niccolò's voice was still soft, but there was a note of urgency in it and he made a convulsive movement with his hands.

Jane could see the pulsing of a nerve in Nicky's cheek. *Yes*, she thought, then she said, carefully, 'It's all right, darling, I've phoned Signora Venturi. She'll go in and, you know, make sure everything's in the right place.'

Let him wonder, she thought triumphantly, *let him wonder whether I know what he gets up to down there on the way back from Rome*. Niccolò looked sharply at his wife, but her face was as smooth and blandly innocent as that of an air hostess offering a complimentary drink. He opened his mouth, then seemed to change his mind.

'I've got to go,' he said, smiled a goodbye to Gina and turned on his heel.

Jane phoned Frank. Nicky wasn't going to be giving anyone a lift, obviously, so she needed him; and after all the trouble Nicky had made about her inviting him last night, it was the least he could do.

'Frank, it was so sweet of you to help us out last night, I am sorry it all ended in such chaos.'

'Well, it could hardly be helped, could it,' Frank said gruffly.

'Well, no, I suppose not. They are such a worry, children, aren't they?'

He was silent.

'Anyway,' Jane went on, 'I wondered whether . . . Are you going down to Rome tomorrow? I thought you mentioned something about going to Nicky's site? If you are, could you take the Siena road and give Gina a lift to Il Rondinaio? It's just that Nicky is so tied up with this awful business and it's quite impossible to get there by train, and I think the poor thing is feeling rather in the way.'

She heard him sigh.

'Fine. Yes, fine. But it'll have to be early. Jane –' she was already saying goodbye, her objective achieved. 'Would you mind if I talked to Ned Duncan? I think I'd like to write a thoughtful sort of piece about young people in Florence, in the wake of this . . . tragedy. Do you think you could have a word with his mother for me, just reassure her about the kind of thing I write?'

Jane thought about it for a moment. What kind of thing did Frank write? She had the nagging feeling she was being manipulated, but she didn't have the energy to resist just now. 'Mind? Why should I mind? Yes, I'll give her a ring. But don't stir things up – and do be careful what you say, won't you, if I'm going to be your entrée? And for God's sake keep us out of it. I don't know what it is between you and Nicky, but I wish you'd both just grow up and get over it.'

She waited. On the other end of the line Sutton did not respond immediately, but then cleared his throat.

'I'll keep you out of it. Thanks.' And he hung up.

Jane Stamp had grown up in a diplomatic household. Literally diplomatic – her father had moved smoothly up the ranks in the Foreign Office until, by the time Jane was nine, he reached ambassador; not Paris or Rome, of course, but a very comfortable tropical posting. From her father and, more significantly, her mother, a quite ruthlessly charming diplomatic hostess, Jane had learnt very early on in life the virtues of discretion and the value of privileged information.

There had been plenty of clandestine relationships carried on in the cloistered atmosphere of the British Embassy compound, and when she was thirteen and looking for her tennis kit Jane had come upon her mother in the laundry room with a man she knew from handing round canapés at embassy functions to be an important war correspondent with wandering hands, foul breath and a fondness for very young women – her mother being, she immediately suspected, an expedient exception to that rule. The subsequent conversation had been very instructive, conferring upon Jane a keen if jaundiced understanding of adult relationships; it had also given her mother a new respect for her daughter's intelligence. So while Jane's suspicions about Nicky's sexual preferences – she had soon understood, for example, that the location of Il Rondinaio, not half a mile from the most notorious strip of road in Tuscany, was far from accidental – occasionally tormented her, they didn't shock her to the core. Now, however, she was beginning to feel unsettled, and angry. Nicky's unfailing charm, and his respect for her position as his wife, were, she detected, beginning to slip, and she didn't like the way he had moved out of her room without paying her the courtesy of an excuse. She thought it was time she reminded him of her virtues, particularly her understanding nature, which was why she had let him know that she didn't mind cleaning up after him, or at least paying Barbara Venturi to do it.

10

The Duncans' villa wasn't much more than half a mile from the outer edge of Florence, across the grimy roar of the ring road running beneath the city wall, uphill between the sad façades, blackened with exhaust fumes, of the once proud apartment blocks built a hundred years before to overlook the city and now exiled by four lanes of traffic, and up the steep incline towards Bellosguardo. The hills surrounding Florence were where the properly wealthy, as opposed to the merely aristocratic, residents of the city lived, raised above the leaden smog and stifling humidity and with a fine view of the Duomo and the distant mountains. Very few of those who could afford the villas in the hills were year-round residents; either, like the Duncans, they were rich foreigners, or they were captains of

Italian industry who owned a place here, one in Rome, a little place on the lakes and an estate by the sea. Hence security was tight: each villa's garden had a high wall topped with barbed wire or broken glass and entry was possible only through heavy, remote-controlled gates; several even had gatehouses and close-circuit cameras to monitor their perimeter.

Vivienne, Lady Duncan, had been very dubious indeed when Frank Sutton called her. Jane wouldn't have recognized Sutton from the careful, considered tones in which he couched his request, for access to Vivienne's son to discuss the murder of Natasha Julius. Vivienne Duncan had, however, talked to Jane already; otherwise, she would have hung up immediately. Most women of Lady Duncan's social position treated the press with lofty disdain, unless they came with a discreetly respectable cheque and a society photographer.

Frank admitted immediately that he was keen to hear Ned's side of the story of Natasha Julius's last night; Lady Duncan would only find, he said, sounding slightly sheepish, that someone less principled would get to them anyway and at least Frank's was a broadsheet newspaper. He mentioned his friendship with Lady Richardson, which seemed to alter the timbre of the conversation for the better, and eventually Lady Duncan – Vivienne, she insisted – agreed that, although at that moment Ned was still asleep – quite exhausted – if Frank were to come up shortly before lunch she would make sure Ned was up and was prepared to talk to him.

After a brief, heavily distorted conversation on an intercom with Lady Duncan, the surly gatekeeper reluctantly allowed Sutton through the gate and directed him up the half-mile of freshly raked gravel drive to the villa. The grass was closely mowed and an unnaturally bright shade of green, and the drive was flanked by huge rosebeds, some already in garish flower. The house itself was vast, and painted a rich terracotta pink; its ground-floor windows seemed to be heavily barred, but a broad balcony with long French windows opening on to it ran around the house at first-floor level. A dark-haired figure could be seen sprawled across a teak recliner on the balcony. A massive door was set dead centre on the ground floor, and Lady Duncan stood waiting beneath its portico, a petulant expression on her flawlessly made-up face.

In the sunlit quiet back at the Manzinis' flat Gina phoned Stephen, at work. She told herself it would be crazy to phone him at home just as he was getting everyone ready to leave the house, when lunchboxes and lost socks and toothpaste would be on his mind. And she wasn't quite ready to hear the background screech and wail just yet. Waking up in Jane's house to perfect warmth, light and quiet, she had felt for an instant as though she had slipped into an alternative universe, in which she had in fact chosen the path of spinsterhood and independence, and was only now awaking from a turbulent dream of motherhood. Or that she'd died and gone to heaven. The absence of a child's warm, oblivious body beside her, or small arms snaking around her neck, came to her only as a poignant afterthought, raising no more than a momentary pang.

'It's me. Are you busy? How are things?'

'Oh, you know. Fine, we're managing fine. No trips to casualty. Dan slept through; got them to school OK; Kath's having Dan while I'm working and helping out a bit after school.'

Kath was the childminder they'd used in the brief and nightmarish period during which Gina had returned to work, between Jim and Dan.

'So they're all right, then, without . . . without me?'

'Yes, well, you know, they miss you now and then, of course, but generally, yes, they don't seem to notice. We had pizza last night but I think I can get on top of the food thing.'

Gina didn't feel as put out as she had expected to by this evidence that she was not indispensable; she even managed to disregard Stephen's implication that her useful role was confined to food provision.

'There is one thing –' Stephen lowered his voice and Gina's heart sank – 'socks, Dan won't wear socks. He says they don't feel right. Any of them.'

'He'll only wear the green and red ones. But it doesn't matter if he doesn't wear any at all.' Then she thought of something. 'Stephen, did you sleep with Jane once – at college, I mean?'

There was a stunned silence.

'Well, I – why on earth are you asking me that now? What's Jane been saying?' Stephen hissed.

Gina laughed. 'Her? Not a word. You mean you did?' she said cheerfully. 'It doesn't matter, I just wanted to know. Stop making a fuss.' And she said goodbye.

Gina and Stephen had been married for twelve years and, Gina had often thought fondly, they had moved beyond conversation; suddenly she was inclined to view the comfortable silence between them less charitably. There were, she realized, plenty of subjects they hadn't raised even when they did have proper conversations; they had never, it occurred to her, talked much about their lives and relationships before they met each other, for one, nor about sex, to Gina's intermittent frustration, for another. Not that she wanted to be married to someone who talked about it all the time, but it might not do any harm to mention it once in a while, just to be reassured that it was something that mattered, still. And in some ways worst of all, whenever she began to relate one of the thousand bitterly frustrating, or even darkly funny, incidents peppering her domestic existence, Stephen seemed, unless it was her imagination, to sigh. Surely she would feel better if she was listened to, now and then. Gina began to wonder whether her little break from the family was going to have quite the effect they had expected.

On balance, Gina had been quite happy to comply with Jane's suggestion that she leave Florence for a day or two. She felt sorry for Beatrice, having a stranger hanging around the house when she was so unhappy, and she was relieved to have been shown a way out. She'd have today in the city, after all, and the thought of it, of a day wandering the beautiful streets unencumbered by responsibilities or obligations, was unexpectedly thrilling. She would, she decided, go shopping with Olympia this afternoon – why not? And she thought of her twenties, in her first job and living in London, waking up on a Saturday morning basking in the delicious prospect of a day looking for the perfect new dress then a party later to wear it at. With Olympia, she had a feeling the experience would be as good. So that left the morning. Gina decided she would go for a walk in the park.

'He says he can't see the point of talking to you,' said Lady Duncan – Vivienne, she reminded him – crossly, and glared up at the balcony. 'But I've told him he must.'

Like her roses, Vivienne Duncan was a fairly gaudy and artificial specimen, and mildly alarming. It would have been hard to pinpoint her exact age, though it was probably closer to sixty than forty. Her hair was a vivid dark auburn, the skin of her face taut but curiously immobile and her china-blue eyes wide in an expression of unvarying mild surprise that even to the inexperienced observer suggested cosmetic surgery. She wore a triple-strand choker of pearls with a fat diamond clasp at her neck, a closely fitted powder-blue suit fastened at the waist with a large gilt brooch, and matching heels.

'You are very kind,' said Frank, carefully. 'It really won't take long. This is such a lovely villa; did you design the gardens yourself?' Vivienne's irritable expression immediately lifted and was replaced by one of complacent satisfaction.

'Well, with the help of an old friend, a landscape gardener, yes. You'd be surprised how many people assume it was professionally done. And the house, too; I designed and sourced everything myself. Do come in and have a look, then Giuseppina can take you up to Ned.'

She offered him her arm, and he took it with barely perceptible hesitation and walked in through the massive, imposing doorway. Giuseppina, an elderly Italian woman in a maid's frilled apron, was instructed in loud and imperious English to make some coffee and take it up to the balcony.

Except for a rather incongruous mural of a vista, part Tuscan, part Neapolitan, in the hall, the interior decoration was so thoroughly fussy English country-house in style, from fitted Wilton carpeting to shirred chintz knicker-blinds, as to have the rather startling effect of almost completely obscuring the house itself. As had been recorded in countless society photoshoots, what was, on the outside, a classic Italian villa became, as the threshold was crossed, a furniture warehouse's approximation of Chatsworth. Lady Duncan showed Sutton from sitting room to breakfast room to dining room before handing him, half suffocated by soft furnishings and small talk, over to Giuseppina, who showed him out to the first-floor balcony and Signore Ned. She stood in the doorway for a moment, watching, then, when Frank turned back towards her, she stepped away into the interior of the house.

Ned Duncan was sitting in a long, teak plantation chair, staring out across the city. He held his temples between his hands, his fingers in his hair, in an attitude of quiet desperation. He looked unhappy, his shoulders hunched angrily under a clean but creased white shirt. He also looked very young. A heavy black fringe flopped in his large, dark, long-lashed eyes.

'Sorry,' said Frank, clearing his throat. 'I'm sorry.' He sounded as if he was surprised by his own sincerity, or perhaps Ned's palpable misery had startled him into regetting his own presence there. Ned turned to look at him, finally.

'That's OK,' he said slowly. 'I suppose there's nothing anyone can do about it now. What do you want?'

Frank remained standing. 'Look, if you don't want to talk about it yet –' he said, with a hint of reluctance.

'Talk about what? What do you want me to say?' Ned sounded listless, rather than aggressive, as though the desire to put up any resistance to the journalist had been drained from him.

'Natasha. Really, I'd just like to know about her. Her life here, and your life, as a group, the children of people like your parents, expatriate children. It must be . . . a terrible shock.'

Ned straightened up, shaking his head. 'There's no group. Just me, and Beatrice and Tash, sometimes a few others come out from home, you know, to do Florence, but they don't stay around for long. But Bea – Bea's shocked, of course she is. She loved Tash – I did too – she's – she *was* – a very special person.'

Frank nodded. 'Her parents –'

'They split up a long time ago,' said Ned, with a hint of contempt. 'They don't . . . their split doesn't explain Tash at all. Don't try to put her down as some poor victim of a broken home. That's the kind of thing my mother would say.'

'So what was she like?' Frank asked quietly. He sat down.

'She could paint. She did textiles. She could speak Italian, French, Spanish, a bit of Russian. German. She was incredible to look at, do you know what she looked like? You must have seen her?'

Frank nodded, and Ned went on.

'There was something about her – charm, I suppose. She made people love her, they couldn't help it. But then she could turn; she liked to push people as far as she could, to see how far she could go before they'd had enough. Like she led Beatrice up the garden path often enough, all darling and sweetie, then she'd leave Bea behind at the drop of a hat, off with someone more fun, to do something more daring. Some people are like that.'

Frank nodded thoughtfully. 'Do you think that's what got her killed?'

Ned frowned. 'I hadn't thought of that. I was just trying to describe what she was like. I don't know.' He turned away from Frank again, towards the view. Beyond the trees the city's rooftops shimmered in the haze of the midday heat.

'Did you have a relationship with her, Ned? With Natasha? Before Beatrice, or –' He broke off; Ned was turning on him.

'How can you ask me that? Whose business would that be? I suppose you want to know how much I'm suffering, do you? Plus, if you knew anything at all about Tash, you'd know she didn't "do" relationships. You don't understand anything.'

Frank nodded, and fell silent. Ned turned away, his hands clenched on his knees.

'What do you do out here, Ned? You're – what, twenty-two? You used to have a great job in England, didn't you, scouting for bands or something? Where's that all gone?' Frank's voice was friendly, in a careful sort of way.

'Yes. I screwed it up, though. I was stupid, and I screwed my whole life up. I'm here to sort myself out, really.' He looked at Frank pleadingly, his eyes shining dark in his handsome face. 'It's not working, though, is it?' He buried his face in his hands.

Frank stood as if to go, but didn't move towards the door. Then he took a measured breath and spoke again, and this time his voice was different.

'Was it drugs? Is that why you left? Did you get drugs for Natasha? And what about Manzini? I think there was something between them, too, wasn't there? Or had been, once?'

Ned gave an inarticulate cry, muffled by his hands, and when he looked up his face was pale with misery. 'She didn't need me to get her drugs. And if you want to know if her best friend's dad was sleeping with her,' his voice cracked, hoarse with emotion – disgust or grief or both – 'why don't you ask him?'

There was a brief, heavy silence, but then Frank went on. 'What if I told your mother you buy drugs from Stefano in the Piazza Santo Spirito, where I saw you last night?' Ned shook his head, mute.

'OK, OK, I'm sorry, Ned. But I'd like to know what happened, on Sunday evening. That last evening; Tash's last Sunday. Was it an ordinary Sunday? Same sort of thing as you usually did?'

Ned looked up at Frank from under his fringe, then spoke, his phrasing terse and cold, as though every word was dragged from him.

'We went to the country. To Niccolò's house. Beatrice's father's house, down in the Maremma. We do that – *did* that – sometimes. Swim in the river, light fires in the woods, barbecue.' He hung his head, shielding himself from Frank's direct gaze, his cheeks wet.

'Then we came back, hung out at Santo Spirito, I took Bea back, Tash went somewhere, I thought she'd gone home, on her own. When I woke up the next morning, Tash was dead.'

'You went straight home after you took Beatrice back?'

'Yes.'

'Was your mother up when you got back?'

'I told the police everything. I don't know if you have the right to ask things like this. Leave me alone, please.'

Frank sighed. 'All right, Ned. All right. Just make sure . . . Make sure you know what you're doing. It doesn't look as though Florence is a nice safe place to sort your life out, after all, does it? I'll see myself out.' And Ned watched, his face suddenly gaunt, older than his years, as Frank walked off the balcony into the villa's flowery, perfumed interior.

'Did you get everything you wanted?' asked Vivienne breathlessly after accepting Frank's thanks. 'If you'd like to send a photographer, I'm sure we could let you have some pictures, too; family shots, you know, and of course the house photographs beautifully. And you will send anything you write to us for approval, won't you?'

Frank nodded absently, but Vivienne seemed satisfied, and squeezed his arm warmly with her heavily ringed and manicured hand.

The gatekeeper's face was sour as he watched Frank leave, walking back down to leave the rose-scented atmosphere of the Villa Duncan for the polluted air of the ring road and the dirty city beyond. He didn't look like a journalist, and he seemed nosier than most. And you'd think, to look at his expression, that he'd just trodden in dog shit, not walked through the most expensively tended garden in Bellosguardo.

Barbara Venturi, her arthritic fingers slow and clumsy, unlocked first the outer iron-barred gate – for security, which Signore Manzini, and Barbara, for that matter, considered very important with all the *albanesi* prowling about, helping themselves to people's private property – then the heavy oak door. Inside Il Rondinaio was silent and dark, but immediately she knew that someone had been there. It wasn't in a mess, and that was sometimes what greeted her, particularly when the young ones had been staying. She couldn't quite put her finger on it; some things had been moved, certainly – a lamp, one of the big oak chairs – and if anything, somebody had cleaned up rather than left the place a tip; had cleaned up but not quite to Barbara's standards. She sighed, then shrugged. She directed her niece to the kitchen, to clean the oven and the heavy iron grill for cooking steaks. She turned and found Giorgio at her shoulder, uncomfortably close, she thought, given the strong odour of wine and manure he seemed to harbour. She shooed him out to cut back the roses and turn on the sprinklers.

'And pick me some parsley, and tomatoes.' She watched him amble off, his white flannel shirt buttoned to his chin, heavily dressed in a handknitted sweater and ancient quilted jacket. *Harmless enough*, she thought; though she had her own opinions about the amount of time he spent loitering along the main road, staring gormlessly at the whores. Giorgio had always had a reputation for being rather simple, and he'd lived with his mother until she died the previous year, but he worked hard, and Barbara could handle him. She turned back to the house.

Il Rondinaio was well fortified, for a farmhouse, up high on its rocky pedestal; the extensive gardens below were enclosed by a stone wall and sturdy stockproof fencing; its doors were double locked and barred, and even the windows presented several lines of defence against intruders, the summer's pervasive heat and, more noticeably, against sunlight. External slatted shutters, mosquito screens, panelled interior shutters and even floor-length net curtains were fitted at every window, and as a consequence one's first impression on entering was always of a deep, cool darkness. Only when Barbara Venturi came blowing in with her dusters and broom were the windows flung open and the warm, fresh air allowed to enter, and she always made sure that everything was shuttered up again before she left.

Barbara hauled her vacuum into Il Rondinaio's huge sitting room; she remembered when it had been a stable, and she wasn't quite sure whether she agreed with all this conversion; you could always tell what it had once been, particularly here with the row of little high windows, now flung open, running all along the outside wall. And she couldn't imagine why anyone would need a sitting room twenty-five metres long. It certainly needed a lot of cleaning, but at least they didn't have too many carpets, not like some of the foreigners she worked for. There was one rug, a shaggy, long-haired white sheepskin by the big fireplace, so she started the vacuuming up there. Almost immediately she heard the rattle of a foreign object stuck in the suction pipe, so, heaving a sigh, she turned the vacuum off to shake the thing out. It was a charm bracelet, cheap stuff, little heathen-looking charms and figurines on a crudely made, tarnished metal chain; it didn't look like the kind of thing she'd ever seen the little Signorina Beatrice wear, but still. Maybe one of her friends. She stuffed it into her apron pocket, and went on.

The kitchen was clean enough; it didn't look like they'd done any cooking, though there were a few wine glasses in the dishwasher. Barbara went upstairs. The big marble guest bathroom and the master bedroom's shower room had both been used and hastily cleaned up; in the latter the mirror had even been wiped, although it was smeared, not rubbed clear, to Barbara's annoyance. Yet still this was unusual: generally the Manzinis were fairly careless, leaving flannels and towels to be washed and even a ring around the bath. Maybe they'd had friends staying without them.

She went to the bedrooms next, Beatrice's first. The room was untidy, as usual, so she stripped the bed and folded clothes, leaving them on a chair. She remade the bed with clean white linen and then, before she forgot, dropped the little broken bracelet on to the centre of the bed, so she wouldn't miss it. The guest bedroom seemed pristine, so after a cursory inspection she left it to enter the huge, rose-coloured master bedroom, which had a connecting door to another, generally occupied by Beatrice's sister. The bed had been made, but it was obvious to Barbara's practised eye that it had been slept in so she turned back the duvet. The sheet below was stained and crumpled, and Barbara tutted disgustedly, but, as she stripped the bed right down to the underblanket and then turned the mattress, she was puzzled, too. Signora Manzini was extremely fastidious about her personal things, and it was unthinkable that she would have left soiled sheets on the bed; unthinkable, too, that it could have gone unnoticed. Perhaps someone left in a hurry. Still, Barbara was well aware that it was not her place to pass comment on anything she might notice at Il Rondinaio, so she bundled up the dirty linen and kicked it down the stairs.

Downstairs Barbara's niece went into the little back sitting room, where the TV was kept; strange, she always thought, that they didn't keep it in the big *sala* but tucked it away in here where there was hardly any furniture. The wire bin in the corner was full, an old magazine, sweet wrappers, wadded-up tissue, so she picked it up and ran her duster over the huge television screen and the expensive video and DVD players. A light was blinking on the video player and, flustered, she pressed a few buttons until it went out. She looked around but the room was poorly lit and she saw nothing else that needed tidying, so she left, the waste-paper bin under her arm.

After almost three hours of scrubbing, bed-making, polishing and straightening, the house was clean and ordered enough even for Barbara, and she and her niece locked up, hung out the washed linen and went to find Giorgio. When they called he came hurriedly out of the garage looking, as he often did, mildly anxious. He still had to skim the pool and turn off the sprinklers, he said, as the lawn hadn't yet had enough of a soaking, so he would stay another half an hour. Barbara took one last look around, her niece climbed up on the Vespa behind her boyfriend, who folded up the copy of the *Gazetta dello Sport* he'd been reading, flicked away his cigarette, and soon Il Rondinaio was behind them for another week or so, the cloud of dust thrown up by their *motorini* still hanging in the air.

On the road below, Mila was leaning into the passenger-side

window of a dusty pick-up, squinting into the car's dark interior, nodding her head mechanically and smiling.

II

In Florence, Gina was hanging out of the window at 36 Borgo Tegolaio, watching life go by in the street below. It made her feel alive, she reflected; back home in England this was the kind of thing you watched a soap opera for, eavesdropping on other people's lives. She saw a handsome, well-built man in his fifties – quilted jacket, thick greying hair, moustache – walk by with a blonde woman young enough to be his daughter, although she obviously wasn't. They stopped at the corner, and kissed. A very old woman, impeccably dressed in a navy-blue suit, with tights and polished shoes, tottered along the pavement clinging to the arm of a young man, dressed in a white shopkeeper's duster coat, who was wheeling two cases of mineral water on a trolley and nodding politely every now and then in response to a quavering question. Then two youngish men who looked like vagrants, with matted hair and layers of dirty clothing, rounded the corner fast, temporarily unbalancing the old lady, who swayed with alarm in their wake. They ran the length of the street in silence before disappearing around the corner, and watching their swift, sinister passage Gina found herself thinking about the dead girl again. Could she have been mugged by drug-addicted vagrants? Could it be as uncomplicated as that? But this wasn't India or Thailand, it was possibly the most benevolent country in the world. Surely that kind of thing didn't happen here.

Gina turned to look inside the room. Down at the end of the corridor she could hear Jane's clear voice, raised in mid-lesson, and, on impulse, Gina followed the sound. Pausing at the open door, she leant against the frame and looked cautiously inside. Jane stood at a small high table at the far end of the room, her hand resting on a large, ornate pasta-roller; seeing Gina she nodded graciously and beckoned her inside without breaking off her instruction.

Along each side of the huge square table Gina had seen Jane surveying the previous night stood four students, all of them women, all over forty, Gina guessed. Each wore a white double-breasted chef's coat buttoned high at the neck, and a kind of little white paper wimple covering their hair. In front of each woman was a smaller, cheaper version of Jane's pasta machine, and a little mound of yellow pasta dough resting on a carefully floured surface. The women stood silent and obedient, just the hint of a twitch of rebellion on the lips of one, a robustly coiffured woman with a square jaw and the suggestion, quelled before it arose by something in Jane's gaze, of a question on her lips. Gina sensed the flow of power down to Jane at her dais, poised and clinical as she lifted a fragile, elastic golden sheet casually with the tips of her long, pale fingers.

The telephone rang loudly behind her down at the far end of the corridor, and Gina jumped and half-turned. She looked questioningly back at Jane, who nodded.

'Could you, darling?'

Gina hurried down the corridor and, surprised by her own decisiveness, plucked the receiver from its holder.

'Hello?'

'Who's that? Is Beatrice there? I need to speak to Beatrice. And my dad.' The voice cracked and broke, fragile and tearful, and Gina frowned into the receiver.

'It's – I'm staying here. Your father's out – he's at the police station with Beatrice.'

'What?' The voice suddenly became clearer, loud and

panicky. 'What do you mean, the police station? Oh. About Tash, is it? I know she's dead, tell him I know.'

'Look – is that Juliet?' Gina was alarmed by the note of desperation in the girl's voice, and turned back, craning her neck to look down the corridor. She could still hear Jane. 'Is everything all right? I mean, I can go and get Jane, she's teaching next door.'

'No, no!' Juliet's voice rose. 'I don't want to speak to her.' She sounded angry. 'Just tell – could you just tell him he'd better call me, tell him I know all about it. I know about Tash. He's really got to call me, or, tell him I'm going to have to talk to Mum. Just say that, will you?' The line went dead, and Gina stood dumbly holding the receiver and wondering what on earth that could all have been about.

Twenty minutes or so later Jane emerged from her kitchen, brushing imaginary flour from her hands.

'So?'

'It was Niccolò's daughter. I mean, the other one, Juliet.' Gina said tentatively, unsure of how to convey to Jane the disconcerting gist of the conversation. 'Is she all right? I mean she sounded very upset about something, she said Niccolò had to phone or she'd speak to her mother, something like that.'

Jane's expression darkened.

'I knew it. She's such an attention-seeker. I expect it's because Beatrice is caught up in all this murder nonsense over here, she's just got to get in on it. And as for begging Nicky to phone her! It's unhealthy, the obsession she has with him. Quite unnatural. You'd think she was jealous, of anyone else he's close to. Me, Beatrice. I suppose –' and she looked pained – 'It's to do with being separated from him.'

Gina reflected that this compassionate viewpoint seemed entirely to overlook the part Jane herself had played in the separation, but she kept quiet. She was beginning to feel rather queasy about the insights she was being afforded into Niccolò Manzini's relationship with his daughters. Surely . . . Firmly she stopped herself speculating.

'I said I'd tell Niccolò, ask him to phone her. And Beatrice.'

'Well, I have no idea when they'll be back from the police station. Really . . .' she frowned at her expensive watch. 'It's nearly eleven. I would have thought they'd be here by now. Anyway, I've got to take my class on their market visit, so I can't hang around. I'll leave a note for Nicky. I'll see you later. Have fun!'

Unsettled by the flat's atmosphere in the wake of Juliet's phonecall, Gina went out looking for a coffee, hoping to find the Medici again. She thought of the bar with fondness, her place of sanctuary after yesterday's journey. The city seemed livelier now; the shops were open, their doorways blocked by customers deep in carefully considered conversation. As Gina retraced her steps through the cool, shadowy streets, only a strip of brilliant blue sky visible between the eaves that almost met a hundred feet above her head, with the occasional shaft of sunlight slipping between the monumental buildings, she couldn't get the phonecall out of her mind. Juliet had sounded frightened, underneath it all, as though she was trying to hold her nerve. She had obviously known Natasha too. Gina found Jane's flat refusal to sympathize with either girl's distress puzzling, but maybe she was underestimating the complications of being a stepmother to highly strung teenage girls. Or maybe she didn't like them because they were too close to Niccolò.

Gina found the Medici easily enough, but when she turned in she was taken aback by the throng at the bar, chattering, gesturing, espresso in one hand, something sweet and dusted with icing sugar in the other, all fitting the last coffee in before lunchtime. She stood, helpless, at the back of the crowd, when Massi the barman caught her eye, and, although he didn't smile, she thought she saw the corner of his mouth twitch upwards. *'Signora?'* he asked lightly, audible still over the extraordinary noise.

She mouthed her request, smiling happily, disproportionately pleased to have been not only recognized but also given special treatment.

Most of the crowd at the bar were women, and as she drank her coffee Gina watched them. Glossy with power and confidence, laughing, mocking, flirting with Massi, they wiped the lipstick traces from their coffee cups with a swift expert flourish. They seemed to know exactly what they were doing, and to be conspiratorial, strengthened by their numbers. Gina smoothed down her hair and straightened her back reflexively, in unconscious imitation. Confidently she drained her own coffee cup and set it down on the bar, smiling a broad goodbye to Massi, who smiled back.

As she walked down towards the Boboli Gardens, Gina found herself slowed by the progress of a small family group ahead, tourists, by their slow trudge and overheated look; two girls linking arms in front, parents behind. As she stepped off the pavement to get past, Gina saw the mother, her hair gingery and frizzed by the humidity, lean forward to touch the semicircle of sunburnt, freckled skin between the younger girl's shoulderblades, tenderly reproaching her. Gina thought of her own mother, who had been to Italy once, for her honeymoon; she couldn't connect her with this woman's gentle touch, nor with the exuberant community of women at the Medici. Gina's mother had only ever seemed happy in her garden, humming absently as she passed below her overhanging roses, standing with her face turned up to the sun, eyes closed.

Gina had not had a tragically unhappy childhood, but nor could she remember anything joyful about it. She had been a tentative, solitary child, and her mother, a frustrated, angry woman, determined to fulfil her duties as a mother and a housewife without having any natural enjoyment or predisposition for either role. Jean had at least had strong feelings for her daughter – Gina knew that, now that she had her own, remembering the awkward goodnight kisses, and hurried, painful embraces – but they had been hopelessly stifled; Gina's mother had found tenderness incompatible with the proper accomplishment of her obligations, the daily grind of feeding, cleanliness and discipline. Gina's father, an engineer, had been often abroad, in Lahore, Riyadh, Oman, building roads and bridges in the desert. He seemed, as his only child grew, to be more rather than less eager to spend long periods away from home, and every time he returned, Gina felt, he would look at her with a frown, as though unable to explain her existence. And then he would awkwardly wave her back to her mother in the kitchen, go into his study and close the door behind him.

And then Gina's mother died, abruptly, when Gina was eighteen and about to start at university, leaving her the moment she could be said to be no longer a child, without a word, without a single conversation about love, or motherhood, abandoning her to raise her own children quite utterly in the dark. Gina's father had been in Jeddah when his wife died, of a brain haemorrhage, and he had flown home for two days before returning to his project: a reservoir, Gina thought. He had retired to the town in which he had been born, in Cheshire, and she had seen him again only three times before he too died, of a heart attack in the library, reading a book on engineering. Gina sighed involuntarily; this was not something she often dwelt on; it was uncomfortable and pointless, to be angry with someone who was dead, and angry with them just for dying at that. It was a knot pulled too tight, an infuriating, stubborn obstacle to contentment; it couldn't be undone.

Gina wondered whether this lack of a role model was why

she found her own life as a mother so confusing, full of setbacks and lurches forward, seductive vistas and dead ends, with the lack of a clear and shining example. But then again, maybe it was like that for everyone; maybe those grand-mothers who knitted and babysat and pointed out family resemblances, if they even existed, would be as much a source of frustration as the absent kind.

As she passed a shop window something caught Gina's eye, something gilded, shiny, and she turned her head just a little and found herself looking into the amused brown eyes of a stocky, attractive man standing in the shop's doorway.

'*Buongiorno, signorina*,' he said, and there was something so blatantly flirtatious and appreciative in his voice and the way he looked her up and down that she blushed with guilty pleasure and hurried on, in her distraction almost walking straight past the big iron gate that was her destination. *Perhaps that's my problem*, she thought, rebuking herself for being so easily pleased; *not enough regular flirtation*. She certainly couldn't remember when she'd last felt so buoyant. Suddenly a swallow appeared from behind her, soared and dipped over the gate, disappearing into the green avenues of the gardens beyond, and Gina felt the small, sad, thwarted ghost of her mother at her shoulder finally evaporate in the warmth of the sun at her back and the glorious prospect of the day ahead.

12

That morning a glazier's van had edged its way down the side of Santo Spirito and the shattered remains of Pierluigi's rear window had been smashed out and replaced with wire-reinforced security glass; behind it sat Pierluigi, restored to his position although having to make do with a Gustavian arm-chair (a good fake) in the absence of his yellow silk *divano*.

The Piazza Santo Spirito at midday was far from the tranquil square of the previous evening. The place was in chaos: most of the market stalls were being packed up for the day so vans were parked anywhere they could fit, ready for loading, and the drunks were at their most active, a couple of bottles down, just enough to make them lively. A good-humoured queue was forming for the opening of the most popular of the restaurants, and the usual dark-blue police van was parked in the corner by the church, an officer leaning nonchalantly against it. He was the *carabiniere* who'd brought Beatrice home the previous evening. A broad-shouldered foreigner whom the policeman might have recognized from Manzini's dinner table, had he been paying attention, separated himself from the mêlée of stallholders, tourists and shoppers, and moved towards him.

The *carabiniere* nodded and narrowed his eyes as Frank Sutton approached. Frank greeted him with elaborate cour-tesy, then asked carefully, 'Have you been able to make any progress? With the foreign girl's murder?'

'Excuse me?' responded the policeman, deep suspicion evident in his tone.

'Natasha Julius. I was at Dottore Manzini's house last night, when you brought his daughter back. It must be tough in a place like this; it's easy for the police in London or New York, all the surveillance they have over there. I suppose you have to go for the old-fashioned methods.'

The policeman bristled at this. 'We are a modern police force. There are cameras, if you know where to look. But there is no need for them, when you have all of these –' And he made a gesture that took in all of the denizens of the square: market traders, the restaurant workers laying out the tables, street-sweepers, drunks and backpackers.

'Some of these guys are here all night. There's always someone here, and even the ones who look as if they're out of it, they see something. Getting them to tell us what they see, that's where it gets difficult. But if you want official police information, you must inquire at the *questura*, at the press office. You are a journalist?'

Sutton nodded slowly. The *carabiniere* looked at him more closely. 'You don't seem too sure.' The journalist smiled stiffly.

The policeman sighed, ground out his cigarette and straightened his back. 'Go to the *questura*, then. But there isn't so much to tell, yet.' Another *carabiniere* approached, and the two walked off together, the market traders pausing to watch them pass, smirking when there was no chance of their being observed – and it was true, there was something faintly ludicrous about the self-importance of their strutting walk, the guardsman's red stripe down their trousers, and the soft, white-leather gloves they held – never wore – like haughty pantomime soldiers. But it was best not to underestimate them. They carried guns, after all.

Cinzia Stallone was sitting in her wheelchair in her usual position next to the Palazzo Guadagni, watching the English guy buy a small bag of dope from the Algerian on the corner of the piazza. She watched him set his sights on her – he was quite cute, really, for an English guy – waiting until she was alone, gazing up at the church and drawing meditatively on her cigarette, before sitting down next to her. She ignored him for almost ten minutes, then angled her wheelchair slightly towards him.

'Yeah?' she said.

'Were you here the night before last? The night the girl was killed? Do you know who I mean?' Frank Sutton seemed shy in the full beam of Cinzia's direct, blue-eyed gaze. Or maybe it was the wheelchair; it had that effect on some guys.

'Who are you? Why do you want to know?' she asked him. He made a gesture of helplessness Cinzia didn't find totally convincing. 'Yeah?' she said.

'My name's Frank. I'm a journalist –' He broke off when she rolled her eyes. 'But I know her friend, the younger girl, Beatrice; I know her parents. She's very upset. And I didn't think – it didn't sound like it was just random.' Then he seemed to remember something, and put the dope in her lap; that clarified the situation for Cinzia at least.

'Strictly medicinal, yeah?' she said, and gave him her sweetest smile.

He couldn't help himself. They never could. 'What happened to you?' he asked.

'Motorbike accident,' said Cinzia, making it clear that was all he needed to know. Then she said, 'I was here a couple of nights ago, yeah. And I saw that girl, Natasha, and her friends. They were here a while, drinking some beers, over there.' And she pointed towards the fountain in the centre of the square.

'Which friends?' asked Frank.

'The same as usual – long-haired guy, sweet guy, Ned, and the other girl, the one you know, Beatrice.' She pronounced it in the Italian way: Bay-ah-tree-chay.

'They talked to Stefano for a bit. She was way out of it, Natasha, stoned. Laughing and laughing about something, she kept putting her arms around the boy and whispering in his ear. The other two didn't look too happy; the little one, she just looked like she didn't know what was going on, but she knew she was missing something. The guy, he looked like she was really winding him up. But then she was a bit of a wind-up merchant, that girl, she was that kind. Gets behind a guy and stokes him up for something, always making trouble.'

'How do you know them so well?' Frank asked, curiously. 'How much time did they spend here?'

Cinzia shrugged. 'Well, there's some foreigners, they come

out for a week, a month, you never see them again. Some come for longer, but they don't come back. Some, like those three, they keep coming back. They disappear off back to wherever it is they come from, but they're always back sooner or later. Don't ask me why; it's a dump, isn't it?'

Frank looked around at the fly-blown square and nodded absently. 'Ever been to England?' he asked.

Cinzia snorted. 'Yeah, right. Sure I have. And Hollywood.'

'I just meant, well, there's nothing like this there. Either you're rich and you stay at home or you're poor and you have to live on the streets. And it's cold there, on the streets.'

Cinzia put her head on one side for a moment, looking first at Frank then along the bench at the church. She nodded. 'Being straight with you, I think it was the stuff they came for. Drugs. But yeah, maybe they liked hanging out, too, just a little bit. Maybe it's us they like. The people of the streets.' She raised her arm in a gesture of solidarity, and from along the bench came a ragged cheer.

'Did you see them leave?' asked Frank. 'That night?'

'Not her. Saw that guy Ned go off with the younger one, around midnight, one o'clock, something like that, taking her home. I had it in my mind he came back, though; I'm sure I saw him back here later – yeah, because I remember, when her dad came looking for her, I remember thinking, *Just as well he missed the boyfriend.* Missed him only by a couple of minutes. You can tell he's not the kind of boyfriend he wants for his little baby.' She rolled her eyes. 'Maybe he's right. Anyway, I think she'd gone by then, the girl who got herself killed, but I was kind of out of it myself, it was late.' She looked away, as though she was embarrassed.

'You're sure you saw her dad hanging around? You know him?'

'Yeah, I know him,' Cinzia said. She looked studiedly indifferent. 'He's a smart guy, isn't he?'

'Yeah, smart guy.' She looked at him sharply. 'But Natasha, the girl who – died . . . You're pretty sure she'd already disappeared?'

Cinzia looked around. The piazza was still busy, and a couple of vans, their canvas awnings thrown up for loading, formed a barrier around them. 'Think so. Like I say, though, I was out of it. It was late.'

'Thanks,' said Frank thoughtfully.

'Any time,' said Cinzia, giving him her special smile again, and watched Frank trying not to look at the bluebird tattooed on her breast, just inside the scoop neck of her T-shirt. 'Want a smoke?' she said. 'Come back to my place?'

His head jerked up. 'Thanks,' he said. 'I've got to go.' And he stood up, then turned and walked away.

He hadn't even got as far as the corner when she called him back. 'Weren't you here too, that night? I thought you were here? Or was it just in my dreams?'

He just smiled ruefully and shook his head. 'Not that late. I wasn't here late enough.'

Cinzia shrugged. *Another time, then*, she thought. *Definitely.*

On the outer edge of civilized Florence, behind the railway station, in the grey hinterland of broad, traffic-choked arterial roads and orderly rows of faceless modern apartment blocks, Niccolò Manzini was walking back to his office from the police station. It was now past midday; they had finished with Beatrice almost an hour earlier, but they had sent her back home without him, escorted by a female police officer, in a patrol car.

Niccolò had then been shown to a different interrogation room and questioned about his own whereabouts on the evening of Natasha Julius's murder and asked, too, some personal questions about his relationship with the dead girl that he had declined to answer. His lawyer had by this time been present, of course, and had objected strenuously when the police officers made veiled references to Niccolò's private life – a car registered as belonging to him being seen in a notorious district of northern Rome, for example. Eventually they had let him leave, with elaborate displays of polite regret at having inconvenienced him. He had decided to walk the mile or so back to work, and he cut a powerful, elegant figure in his deep-blue suit and finely striped shirt, his dark, thoughtful face the image of calm and composure amid the chaos of the midday traffic roaring around the city's perimeter.

One of Niccolò Manzini's strengths as a businessman, if not always as an architect, was his ability to compartmental-ize his life and to hold in concealment his personal tastes. Thus the demands presented by, say, the construction of an elegant, functional cemetery complex as a government commission could be met just as readily as those of a cou-ture designer's baroque-fantasy palace and leisure park. He rarely showed emotion and this had earnt him a reputation, perhaps undeserved, for coldness. But it was only with con-siderable effort, this time, in exercising his talent for over-looking the uglier aspects of his life that Niccolò was able to put out of his mind the intrusive questions the *carabinieri* had put to him. But as he walked back to the south of the city, past all the banal, corrupted buildings he usually man-aged so successfully to avoid, towards the perfectly propor-tioned and ordered environment of his office, he felt his head clear.

The office of Manzini & Partners (the partners, in this case, being of the sleeping kind) was tucked between the Palazzo Vecchio and the river in an exquisitely plain sixteenth-century palace built around a spacious, light-filled courtyard. Manzini's career had had its vertiginous beginning in London with his commission, when he was twenty-six and barely qualified, to build a high-profile, ultra-modern glass-and-steel skyscraper for a foreign bank in the City. Later, his leaving London at a time when all eyes were on the capital's architecture had been seen as eccentric, for he did not even head for Milan, his father's birthplace, but for Florence, where, because of the labyrinthine planning laws, the difficult terrain, and the weight of regional bureaucracy, virtually no new buildings were ever accomplished. The reason he gave for the move, when asked, was that he felt that Florence's incomparable architectural legacy was the perfect complement to his modernist leanings; that the austere purity of Brunelleschi and Vasari, Alberti and Cronaca informed his work. But in fact what Niccolò Manzini most valued about Florence was, rather surprisingly, its seclusion. The old city, encircled by hills, its climate infamously humid and hostile, its streets dark and narrow, seemed to repel intruders and to allow its residents privacy. Even the permanent flow of tourists, with their guides holding up sunflowers or umbrellas or flags to distinguish themselves from the masses, couldn't penetrate the city that existed behind the great wooden doors, incurious as they were – as their crowded timetables allowed them to be – about anything but the main attractions. So Niccolò felt, in his sunlit courtyard, his vaulted office, the rooftop studio with its rows of tilted drawing-boards and pale northern light, that he could get on with his own business.

Manzini let himself in at the base of the discreetly massive stone building, and nodded to the porter. His PA, Claudia, was waiting for him in the lobby, leaning against her desk, a slab of limestone he had designed himself. Her resemblance to Niccolò's wife, or rather to a younger version of his wife – as even Jane's carefully maintained complexion had not quite managed to hold back time by twenty years – was striking: her skin very white, her eyes large and blue, her hair a glossy light blonde. Claudia's edges were a little sharper than Jane's, her hair cut shorter, in a discreetly asymmetric bob, and she invariably wore severe dark trouser suits, in charcoal or black, with a hint of crisp white shirt at the neck. Whether from preference or good sense, Niccolò never made remarks or overtures of a personal nature to Claudia; the architect looked on his personal assistant as a particularly highly developed piece of office equipment, and her appearance, like his wife's, met his requirements aesthetically rather than on a more primitive level.

Claudia, for her part, was grateful for his lack of interest; she was unsettled by her boss, for reasons she could not entirely articulate but which were to do with the coldness that in Claudia's mind concealed something, some unsettling and powerful carnal interest she did not recognize. Also there was his unvarying ruthlessness in business and the edge of disgust she sometimes heard in his voice when talking about certain women – female clients who flirted with him, women he considered overweight or badly dressed, women who drank, and, sometimes, even his own wife. There was no laziness, no good humour, no indulgence in Dottore Manzini, and sometimes she wondered if he really had any Italian blood at all. His father was from the north, and perhaps that was the explanation: the Milanesi were, in her opinion, bad-tempered and cold. However, he paid her very well, she enjoyed her work, and he never touched her, so the bargain she made with her apprehension seemed worth it, for the moment.

'Dottore, there have been messages, some of them urgent. Giuseppe telephoned from Rome; the *guardia di finanza* wish to make an appointment to examine your books and he would like to speak to you about this. Your daughter telephoned from England and she –' Claudia paused, knowing that Manzini would not wish her to express her opinion about his daughter's state of mind. 'She would like to speak with you urgently.'

Manzini's narrow, handsome face darkened. He seemed particularly impatient today. 'Anything else?'

She hesitated. 'A journalist. Frank Sutton. He said he knows you . . .' She could not help but sound sceptical, as the one thing she knew for sure about her employer was that he loathed journalists. 'He would like to visit the site in Rome some time, to write something about it for his newspaper in London.'

She was surprised by Manzini's sharp intake of breath. If she hadn't thought her employer incapable of it, she could have sworn he was afraid of something. 'No?' she said, unable to resist pursuing it. 'Shall I tell him you are too busy?'

'Don't tell him anything. Nothing. Leave him.' He made a noise in his throat, a soft growl of impatience.

There was no arguing with that. Claudia shrugged, but she wondered what kind of man Mr Sutton could be. 'Also, will you be lunching at Pici? I have a table booked for you but I thought perhaps you would need the time for other things today.'

Niccolò nodded, apparently restored to calm, although not, Claudia thought, without an effort. 'Yes. I have a meeting over the river. I'm going there now, so you can cancel Pici. I'll call the others from home. I'll be going straight on to Rome this afternoon.'

She smiled and nodded, relieved to be free of him, though she was careful not to make this obvious. Manzini walked into his office and she glimpsed him at the filing cabinet to which only he had the key before his door swung slowly shut behind him. Claudia slowly returned to her desk. *Perhaps*, she thought, *it is time for a change of scene.*

13

Frances arrived at the market later than she would have liked on this particular morning; once the warm weather arrived, she preferred to be on her way back home by eleven, and not just because she didn't like to walk home in the heat. The ground floor of Florence's central market, a huge, highly decorated wrought-iron hall like a Victorian railway station, incongruously planted practically on the steps of the Medici chapel, was given over largely to butchers' counters. Whole sides of beef and pork were wheeled through the aisles and laid out on marble slabs, there were cooked-tripe stalls shrouded in steam and poultry hung in rows, and in summer the smell, which even in winter was not for the faint-hearted, was intense and cloying. Frances often saw the more refined visitors – in particular the English-speaking ones – recoil as they entered, greeted as they were not by bright pyramids of fruit and vegetables (these were upstairs) or delicatessen counters (restricted to one banquette) but by this carnivores' feast; rolls of meat larded with fat and garnished with rosemary, slabs of glistening pink veal and rows of chickens hanging up like Christmas decorations, complete with heads and feet. However, even though the smell was sometimes too much for her, Frances didn't at all mind the spectacle; when she had first arrived in Florence it had transported her back to the England of twenty years before, when supermarkets had barely existed and the consumer was prepared for his meat to reveal quite clearly the animal it had once been – altogether a more honest state of affairs, in Frances's opinion.

Today, Frances wanted chicken and fresh pasta; barely worth the walk from home, but she liked the sight of other elderly people, who tended to favour the market for their shopping, still happily carrying on their lives despite infirmity and even, for some, frank dementia. They were not troubled, as they perhaps would have been had they lived in England, by the thought that most people would prefer them to be tucked away in a home and spoonfed instant mash by a 'carer' rather than cluttering up the queues of able-bodied shoppers with their dithering, their illegible shopping lists and their arthritic fingers.

With asparagus tortelli for her dinner with Lucienne and Nino and gnocchi for one nestling soft and heavy in her little rucksack, Frances stood in line to buy her chicken at one of the farmers' stalls. Yellow-skinned birds were plucked and stacked against the glass, rosettes testifying to their quality and origin pinned to their plump breasts. Ahead of Frances stood a tall, strongly built Nigerian girl dressed in a short, skin-tight purple dress and carrying a bulky string shopping bag, waiting as the countrywoman, her face stony with resentment, dismembered five chickens and chopped them into small pieces. Frances wondered idly how the meat would be cooked, a gigantic stew or casserole, perhaps, to feed how many people?

The farmer's wife, or mother, perhaps, paused in her chopping and looked at Frances with an obsequious, apologetic smile, and Frances, embarrassed, tried to convey with a gesture that she didn't mind waiting. The girl ignored this exchange, and simply indicated that the pieces of meat were not small enough, her eyes hooded and incurious as she looked through Frances out to the street, where the North African market traders were hawking handbags and ivory chess-sets and fake cashmere. The illegals Frances came into contact with were, she knew, only the tip of the iceberg; if you believed some of the country people, the Chianti hills were swarming with villainous Albanians, sleeping rough in shacks and caravans and old railway carriages and murdering people in their beds, the country roads lined with prostitutes, as thick on the ground as the litter thrown from passing cars.

This queasily ambivalent attitude was where she stopped even pretending to understand the Italians; this was where she felt the last traces of the northern puritan reassert their presence in her blood. At first sight it seemed as though the new residents of Italy – and there were many more, legal and illegal, than there had been when Frances arrived – had carved out a place for themselves. Certainly they were visible everywhere, carrying on their lives, buying chicken in the market, riding around in battered cars; Sri Lankans sold roses to alfresco diners, Nigerians sold handbags on the Ponte Vecchio, they all chatted on street corners. But, if Frances looked closer, it was clear that for the most part they floated on the surface, excluded from the patterns and habits of Italian life laid down over thousands of years, from a way of living that had been honed to comfortable perfection and would not readily admit to change. Perhaps it was just a matter of time, and eventually the immigrant children who played alongside Florentines in the city's schools would be seen to belong here, and Albanian, Croatian, Moroccan or Somali communities would flourish among the vineyards and olive groves, but in the meantime it sometimes seemed to Frances that the city was overloaded to bursting point with unassimilated aliens, from gypsy beggars to Sri Lankan pedlars, and the traditional Italian smile of welcome was looking a little weary.

Frances looked away, down towards the delicatessen counters, thinking idly that she should buy wine and olives, and saw Jane, standing straight and imperious at the head of a crocodile of her cookery students, who were pressed admiringly up against the glass of the most expensive gourmet banquette in the market. Over the head of the stall's proprietor, Luca, was suspended a stuffed, tusked wild boar with a coarse hairy hide as sleek as a seal's and a malevolent gleam in its glassy eyes. Luca sold a hundred different kinds of cheese (including Stilton, to the obvious suspicion of one of Jane's students); vast, meaty salamis and giant wax-covered *provolone* hung down beside the boar, the countertop was covered with baskets of dried porcini and, in tissue paper on a gilt server, two little wizened black nuggets reverently advertised as truffles from Piedmonte. Even Frances, with her hazy grasp of *haute cuisine*, was fairly sure that May was not the truffle season. Jane was explaining that her students would be well taken care of by Luca, who would ensure that only the best produce at the most favourable prices – including a ten per cent discount only for the students of the school – would be offered to them, and if they wished he would vacuum-pack it for their journey home. Jane and Luca exchanged a satisfied, mildly flirtatious smile, and Frances wondered whether Jane ever had affairs. Probably not, she reflected, thinking of Jane's carefully preserved cool and how little she liked it ruffled; she also considered how Niccolò Manzini might respond to betrayal.

Frances herself had had an affair, in her twenties – perhaps, she thought in retrospect, because she had no children to tether her more securely to Roland, perhaps as an act of revenge for his own irregular and, she thought, highly casual infidelities. She could still remember going, confused and miserable, to meet her lover in some pub or other in Soho or Fitzroy Square, unable to convince herself that she had a right to this kind of mixed pleasure, this kind of flattery and solicitude. It hadn't endangered her marriage; in fact, although her lover had been very attentive, she had ultimately found him shallow and vain and very much less likeable than Roland. He was quite well-known now, the lover, an august human-rights lawyer, and she came across his name now and again, never without a shudder, in the occasional English newspaper. She had retreated from the relationship in a confusion of shame and disquiet and was never tempted again.

Frances wondered, sometimes, how Roland's affairs had ended; she had had a shrewd idea of who one or two of them were, but was aware that there had been plenty more whom she knew nothing about; such things had been almost accepted, then, for a childless couple, and she had managed not to feel shamed by them, eventually. All the same, she had always wondered what deficiency in her was compensated for by them; in what way she failed him. And then quite suddenly a time had come when she knew it had stopped; when Roland came home one evening to their flat in Rome, put his arms around her from behind and rested his head wearily on her shoulder, his whole body leaning on hers, and she knew it was, at last, just them.

'*Signora?*' Frances, who had been gazing at Jane's profile across the aisle, was brought back with a start to the matter in hand by the farmer's wife, who held up a chicken and gave her an inquiring smile. There was no sign of the Nigerian girl and her three kilos of meat. Frances asked for hers to be jointed, the head and feet removed, and for half a dozen eggs, and looked over again at Jane, now knowledgeably answering questions about Tuscan curing methods and the virtues of wild-boar sausage over venison. She shook her head at the thought of Jane's life; how little fun she seemed to have. Other people's marriages, she supposed, were always mysterious, but even so. She thought of her life with Roland, posted here and there, of how he had always wanted to find the most outlandish parts of foreign towns, the souks and slums, battle-zones and red-light districts, dragging Frances with him; really it was quite surprising that he had risen as high as he did in the diplomatic service. People had to be so strait-laced these days, and they seemed to find their amusement in the most peculiar places. Cooking, of all things, raised to an art form and performed for an audience; she wondered sadly what had happened to the noisy, convivial gatherings of her early married life, fuelled by a messy heap of couscous, bread and sausage, or Jimmy's greasy lamb stew, a sink piled with dirty plates and a crusted bottle with the dregs of a filthy Greek liqueur in it. What did they mean by 'party' these days? Interior design, the creation of rooms with almost nothing in them, and the inviting of guests around to admire the almost-empty rooms. Extraordinary. And so dull. She paid for her chicken and wandered outside, escaping with relief both Jane and her acolytes and the carnal tang of the butchers' stalls, out into the tourist market's choked alleyways.

By midday or so Gina had reached the top of the Boboli. The baroque gardens, laid out across the slope that rose up steeply behind the Pitti Palace, seemed to her quite unlike any other park she had seen; almost entirely without flowers, for one thing. She had wandered up through a maze of tall evergreen hedges, occasionally rewarded by a tantalizing vista, a glimpse of a tower or a dome framed by bay and holm-oak, but more often finding herself baffled by dead ends and winding alleys snaking off in the wrong direction. Most mysterious of all, the place seemed quite empty; she only ever glimpsed other walkers fleetingly, at the end of a tunnel, or overheard them on the other side of a hedge. The overall effect was soothing, and mildly surreal.

Gina had almost resigned herself to being pleasantly lost when she came upon a low tunnel of ancient trees arching overhead, brightened by the shafts of sun occasionally filtering through to produce a lovely greenish light. She walked to the tunnel's end, reached the broad, steep cypress avenue that stretched from top to bottom of the gardens, and knew where she was. Looking back down she could see a great circular pond, a fountain surrounded by luminous green water, then the city's edge defined by a great thick wall, and a mass of tenement housing backing on to the parkland, balconies and terraces, where potted geraniums were piled up on top of each other and scrambling for light and a bigger slice of the view.

Turning to look uphill, Gina was daunted by the slope and the long way still to go; but once at the top she sat, breathless with excitement, on a stone bench beneath the trees and looked down at last over the full extent of the city. Stretching away to the distant forested Appenines, the city seen from above had an open, sunlit character quite unlike the dark streets below; softened here and there by patches of green, the spread of terracotta tiles and soft grey stone was dotted with bright spires and domes and towers and at its centre the huge bulk of the cathedral as if floating, gigantic and serene as a sphinx, above even its tallest neighbour.

Gina couldn't have said how long she sat there, getting her breath back and absorbing the view, trying to orient herself. She looked for Jane's loggia, and thought she could see it down to her left, tiny and presumptuous as it stood proud of the surrounding buildings. She decided to go back; she was hungry now, and hot. She walked down between the cypresses, slowly this time, and at the foot of the slope she turned right, expecting to see the gate by which she had entered. Instead she found herself looking down an avenue of towering plane trees towards a building she had not seen before. At the building's centre, facing Gina at the far end of the avenue, was an immense, arched doorway, its double doors standing open to reveal an interior in deep shade.

In front of the building was a small formal garden, beds of foxgloves, roses and peonies enclosed by box hedging, and high iron railings with a central gate which also stood open. A wooden trolley rested by the doors to the building, and on it stood four or five lemon trees in swagged terracotta pots; the building, Gina deduced, must be the orangery, and the gardeners must be bringing out the fruit trees. Cautiously she approached the great doors, nervous that she wasn't authorized to enter, but Olympia had been very enthusiastic about the beauty of the building and there seemed to be no one to prevent her. She stopped in the doorway, and peered in. At first she could see nothing in the deep gloom, but she could smell. An extraordinarily powerful and delicious scent hung in the air, of marmalade and sweet fermentation, tangerines and lemons and grapefruit and oranges, sharp and tangy and as rich as wine.

Gradually Gina focused in the darkness and saw that one or two trees remained to be brought out, their fruit glowing like treasure among the glossy dark leaves, standing on a broad stone shelf that ran along the great dark length of the orangery and extended at least fifty feet to either side of Gina. It was a tall building, but not deep, like a primitive church, with chestnut rafters, and long leaded windows, now standing open in the heat, which allowed light in at regular intervals. At first she had thought it empty, but just as she was about to turn and leave she heard something, a voice lowered but talking urgently, down at the far end to her left, and automatically she turned to look.

Gina could make out a man's head, hair shoulder-length and silver, or blond, above a tall, spare figure in a leather jacket; she couldn't immediately see who he was listening to, as he was blocking her view with his body. Then he shifted slightly and, her eyes finally adjusting to the light, she saw that his interlocutor was Niccolò Manzini. Instinctively she moved backwards in the doorway, out of his field of vision, but she didn't leave. She waited, and listened, feeling a guilty thrill of excitement. She wondered whether Manzini had seen her; as the conversation continued without a pause, she assumed he had not. In the still, hot noon the birds were almost silent now, the traffic a distant hum. They were talking business; the white-haired man was speaking now.

'I'm just saying, *dottore*. You wouldn't want the *carabinieri* on your back, not just now, would you? An anonymous tip-off about what you get up to down in the country? Not to mention what you were doing on Sunday night?'

Niccolò shook his head. He spoke softly, and Gina had to strain to hear. 'Why would anyone take your word over mine, Stefano? Listen: what you sell, I buy; that's a business relationship. You use that to threaten me, and you're a criminal. But then that's something the police don't need telling.' He did not seem able to restrain his disgust.

'Now, now,' said the other man, mildly. 'You want to be more discreet, you know that? A tip-off, to get them looking into your business? Wouldn't have to come from me, would it? And it would make plenty of trouble for you.'

'That's blackmail.' She had to puzzle over the word Niccolò used, using what remained of her A-level Italian. *Estorsione*: extortion.

'No, no.' The man's voice was soothing. 'Just a bit of advice. But you know, a little quid pro quo wouldn't hurt. A little give and take.'

'No.' Gina moved closer, and she saw her shadow appear ahead of her in the semicircle of sunlight that fell through the great doorway into the orangery. There was silence, then when they spoke again it was too softly for her to hear. They knew someone was there. A gardener appeared behind her, moving towards his trolley; he picked up the iron handle and rolled it inside to collect the remaining trees. *They'll come out now*, Gina thought, *once they see him*. She backed out of the doorway, turned and walked away, without looking back, past the flowerbeds, out through the iron railings and back to the street.

No more than five minutes later Manzini emerged through the same gate and looked thoughtfully after Gina before turning to walk in the opposite direction, towards the city's walls.

*

'Look, what can we do now?' Giannino spread his hands. 'Just relax. If it was a warning, it was a warning. If you ask me, it wasn't. Do you know anyone who would do that? No. We keep our heads below the parapet for a while, no problem.'

The gathering of Pierluigi and his cronies was a more subdued one even than the previous day's as they sat at their corner table at the restaurant eating a late lunch, picking desultorily at a plate of fancy breads and *insalata caprese* and gloomily helping themselves to wine from the little carafe. It was a beautiful day, and the sun poured through the long window, its golden light playing across their long faces.

Pierluigi was still fretting. 'I'm trying to think, the last couple of jobs. There was that Milanese banker, that nice little villa out towards Scandicci. I've always said it's a mistake, ripping off the Italians.'

'But Jesus, Pierluigi, it was only that little piece of jade. And he's got so much stuff I don't suppose he's given it a second look yet.' Leo was beginning to lose patience with Pierluigi and his lugubrious fatalism. 'If you want, I'll talk to Stefano. You know, I think he knows more than he's letting on about that girl. After all, she spent most of the night in the piazza with him and his junkies, and Stefano always has his wits about him.'

He forked a piece of mozzarella into his mouth and chewed it, an expression of disbelief on his face. 'Hey, Franco, where do you get this stuff? Says *mozzarella di bufala* on the menu; if this has ever been near a buffalo I'll eat my grandmother!' Standing by the hatch to the kitchen, Franco went on polishing glasses and didn't gratify Giannino with a response.

Four platefuls of gnocchi arrived, and Giannino signalled to Franco for more wine. Giannino looked uncharacteristically thoughtful.

'You know, perhaps that's not such a good idea after all. I think he was tied up with that girl, somehow, more than just getting her drugs for her, too; I saw him talking to her like he was having a word, you know, very familiar and just a little bit put out. Maybe she was working for him – she had to pay for her habit somehow, didn't she? Maybe he did it himself – violence wouldn't be unknown for Stefano, would it, if she wasn't paying? And we don't want to get ourselves into all that.'

Roberta was incredulous. 'I can't believe she was doing that, you know, prostituting herself. She was classy; her friend, she's that big-shot architect's daughter, and that young guy, the long-haired boyfriend, his father's an English lord, did you know that? I did some work up at their villa in Bellosguardo, she was always up there.' She laughed rather sourly. 'Not that that meant he had any taste, as far as I remember. There wasn't much worth going after in that place, unless you've got a customer who's particularly interested in nasty repro.'

Leo cut in, poker-faced. 'Now, now, where would we be without customers interested in nasty repro, eh?' And they all hooted with laughter.

Franco smiled as he heard the sound and looked over, pleased to see that his favourite diners seemed to be recovering their good humour, at last.

Frank Sutton was still in the Piazza Santo Spirito when Stefano turned up, sitting outside at one of the bars, the Cabiria, a funky, eclectic sort of place, with an American jukebox, beaten brass walls and staff with a lot of body piercings. They had a couple of cheap aluminium tables under the trees, and Frank was drinking cold beer.

Stefano strolled into the square, walked over to the Borgo Antico and sat at a table. Had he been a casual visitor, he'd soon have been turfed off, told to wait his turn or that the only free tables were inside. But as it was, a bowl of *spaghetti alle vongole* and a beer appeared in front of him in less than five minutes, the waitress smiling at him warily. She couldn't quite work him out today, he was distracted, so she kept her distance. Frank wasn't so restrained, though he waited until Stefano had finished eating before draining his beer, tucking 10,000 lire under his empty glass and walking over.

'May I?' Frank asked, pointing to the empty seat. Stefano shrugged and took a drag on his cigarette. The waitress set an espresso in front of him and he sipped it meditatively, then leant forward, his lined, dark face set and angry.

'You want to know about the girl that died? Cinzia says you've been asking.'

'Yes.' Frank looked taken aback.

'She was very stupid. I mean, really stupid.' Stefano shook his head, regretfully, but there was a hard edge to his voice. 'She went too far, she didn't treat people with respect. Plenty of people would have been happy to give her a smack for the way she treated them. I don't like the way they behave, those rich kids, they like a bit of rough, like to walk on the wild side but they haven't got any guts when it comes down to it, and they don't like to pay for their fun. Think they can walk on water, but she found out different, didn't she?'

'Did she owe you?' Frank asked. 'She bought her stuff off you?'

'Yeah, that, though it was mostly her boyfriend – sorry, he's not her boyfriend, is he, he's supposed to be her best friend's boyfriend.' He paused, as if to make sure Frank had got his inference, and when Frank nodded he went on. 'He liked to be the one who bought their stuff; maybe it made him feel like a big guy. Did Cinzia tell you what was going on here that night?'

'She said they were arguing – at least, Natasha was winding him up about something, but Cinzia didn't know what.'

Stefano leant towards him again across the table, pointing at him with a thin brown finger. He spoke slowly, enunciating carefully. 'You know what, I think you want to check out what they get up to down in the country, when they go down to Daddy's country cottage. I think that was what they were arguing about. You ask me, Daddy's not as clean as he makes out, either.' He spat the last phrase and downed his coffee, already pushing his chair away from the table. Then he turned back.

Frank said nothing. He was leaning forward himself now, waiting.

'I saw Manzini out in the country, doing some business by the side of the road with one of the girls, a girl who's since disappeared. These things happen, you know? Funny thing is: little Natasha, sounded from what she was saying that night, she was down there too. And now she's ended up in the same place as I reckon that little roadside whore got to. The morgue. Makes you wonder, that's all, what went on.'

Frank stayed at the table as Stefano strode back across the piazza, to take up his habitual position underneath the Palazzo Guadagni. Frank seemed composed, his face calm and blank of emotion, but there was something about the way he was looking fixedly at a spot on the wall opposite and tapping his fingers, one after another, on the wooden table, that implied that a considerable amount of calculation was going on behind his unfocused eyes. The waitress returned to the table, and Frank paid for Stefano's lunch.

14

Ned Duncan lay on his bed in the near-darkness of his room, the long windows that led out to the balcony shuttered against the heat. At two o'clock, the temperature in the city had climbed to its daily maximum, stifling most activity, and even the sound of traffic on the *viale* was muted. Downstairs he could hear the ring of expensive crystal, the reverent placing of bone china on his mother's gilt-and-marble dining table, her horrible, tinkling laugh as she gossiped with Sonia Bradford. He couldn't stand them, those women his mother spent time with – Sonia, or Giulia Braganza (a contessa, you know, darling), or whoever. With their terrible, lifted faces, usually caved in around the eyes by now, or so taut they could barely speak, their hair elaborately arranged to cover the tucks and seams – and this afternoon he hated his mother most of all.

'Early siesta, darling?' she had commented sarcastically when he mentioned that he was tired and wouldn't be wanting lunch. She had turned to share her amusement with Sonia, and the maid; no doubt she'd have shared it with Frank Sutton, too, if he'd been there: Ned's life was her property.

'Just have a little lie down, there's a good boy. You'd only spoil our lovely lunch, with that long face. Giuseppina will bring you something if you're hungry later.'

Having dismissed him, Vivienne had turned back to Sonia and seized her ropy old forearm with a manicured hand, greedy for a piece of gossip from Rome.

In the dark Ned groaned. He turned this way and that on his heavy, damask-covered *bateau-lit*, unable to sleep with the sound of his mother's breathless, girlish banter downstairs, lowering her voice huskily to convey a particularly salacious piece of slander, then squealing with feigned horror at the response. His head throbbed, thinking about Natasha, and about the journalist, Frank Sutton. He wondered what he was after, really.

There was a lull in the conversation downstairs, and Ned detected a new sound: the crunch of footsteps on the gravel outside followed by a tentative knock at the door below his window. Then his mother's voice, no longer lowered in conspiracy with Sonia, but raised in greeting, her best, gushing hostess voice.

'Darling! How have you been? You poor child, look at you.' Then a summons. 'Ned! Beatrice is here.' It was obvious to him from her voice that, far from being glad to offer succour to Beatrice, Vivienne was furious that her lunch had been interrupted and wanted the girl off her hands so that she could get back to it.

'Send her up,' he called, his voice cracking. He wasn't sure he wanted her either. Poor Bea. He let his head fall back on to the pillow and stared sightlessly at the ceiling.

Ned could hear Beatrice walking slowly, first up the huge baronial staircase that occupied the centre of the house and then along the gallery to his door. The sound of her hesitant footsteps irritated him. She put her head around the door and whispered: 'Is it all right if I come in? It's just that –' She burst into noisy tears and flew across the room, dropping on to the bed beside him.

'I've been walking around. I didn't know where to go; Dad's not at home, they kept him there, I had to go to the police station today to talk to them about Tash, about what we did on Monday, when I last saw her –' Again she broke off and sobbed, her face pressed against Ned's shirt. He felt hot and uncomfortable, the feel of her damp cheek and convulsive movements setting his nerves on edge.

'What did you say to them?' His voice was steady, his eyes still fixed on the ceiling.

'I just told them we went walking in the woods. That's what we did. Said you took me home. We last saw her . . .' Her mouth turned down, twisted with misery. 'Last saw her laughing in the square, talking to someone, some biker guy we didn't know. Do you think he could have done it? I mean, why would someone hurt Tash? She didn't have any money or anything.' She cried again, and Ned wondered when it was going to stop, all this. He put his arm around her and gently rubbed her trembling back, drew her round to him and pressed his face against hers, their cheeks wet against each other in the darkened room.

Somewhere on the Via de' Tornabuoni, a couple of hours into her shopping trip with Olympia, Gina leant back on a huge black-leather sofa and smiled up at the younger woman's back.

Olympia stood in front of a mirror-covered wall and contemplated the sight of herself in a draped column of black velvet, one long, brown arm resting on her hip. At the front the dress hung elegantly from the shoulders, the neck was cut straight across, revealing only her long neck and a delicate suggestion of collarbone. At the back, however, it was cut low, skimming the base of Olympia's spine, and hinting decadently at corsetry with a cross-lacing of satin ribbon all the way down. Olympia seemed very pleased with it; Gina was awestruck.

Gina had returned from the Boboli for a siesta at the Manzinis' flat, shuttered and cool – the students off on a field-trip somewhere, she assumed – to find a message in Jane's neat, meticulous hand to the effect that Olympia would pick her up at four; and at three minutes to, there she had been, golden-skinned, braceleted and fragrant, ready for action.

Shopping with Olympia was turning out to be a pleasantly sociable experience, frequently punctuated by gossip and tiny cups of strong coffee. She seemed to be well known in all the shops they had visited so far, and Gina had been able to wander through racks of staggeringly expensive and beautiful clothes without the fear of being challenged in clipped Italian as to her intentions, while Olympia allowed the sales assistants to bring her anything new and daring for her careful consideration. Olympia's tastes, as Gina might have predicted, turned out to be theatrical and very bold, and Gina was beginning to think, not without some relief, that perhaps the afternoon was going to be more of a spectator sport than anything demanding her participation. Gina didn't think she was quite ready – or, rather, she thought she was no longer prepared – to wear an embroidered chartreuse-satin djellabah, velvet lounge pyjamas with marabou trim or even the kind of plunge-backed weapon of war Olympia was currently contemplating with a serious frown.

'What do you think, darling?' she asked Gina.

'It looks wonderful,' Gina replied, honestly. Olympia broke into a smile, and nodded at the girl standing patiently beside her.

'*Si. Questa,*' she said, and skipped gleefully back into the changing room.

Gina sat back, and gazed out of the plate-glass window. Dusk was falling in the warm city. She felt only a mild suggestion of disappointment at not having found anything to buy, and she began to believe that perhaps just watching the whole sensuous drama unfold, Olympia's pursuit of the perfect garment, might be pleasure enough. All the same, as they came out of the shop, arm in arm, into the gathering darkness of the Via de' Tornabuoni, its windows posed and spotlit tableaux for the passersby, Gina felt a wistful pang at the sight of Olympia's jubilant expression. They walked on a little while in silence. They had reached a corner and were hesitating when something caught Gina's eye down the narrow street to her left and she turned her head. A shop.

She drew nearer and stood, gazing wordlessly at the dress in the window. It was very plain, slippery, almost-white silk, gleaming like the inside of an oyster shell. Olympia nodded, and pushed her through the door.

The dress was perfect, clasping her just beneath her breasts and falling to just above the ankle, sliding over her hips without clinging. The saleswoman came up behind her, and smiled with satisfaction, holding out a heavy wrap of dark, damson-coloured linen, fringed at the edges, and a pair of tiny velvet sandals, dyed to match the linen and embroidered with silvered beads. As though in a trance blinking only slightly as she registered the price, Gina handed the shimmering, gorgeous heap of garments to the saleswoman. She didn't even have to remind herself of the ten years spent in ill-fitting jeans; she knew she needed to buy the dress. And Olympia seemed almost as thrilled by Gina's miraculous success as she was, hugging her as they left the shop together, Gina holding her crisp, tissue-filled carrier bag, eyes glittering with triumph in the streetlights.

'Now,' said Olympia, 'let's celebrate. Do you know Procacci? It's glorious.'

Olympia pointed to an old-fashioned shop-front, golden lettering overhead, displaying wine bottles and jars of delicacies, truffles and pâté and whole hams. Inside Gina could see a long marble counter and a couple of little tables. Olympia pushed open the door and Gina followed her in. They sat down, Olympia said something to the waitress, who wore a white waiter's apron tied twice around her waist, and she came over with two tall glasses of cold *prosecco* and a plateful of tiny glazed finger-rolls. Olympia sighed contentedly and took a sip of her wine.

'Do you know,' she said, looking at Gina thoughtfully, 'I think we should pay a visit to Frances. Wouldn't you like to meet her, before the party? She is heavenly; you'll love her.' She smiled and squeezed Gina's hand.

Gina shook her head and laughed. 'Maybe. Yes, I should, shouldn't I.' She took a sip, and a mouthful of one of the little sandwiches, its delicious, musky savouriness, a taste quite unfamiliar to her, taking her by surprise. Olympia laughed. '*Panini tartufati*. Truffle sandwiches. Almost as good as *prosecco* for stimulating reckless behaviour.'

At the other table sat a pair of women who seemed to be taking the whole business of celebration far more seriously. Both had dazzlingly dyed hair, one platinum blonde, the other a flaming, pomegranate red, and they wore identical expensive black suits. The blonde had a huge diamond on her ring finger, whose red-painted nail was tapping a lazy tattoo on a minuscule mobile phone on the marble table in front of her. Their plate of panini sat untouched beside it.

The ladies' dainty feet, one pair shod in patent-leather stilettos, the other in high-heeled crocodile sandals, were surrounded by a whole flock of expensive, shiny carrier bags, tied with ribbons, embossed with gold, standing stiffly proud of their exclusive contents. Looking down, rather to her surprise Gina discerned the lumpy outline of a gold ankle bracelet below the slender calf of the redhead. The tiny phone bleated, and the blonde picked it up and barked into it in bad-tempered Russian. At least, it sounded like Russian to Gina. She looked sideways at Olympia, a question in her eyes. 'Russian Mafia. Mistresses,' mouthed Olympia.

Gina sat back, impressed. She had expected her holiday to bring her into contact with nothing more glamorous than Jane's cookery students, but Florence was proving a city of many more undercurrents than she had anticipated. She thought of the shopping on her local south London high street: Woolworth's, a miserable greengrocer's, discount butcher's, three charity shops. Old ladies with dun-coloured raincoats and worn-down shoes, women in tracksuits with a clutch of children grimly hanging on to a pushchair.

Within five minutes of the blonde's phonecall, a sleek black stretch-limousine drew smoothly up at the kerb outside and the Mafia mistresses gathered together their crackling bags, haughtily slapped a large-denomination note down by the till, and swept out. Olympia looked at Gina's awestruck face with amusement.

'Did you only expect to meet art historians and architects?' she asked. 'Florence is full of that kind of thing, you know; those two were at the top end of the scale, but you get all sorts. That's why I live here. Now, tell me – were you really at university with Jane? I'm dying to know what she was like. Just can't imagine her as a student, somehow.'

'Well, she wasn't much like one even then, you know.' Gina laughed nervously, half expecting Jane to walk in and reprimand her. 'She was much more polished than everyone else. And she was, I don't know, intent. She had an agenda. I think she's got what she wanted now. A powerful man, that's what she was after, someone who could make big things happen, I don't mean someone to dominate *her*; more a mover and shaker. A man of influence. That's what he is, isn't he?'

'Do you think so?' asked Olympia curiously. 'Yes, I suppose he is. I think of him more as predatory, something a bit more sinister than powerful.'

'Maybe Jane likes that,' Gina said uncertainly.

'Do you really think so? I think they're horribly ill-suited. They look good, that's true, both beautifully presented, she's the perfect hostess. But he's . . . he's so cold with her. I –' Olympia broke off.

'What?' asked Gina. There was something loaded about Olympia's sudden silence.

'I slept with him once, you know. More than once, actually. A long time ago. Don't tell Jane – though she probably knows; I wouldn't put it past him to have told her.'

'No!' said Gina, aghast. 'But surely she wouldn't–'

'Still invite me round to dinner? Oh yes, she would. And it was more than ten years ago now, just after I arrived here. I was nineteen. You know, I'd put it out of my mind – you do, don't you?' Gina didn't know. She gazed at Olympia with horrified fascination.

'I think it was this, this murder thing, I don't know why, it made me think . . . I hated it, you know. It made me feel sick, sleeping with him. At first it was kind of a trip, you know, this great architect – he was really something then, an *enfant terrible*, very famous – wanting me, just an art student. He took me to Venice, to a flat he borrowed there. It was very cold, March, in this minimalist flat in Venice, not a rug or a curtain. I ended up scared stiff, too, he was so . . . controlling. I think he would have liked me to be even younger. More malleable – Jane's not what you'd call malleable, is she? He wanted to move me around like a doll, you know, put me in poses. He liked making videos of us.' She shivered, then gave herself a little shake, and drained her glass.

'Now,' said Olympia. 'We're going to see Frances.'

Jane was sitting quite alone in her drawing room as the sky grew dark outside, dressed from head to toe in striped silk Missoni, an iced vodka martini on the table at her side. *Bloody women*, she thought, cursing her cooking students, who had this afternoon grown audacious and asked her whether her husband lived in Florence or in Rome.

Jane was well aware that part of her school's appeal could be put down to her husband's reputation, his good looks, the fact that he had designed her much-photographed professional kitchen and the rooms in which the students slept. She also knew that a good proportion of them came in the hope of catching a glimpse of them, the golden couple, in the flesh and that, as most of them were women, they were more interested in seeing him than her. The perfect pizza dough, her artichoke lasagne, her zabaglione, all were secondary to the students' desire to return home with a few knowledgeable remarks, hinting at intimacy, about her dress sense, his green eyes, the particular shade of limestone she used for her work surfaces, and the phone number of the man she used to lay the *terrazzo* flooring in the annexe. She curled her lip at their vulgarity, and took a long draught of the ice-cold

154

vodka, just a ghost of vermouth, a sliver of twisted lemon peel.

Still, today it was all a bit close to the bone. Where the hell was Niccolò? She hadn't heard from him since he went off to the police station; he hated her to call him and generally kept his mobile turned off. Beatrice, the miserable child, had come back in a police car at lunchtime, scowled at her, asked for money, then gone off 'to see some friends'. She'd said that Niccolò had stayed behind to talk to the police; and, remembering this now, Jane quelled a feeling of profound suspicion. What had he done? She stifled the thought before it was born.

Nicky wasn't a physically violent man, she was as sure as she could be of that. Of course, he had strong feelings about certain things – the way things should look, the aesthetic. He had to be tough with the people who worked for him, the stonemasons and suppliers and construction crews and site managers, particularly here. If he wasn't he'd be robbed blind every time he turned his back; they'd cut corners, substitute cheap materials, labour would keep disappearing to moonlight somewhere else. He had to be ruthless, and his vendettas could last for ever, but was he dangerous? Jane mulled that one over, thinking back to their early days together, before she'd learnt where to tread and how lightly. Dangerous, well, yes, he could be dangerous; that was part of the appeal. She reached for her glass, but to her surprise it was already empty. She was on her feet and heading back to the kitchen when the phone rang. *At last*, she thought.

But it wasn't Niccolò. 'Hello?' she said again, sharply this time, because she knew there was someone there. She could hear ragged breathing, a snuffling, miserable sound.

'Oh Christ, I don't want to talk to you!' the voice sobbed furiously, and Jane knew it was Juliet. She exhaled impatiently.

'I'm sorry, Juliet. Your father's out, not back until Friday. If you want him, you could try the Rome flat.'

'What about Beatrice? I need to talk to Beatrice, or – him. I've done something . . . they need to know about. Oh, what does it matter, he'll know soon enough. It's too late now.'

What the hell has she done now, thought Jane. *Christ, I'm tired of these girls and their tantrums.* 'Beatrice is out too. With friends. I can always take a message,' she said, a little sharply, reckless as to whether her voice betrayed her annoyance.

This seemed to enrage Juliet; Jane heard a sharp intake of breath. But when she spoke again she sounded unnaturally calm, and strangely like her father.

'Well, you might as well know, too; let's face it, you were only ever Dad's glorified secretary, so I suppose you can at least take a message. Here it is: Dad had an affair with Natasha. When she was fifteen. Didn't know that, did you? Not even Bea knew; still doesn't. Why d'you think I haven't been out there in a while? He disgusts me. So when I heard she was dead I told Mum; I didn't feel like keeping it to myself any more. And Mum's told the police.'

The silence that followed echoed down the line and around the room. Jane could feel it shift and hum around her and she was barely aware of the click on the line as Juliet hung up.

15

Out on the S223 it seemed to Mila that darkness fell more suddenly than it did in the city. One moment the road was bright with the last rays of sun, the ridges of the misty blue hills repeated one behind the other into the far distance more sharply defined even than in the brilliance of midday, then before she knew it the shadows from the woods behind her had crept forward, across the road, and cars' headlights were dazzling her out of the darkness as they rounded the corner.

Mila hated the sunset; this time of year, it turned cool and creepy quite suddenly and the punters came crawling by thick and fast. Most of them didn't really like pulling in in broad daylight, even though they only ever stopped for ten minutes. They knew what it meant, a car left empty – some of them even left the sunshade across the windscreen, on this stretch of road – and if anyone they knew passed by and clocked the car they'd never hear the end of it. Only drivers from out of town would risk it, and they too were a lot happier after dark. But Mila wasn't, and especially not tonight. She still couldn't quite shake that feeling, the jitters she'd got after she'd come out of those bushes at the back of Evelina's pitch. There was only so long you could go, assuming it wouldn't happen to you, telling yourself there was nothing out there that wanted to harm you. Sooner or later a girl would disappear, just like Evelina, her life already turning into garbage by the roadside.

Seven o'clock, and it must have been an hour since the road-maintenance crew had packed up and gone, trailing past her in their vans, some of them having a good look. She had felt like asking them to take her with them, get her out of all this. She hadn't thought that way for years, thought about how it could have been with a decent life, another life, growing up with her kid back home, a bit of money and a guy coming home from work every night. But she didn't need telling how that kind of fairy story always ended up, same way it had for her mum and her sister and every other daft little girl in Tirana. Five kids, six abortions, a different broken bone every Friday night and holes in your shoes all winter. She shook her head angrily as she felt her eyes well up. A fix'd sort her out. But, it'd be two hours at least before she saw Stefano again, so she'd just have to deal with it.

The darkness seemed to be getting denser every time a car's

lights faded out at the end of the road, and the noise from the bush was deafening. The *cicadas* during the day buzzed loud enough, a sawing, rasping kazoo that made the woods vibrate, but at night the noise became more high-pitched, a ringing sound, like a zillion mobile phones all going off at once. Mila found it spooky that you never saw them, the *cicadas* or crickets or whatever they were, and sometimes you could be sitting under a tree when it would suddenly stop, silence, so you knew it must be just one tiny little bug making that huge sound, maybe just a handful of them making the whole forest hum, and the thought of that one little creature sitting up there watching you was weirder than a whole cloud of locusts swarming.

Mila looked across the road, down into the valley, to the same couple of distant lights that came on around this time every night. There was a big farm right over the other side, all lit up, a couple of barns full of pigs and some long-horned cattle, expensive tractors moving slowly back and forwards all day across the fields. A small restaurant up on the ridge, too, but it was closed all winter, only opened up in June. The funny little guy, the *contadino*, with his strip of vines, just a handful of grapes, some olive trees, tomatoes. Kind of creepy, living out here in the middle of nowhere, all alone except for those dogs. He had an orange light over his back porch. Along the road she could see just the edge of a glow from the roadhouse, the Hotel dei Bagni, and thought longingly of the bar, a little glass of something to take the edge off, some company, not that they'd give her the time of day down there. Took her money, though.

Unwillingly, her thoughts turned back to Evelina. She was just a kid. Mila had a suspicion that she was around fourteen; certainly without her platforms she wasn't five foot tall. And she had that look, like she wasn't sure of what was happening to her and she was just hoping it would all go away. A few turned up like that, not just from Africa; from Slovenia, Albania, all over. Mila didn't know what story they told them. Maybe they told the parents they'd put the girl in school over here, or maybe give her a waitressing job, or get her looking after kids.

She thought of Evelina trudging past every morning from the mini-market back down the road, with her bottle of water and a bag of biscuits, barefoot because she couldn't walk in the platforms. She would look at Mila, but Mila never cracked a smile. You just don't mix, do you. But now . . . She didn't want the kid to be hurt. And there was no one to look after her; Betty got a different guy every day to pick up those African girls, it seemed, and none of them could care less.

A tailback of cars went past led by a slow-moving caravan, an impatient big Audi edging out behind him to get past – they just couldn't wait; the number of near misses she'd seen in front of her eyes you'd think they'd have more sense. She blanked her expression to meet the stares, and leers, her best poker-face on, then a truck swung in, taking her by surprise and blinding her, his lights right in her face. Money, she registered, and flung her arm up across her eyes and squinted up at the cab as the driver climbed down.

He was a big guy, thick-set and smelling of sweat and diesel, like they always did; she knew he was trouble when he opened his mouth. Albanian, three days on the road and with a filthy temper he liked to take out on whores who spoke his own language. All she'd done was ask him to use a condom. The next thing she knew, Mila was on her back on the ground. *Shit*, she thought, *one of those*, as she heard him muttering obscenities. She could feel the stones digging into her back and her face felt wrong, as though her jaw had been dislocated when the man's fist connected with it. And he was on top of her, blotting out the stars over her head. Mila stayed as still as she could, she just let him do it. The sex, then the beating. It was all the same to her; it was just a question of waiting till it was over, she told herself.

She saw her world narrow, her peripheral vision went, and she knew she was going to pass out. A foot like a great blunt instrument connected with Mila's ribs, and she was over the edge, and falling, down into the blackness, down on to the rocks and the river.

Night had fallen by now on Evelina's body, lying still undiscovered, except by the minute investigations of insects and the bolder forest-dwelling creatures, 300 feet below Mila's hiding place. Beyond the cultivated part of Il Rondinaio's garden, a section of the hillside had once, long ago, broken off in a landslide brought on by heavy spring rains and had fallen into the ravine leaving a raw, sheer slope to which a few scraggy myrtle and gorse bushes now clung. At its foot, in the deepest shade the valley held, Evelina lay between the rocks, her body starting now, after two days and three nights in the warm spring air, to show the marks and processes of the first stages of decomposition.

As the city sky began to take on the electric brilliance of dusk, a luminous deep blue full of the tiny movements of swallows and bats and insects, Frank Sutton was still on the street. All he'd eaten for lunch was a handful of nuts and olives with his beer at the Cabiria, so perhaps it was hunger that led him down to the Pizzeria Dante by the river. The most direct route there, it so happened, took him down past the scene of the crime; the back of Pierluigi's shop.

Frank turned into the alley – Vicolo degli Innocenti, it was called, 'little street of the innocents'. There was a kink in it that meant you couldn't get a direct view down it from the piazza, and although you could see the window of Pierluigi's shop, you couldn't see it all, and you couldn't see any further down. It led all the way through to the Via Santo Spirito, where there were a couple of bars, and further, to the river, and seemed, at least this evening, to be a well-used little cut-through. It wasn't somewhere you'd plan to murder someone, not even at one or two in the morning when the city generally still had some life left in it. Frank was walking slowly, looking up at the eyeless houses, all of them shuttered. No one was leaning out to chat to a neighbour or call to a friend in the street; the houses might have been uninhabited for all the life they showed, and there was something dead, something abandoned about the alley.

In the golden light of the piazza, just visible at the end of the street, the usual motionless figures were stretched out in their sleeping bags along the side of the church, a handful of ragged travellers in a circle on the steps, heads bent in concentration as they rolled up by the light of the nearest street lamp, and a cluster of excited Japanese girls walking out to dinner arm in arm. None of them cast a glance down the Vicolo degli Innocenti at the motionless figure standing so close to where the murdered girl had lain, so absorbed were they in their own evening's entertainment. After some moments Sutton turned back and walked down the alley, glancing up at the shuttered windows as though to see if any inquisitive eyes followed him down to the Via Santo Spirito, but no one was watching.

There was no sign of Natasha's passing; the window glass looked as good as new, today's litter on the pavement eclipsed yesterday's, and a towering chandelier formed the new centre-piece in Pierluigi's display. Opposite the shop was an all-night car park, a glimpse of Ferrari scarlet and the flare of expensive tail-lights disappearing down the ramp; Florence was full of garages, as the narrow, crime-ridden streets, even if you could find a legal place to park in them and had the right permit, were hardly the ideal home for a valued vehicle. There was no manned booth that might have held a witness to Natasha Julius's last moments, just a striped barrier and a machine to read your card and allow you access.

Outside the Pizzeria San Frediano, just south of the bridge, evening strollers were on their way back from window-shopping among the boutiques over the river. A pair of women walked past the restaurant's plate-glass window, their heads thrown back as they laughed at something, arms linked, a flash of high cheekbones, white teeth and triumphant pleasure. The women were Olympia and Gina, clutching carrier bags and looking as young and happy as a pair of schoolgirls. Frank Sutton, at his seat in the window, looked up as they passed, and watched as they crossed to walk away down the Via Maggio.

Brimming with *prosecco*, the women had dispensed with the niceties.

'I can't believe it!' Olympia was aghast. 'You mean you've never – when you met him you'd never . . . No! I don't think I know anybody who's only ever slept with her husband. That's almost miraculous.'

Gina laughed shamefacedly. 'Sorry. Actually, sometimes I think I really am sorry; it does make me feel very . . . naive. But you don't realize that the time for experimentation will be over, once you've met the one, the father of your children; that it's too late then. You can't go back and have another go. Well you can, I suppose, but it's not usually happy ever after.'

'No, no.' Olympia recovered herself, realizing the effect her theatrical response had had on Gina. 'No, you're lucky, that's all. Most of us never are sure enough about the one.'

'Mmm,' said Gina. 'Yes. But you do wonder, all the same. What it would be like.'

'I imagine you do.' Olympia laughed. 'But believe me, it's rarely worth it.'

Suddenly Gina thought of her hostess. 'Olympia, hadn't I

better phone Jane?' Olympia shrugged, then, looking at Gina's anxious expression, she sighed, withdrew a tiny mobile phone and handed it over. Jane answered on the first ring, and there was something odd about her voice. She was subdued.

'Oh, darling, of course, that's quite all right. In fact I –' Jane seemed to falter, as though confused. 'I hadn't got around to cooking yet. Just let yourself in, darling, won't you? And if I don't see you, Frank's coming early in the morning to pick you up, do remember.'

Obediently Gina agreed, and clicked the phone shut, unsettled by Jane's distracted air; she hardly sounded like the same person.

The antique shops on the Via Maggio were all still open, and Olympia and Gina gazed in at their displays: Roman jewellery, an engraved samurai helmet and sword, a velvet-covered day-bed on which a portrait was propped. As they passed Pierluigi's shop, he was kneeling behind his front door locking up, a pretty but cross-looking redhead standing behind him with her arms folded. He looked up and, seeing Olympia, kissed his clasped fingers and held them up to her like a flower. She waved happily back, ignoring a nuclear glare from the redhead.

'I do hope Frances will be inviting Pierluigi on Friday; he is pure heaven. The problem is making sure you've only invited one of his girlfriends. It's always daggers when they come across each other. They all know who they are.'

Gina was beginning to feel a little apprehensive about meeting Frances; Olympia seemed very confident that they would get on, but after an evening with Olympia Gina had learnt that confidence, about everything, was her hallmark. They stopped.

Frances's front door gave no clue as to her personality; the building in which she lived was, like almost all the others in the Via delle Caldaie, one of those shabby, peeling façades whose neglected, unprepossessing appearance had so struck Gina on her arrival in Florence. They even had to shove aside a dumpster to get up to the front door, but when Olympia announced their arrival the sounds of joyful surprise through the crackle of the entry-phone were very reassuring.

When they reached the top of the stairs the door was already open. Nino, beaming, stood back modestly to hold the door wide for them. The room thus ceremonially presented to them could not have been more different from the spare brilliance of Niccolò Manzini's huge apartment. It glittered and glowed in the light from a hundred different sources – lamps with tattered silk shades, candles on the huge oak table that ran down one side of the room, in gilded sconces against the cracked soft plaster of the wall, and even an ancient, intricate pink glass chandelier that hung low in the room's centre.

Straight ahead of Gina, between two of the long, teardrop-arched windows, was a huge gilt-framed portrait of a stout, dewlapped cardinal in scarlet damask. At either side of the portrait, beneath the windows, in little bergere armchairs upholstered in the shredded remains of what had once been gold-coloured silk, sat Lucienne and Frances. Gina couldn't help but look at Lucienne first: crop-haired, tiny and dazzlingly coloured, like a hummingbird in an embroidered turquoise tunic and red chinese trousers, her bright, brown eyes alight with interest at the arrivals. Then Gina looked at Frances, her silver hair swept back, sitting composed and still in a long, soft, dark garment, her hands relaxed and open in her lap and on her face a smile of such irresistible sweetness that Gina found herself smiling back.

For a moment they looked at each other, then Frances leapt up, kissed Olympia warmly then took Gina's hand gently between hers. Gina felt all her apprehension disappear, and she leant into Frances's soft embrace, breathing in her sweet, elusive scent, of smoke and patchouli and jasmine.

'How lovely! Another guest for my party! Do you know, I think the surprise guests almost always turn out to be the best. Sit down, and have some *mirtillo*, it is so delicious.'

Olympia and Gina sat obediently on the coral-velvet sofa and accepted the *mirtillo*, dark, sweet and sticky, and brought to them by Nino in tiny, jewel-coloured glasses, and Frances raised hers to them.

'Olympia, darling. How is that lovely James? Will you make an honest man of him one day? Give us another party? Just imagine what a party that would be!' Frances smiled in mock-beatific anticipation, and Olympia and Frances looked at each other and laughed like schoolgirls. Frances leant in towards Gina.

'You have children, don't you? Who did I hear that from? Frank, perhaps; you made a great impression on him, I could tell. Do you have a picture of your children?'

Gina blushed at the memory of the previous evening, alarmed to think precisely what impression she might have made, and to disguise her embarrassment she fumbled in her bag and withdrew a dog-eared photograph of her children from the pages of a book. As she saw the three bright faces, crowded together on a garden bench, she felt an involuntary convulsion of longing, her eyes hot with sudden emotion, and she frowned in an attempt to disguise it. Frances looked at her quickly, then moved closer and carefully took the picture from her hand.

'Ah. How beautiful they are,' she said quietly, smoothing the photograph's corners. 'He looks very serious.' She drew her finger under Jim's solemn chin, his head on one side and in his dark eyes an expression Gina knew only she could recognize. 'Is he looking at you? You were taking the photograph?' Gina nodded dumbly, and Frances smiled and nodded, as if she understood. She sat looking at the picture for a few moments more, then gently handed it back to Gina.

'And on Saturday you'll see them again. How lucky you are. And clever, too; they're wonderful children.'

Gina smiled gratefully at Frances, her smile broadening as she thought of them.

'So we must make the most of you while we have you,' said Frances, Lucienne leant in to agree, and all at once they began to talk about the party, and the preparations for it. Olympia and Gina were invited to eat; after repeated exhortations and assurances that there was plenty to go around, they agreed. Companionably they sat around the long table in the candlelight, eating tortelli and chicken and salad and white peaches.

There was something subtly festive, an undercurrent of ceremony about the glowing room and the laid table; the old white napkins, Frances's silver, dented and battered but bright with polishing, the chipped plates with their painted garlands and gilded roses. Gina looked across at Olympia, who smiled conspiratorially like a subversive younger sister. And she felt young herself for once, among the smiling, elderly people, as they leant and touched her arm, beaming at her, passing her dishes and condiments and refilling her glass. Gina felt as though she were participating in an eccentric family gathering of some kind, a reunion, with her cast in the role of child returned. Lucienne, Nino and Frances were talking about the old days, about their youth together in Paris, visits to Budapest and Prague and London, and the glamour of the world they evoked drew Gina in, fascinated. Frances took an odd little cigarette, hand-rolled, from a cedar-wood box, and lit it. She turned to Gina.

'So, tomorrow you're off to the Maremma? It's very wild down there, you know. Poisonous snakes, boar, cowboys. People who live in the woods. I think you'll have a wonderful time. I think you could do with some time away from civilization. What do you think?' She smiled, merry, her blue eyes alive with interest and mischief, and Gina laughed with pleasure in response. *What an extraordinary person*, she thought, almost mesmerized.

Then Lucienne, who had been sitting back in her chair and observing them, turned towards Gina, something in her bright, questioning eyes that Gina couldn't pin down, and asked her about herself.

Awkwardly at first, then more fluently as she understood that Lucienne's inquiry was sincere, Gina found herself telling them what she considered to be the humble and uninteresting story of her life, growing up in a London suburb, her mother's death, meeting her husband, returning to a different London suburb to generate a family of her own.

'And your father?' Lucienne asked.

'He died years ago, not long before I was married,' Gina replied, flatly, feeling unable to convey the distance between herself and her father and the sense of frustrated confusion she had felt at his death. 'We were never very close; he spent a lot of my childhood working abroad. He was an engineer. He wasn't . . . He wasn't a demonstrative man.' She frowned at the question, wondering why Lucienne should be interested, but also at her own reply, which suddenly seemed a sad, thin little answer.

She saw Lucienne glance at Nino, then at Frances, a look perhaps of remorse at having broached a painful subject. Then Lucienne sprang up. 'Bridge! We could have a hand, surely. Or something else, so we could all play?'

Gina watched as the others played an exuberant game of bridge, then joined in for whist, and poker, and pontoon, surprised by the older people's enthusiasm and stamina. After a while, though, she retreated to the sofa again, laughing at her hopelessness at cards, and Frances came with her.

Frances settled herself comfortably next to her on the red velvet. Gina felt tired but relaxed; there was something about Frances – she was clever, Gina decided, that was it. And curious.

'So. You were why Jane invited Frank to dinner, then, Gina.'

'Was I?' Gina felt obscurely pleased, perhaps that she was still a female requiring a male to squire her, not just a worn-out housewife. 'Oh dear, poor him.'

'Nonsense,' Frances said stoutly. 'Lucky Frank. I'm beginning to despair of him; he's going to turn into an old maid, if he doesn't watch out. I sometimes wonder whether he isn't already quite odd sometimes. What did *you* think? Of him?'

Gina couldn't help smiling. 'I liked him. He didn't talk to me very much, though. He seemed rather – tense. Especially after Niccolò arrived.'

Frances sighed. 'Yes. It's an old story, that one – they were at school together, you know – that's why I was so surprised Jane invited him.'

'They're old enemies, then? Since school?' Gina thought of Jim's face after school sometimes, too angry to speak, or frozen with unhappiness about something someone had said. Could that go on for thirty years? She didn't believe it.

Frances nodded. 'I don't know what happened between them; something quite insignificant, probably. You could always ask Frank tomorrow, if he gives you a lift. But at that school – I expect you've never heard of the school, it was quite well known at the time. The Grange.'

A memory stirred, when Frances said the name; had she seen it on television? A picture came into Gina's mind, of adolescent boys, their faces painted, running through a wood. She nodded, sleepily, and Frances went on.

'It was one of those experiments in the sixties, they allowed the children – young people – to decide all sorts of things, gave them a student council, they could choose whether or not to go to classes. It didn't work very well, by all accounts. It closed down, oh, long ago. When you were still a child. There was a scandal; a girl was – oh, it's a nasty story. You don't want to hear it.'

Gina nodded, yawning, feeling quite a child herself now, ready to be carried to bed. Frances shook her head at her gently.

'Time for bed.'

At this Olympia looked over her shoulder from the card table, at the pair of them leaning close together on the red velvet. She clicked her tongue against her teeth in stern disapproval.

'Come on, then. We're keeping you up, too, Frances, aren't we?' And she set off briskly around the room collecting their packages and cardigans and scarves while Gina smiled and let her get on with it.

'I am so glad, darling, that you came to see us, and that we'll see you again at the party.' Frances smiled gently into Gina's eyes, and pressed her soft old cheek for a long moment against the younger one. She stood, silhouetted against the pink light that suffused the room behind her, and watched them go.

It was something Lucienne had said, about Gina. She'd said she looked familiar. Then Lucienne had looked worried, a look Frances had recognized, as though she had said the wrong thing. It had been a light-hearted remark, and she seemed to think Frances might have taken it too seriously. Lying in her bedroom in the dark, her guests dispersed, Frances smiled; Lucienne need not have worried. It wouldn't have been the first time since his death that she had been transfixed by the sight of Roland's high, arching eyebrows or his wide, laughing mouth on a stranger's face.

It was of course possible that Roland could have been Gina's father; she was roughly the right age and Roland had been in London at the right time; she knew he had had mistresses and one of them could have borne him a child. She knew it wasn't true, all the same; Frances did not believe that such a child could lose a mother and then discover Frances in that mother's stead. It was too close to the thing she had longed for, too transparently a wish fulfilled.

Frances thought of Gina, slowly unwinding in the warmth of the evening, helping herself to the food Frances might have made just for her, such a marvellous luxury had she seemed to find it. There was something neglected about the girl – Frances thought of Gina as a girl, unspoilt and impressionable – something that needed to be indulged, nurtured. So much quieter and more tentative than the people she usually found herself among – the sort of noisy, entertaining people Frances had spent five decades gathering around herself, with whom to furnish her dinners and her birthday parties, her picnics in Hungarian forests, her boating parties on the Douro; expansive, indiscreet people to enliven the deadliest embassy cocktail party and keep the scandal sheets in business. People like Roland.

And then it came to her: it wasn't because Gina was like Roland that Frances was drawn to her; it was because Gina was like *her*. Gina was like the shy, sixteen-year-old Frances, in Florence for the first time, and suddenly Frances thought that, with luck, the old city might act upon Gina as it had acted upon her, working its way into her affections, filling her life with romance and possibility. As she lay on her high old bed and gazed up at the faint, faded outlines of her frescoes, remembering the golden evening the five of them had spent like an odd sort of family around her table, Frances willed it to happen; and, warmed by the thought that her life could still surprise her with opportunities, she slept.

*

Far to the south, beside the dark country road, the moon had moved right across the sky by the time Mila stirred, trying to raise her head, to move away instinctively from the gurgle of the river below, but even the tiny movement she was able to make sent her head spinning. How long had she been out? Mila couldn't gauge whether it had been a few seconds or hours, so she listened. Then she realized there was no traffic noise, and on the S223 that meant it could only be between two and four in the morning. He must have gone by now. The cheap bastard. For some of them, it was part of the service, she thought sometimes, blow-up doll and punchbag, then get away without paying for it. Gingerly she sat up, and began to crawl up the hill towards the light.

Almost half an hour later Mila staggered into the lay-by. She scrabbled behind the bush where she'd hidden her stuff, and it was there, her bag and her mobile. She dialled Stefano's number.

He took a long time to answer, and when he did he was cold and indifferent; angry with her for wasting his time. She tried to tell him about Evelina, but all he said was that it was none of her business – and none of his either. She wasn't one of his girls, was she? Even if she had been, what was he going to do, call the police?

'Evelina's Betty's girl. If I do business with Betty, she can ask me to sort out some girl who's gone missing. And you can just keep your nose out of it.' His voice sounded ominous, but Mila had to go on. Trying to keep the pleading note from her voice, she asked him, in a whisper, if he'd come and get her.

'You've got to be kidding. I've been down that road once tonight, you know. If you think I'm going to come and get you every time you decide you want to go walkabout, you can think again, I'm not your daddy,' he sneered. 'I'll come and get you in the morning, and don't think you'll get a day off, either.' He hung up.

Mila pounded the mobile into the dirt of the road with her fist, screaming at it. Five, six hours freezing her arse in the middle of nowhere, waiting for that miserable bastard to come along with a change of clothes so she could go back to work. Oh, maybe he'd bring a bit of make-up, to cover up the bruises – not that the punters could give a stuff what your face looked like. She grabbed her carrier bag, pulled out her cardigan – home-made, brown and bobbly, only for cold nights – and put it on. No. She wasn't going to hang around waiting for Stefano. Not any more.

Mila felt in the bushes for her bag. It was still there, and she pulled it out triumphantly. There was a torch – a big heavy one, made her feel safer – and another old cardigan. No decent shoes. She looked up at the hillside, scanning the darkness for something that might offer shelter, and without a backwards glance she began to climb.

Wednesday

16

Gina opened her eyes to a room flooded with early-morning light, having woken from a sleep so deep and thick with dreams she didn't know where she was. At first the outlines of the room, clean and perfectly unadorned as they were, seemed to be like a hospital's, or a scene from science fiction. Then she focused on the sunlight through the shutters and registered the sounds of the street and, with something like relief, the presence of the real world. She immediately looked at her watch, remembering that Frank was to pick her up at eight to take her down to the country. It was seven-thirty. She tried to recall the night before; the day, which had been so filled with pleasure, had somehow so worn her out that she had barely managed to fit her key in the Manzinis' lock and stumble up to bed. She marvelled that she must have slept for nine hours, her limbs deliciously warm and heavy. Sighing with profound contentment, she stretched luxuriously in the soft white bed.

There had been no sign of Niccolò last night, but she did dimly remember Jane telling her earlier in the day that he was going back to Rome. The drawing room had been dark, and when she had located a switch it illuminated a pair of martini glasses, each still with a twist of limp lemon peel marinating in the last drops of viscous liquid, standing on the little Indian teak table in the centre of the room. This had struck her, even late at night and given her slim reacquaintance with Jane's fastidious habits, as uncharacteristic. Perhaps she let things slide a bit when Nicky was out of town, but Gina wasn't convinced. And two glasses? One way or another, that would indicate a vice to which she had not previously thought Jane susceptible. There had been no evidence of Beatrice, either, but Gina hadn't found that surprising. For all Jane's insistence on her status as a substitute mother, the two seemed to harbour an intense mutual dislike that kept them apart unless Beatrice's father was present to filter it.

Reluctantly, Gina got out of bed, showered and dressed. She had barely unpacked so it seemed simplest to just stuff everything back in the case for her two days at Il Rondinaio. She caught sight of the expensive carrier bag she had placed the previous night at the foot of her bed; leaning over, she carefully removed the dress from its tissue paper, hardly daring to look at it. She felt its slippery silvered weight drop from the straps she held by her fingers as she hung it reverently in the cupboard, folding the dark linen around its shoulders and placing the beaded sandals at its feet. She stroked the pale silk, which still held the perfumed air of the boutique in its folds, and wondered what Frances's party would be like. She looked at her watch; five minutes, just time to phone home before Frank arrived.

'Darling,' Stephen sounded relieved. In the background Gina could hear no alarming noises, no crashes or screams, just the clatter of breakfast bowls and a laugh, Dan giggling, something about Coco Pops. She could imagine him, crawling under the table with the box on his head, or jumping on Jim's back as he tried to eat his breakfast, and she felt her stomach twist with love.

'Everything all right? It's lovely here, weather's wonderful. I just phoned to say I'm going down to their country place for a couple of days, but I think they've got a phone down there so I'll call again. Maybe tomorrow.'

'Yes, er, everything's fine. Parents' evening tonight; Kath's going to have them. I was just a bit worried about you, um, you know, the last conversation we had you seemed, not your usual self.'

Gina frowned, trying to remember. She almost laughed out loud when she realized he was worried she'd been talking to Jane about him, so completely had their affair gone out of her head.

'No, no. But maybe you should start worrying – I went shopping yesterday and bought rather an expensive dress.' *That should get him going*, she thought mischievously. But she was wrong.

'Good, good,' Stephen said, absently. Perhaps he was more worried about her digging up any more old flames than he was about the size of her credit-card bills. 'We had roast lamb last night. Kath only helped me with the vegetables.' Gina detected a note of pride in his voice, and in her imagination set him up with Kath, who wore neon-blue eyeshadow and a stiff blonde beehive and was about fifty.

'But –' He stopped. 'The washing machine. I'm afraid there's going to be rather a big pile of washing when you get home. I haven't had time to work out the settings, how the machine works.' This time Gina did laugh. The entry-phone screeched.

'That's great. Never mind about the washing. Look, I've got to go. I'll phone again, not sure when, and speak to the kids. Give them a hug from me.' She put down the phone, picked up her case and went to the door.

Less than half a mile away, Stefano was walking past the grimy, desolate shop-fronts of the Via Romana, looking their dingiest in the clear morning light. He stopped in front of a splintered brown front door beside the winking neon of the late-night supermarket and leant his fist on the bell. The supermarket manager, gloomily unlocking his steel shutter, gave him a jaundiced look; Stefano ignored him and turned his attention to the door in front of him. The lock clicked open, but before he pushed open the door, his dark face a picture of resigned disgust, Stefano looked sharply upwards and the two girls who had been craning their necks out of the third-floor window jerked back inside, hastily pulling the windows closed behind them.

Betty had been in the Medici that morning, early, and when Stefano walked in she had scowled at him. 'If you want your money, you can take my girls down to work today, mister. I got hung out to dry by that Albanian; I paid him to take them all week, but he didn't turn up again. I bet the cops have had him, the little bastard.'

Stefano had just nodded, giving nothing away, as usual. As he had to get down there this morning anyway, to sort that silly cow Mila out, he might as well make a few extra lire out of it.

He wasn't sure now if he was happy about the decision. Stefano's own flat was in a clean modern block in the southern suburbs, and he wrinkled his nose as he entered Betty's hall-way. The building opened directly on to the bumper-to-bumper rush-hour traffic of the Via Romana to the front, and at the back it had a lightwell streaked with greenish mould for a view; inside it was airless and smelt of damp. It wasn't the kind of building where the residents paid for the communal areas to be mopped, either, and the hall's only light source was a skylight, four floors up.

Once in a while, Stefano ran the Nigerian girls to the country. Betty used a few different cars – she'd had a deal with a taxi firm for a while, and sometimes an Albanian guy took them; sometimes she made them go on the bus. She liked it that way; she kept a tighter hold on them. They couldn't form alliances with their driver, and if she used a Nigerian guy they'd all seemed to fall in love inside a week and start planning to run away with him, or at the very least give him for free what they should be charging for in order to pay Betty back for their passage over.

The girls were all scared of Betty, too scared to run away, at least. Some kind of African voodoo, but it worked fine, most of the time. Stefano squared his shoulders; he didn't like business done indoors, it made him feel claustrophobic, and the third-floor flat the girls inhabited – three of them, in two windowless bedrooms, sharing a shower and a tiny kitchen – was suffocatingly small, piles of cheap, bright clothes everywhere, and magazines. As he entered his throat contracted against the sweet, spicy smell of last night's curried chicken combining uneasily with the ripe, heavy scent of women living too close together.

They were waiting for him in the kitchen, Betty and the other two, lined up with their backs to the grimy window and staring at him sullenly. Both the younger ones were nineteen, and from the suburbs of Lagos. Glory, the tall one, her head covered with tiny braids, was almost six foot in her platforms, and she never smiled; Victoria, shorter and plumper, was lightly scarred on both cheeks, and her hair was long, straightened and highlighted with golden streaks. Neither of them knew more than a handful of phrases in Italian, and all of those concerned the tariff on their services; after six months or a year of watching Italian TV, which was all there was for them to do when they weren't working, they'd pick up a bit more. Betty, who'd been in the country almost ten years and was the only one of them who went out into the city, had a good, aggressive grasp of the language, and she used it.

'They don't want to go. They're freaked out. They know Evelina wouldn't run away, she's just a kid, she'd never have the nerve. Someone's had her, and they're afraid he's coming after them next. You've got to sort it for me.'

Stefano sighed.

'Listen,' he said. 'First things first. You owe me already,

remember? I don't give out that stuff for free. And it keeps your girls happy, doesn't it?' He nodded at them. 'Most of the time, anyway.'

Betty glared at him sullenly, then reluctantly she nodded, and pulled out her bag, brightly printed African fabric, with a drawstring. She handed Stefano a wad of notes, and without counting them or even looking he put them in his pocket.

'Right. First of all, you tell them, they don't go out and work, they're dead anyway. Are you going to feed them if they don't work? They've got their mobiles. They can work together, and those psychos only go for girls on their own. Plus, I'll deal with it.'

Betty looked at him. 'You know who it is?'

Stefano shook his head slowly. 'I saw that guy, Manzini, pick her up Sunday evening, when I was on my way to get Mila; he lives in Borgo Tegolaio but he's got a house down there. I think he's a regular. On my way back past she still wasn't there, so . . . You know.'

Betty looked sceptical. 'So you don't know who it is?'

Stefano looked at her levelly. 'I'll find out, don't you worry. I've let him know I know what he gets up to. That's enough for the moment. Do you want me to get them to work or not?'

Betty spoke for a few moments to the girls, their faces puffy with sleep and tears. Their unhappy, mulish expressions remained unchanged. They shook their heads and said something to Betty he didn't understand, though he could tell they were begging. She shook her head then casually, with her open hand, slapped them both hard on their cheeks. Stefano turned for the door, and Betty pushed them after him.

Jane groaned as she heard the squeal of the bell, then the click of the door down the hall as it closed behind Gina. She lifted her head slowly from the pillow, and felt pain clamp around it like an iron band. She let it fall back and waited a long moment before she opened her eyes, bracing herself against the stab of the sunlight through the shutters. She stood up carefully and walked to the door, pausing to collect the empty vodka bottle on the way. At least she'd changed into her nightdress before falling asleep – although, she noted sourly as she approached the bathroom mirror, she apparently hadn't got as far as removing her make-up or applying the night-cream that formed the bedrock of her elaborate beauty regime. She opened the chrome bathroom cabinet, reached for one of the many bottles it contained and some cotton wool and, wincing with distaste, began to dab at her face.

Half an hour later, Jane's face was repaired and made-up and her hair curled prettily under her ears once again as she grimly swigged her way through her second litre of mineral water. Wouldn't do to give the students any more to gossip about than was strictly necessary. Wednesday: almost halfway through. This morning, a short lecture on Italian animal husbandry and slaughtering methods followed by a coach trip to the Val di Chiana to visit the award-winning herd of organic cows that supplied the school with Fiorentina steaks, and to observe the butchering, seasoning and roasting of a suckling pig. Gathering wild fennel in the hills and then back to Florence with a handful of brochures advertising the butcher's Internet ordering service. Jane smiled thinly; all that butchery would sort the men from the boys. Jane herself had a stomach of cast-iron; even Nicky had winced when he had witnessed her decapitation of a diseased rabbit – a mercy killing – on one of their walks in the hills.

As her thoughts returned to her husband, though, Jane's composure faltered; she gritted her teeth and exhaled angrily. She reached for her mobile and dialled the Portakabin on the Rome site; an answering machine, and, as she didn't want Giuseppe picking up this particular message, she hung up before she heard the tone. The same went for the flat in Rome – Jane was aware that plenty of casual visitors passed through there.

She called his mobile; it was, as she had expected, also switched to its message service. Nicky disliked being at her – or anyone else's – beck and call so he kept the thing switched off.

'Niccolò. You had better phone Juliet. Now. She's told me something, about you and – and Natasha. And she's told Melissa, and Melissa, she says, has gone to the police. And when you've phoned her, you'd better phone me.'

17

At eight o'clock sharp on Wednesday morning, the rush-hour traffic into Florence was terrible. Nose to tail, the commuters sat patiently in a steaming queue of cars that tailed back from the Piazza San Felice at the head of the Via Maggio, through the colossal brick arch in the city's mediaeval walls and then another five miles or so out through the suburbs right back as far as the motorway tollbooths, swarms of Vespas weaving noisily in and out of the line wherever they could find a crack to squeeze through. As Frank and Gina drove past them, heading in the opposite direction, blissfully unhindered, Frank shook his head.

'Sometimes I'm glad I haven't got a proper job. Twice a day, every day, then the same again only ten times worse when they all decide to go on holiday at the same time. They don't look angry, do they? You'd think they like it. Everyone seems to think they're fiery, impulsive Latins, always swearing and shouting at each other, but in fact behind the wheel of a car I'd say the average Englishman has a much shorter fuse.

You wouldn't catch an Italian jumping out of his car to brain someone with a monkey wrench for cutting him up.'

Gina nodded absently, watching the drivers as they smoked and chatted and exchanged mild gestures of impatience or helplessness. Frank's battered Alfa was climbing now, up through the suburbs scattered across the hills on the city's southern edge, pretty little villas with comfortably wide balconies, vine-covered terraces or little striped awnings, their gardens thick with tropical foliage, palms, bougainvillaea and citrus trees.

'Yes,' she said wonderingly, thinking of the taxi driver who'd jumped out of his cab and smashed his fist against her window when she was on the school run one morning because she'd pulled out in front of him without showing the right kind of respect. 'They seem so laid back. But even after ten years in London I've never knowingly been as close to a murder as I was on Monday night. Isn't that strange?'

Frank shrugged, and smiled at her. 'Oh, they're not all harmless, that's not what I meant. It's not all art galleries and cappuccino. A lot of poor people, a lot of people with nothing to lose and no official status. I –' He stopped, gazing out of the window.

'What?' Gina looked at him curiously.

He shrugged uneasily. 'Nothing. It could have been drugs. Or it could have been someone she knew, from what Jane was saying. That kind of thing happens wherever you are.'

'But in a way, isn't that more frightening?' said Gina, frowning. 'If it's someone she knows, then it might be someone they all know. Someone Beatrice knows, too. If she was my daughter, I'd be scared for her. There doesn't seem to be anyone to look after her here.'

'Yes,' said Frank. 'Well, Jane's probably exaggerating. I don't suppose she knows the first thing about Natasha Julius's friends, really, and I can't imagine she knows much about the drugs scene, either. Jane's pretty good at not seeing what she doesn't want to see.'

That was a rather odd way of putting it. Gina looked at him, curious. 'What do you mean?'

'Well. Married to Niccolò.' He looked scornful.

'You don't like him, do you?' Gina was cautious.

'Not much.' Frank was tight-lipped. 'And I know him better than most. Knew him.'

'From school?'

Frank nodded.

'Maybe he's changed,' Gina ventured. 'People do. And it would be awful never to be allowed to forget what you were like at fifteen, wouldn't it?' Gina thought about herself as an adolescent; self-conscious, timid and studious, she had felt perpetually unloved and suddenly she brightened as it occurred to her that her life had in fact been transformed.

Frank snorted. 'I don't think he's changed.' He fell silent.

Niccolò Manzini obviously didn't bring out the best in Frank; his dislike was startlingly uncompromising and Gina felt excluded by it entirely, excluded from the pleasant, easy-going man who'd sat next to her at dinner on her first night. But then Frank sighed, and spoke again.

'Niccolo and I were both expelled from that school, and effectively we closed the school down. We did something very bad, and it was shocking enough, even at that place, to close it down. I can't – I can't deny that I shared the responsibility for it. Not now. But Niccolò – well, I know how I got into that situation; I was a child, really. But Niccolò Manzini, he's something else. Even then, there wasn't anything naive about him.' Frank stopped abruptly; he looked at Gina, whose face had turned quite pale. He shook his head as though reproaching himself and smiled at her awkwardly. She couldn't help but want to reassure him, so she smiled back.

'Look, I'm sorry. It was a long time ago, and nobody died.' Gina opened her mouth to ask for more information, but Frank's expression, closed and stern, and the finality of his tone stopped her. He shook his head slightly. 'And you mustn't let all this spoil your holiday,' he said. 'The murder, I mean. Florence isn't a dangerous place, generally, only a bit rough around the edges. South of the river, well, there are a few problems, but at least it's all out in the open. Nothing's hidden.' He looked up, and smiled. 'The countryside, now, that's a different matter.'

By now they were on the *superstrada*, driving fast through dense deciduous forest, lush and green where it overhung the motorway. To either side gentle hills striped with the marks of cultivation, terraces of olives or vines, rose above the trees, occasionally surmounted by a crenellated villa or miniature castle. It didn't look at all sinister.

Gina laughed.

'All right, it doesn't look very dangerous.' Frank smiled. 'Are you having a good holiday, so far? Away from your family?'

'Mmm, yes, actually.' Gina wondered why she felt so relaxed with someone she hardly knew. She realized that it was quite a long time since she'd had a proper conversation with a man other than Stephen; perhaps that was it. It seemed so easy when compared with all those barbed conversations with other mothers, every other phrase freighted with an unvoiced criticism or an unflattering comparison. Not the gentler sex at all. Or perhaps she just didn't understand men.

'I mean, of course I miss them, but somehow I am managing to forget all about them for quite a lot of the time, much more easily than I'd expected. Of course, all the excitement helps. Not to mention the shopping. And it's – it's just great to have someone to talk to.'

Frank looked surprised. 'Don't you talk to anyone in London? Your husband?'

'Oh yes.' Gina was quick to defend Stephen; she hadn't meant . . . Well, she wasn't sure what she had meant.

'Yes, but, he's at work till seven, and there isn't really anyone much else, unless you count the children. Here people talk all the time, in the street, in the bar, in the shops. Perhaps you've forgotten what it's like in England. It's a sign of mental instability to strike up a conversation with a stranger. Unless you're drunk in the pub, and I'd need a babysitter for that.'

As she said this Gina realized that she was in fact already revealing a great deal more than she was used to. It was rather liberating, to be talking to someone who knew so little about her circumstances; someone who didn't automatically associate her with her children, or school, or her husband, as someone's mother or someone's wife. She wondered whether she was sounding pathetic. Just a bit, she decided. She was going to have to get out more.

Frank looked at her pensive, crestfallen face. 'It's a good thing you came, then. Pity you've got to go back.'

Gina smiled despite herself, glancing sideways at his profile. He was looking straight ahead at the road, giving nothing away.

'Now,' said Frank, indicating to turn off the motorway, 'I need a cup of coffee and you're going to tell me all about Jane at nineteen. Did Manzini turn her into a monster or has she always been like this?'

Jane was trying to remember when she'd last seen Beatrice. She gave up shouting down the corridor and marched into the girl's silent bedroom, throwing open the door furiously. The room was cool and dim, the shutters closed. The bed was neatly made, and empty.

With her head still fuzzy with the previous night's toxins and just ten minutes to go before she had to go into the school kitchen and deliver her meat lecture, Jane was having difficulty remembering. *Bloody girl*. Lunchtime, when the police brought her back after the – the interrogation or whatever it was. Where had she said she was going? To see friends. That meant Ned Duncan, though she wouldn't have said so, knowing the reaction she'd have got. Jane looked at her watch. Too early to phone the Duncans now; perhaps she could do it before leaving for the Val di Chiana. What did the girl think she was doing, disappearing for the night without a word? God, how she resented having to nursemaid Nicky's daughter day and night and run a business at the same time.

Jane went over to the Venetian mirror in the hall and smiled slightly at herself, head tilted to one side, in the rippling, watered glass. She ran her fingers through her hair and widened her eyes, eye exercises to mitigate the ageing effects of the previous night. *Lack of sleep*, she thought. As she turned towards her kitchen, she heard the doorbell go, and wondered for a moment whether it was Beatrice, lost her keys again. It wasn't.

She opened the door to the two policemen, who smiled at her politely and asked her permission before entering.

'What is it? I'm about to begin a class,' she snapped, heedless of courtesy by now.

'Please accept our apologies, Signora Manzini,' said one of the *carabinieri*. 'However, you must remember that we're conducting a murder investigation. There have been certain allegations made by Signore Manzini's daughter in England that have been communicated to us, as they relate to the murder victim, Signorina Julius. I'm afraid we must speak with him again. Is he at home at this moment?'

'As far as I am aware, he is in Rome, at his work. I have been attempting to get through to him myself.'

Jane drew herself up, aware of how it looked, her inability to make contact with her own husband. 'I can give you his numbers, at work, at the flat in Rome, the *telefonino*.'

'We understand you also have a house in the country, in the Maremma? Is it possible that he may be there?'

Jane looked at them blankly, wondering how they knew about Il Rondinaio. 'I doubt it. It's for holidays. But have that number too, why not. Now please, may I continue with my work?'

'By all means,' said the *carabiniere*. Jane registered that he was the same man who had brought Beatrice home two nights before, when this nightmare had begun. He bowed slightly, and Jane looked at him narrowly, suspecting him of sarcasm. She moved towards the door in an effort to usher them out before her students arrived in the kitchen behind her – the door to which, she was uncomfortably aware, remained open. However, the *carabiniere* didn't seem quite ready to go. He held up his hand.

'Just one thing, *Signora*. We also need to speak with you in relation to this inquiry, of course. Your husband mentioned one or two things we would like to check with you, and also we need to confirm your own whereabouts on Sunday evening, just as a matter of routine, naturally. If it isn't convenient to come with us now, then perhaps this evening? We'll expect you at the police station. If you wish we can send a police car for you?'

Jane gaped at him, incredulous, for a moment. Then, deciding she didn't have time to express her full outrage and indignation, and that it was unlikely to do her any good in any case, she rearranged her clenched and furious jaw into a smile. Suddenly the *carabiniere*, smiling back politely, no longer appeared to her as a faintly laughable, pompous little toy soldier; he now looked like something more sinister, with the power to interfere with the life she had worked so hard to construct. She found herself looking at the heavy gun hanging from his belt in its holster.

'You're very kind. I appreciate your consideration, but I think I'll be able to find my way on my own. Now, I can hear that my students have arrived and I would like to go to them.'

Jane opened the front door and the policemen left, at last, but with what seemed to her to be a deliberate, calculated slowness, as though to indicate to her that it was for them to decide when the door would finally close behind them.

Although, as Frank wryly pointed out, nothing could have marked them out more clearly as tourists, and gullible ones at that, Gina and Frank were drinking their cappuccino sitting outside in Siena's main square instead of standing at the counter in one of the cheaper places in the steep, narrow side-streets or, better still, a roadside truck-stop. But when Gina had mentioned, with a wistful look, that she'd last been here as an Interrailing student almost twenty years before, Frank had seemed to reconsider.

As Gina remembered, it was not square at all, scooped out of the centre of the old red city, a piazza as curvaceous and perfect as the inside of a scallop shell. The tall, slightly misaligned buildings of faded, crumbling pink brick curved away from them, following the sweep of the piazza with their elegant clover-leaf windows and delicate ironwork balconies. The waiter set tall glasses of iced water in front of them on the metal table.

That summer, the end of her second year at university, she should have been here with Jane, but the plan had fallen through and she'd come away on her own, for a month, her first time in Italy. Jane, she remembered, had very convincingly developed a mysterious and debilitating stomach condition to excuse her poor performance in their end-of-year exams. The illness had begun at the outset of the summer term, and with hindsight Gina suspected it had been originally intended to get her out of sitting the exams at all, but her tutor, not as susceptible as some to Jane's self-mythologizing, or perhaps he'd seen it all before, was having none of it.

'She said she couldn't eat a thing, all summer. She kept throwing up. She was very thin, by the end of it; I remember thinking what a useful sort of illness it was, getting her out of exams and losing weight at the same time. I suppose it's possible she was actually a bulimic, now that I know such things exist, but somehow that seems too much of a victim thing for Jane to get into. It seemed like a clever strategy to me at the time. That sounds bitchy, doesn't it?'

Frank just smiled at her, one eyebrow raised. Gina sighed. 'I don't quite mean it like that, not entirely. She's interesting, admirable in a way, you know. She's so determined. She never stopped, not at university, not once we'd all started work afterwards, just moving upwards, working through the opportunities, never resting on her laurels. She was a monster to live with, though. Not that I ever did. But some friends shared a house with her at the beginning, and she was impossible. Ordered them all around, organized rotas she never appeared on, made sure she had the best room, got money out of them for stuff she wanted for the house, in that steamroller sort of way she has, just through strength of will.'

'After all this time, you remember all this?' Frank said.

Gina was shamefaced. 'It's just that she was memorable. She stood out. When we were all just loafing about in hopeless jobs, never saving money and eating takeaways, assuming life would come along sooner or later, Jane was in a different league. Dynamic, no room for self-doubt, desperate, in a way. It was so important to her, to be somebody, to be in the driving seat. And absolutely extraordinary in a crisis; you can imagine her evacuating the *Titanic*. Perhaps that's why Stephen –' She broke off.

'Yes?' Frank leant forwards, elbows on his knees, and looked into her face. She smiled awkwardly, and shrugged.

'Why he asked her to have me. I was . . . In a bit of a mess, staying at home, the children, they were getting me down. Kept bursting into tears, you know.' She grimaced at the inadequacy of her description and Frank looked at her quizzically. Gina burst out laughing, feeling some kind of release. 'Kill or cure, maybe, a week with Jane. Actually, I think it's working; I'm starting to see the point of Jane, now. Anyway, back then, none of us could stand her for long, and we were afraid of her, but she was fascinating.'

'She married the right man, then, do you think?' Frank said.

'Oh, yes, he was perfect. She wouldn't have settled for anything less,' Gina said, thinking of the suitors Jane had turned down, and her triumphant wedding, choreographed and exquisite down to the last rose petal floating in the last finger bowl. Then she realized that might not have been what Frank had meant, exactly.

'I suppose he *is* just like her, isn't he. He is . . . charismatic, in a frightening sort of way. At the time, he was *so* famous, so powerful – he'd had that glass tower built in the City, he had commissions all over the place; they were always going to parties and being photographed. She couldn't have married anyone better, we thought. But then they came out here; wasn't that rather odd?'

'A bit, maybe,' Frank said. 'But . . . it has its charms. We all have our reasons for staying out of the mainstream. For Manzini, well, it's a lot easier to keep your private life private here. No tabloids to doorstep you if you're indiscreet with your girlfriends.'

Gina wondered whether Frank knew about Olympia. 'Girlfriends?' she asked, cautiously.

'Well, you hear rumours,' Frank said reluctantly. 'And it wouldn't be a first for a powerful man like Manzini, to choose a trophy wife like Jane then go somewhere else for sex.' Frank stopped as though worried that he might have embarrassed her, but Gina was frowning with concentration.

'It almost makes me feel sorry for Jane,' she said finally, looking up at him.

Frank looked at her serious face, and took her hand in his. 'Come on, let's go. I want to show you something.'

And they stood up together, turning away down a steep side-street and leaving the rose-pink piazza behind.

The smell of dust and mildewed straw in her nostrils, the sun already high in the pale, scalding morning sky and shining in through a gap in the broken planking, Mila lay still with her eyes slitted against the light; her head ached as she tried to pick out the reality from the night's feverish dreams.

Il Rondinaio, the Manzinis' celebrated and much-photographed country house, had a number of well-kept out-buildings, containing garden tools, wooden sunloungers, large canvas umbrellas, a mini-tractor. There was a laundry room, with washers, dryers and drying racks, and there was a corrugated plastic lean-to which sheltered an ancient Fiat 500, whose door Mila had tried almost instinctively the night before, and found locked, like everything else, as she had circled the massive stone house in search of an entry point. In the end, a wooden shed so dilapidated she had originally walked straight past it, more like a pile of reclaimed planks than a building and, judging by the smell, once used to house goats, offered the only shelter. With something like gratitude, she had crawled inside and it was only when she felt the meagre protection of the shed around her that she had begun to shake, her body betraying her at last. Then she had heard the car.

It was further down the hill, but moving slowly, as though it was looking for something. The road up here must be a *strada disessata*, an unmade road, just gravel and potholes by the sound of it, the car bumping and lurching through the overhanging hedgerows. It had come nearer, infuriatingly slow, winding up towards the ridge until Mila could see the beam of its headlights swinging around, illuminating trees and sky at random as the car dipped and swayed on the uneven road, then it had stopped at the foot of the drive, and the lights went out.

A man – she had known it was a man, from the heavy crunch of his feet on the gravel – left the car and as he approached the house the blue-white glare of a row of high-wattage security lights suddenly, noiselessly illuminated every-thing for fifty yards around the house. Mila had flinched, horrified suddenly to think that all the time she had herself circled the farmhouse, she might at any time have set off these merciless lights. She could see the man's back at the door; he was tall, and there was something smooth about him, his hair cut short and clean, and he was dressed in a very sharp suit. He was unlocking the door, his head bent in concentration. He went in, leaving the door open behind him, and the security lights went off, to be replaced by a dim external lamp over the porch. For a second Mila wondered whether she should try to slip in after him, but shook the idea off; there was something about the guy, something dark, the way he was acting, his sure, careful step, his quick, surreptitious movements, made her think he perhaps wasn't a kindly foreign visitor, a soft touch that might take pity on a poor abused whore if he found her sneaking through his front door after him. So she stayed put.

A moment later he had come back out holding a box of something that looked like books, their spines facing up, or maybe videos. Above the box she could see the delineament of his face in the dim light; haunted, narrow, the beginnings of a five o'clock shadow emphasizing the hollows beneath his high cheekbones. He put the box down at his feet and turned, extinguishing the porch light and locking two sets of doors.

Despite her fear, Mila had cursed his security precautions in the night chill, but she felt very relieved when she heard his footsteps pass below her in the drive, the solid clunk of his door shutting behind him, and saw the car's taillights heading away from her through the trees.

Now, by daylight, Mila went over the scene in her mind before she ventured outside, as a precaution. Had he really gone? Or had the whole thing been her imagination? Not that, at least; Mila had sorted her imagination out long ago, you had to, doing what she did. Now, though, her throat dry and her head pounding, the need for water was overriding. Satisfied that she was alone, she squeezed out through the hut's mis-shapen door into the warmth of the morning sun, and looked around her.

The house was high up, and that pleased Mila. She looked down with a kind of triumph at the river, and the busy S223, far below, and was surprised by how far she had climbed. She could see the solid stone terracing of the garden below, the roses, the well-kept lawn, and, looking back, the comforting bulk of the house. A rich man's holiday home; carefully secured, well-equipped, and empty, for the moment at least, and that, she thought, should suit her very well.

18

Frances had got up early to walk to the flower market, and in the calm atmosphere of morning, the warm, golden light that blessed the open spaces as she walked through them and the comforting bustle of the cool, dark streets, she found herself thinking about the previous evening, and about Gina. A new friend.

It was often said that Frances had a great gift for friendship, and it sometimes seemed to her that her whole life had been an effort to compensate for the silence and solitude of her childhood. She was industrious in her relationships; she paid them careful attention, remembered birthdays, wrote thank-you letters, listened with great interest to the stories of her friends' lives. Frances could not imagine a time when she would consider herself too old to make a new friend, and a friend once made was never dropped; she considered good company to be too valuable to be treated lightly. And the discovery of someone new to find out about always seemed to Frances to be something akin to a miracle; she hesitated, being ignorant of childbirth, to make the comparison, but it seemed to her that the glimpse into another life that the establishment of a friendship afforded was a little like having a child, a manifestation of the world's delicious variety.

Gina, now. If ever a friend needed drawing out, it was Gina, and Frances felt quite excited at the prospect. Frances thought of how she had looked at the photograph of her three children, all looking back at her, her reflection in their eyes. Perhaps, Frances thought, those bright-eyed little children would like a surrogate grandmother in Florence; someone not too close, not too importunate. She imagined them clambering on her ancient furniture, opening her little boxes, playing with her ivory elephants, playing hide-and-seek in the Boboli Gardens while she sat on a bench in the sunshine. Then she smiled at herself; *First things first . . . The party.*

Frances wanted lilies, the long furled trumpets of arum lilies, tuberose, lemon trees in pots, and at least thirty gardenias, for their scent and waxy white flowers. She imagined the lemons standing guard at the great oak doors to the Casa Ferrali, thrown open for once, and the gardenias laid out beneath the trees, gleaming from out of the darkness and filling the air with their heavy, tropical perfume. The expense did not even occur to her, as she crossed the bridge of Santo Trínita, crossing from the Oltrarno to the wide boulevards of the northern city beneath another day's brilliant blue sky. She looked along the row of sunlit façades fronting the river and up to the mountains beyond, hazy in the soft spring light. She saw the golden ochre and crumbling balustrades of the Palazzo Corsini, its terrace crowded with baroque statuary which always made her think of parties, evenings spent drinking champagne and looking down the river hung with lights. Frances was in a mood for celebration.

Once a week the flower-sellers laid out their banks of mimosa, tulips, and lilies, potted jasmine, Japanese tree-peonies with tissue-paper blooms, pink and yellow roses, filling the vaulted space beneath the massive marble art-nouveau arcades along one side of the Piazza della Repubblica, and flooding it with colour and scent. Once the warm weather had arrived in earnest, as Frances felt, today, that it had, the atmosphere of the flower market became intoxicating; perfumed and opiate, and even when a summer downpour would fill the piazza with pelting rain, beneath the arches it felt like an Indian bazaar in the monsoon.

Frances looked up at the clear sky, and wondered whether the weather would hold for another two days. She didn't have much of a contingency plan in case of rain on Friday evening, but awnings could be put up over the trestles easily enough, and the trees would provide good shelter unless, as was quite possible after a spell as warm and humid as this, there was a full-blown thunderstorm. They could always retreat to the house, though, and anyway Frances enjoyed the exotic spectacle of Florence's violent storms, when lightning would illuminate the hills all around, and the rainwater gulleys at the centre of the steep, winding streets leading down into the city would become torrents.

Her arms filled with lilies and a great bundle of someone's

pale back-garden irises, Frances bargained gently, courteously but with great persistence with the gardenia-seller, and after much smiling and nodding they agreed on a price, including delivery to the Casa Ferrali that evening, a couple of potted lemons thrown in at the last minute. Delighted with her success, Frances decided to reward herself with a cappuccino taken sitting down outside the Caffè Gilli, in the far corner of the square.

For the rest of the week, deprived of its flowers, the Piazza della Repubblica was an uninspiring square, dauntingly grey, monumental and Victorian. Emblazoned with solemn, triumphalist slogans about modernity and hygiene, it had been carved out of the old ghetto more than a hundred years before, in a mercifully short-lived bid to drag Florence out of the middle ages. To Frances's mind, the flower market aside, Gilli was the only reason to stop here. Wood-panelled, gleaming with polished silver and crystal, it reminded her of Fortnum's in the forties; a refuge from privation, a provider, at a price, naturally, of impeccably old-fashioned luxury and good manners, although it cost as little to stand at Gilli's huge green marble bar as it did at the Medici. Today, burdened as she was, Frances decided she would take the more expensive option and sit, beneath the jasmine on the deep, shaded terrace, to rest and eavesdrop and glimpse the passersby through the hedge of bay that enclosed the pampered clientele. She ordered coffee and the café's proprietary pastries, delicate and buttery, reputedly the most delicious in Florence.

Gentler than its competitor, Rivoire, which was situated at the tourist epicentre of Florence, the Piazza della Signoria, and which was so central to the mainstream that it forced the tide of tourists to part and flow around it, the Caffè Gilli appeared to have retained as its core clientele the moneyed elderly Italians, either visitors to the city or the last of the Florentine aristocracy, whose tall daughters still pushed huge prams up and down the Via de' Tornabuoni dressed in Edwardian tweeds, shopping at Loretta Capponi for a satin negligée or a christening gown embroidered by nuns. Frances had only once visited Loretta Capponi, to buy a lace bib for a god-daughter, and had found herself stalked by a fierce saleswoman in black taffeta, as though if left alone for a moment she might sweep an entire layette from its mahogany display cabinet and into her bag.

Frances found it particularly interesting to observe these gentlewomen, the impoverished remnants of Tuscan high society. They seemed monstrously snobbish, and far more antique than their English counterparts in their habits of dress and behaviour, and they could be heard complaining ceaselessly to each other about the trials of modern life. They complained about the vulgarity of the foreigners to whom they were forced to let their annexes and converted stables in the country, about the cost of running a swimming pool, the plague of immigrants, the dishonesty of their servants and the iniquities of the Catalogo delle Belle Arte, the historical preservation authority that insisted on listing their Renaissance statuary so that they could no longer discreetly sell it on the Via Maggio, to someone like Pierluigi.

Today in the sunshine and bustle of the square's busiest day, the terrace was crowded with rich women of late middle-age, all beautifully suited and shod. To her delight, Frances's nearest neighbours were Giulia Braganza, whom Frances knew slightly, and Vivienne Duncan, both exclaiming bitterly about the exorbitant cost of the pair of gaudy red camellias they had, all the same, been unable to resist. They looked around themselves busily to see whether there was anyone worth acknowledging, and nodded perfunctorily to Frances. She inclined her head and lifted a hand in greeting. The two women then turned from her and began to talk about their children.

'Giovanni is so tiresome these days!' Giulia Braganza put a hand to her brow in a sorrowful gesture. She was referring to her son, a lazily handsome playboy whom Frances had once or twice invited to her parties; he was narcissistic but charming, and she found him considerably more agreeable than she did his mother. Giulia went on: 'Would you believe he's almost forty, and yet he will do nothing useful. He has so many expensive cars, and he is always flying to New York to enjoy himself and leaving the business to carry on without him. His father is at his wits' end. And as for finding a good wife! Or any kind of wife, for that matter.'

'I know,' agreed Vivienne Duncan with a sigh. 'Of course, Ned is very much younger,' she paused, as though to allow Giulia to make the obvious calculation about their own respective ages, 'much too young to think of marrying – thank God, if you look at some of the specimens he drags home – but I do wish he would do something, and stop . . . stop hanging about the house all day!' Her voice was raised and querulous, and Frances could see Giulia Braganza's head turn in mild surprise at her friend's uncharacteristic vehemence, at the weight of frustrated incomprehension behind Vivienne's outburst. It was not like Vivienne Duncan to betray any dissatisfaction with her son.

Vivienne made a gesture of impatience, and looked away. 'He has had such a wonderful education. His father was determined that he should have every advantage.' She shook her head, and Giulia Braganza nodded, but it was clear to Frances from her bland and tolerant smile that Giulia was rehearsing the arguments against English boarding schools – The brutality! The absence of a mother figure! The lack of proper hygiene! And, of course, the prevalence of homosexual behaviours! – behind the mask of indulgence she turned towards Vivienne. *No wonder the poor child went off the rails*, she seemed to say, *and don't think we don't know why Ned was*

removed from that particular privileged place of learning. These
English . . .

Vivienne seemed to be gazing at some far distant object, however, and did not appear to register Giulia's expression at all. 'And sometimes it does seem to be too much that I am left to deal with all this on my own. Of course, if his father –' She stopped, frowning. Giulia Braganza looked at her for a moment contemplatively, then sighed and patted her on the hand.

'I know, my dear. It is a great sadness. But sometimes these things happen in families. Silvano refused to talk to Giovanni for a whole year, when he lost all that money investing in the flying school. Things change.'

Vivienne Duncan looked at her narrowly. 'Giulia, darling, this has been going on for three years already. Sometimes I think my husband hates his son. I mean, everyone has a little trouble with drugs, almost everyone I know has a child who has been through this; there is no need for all this.'

Giulia nodded sympathetically. 'Of course.' She looked at her companion expectantly, and with a sigh of resignation Vivienne went on.

'George simply won't come to Italy any more. He says he can't bear the heat, and the estate doesn't run itself . . . There's always one reason or another. And I can hardly stand to spend more than a week or so in England these days, not with Ned, the atmosphere is so ghastly. And Ned has taken it so hard. He always wanted to please his father, as a little boy, and George – well, he is not a demonstrative man. His upbringing, you know. And of course he never got on with his own father after we . . . when we were married. Ned has become very – unhappy. I sometimes wonder whether there's something . . . whether he's depressed. Or perhaps he could have one of those, you know, those illnesses. Some kind of syndrome.'

There was a trace of something so uncharacteristic, anxiety, or uncertainty, in Vivienne Duncan's voice that Frances craned her neck in an unsuccessful attempt to see her expression. She saw Giulia Braganza's stiff, glistening helmet of hair tremble as she shook her head and tutted in sympathy.

'It is so galling, when one has given them so much, these children, and they simply waste it. It is not as if we haven't set them a good example; after all, Silvano and I have never ceased to work, on the villa and the business.'

Frances smiled as she overheard this, Giulia Braganza's idea of work being wandering through Zoffany selecting curtain fabrics for the family villa outside Lucca. And as for the business, it was well known that the Braganzas had spent the last forty years running the ancestral handbag-and-leathergoods business into the ground, and as a ne'er-do-well Giovanni Braganza was only following dutifully in his father Silvano's footsteps, with his flat and mistress in Monaco and another in Rome. Frances was more interested to hear about Ned; on reflection she felt, like Frank, that there was something veiled and unreadable about him – although, with a bully of a father and a mother of such brittle superficiality, perhaps it was unsurprising he kept his feelings to himself. She leant closer to hear Vivienne's response.

Vivienne's voice had become more sober in tone; she was talking about Natasha.

'We saw the girl very often at the villa, of course. Her parents really permitted her to run wild out here, her father in Germany, her mother in London, quite frightfully irresponsible. Of course I did my best, in loco parentis, you know, and she could be – very sweet. But she was a troubled child, very troubled.' Vivienne lowered her voice so that Frances had to strain to hear it at all.

'You know she spent a great deal of her childhood with her father, in Hamburg. Really not a healthy city for a child. The Reeperbahn . . .' She sat up and went on, brightly, 'Ned was such a friend to her; I think he saw more of her than he saw of his own girlfriend, little Beatrice. And she always seemed so much better after only half an hour with him, I do believe he has quite a gift.'

'Yes, it is a shame they don't seem to be as sweet with us. He was really quite unfriendly with me the last time I visited the villa,' Giulia pouted.

'Well,' Vivienne smiled charitably, 'I think perhaps he's suffering; he's hardly left his room since – it has been traumatic for all of us, a murder on our doorstep. And of course he's having to take on the burden of poor Beatrice, moping about. She was with us for hours yesterday; they were shut up together upstairs, and I could hear her going on and on.' She shook her head. 'It is a bore, all this. But –' and she leant closer to her companion – 'I hear they also questioned Manzini, the father! And they may even have to talk to the stepmother.'

At this Frances turned away, uncomfortably aware that, avid as she was for information herself, she could hardly take the moral high ground. She made an effort to shift her concentration to higher things, and under the circumstances flower arranging seemed noble enough. She signalled to the waiter, gathered up her armfuls of blooms, inhaling their fresh light scent with relief, and turned to go. Frances walked slowly down to the river and crossed back to the south, where the Via Maggio unfurled at her feet, its rafters meeting overhead like a wedding arch as she walked down it with her flowers.

Soon after Siena, Gina felt her surroundings shift in shape; the Alfa went into a tunnel through a modest hill and when they emerged at the other side the landscape had changed. At first it was bleak and bare, and flat enough for paddy fields to appear briefly beside the road, then a garish roadside restaurant appeared, a fleet of container lorries filling its concrete parking bays, and beyond it rose a great dark range of hills, their dense covering of trees black against the limpid sky. Gina felt something prickle at the back of her neck, and she gave a sudden shiver in spite of the warmth. Frank looked at her.

'It's quite beautiful, actually, once you're there. Wild, very unspoilt. There aren't many holiday homes; it's mostly just a few farmers, some wild boar and a lot of empty forest. Very peaceful.'

Gina nodded. 'Just what I need, perhaps. A retreat.' She didn't feel as sure as she sounded about the prospect of silence and solitude, but it was growing on her. She looked out of the window and into the woods that now enclosed them; then, as they flashed past a lay-by, she did a double take and craned her head back over her shoulder, uncertain of what she had seen. Fast receding behind them she saw two tall African women – girls? – in brightly coloured stretch minidresses, standing in the shade of a large golfing umbrella at the side of the road. She opened her mouth, then closed it again, looking at Frank, who laughed reluctantly.

'Well, that's partly what I meant about the country having a dark side.' He looked embarrassed.

Gina looked out at the woods again, now innocently, idyllically empty, shafts of sunlight falling through budding oak and elm on to the leaf-carpeted forest floor. Then the car emerged briefly from the trees enclosing it, and in a field of maize on her left Gina saw another girl, standing in the tall green plants like a scarecrow, her face turned to the road as a sunflower to the sun, and her hand on her hip in an unmistakable pose. She was certainly a girl, this one, no more than sixteen or seventeen, and Gina caught the expression on her face, a poignant mixture of fear and defiance, incongruous above her strong, slender body in its tight cropped T-shirt. Gina had barely had time to process the image before they passed two more girls, on the other side of the road this time, a forested hill rising up behind them, and then the Alfa was swallowed up in another tunnel.

'Where do they come from?' Gina asked, aghast. 'There are so many of them.'

Frank nodded. 'They're mostly from Nigeria. Some from Eastern Europe. A lot of them don't know where they're going when they leave home, or what they'll be doing. Once they're here, they're completely dependent on the people who brought them here; they have nothing of their own, no papers, no money, they have to pay back the madame who brought them over, millions of lire sometimes. They're locked up in an apartment in the city somewhere to keep them out of sight.'

'And they . . . they work out here, in the middle of nowhere? Who stops on a road like this?' She stopped, thinking of the fleet of lorries at the truck stop, the empty woods, the fear on the girl's face. 'It must be so dangerous.'

Frank nodded, his face clouded. 'Yes.' He seemed ill at ease, Gina thought, as he continued. 'They've mostly disappeared by high summer, they move on down to the busier tourist roads. And they're not out here in the winter. It's not usually as bad as this.'

'I had no idea.' Gina said, lost for words. 'It's so . . . unexpected. Bizarre, not the image I've ever had of Tuscany; it doesn't fit in.'

Frank shook his head. 'Tuscany is more . . . interesting than people think, there are more layers. A lot of what goes on isn't visible to us, to foreigners, or we choose not to see it. Do you remember Il Mostro? He hacked up courting couples, mostly foreign, in the hills around Florence. He came from San Casciano, the richest, prettiest part of Chianti; not that he was a rich man – a bit of a culture clash, there. And because there's money here, tourists, a lot of the immigrants end up here so, you know, with a lot of the locals still – *traditional*, let's say, it's not a happy mixture. I've thought about writing a piece on it.' He shrugged, and looked at her askance, as though challenging her to laugh at him.

'About the – women who work on the road?' Gina took him seriously.

Frank nodded uncertainly. 'There's certainly a traffic in women. And it shocked you, didn't it?' Gina nodded, waiting for him to go on.

'So perhaps it is something people want to know about. Or should know about. At first I was going to write about it, it seemed so extraordinary. But it's just – it gets so you don't notice, I suppose.' Frank looked perturbed. 'It should always be shocking, but after a while, they become invisible. You stop registering the danger they're in, the duress they're under.'

'So what do you write about?' asked Gina. 'I'd have thought journalists write about this kind of stuff all the time.'

Frank laughed uneasily. 'Well, not me. Not so far, anyway. I've spent a long time writing pieces about – nothing much. It's a nice life. Gossip, stuff about food and fashion and people who come here on holiday, British politicians, Eurotrash. A virus hits Tuscany's cypress trees, Florence has too many tourists. Hardly news, is it? There are Mafia stories, of course, I interviewed a Mafia supergrass about five – no, nearer eight – years ago.'

Frank paused as if to consider his Mafia investigation, but he didn't seem convinced that this piece of hard news redeemed him. He seemed to be talking to himself now, rather than to Gina. He went on: 'So really, I suppose, I've got to the point where I look at what I've done and it doesn't amount to much, on paper. It's a living.' He glanced at her then, and smiled ruefully.

'Come on,' she said, putting her hand on his arm. 'There's time yet.'

Frank nodded, his eyes back on the road, and they flashed past another lay-by, occupied this time by a European woman who looked as though she might be Gina's age, sitting glumly on a camping stool in the shade of a moulting pine, looking down at her hands.

'So what do the locals think about this, then?' Gina asked incredulously, nodding back towards the woman as she receded behind them, gazing sightlessly after the car. She wasn't trying to provoke Frank into writing the piece he obviously should write; it was just that she found it hard to ignore the women stationed by the road like so many milestones.

Frank sighed. 'They act as though they can't see them. They bad-mouth them. Then, after dark, I suppose, some of them are out here picking the girls up. They're not just here for the tourists, after all, these women. Not here for the English families on holiday, or the elderly French ladies following the Piero trail.' He looked at her quickly, as though reminded, Gina thought, that she was part of a family, that it was a fluke that she was here alone, with him. But she was – perhaps for the first time – she realized, enjoying being without her family.

They rounded a bend, and a deep, wide valley opened up ahead, bridged by a huge viaduct that stretched away in front of them as far as they could see. Far below Gina just glimpsed the silver glint of a river, then abruptly Frank swung the car off the fast road, and down a steep, narrow track.

Frank negotiated the sharp bends leading them down to the valley floor as though he'd done it before. They dropped a hundred feet in minutes, twisting through trees and dense scrub, past a couple of silent, shuttered stone cottages and the occasional decrepit, rubble-built barn. Further down, the slope flattened and the flayed red trunks of the cork plantations lined the narrow track, while high above them the fast road roared across the colossal bridge on its way through the valley to the sea. The road was sunlit and empty down here, the dense forest left behind them now, and Gina could smell the river, down to her left below the hazel and willow that clogged its course, a faint scent of decomposition, the still air of the valley floor combining with the cool, mineral tang of the water from the mountains as it trickled down through aromatic vegetation and rusty earth.

'Here we are,' said Frank, turning sharply downhill, and Gina, her face turned to look out of the open window, suddenly recoiled as another, overpowering odour flooded the car. Sweetish, the thick, foul air of the school science lab, rotten eggs and stink bombs, it was at startling odds with the fresh green of the hillside rising to either side of them. Gina spluttered.

'Sulphur, in the water. It's the hot springs. You get used to the smell after a bit.' Frank pointed down towards the river, and Gina saw a clotted, rag-wrapped pipe emerging from the rock, a steaming white waterfall pouring from it down the riverbank. Frank stopped the car; a handful of others were parked against the rocky flank of the mountainside. Gingerly Gina got out and together they walked towards the steep bank, the river itself still not visible. As they approached Gina could see that the sulphurous water was pouring into a succession of stepped pools formed out of a strange, smooth, luminously white material, perhaps the accretions of minerals from the volcanic springs, and emptying at the bottom into the river itself, which had swollen here to form a bathing pool of dark green water. There were five or six people there, an elderly couple in wrinkled, sagging costumes, some teenage boys splashing each other in the river and a man – Nigerian, Gina thought, though she couldn't be sure – who was standing motionless in the river and allowing the scalding water from an ancient pipe to pour down between his shoulderblades. The boys stopped their splashing and looked up as the water's surface grew still around them, and the old couple smiled a greeting. Gina quailed.

'Are we going in?' she asked. 'Is it better than it looks?'

'Oh yes. I think so, anyway,' said Frank. 'Tell me what you think when you've tried it.' He pulled his shirt over his head in one easy movement.

Rooting about in her case Gina found her swimsuit easily enough, though she regretted its faded shabbiness and the soft pale thighs it displayed; she had put it in only as an after-thought, and she certainly hadn't anticipated an audience even if it had proved warm enough to swim. *Still*, she thought, *it's not exactly San Tropez*; and she felt comforted by the realization that at least she'd look younger than the septuagenarians. As she wriggled into her costume behind the shield of the car door, she saw Frank walking down to the bank, already changed, so she hurried after him, uncomfortably aware of her pale body.

To the left at the top of the bank a woman of roughly her own age, her long hair greasy and unwashed and threaded here and there with beaded braids, sat in a grubby kaftan at a plastic picnic table smoking a joint. Beside her was a clothes rail hung with limp, faded, obviously second-hand ethnic clothing for sale, screen printed with Buddhas, and tie-dyed and batik, and beyond her stood a dirty, lopsided teepee. For a surreal moment Gina wondered whether the woman was there in some kind of official capacity; the set-up was so unexpected that she seemed an appropriate enough ticket-collector.

Gina stood next to Frank as he looked down at the river, their warm, bare skin almost touching. She felt a kind of static on her forearm and looked down to see the hairs rising to meet Frank's. He took her hand to help her down to the water.

Underfoot the bank was dry and powdery, smooth from the passage of feet and knotted with the roots of the trees that overhung the river. Gina gasped as she put her foot into the water; it was much hotter than she had expected, and stung her skin slightly to begin with, but was surprisingly clear, with a bluish tinge. It looked as suspiciously inviting as a magic spring, and the illusion was complete when the old woman, sitting further down the bank, smiled at her encouragingly. '*Fa bene, fa molto bene,*' she said.

It's good for you, is it? thought Gina. *Well, I'm not so sure.* But all the same she lowered her body into the long, narrow pool and let the water cover her, all but her shoulders. She closed her eyes, and felt the scalding, pungent water enclose and support her body. Despite herself, a sigh of deep contentment escaped her, as every thought emptied from her head and she felt her skin, her nerves, muscles, tendons soften and relax, and she saw Frank look down at her, at the sound of her sigh. She looked up, at him, at the bright sky, almost white with the midday sun, at the dark green of the trees climbing up the hills to either side, and at the swallows whistling down the length of the river, swooping low over the water then up again to disappear into the brilliant light of noon. Frank lay in the pool next to hers, and looked at her, smiling. 'Hey,' he said. 'So what do you think?'

'I think you were right,' said Gina dreamily. Frank closed his eyes and lay back and Gina, her face sideways, resting on the rocks, looked at him and was taken by surprise by the desire to wrap her arms around his neck, to twine herself around him and sink with him below the surface of the dark water. *No,* she thought, *no, no, no.*

After a while she stood up and carefully climbed down to the river. The boys who had been horsing about had gone and the dark water flowed uninterrupted and empty past the hot spring. It was pleasantly cold and deep, and the broad bathing pool stretched back up the river fifty yards or so to the massive pillars supporting the viaduct 200 feet over their heads. Beneath the bridge the air was dark and still, the reflections of the slow-moving water sliding and shimmering on the concrete columns, and the roar of the cars transmuted into an echoing, ululating whisper. Gina swam her careful breast-stroke as far as she could, twisting and treading water in the cavernous gloom, looking back to where she had come from. She saw Frank sitting on the bank, looking at her, a stranger again suddenly, his face turned blank by the sun's glare, and she wondered what she was doing there, alone with him. She shivered, suddenly feeling the chill in the shadow of the bridge, and swam back into the sunlight where Frank now stood, waiting for her.

Not much more than a mile away, now, Mila was circling the farmhouse, one ear cocked to listen for the access road. Her body ached from sleeping rough, her hair was greasy and now she was beginning to stink as well, of goat. She grimaced.

Half-heartedly she rattled the security grille over the front door, then moved round to the side, into the courtyard where she felt less exposed, the house shielding her from the road and the surrounding countryside. She found a tap, set in the wall beside a back door and half concealed beneath the creeper that covered most of the house, and stripped off, carefully folding her torn and filthy clothes, to wash herself. When she'd finished, dripping and goosepimpled from the shock of the freezing water, Mila wasn't much cleaner but she felt a lot better. She shook herself like a dog and laughed at how she must look, then couldn't stop laughing, hiccuping and gasping, with a mixture of exhilaration and hysteria. She put on her clothes, then, even though she was still damp, before someone turned up and took her for a crazy person.

Although she'd been round the house in the day before to see if anything had been left open, the light had been failing by the time the old *contadino* had gone about his business, and besides, she thought the guy who'd turned up to collect his box of whatever it was, maybe he'd left something open.

Nothing. She could see inside some of the windows, though, and she felt like crying at the sight – a sofa to sit on, water from the tap to drink, a fridge full of food. One of the rooms had a giant TV screen, a whole load of video equipment, and not much else. Mila didn't know what to do. She was starving and her clothes were in rags; if she wasn't going to get any joy here then she should get going, walk back down to the road and take the bus even if she did look like a filthy beggar. But she was beginning to feel weak, and on the verge of tears, and she sat down. Just for a while, in the sun, then she'd think about what she was going to do.

Claudia listened to the buzz of conversation drifting down the cantilever staircase from the rooftop studio where the junior partners worked, a sure sign that Niccolò Manzini was not on the premises, as he demanded as close to complete silence as was compatible with the efficient functioning of the practice. She couldn't hear what they were talking about, but she knew, anyway. Manzini talking to the police, rumours that he had been having an affair with the girl found murdered in the Oltrarno. That she could believe, but surely that didn't mean he was also capable of her murder? None of the juniors upstairs liked Manzini, and Claudia wasn't surprised, for she'd heard their complaints: he was grudging in his praise, didn't share the credit for the practice's achievements, he was demanding and ungenerous. She'd seen him with them, too, cold-eyed and often harshly critical, as he could be with her if she'd done something he considered stupid, or had presumed to ask the wrong kind of question. They worked for him only because he was good, and therefore they gained, if only by association, and as soon as they could, they moved on. Did that mean he was a bad man?

Claudia sighed, shuffling the papers on her massive stone desk, whose chill she could feel seeping through her hands and into her bones, even on so warm a day. She looked out of her long window across the rooftops, where the light curved and rippled in the heat haze, and wondered when the weather would break. She thought of the weekend with longing, a *passeggiata* with her friends, Sunday afternoon basking on her terrace, all thoughts of her employer and his dirty secrets banished from her mind. It seemed a distant prospect.

Claudia hated to feel this helpless; fourteen messages for Manzini, and not a word to let her know where he was. She could at least take comfort from the fact that his wife didn't appear to know either, as three of the messages were from her. The daughter in London had given up trying, but the little one, Beatrice, had called yesterday afternoon, and Claudia had told her her father was on the way to Rome. *Poor child*, thought Claudia, whose well-groomed exterior concealed a maternal softness of heart, and an old-fashioned yearning for children of her own. Beatrice had sounded so lost, quite desperate and frightened. And no wonder: this dead girl was her best friend. What a mess.

The other messages had been from the police (several times) and, ominously, from Giuseppe in Rome, so Manzini obviously wasn't at the office if he was down there at all. A smooth and rather menacing-sounding person called Stefano. The construction company in Rome, wanting to know if they'd won the contract. Claudia had had enough of thinking up convincing excuses, pleading innocence, and telling out-right lies, and she was about ready to jump ship when the phone rang again. It was Manzini.

'Signore Manzini, at last. Do you wish to hear your messages?' This was as far as Claudia could go to express her furious frustration; her relationship with Manzini would not permit her to ask him where he had been.

'Let me guess,' said Manzini. 'Giuseppe. Well, I've spoken to him; in fact I've given him his cards. My wife. Ferrucci

Construction. And the police?' Claudia assented. 'As for Stefano, if he phones again tell him to do his worst. Tell him it's too late.' He sounded strange; his voice was flat, unemotional, but there was an undertone of something else, as though he'd gone past the point of no return.

Claudia bit her lip, then blurted out, as though despite herself, 'Who is he? This Stefano?'

Manzini sounded cool. 'He's no one, Claudia. He's a – a person from the streets who thinks that, because of all this police business, he can extort money from me. This is how people are; if a strong person weakens, then they swarm all over him, like flies.' She turned away from the sound of his voice to look out of the window, at the terracotta segment of Brunelleschi's perfect dome that curved across the view.

Claudia swallowed. 'What shall I say, Signore Manzini, if anyone else calls? Where can I reach you?'

'You can say I can't be contacted at the moment. There's a lot I need to sort out; Giuseppe hasn't been handling things on this site as I would have wished. He was making promises he couldn't keep. The police –' He broke off. 'Claudia, on Sunday evening I was in the office. Were you aware of that?' Claudia frowned, trying to remember how the office had looked on Monday morning. There had been something – had his door been left open? 'Yes . . .' she replied slowly, uncertain what he was asking of her.

'I arrived back from the country at about eight in the evening, and I came straight here to get some preparation done for the planning meeting on Monday. It may be that the police would like to see the security tapes of the lobby, to check against my statement. Please would you make sure that they are kept?'

'Yes,' said Claudia, bewildered.

'I may not be back – for some time. I've got to speak to the police. It's very important that you know where all my personal papers are, in case I am no longer able to handle things.'

It sounded to Claudia as though he was speaking in code. Was he trying to send her some kind of message? She couldn't imagine the circumstances under which Manzini would no longer be able to handle things, not even police custody. 'Signore Manzini,' she said, 'are you all right?'

He seemed to recover himself. 'Yes, I'm all right. This is a very complicated situation, and I may need time to sort it out. I am simply asking you to ensure that the practice continues to run smoothly in my absence, Claudia. Now, I've got to go.'

Claudia held the phone in her hand for several minutes after he had hung up. She had a bad feeling about this; until this point she had assumed that, as so often happened, the rumour, once begun, would do the rounds and then disappear, revealed as a ridiculous fiction. This was too much, however; she felt as though the ground was shifting beneath her feet. The girl's death, the *carabinieri*, the tax police, even the debts to Ferrucci. She could imagine Manzini being perfectly able to shrug off one of these, but all at once? She had never heard anything as close to desperation in his voice before, and she wondered what he was planning to do. If she had considered him an impulsive man, she might have been worried. She dialled the concierge.

'Umberto? It's Claudia. Signore Manzini may need the security tapes for Sunday night, from about seven o'clock. Could you put them aside for me?' She paused, then: 'On second thoughts, would you bring them up now, just to be on the safe side? Thanks.' She put the phone down, and waited for Umberto to arrive.

19

Frank and Gina, their heads bent close together over Jane's huge bunch of keys, were laughing with relief; they had found Il Rondinaio at last, after some difficulty with the chatelaine's directions and the inauspicious sight of a pair of magpies pecking ravenously at some pulpy, unidentifiable carrion at the entrance to the farmhouse's avenue of cypresses. Gina stood on the doorstep, in the centre of the house's massive stone frontage, and gazed down at the view. The neat terraces of the garden led down to some wild fruit trees and tangled shrubs, then below that the hillside dropped away and the vista opened up. She could just see a part of the viaduct, stretching across the valley; it looked almost dainty from this distance, elegantly elongated and austere in design, not the roaring concrete giant that had dwarfed her as she swam below it. Otherwise the black hills seemed quite empty, as Frank had said they were. She turned and entered the house after him.

Il Rondinaio was very dark and cool inside, every window shuttered against the heat, and the floor beneath Gina's bare feet was rough, soft brick, pitted and pale. She entered what seemed to be a huge kitchen and dining room, at one end a slab of marble fitted with a stone sink, and burners, a griddle built in, even what seemed to be a wood-fired oven beneath a low clay chimney at the far end. The long room had floor-length windows, hung with fine gauzy curtains inside the shutters, a broad oak table at its centre, and on the table a pewter jug filled with branches of bay. The sombre, aromatic, grey-green leaves and berries against the dull gleam of the jug, the silence and the vaulted gloom in which a few dust motes disturbed by their entrance hung suspended in the broad shaft of sunlight that fell through the open door, gave the room a ceremonial, almost religious air, and Gina felt as though she should whisper.

It was strange, Gina thought, if what Frank implied about his private life was true, that Niccolò Manzini should be so committed to austerity in his work. Even his appearance verged on the monastic, although Gina wasn't entirely convinced by it, still having a residual Protestant mistrust of that kind of theatrical asceticism. Then Frank threw open a shutter at the far end, then the windows themselves, and the great vaulted space was revealed as nothing more spiritually significant than a well-proportioned, handsomely decorated dining room.

All at once wanting to postpone the moment at which she would be left alone, Gina offered Frank some lunch; it was almost one o'clock and she felt ravenous suddenly. Frank went out, and soon returned with a handful of tomatoes from the vegetable garden, and they sat at the table outside and ate them in silence with the bread and hard sheep's cheese Gina had bought in Siena, and some beer.

'You'll be all right on your own? I quite envy you, all this silence, and the pool – have you seen it? Around the back.' He fell silent for a moment, then said, carefully, 'I could leave you my mobile number, then if I'm passing back through tomorrow evening I can give you a lift back to Florence. I'd like the company.'

Gina felt happier with this thought than with the prospect Jane had offered her, of driving the ancient Fiat 500 back to the city. She'd even been considering taking the bus back rather than braving the terrors of an Italian *superstrada*, never having driven in a foreign country before, and she couldn't help being pleased that he liked her company enough to offer. She blushed at the thought, looked up to disguise her confusion and suddenly the sky was filled with swallows wheeling overhead, calling to each other.

'Look, oh, look!' she cried, gazing into the sky. Frank looked, but not at the sky; he looked at Gina's upturned face. After a moment she turned back, and caught him looking at her, but he didn't look away. He smiled, then stood up.

'I'd better go,' he said gravely, 'if I want to catch anyone out on Manzini's cemetery site. I bet they all knock off early down there in this heat.' He stood up, and before she could think of how to react, put his arms around her briefly and kissed her cheek. His smell, of warm skin and cigarettes beneath the bitter mineral overtones of sulphur and river water, took her by surprise, so alien and intimate. She was so used to Stephen she couldn't have said what he smelt of; washing powder, soap, the faint scorch of an ironed shirt, perhaps. He walked away and got into the car, and Gina watched the Alfa rock and sway down the hill in a cloud of dust. She turned and went inside.

Jane was feeling sick. Giorgio Biagiotti, the affable butcher from the Val di Chiana, was going through the beef spiel with his usual practised showmanship, pointing out to her students the grain of the meat on the great slab of T-bone, its deep red, the precise thickness to which it was cut. She stood beside him, a crisp white apron defining her flat hips, her sleeves carefully rolled, ready to cook the steak on Giorgio's massive wood-burner, which was surmounted by a heavy blackened griddle. It wasn't the meat that was turning her stomach, however.

If Niccolò had been having an affair with Natasha Julius when she was fifteen, that would have been around the time she'd been trying to talk him into their having a child of their own. Four years ago, the school had just begun to run itself, and there had been talk of a government position for Nicky, and, contrary to what she'd told Gina, it had bothered her, then, that he'd had children with Melissa but not with her. She'd worked around it from a few different angles, her biological clock, cementing their relationship, but it had come down to wanting something Melissa had that Jane didn't have, though of course she hadn't used that one on Nicky. He'd flatly refused; he'd said she knew he didn't want any more children, it had been one of the conditions of their marriage. He'd had a vasectomy the week before they married; his present to her, he said, although it was a present he hadn't revealed to her until nine years had passed, nine years in which she had assumed either of them might have changed their mind about having children.

Giorgio Biagiotti reverently handed her the oiled steak, and she slapped it on to the griddle, smiling through the hiss and smoke at her assembled students.

'The fire must be very hot. Wood is better than charcoal, but you must make sure all the smoke has gone before you put the meat on the griddle. Don't salt the meat before you cook it – it will become tough; you can season it with pepper and oil.'

She surveyed her class. The woman from Wiltshire, the one with the lantern jaw and the Provençal olive-picker's basket in which to cart about her collection of pashminas and ostentatiously high-brow reading matter (Elizabeth David on ice-cream-making in the eighteenth century, and *Barchester Towers*), was squinting intently at her through the smoke, building up, Jane could tell, to a question designed to show off her superior knowledge. Sure enough, she was asking about BSE in Italian herds, and Jane, after making reassuring noises about the exemplary standards of stock elevation, feed-quality control and slaughtering methods, wearily handed the question over to Giorgio. The elaborate courtesy of Giorgio's reply to the woman, she could tell, disguised a deep umbrage at the question, and serve her right.

Fifteen. Well, the girl was almost of an age – there were

societies in which girls were married and bearing children at twelve. Even as she rehearsed the words, she knew she was deluding herself. Natasha Julius had been a child. And Jane's stomach churned with misery and humiliation at the thought of the betrayal, all those trips to London he was making at the time, bringing her back chocolates from Charbonnel and Walker, that diamond eternity ring from Bond Street, to keep her sweet. Whores were one thing; no one could say they were competition, and his using them could even be seen as a mark of his European sophistication. But his daughter's best friend? To Jane that was so bizarrely reckless that it spoke to her of debility, of Niccolò's being unable to control an impulse, and that she couldn't stomach.

The steak was cooked, by continental standards at least, and she forked it on to an earthenware plate on the long rustic table beneath Giorgio's vine-shaded terrace, and cut it into little bloody chunks for tasting. She watched as her students clustered around the meat, each one of her finely tuned senses in fastidious revolt against their avidity and against Niccolò's treacherous, humiliating weakness.

Gina sat beneath one of the umbrella pines on Il Rondinaio's lawn, the shade cast by its circular canopy as delicate and symmetrical as a snowflake, and gazed out at the view. After her bathe in the hot springs her skin felt smooth and warm, like a child's after a bath. She lifted her forearm to her nostrils and breathed in the lingering traces of sulphur; it didn't seem to her any more to be the smell of decay, more of purification, a faint whiff of burning, matchheads and sparklers. A light breeze blew up here on the ridge, and Gina let it cool her skin as she surveyed the hills, a few wheeling birds hovering, waiting for something, and the distant viaduct following the curve of the mountainside. Then she stood to go inside.

Once her eyes had adjusted to the dim interior, Gina found

it soothing, like a darkened room for an invalid, after the glare outside. The house smelt fresh, of polish and ironed linen, and she thought, faltering a little, of home, the atmosphere thick with layers of cooking and unmade beds and children's trainers. It seemed to her still miraculous, after three days away, that she could move through a space without having to pick up toys and books and cups, without sighing with exasperation at spilt juice or a grape crushed into the carpet or at the futility of her attempts to restore order. On her own she seemed to take up so little space, to have so little impact on her environment as she moved through the house's neat, organized calm, that she barely disturbed the dust that hung in the air.

Gina took her case, and put it in a large whitewashed bedroom at the top of the stairs that seemed neutral and empty enough to be a guest room, then began, tentatively, to explore the house, the polished *cotto* of the floor smooth and warm to her bare feet. A narrow corridor led to a comfortable upstairs sitting room with a raised brick fireplace, and off the sitting room a number of further bedrooms, each with its own tiny lobby and some with connecting doors. Everywhere there was evidence of a ghostly, well-ordered life; the windows all had mosquito screens, rubber chocks held doors open to allow air to circulate and, perhaps, to allow a nervous child a glimpse of light through her door at night, or for her parents to hear if she woke. There were no patches of damp, the woodwork was all freshly painted; Gina thought of the close-cropped, watered lawn and the wood neatly stacked in the shelter of a lean-to outside, the gleaming saucepans and unchipped crockery in the kitchen, all testimony to a careful, interested, painstaking hand in every detail of the hospitality the house offered. Gina wondered if it was Jane's or Niccolò's. She decided to go for a swim, and went inside to put on her costume, still damp and pungent with sulphur.

Gina hadn't yet been round to the back of the house, where Frank had told her she'd find the pool, so when she rounded the rough stone of the corner, she gasped at the sight. She supposed, in retrospect, that she might have known the Manzinis wouldn't be content with just any old tacky Los Angeles blue rectangle, but this was something else entirely. From the back garden the view across the landscape stretching away to the north was more Tuscan, more benign, than the black mountains of the Maremma one could survey from the front; rounded, golden hills ribboned with cypresses undulated as far as the eye could see. Three pairs of long glazed doors opened from the house on to an old stone terrace facing this open, sunlit vista; the land dropped a foot or two lower beyond the terrace and opened out to accommodate a perfectly flat rectangle of black water, surrounded by smooth, dark-slate flagstones and hedged on either side with tall, clipped, fragrant bay, the deep, sombre green of a mountain pool. Beyond it the land fell away sharply right at its edge, so it looked as though the brimming water was about to overflow into the ravine below.

Solemn, formal and fathomlessly dark, the oblong of still water shielded by the severe planes of the hedge, the dense black of the flagstones and the brutal, dizzying drop seemed to Gina both beautiful and ominous, an ordained space of sinister significance, like a pagan temple or a place of sacrifice. She walked to the edge of the pool, and sat on the stone, hesitant to put her foot in the water, trying to shake the feeling that it might turn her warm flesh to stone.

The sun had long since left this side of the house, but the soft pale hills in the distance were still bathed in its glow, and the earth at Gina's back still held the heat of the week's long, warm days. The air was stickily humid, and Gina could feel the moisture at her temples and between her shoulderblades. She took a deep breath, and slipped into the water. It was deep and very, very cold, and she gasped with shock, pushing herself away from the side and beginning to swim. The house was behind her and in front of her the horizon of water that seemed to tip over into the valley below, and as she swam towards it with her slow, old-fashioned, graceful breaststroke she felt as though she might swim right over the edge. She stopped to tread water and looked down at her body, its watery outline fluttering palely beneath the surface, and silvered with tiny bubbles. At the bottom of the dark water, something glittered up at her, its image broken by the shifting, rippling surface; a golden hoop, maybe an earring, or a bangle. She was about to dive down for it when she heard a crash from the other side of the house, and paused, wondering at the echo the sound, startlingly loud, sent around the courtyard. A door blown shut in the wind, perhaps. Reluctantly she climbed out of the water, black pools forming at her feet on the slate and she shivered suddenly, goosepimpled though the wind was warm.

As Gina turned the corner, a big, soft towel wrapped around her shoulders, she saw that the doors had blown wide in the wind. Then suddenly the doorway wasn't empty and she found herself face to face with a woman of about her own age and build, perhaps thinner, certainly in the face; large, expressive dark eyes, wide with alarm, the pupils dilated; a tangle of hair, slender wrists and thin hands clasping what looked like the remains of Gina and Frank's lunch to her chest.

Gina had caught up with her before she even reached the edge of the lawn. After barely a second's hesitation she had set off in pursuit with a mixture of surprise and curiosity, rather than anger, fuelling the chase. The stranger had not looked intimidating, certainly not by comparison with the average passenger on a south London nightbus (Gina's yard-stick for the measurement of aggression and desocialized behaviour), and she was obviously starving, distressed and ashamed. She kept her face hidden as Gina relaxed her grip and gently put her arm around her thin shoulders.

Now Gina sat opposite Mila at the kitchen table, and watched her eat. The woman must have been ravenous, to judge by the speed with which she devoured the plate of bread and ham, some olives, and a piece of the hard cheese she had stolen; but, catching Gina's astonished gaze, she slowed her pace and made herself use her knife and fork, smiling awkwardly at her through a mouthful.

'Are you all right?' Gina tried again, in Italian, and the woman turned her face up at last to meet Gina's eyes. The grime and dust on her cheeks were streaked with tears, her nose looked as though it might have been broken, her eyes were puffy and the flesh around them turning the deep yellow of a fresh bruise, suffused with tints of green and dark purple. She was cut on one cheek, and her arms and legs were scratched. She looked as though she'd been badly beaten.

'What happened to you?' Gina had asked, horrified, when she caught up with her. In broken Italian and with painful gestures, pointing to the gorge below and to the road, the woman, Mila, as she now knew her, had seemed to be saying that she'd been pushed down the hill, that she didn't want to go back, she had nowhere to go. Gina had coaxed her back up to the house, surprised by her own composure. Feeling Mila's hunched, warm, thin shoulder beneath her hand, she had wondered at herself, she who would normally be too timid to give money to a *Big Issue*-seller. Watching now as Mila finished off the greater part of the provisions they had picked up in Siena, she pondered what she should do next; could she offer the woman a bed? The thought made her uneasy; this was not, after all, her house. Not that, then. But still she felt uncomfortable, as though she had an unexpected guest and should do something to entertain her. She sat back in her chair and took advantage of Mila's preoccupation to look at her more closely.

She was very pretty, in a tired, damaged sort of way; her eyes, beyond the bruising and dirt, were large and black, her cheekbones were pronounced and her hair was long and thick, not a single grey hair, Gina noted wryly. She was wearing a brown silk dress, torn and dirty now but too showy, all the same, to be the uniform of a countrywoman. At first Gina speculated that perhaps she was the battered wife of a violent local farmer, but that didn't seem to fit; she was too pretty, too delicate, and obviously not Italian. Then it clicked: she was one of *them*.

20

Niccolò Manzini's cemetery project was to the south of Rome, on the site of a third-century battlefield that had found itself fought over again in 1944 and was now a bleak, treeless plain. Frank Sutton's Alfa struggled round the vast, clogged ring road in the customary chaos of Roman traffic, then he decided to break loose and drive the last part on the Via Appia. Even on a warm spring day there was something ghostly about the ancient highway; the surreally shapeless ruins to either side, the vast blocks of volcanic stone that paved it showing the ruts made by Roman carts, the sound of birds accentuating the silence around them. Only a small section of the old road was open, but it led Sutton to within a mile of the Cimetero del Popolo, and when he arrived at the wire security fencing the site was quiet and apparently empty.

At first sight, Manzini's great and ambitious undertaking looked very much like any other building site, although, crucially, without any sign of activity. The link fencing enclosed a large area of churned earth, not all of it immediately visible, but a row of giant dumper trucks, motionless excavators and level-graders stood along one side, and next to them a couple of curtained Portakabins. Tall floodlights flanked the steel gates at the head of the access road and stood at intervals around the fence, along with warning signs indicating that the area was patrolled by guard dogs. Frank put a hand to the gates and shook them, and a clinking and rattling reverberated along the fencing to either side. For a moment or two nothing happened, then, 500 yards away, a door opened in one of the Portakabins planted in the hardened mud, and Niccolò Manzini emerged and stood in the doorway looking at Frank.

For a moment or two neither man moved; Frank, with his hand to the wire fence still, looked steadily at Niccolò, whose pale, slender face was almost expressionless; only a faint enigmatic smile, as though he had just finished telling an amusing story, or possibly was enjoying some secret pleasure at the sight of the journalist's petitioning stance at his gate. Then Manzini walked over to the padlocked steel gates and with a quick, fluid movement unlocked and swung them open to usher Frank inside the compound, one arm dipped in a regal gesture of welcome. Sutton walked through and the gate clanged shut behind him. The architect didn't bother to lock it.

'Mr Sutton.' Niccolò held out his hand and with barely perceptible reluctance Sutton shook it briefly, his own hand dropping quickly back to his side as soon as the gesture of greeting could be said to be complete.

'Manzini. Am I – interrupting? I did leave messages with your assistant. Claudia?' Niccolò Manzini nodded slowly, and his face darkened, the expression of amused tolerance with which he had greeted the journalist still in place, but barely.

'Yes, she did say something. It's not quite – we'll have to sort something else out. Look in the diary.' Manzini gestured towards the Portakabin, and the two men began to walk across the churned earth to the ugly brown box. At its entrance the architect hesitated, his narrow, angular frame in the doorway partially blocking Sutton's access. Inside, a stocky man in a leather jacket, dark-skinned and unshaven, stood over a ledger that lay open on a cheap veneer desk. He glanced up and sideways at Frank over Niccolò Manzini's shoulder.

Standing there, his head silhouetted against the harsh overhead lighting, the architect did not look quite at home in this makeshift environment; his perfectly cut dark suit and high cheekbones out of place among the Portakabin's cheap materials and distorted angles, and there was something uneasy about his stance. Sutton took a step forward, into the doorway, and the thin flooring creaked beneath his weight, the doorframe distorting with the movement. Manzini retreated slightly.

'The diary?' Frank's inquiry was light, to all appearances well-intentioned. Niccolò nodded, his eyes veiled; he reached up to a shelf, pulled down a leather desk diary and abruptly turned his back on Frank to look at it. He shook his head slowly.

'Nothing. There's nothing I can do, not really. I'm here on site all today, but there's too much for me to do. This is a critical time. My site manager, Giuseppe Glave.' The architect made a perfunctory gesture of introduction towards the thick-set man in the Portakabin's far corner, who nodded curtly to Frank, his expression guarded, before turning back to the desk.

Niccolò's eyes rested briefly on the site manager's back before returning to their appraisal of Frank Sutton. 'There are things Giuseppe and I need to deal with together. Then I'm driving back up to Florence tonight, I think, and I may . . . I may have to be in London. I may have to take Beatrice back to her mother, and there are meetings . . .' He shrugged apologetically, allowing his voice to tail off. At the ledger Giuseppe still had his back to them, but there was something attentive about the set of his shoulders, a kind of tension.

Frank nodded, his face a mask of polite attention, and half-turned as if to leave. Then something seemed to occur to him.

'Look, I'll be in Rome this evening. How about just – an informal meeting, before you head back to Florence? I've seen the site now at least. A coffee? I could meet you at the Tre Scalini at about nine?'

Sutton opened his hands as if to evidence his good intentions, and certainly the Tre Scalini, whose tables were set out in the prettiest corner of the Piazza Navona, was about as benignly public a place as Rome's crowded streets could offer. Niccolò Manzini eyed the journalist narrowly, then looked away from him, out of the cramped little ersatz structure in which the two men stood in uneasily close proximity, and towards the horizon. He sighed, then took a step back out of the Portakabin, Frank at his shoulder. Reluctantly, he nodded.

'All right. I can't promise – but if I finish up here in time. The Tre Scalini at nine. Now, if you don't mind, I think I should get on.' This time Niccolò Manzini did not offer Sutton his hand, but instead gestured towards the perimeter fencing. Sutton nodded, turned and walked away, his stride suddenly buoyant. As he let himself out through the gate, its padlock dangling, he looked up and back towards Niccolò Manzini, who stood motionless at the entrance to his site office, cradling a mobile phone in his hands and gazing into the distance at his work in progress.

21

At the Villa Duncan, nestling on the soft green slopes of Bellosguardo, it looked like Ned might be leaving home. His car, a dented silver Mustang with a hole in the exhaust, California plates (it was said he'd made his mother ship it over from Los Angeles, just to see if she would, although Ned always denied it) and chipped paintwork, was parked around the side of the Villa Duncan and it stood with the boot open, waiting for him. He emerged from the house by the kitchen door, carrying a small green-canvas holdall and a black bin-bag, which he held by the neck. He put both in the back of the car, then the gatekeeper called his name from further down the drive and Ned walked round the Mustang and looked towards the sound.

On the narrow road outside the gates below Ned stood a dented and dusty brown Datsun, its motor running noisily, and on the drive Ned could see Stefano walking up towards him. Despite the battered leather jacket he never seemed to take off, Stefano didn't look as though he was feeling the evening heat; he walked easily up the steep incline and his expression, framed by the long silver hair, was characteristically unruffled and calm. But even to the inexperienced observer his well-worn brand of street credibility looked out of place against the expensive brilliance of the gardens of the Villa Duncan, and Ned frowned slightly as his visitor drew closer.

'Hey,' he said softly. 'You nearly missed me. I'm just off.'

'Oh yeah?' said Stefano, mildly, pursing his lips slightly and nodding, as though in agreement. 'Somewhere nice?'

Ned frowned again, more deeply this time. 'I just . . . I needed to get away for a bit. Out of here, you know?' He gestured down at Florence then broadened the sweep of his arm to include the hills around. 'It's been a bit rough, with Tash – all that.'

'Yeah, yeah,' said Stefano absently. Then he seemed to collect his thoughts. 'Oh, you mean her getting herself murdered? I guess that was pretty difficult. Any ideas who might have done it?' He inspected Ned for a reaction, and Ned's face darkened at Stefano's light-hearted phrasing, as though the dealer might have been asking the time.

'If I knew – if I had any idea who'd done it – do you think I'd be just standing here?' His voice was fierce, but it seemed to have no effect on Stefano, who stood there smiling slightly as he observed Ned's distress.

'I suppose that's right,' said Stefano. 'Sure. I just thought, with you being there, in the square, you might have seen something. Seen who she left with. She put it about a bit, we all know that; not wanting to speak ill of the dead, but it could have been anyone, couldn't it? And, let's face it, it solves a lot of problems. No more baby-talk for a start; I was getting bored with that, weren't you?'

He cocked his head on one side, still looking calmly at Ned. Ned clenched his fists at his sides, but he made no move, and Stefano continued.

'Anyway. I brought what you wanted. Just to save you a journey.' He handed Ned a little brown paper bag, folded over at the top. 'It's good stuff, very pure.' Ned made a noise, a snort that combined anger and disgust, and Stefano looked faintly offended. He looked around himself and up at the house. 'Nice place. You should have invited me up here before.'

'I didn't invite you now,' said Ned through clenched teeth. 'Did I?' His tone was final. 'I don't want you here. I don't want to see you here. And Natasha –' he pronounced her full name gently, carefully – 'Don't talk about her. As if you had nothing to do with it.' He looked at the brown paper bag for a long moment then reached for it.

Stefano let him take it with a narrow smile. 'Why don't we say you pay me later. When you get back from wherever it is; I can see it's not quite convenient just now.' He nodded up at the house. 'Anyway, I've got to get off, too. See myself out?' And he turned and walked away down the hill.

Ned stood, a slight figure, almost boyish, leaning against his car, and watched Stefano go; he gazed over the rooftops towards the great dome as the sun slipped down behind him. He could see down the dark, straight length of the Via Romana, leading into the city, the pale stone of the great mediaeval wall that curved around and enclosed it, and as he looked, his face cleared. He flexed his shoulders and rubbed his neck as if he was stiff after carrying something a long way, and climbed into his car then drove away from his home, down between the rosebeds, which glowed in the twilight with day-glo orange and pink. The gates swung open silently at his approach, and the old Mustang coasted through them slowly and without its customary, insolent roar, the exhaust only coughing once as the big car slid away down the hill.

With hooded eyes the gatekeeper watched the car disappear, his expression of dislike undisguised once his employers' son had left the premises, as usual without acknowledging him. Perhaps, too, he was wondering about Ned's visitor, whom he had, of course, recognized. Everyone knew Stefano, and what Stefano did. The villa appeared to be empty now – at least, no other cars stood on the gravel apron in front of its imposing façade. The windows to Ned Duncan's first-floor room stood open, though. Their long lace curtains billowed out on to the balcony in the delicious evening breeze that could be felt only up here, in the hills, a privilege of the rich, like the security cameras and the gatekeeper and the high walls topped with broken glass.

The heavy, low-slung American car wound its way between the olive trees down the narrow road, which, had it not been for the hum of the great city over the brow of the hill, would have seemed for all the world like a country track in the middle of nowhere, so carefully preserved was this microclimate for the wealthy. But after a mile or so the Mustang emerged on to the glare and bustle of the Via Senese, filled with shoppers and the roar of cars on their way out of the city. Ned turned south, joining the flow of traffic; on the street corner stood some adolescent boys, who let out a cheer of admiration when they saw the car. Ned broke into a smile, suddenly relaxed; he thrust his hand high out of the window to give them all a high five, each boy's hand slapping his as he passed.

When he reached the *superstrada* Ned abandoned the silent crawl and low profile he had adopted through the city's outskirts, and the car accelerated with a roar, shaking off Florence's dark, dirty streets and heading down into the dark woods of the Val di Pesa where Chianti began, past Siena, into the forested mountains of the Maremma.

Jane climbed out of the dark-green leather and walnut interior of the lead Range Rover, which was parked up on the narrow pavement of the Borgo Tegolaio, one of a small fleet the school hired for day trips. Her students, clutching their information packs and clipboards, were eagerly discussing their evening, part of the course, a meal at a restaurant in the Borgo San Jacopo where the kitchen, which specialized in meat grilled over a wood fire, would this evening be cooking the steaks the class had brought back with them from the Val di Chiana. Jane never accompanied her students on this outing; instead she paid the restaurant owner handsomely to allow them a glimpse of the kitchens and to make sure they were kept happy at the table, with a personal visit from one of the chefs and solemn, careful explanations of the menu. And this evening, of course, she had an appointment of her own to keep anyway. She nodded and waved a stiff goodbye, and let herself in at number 36.

As always, the first sight of her lovely apartment afforded Jane a frisson of pride, this time with an admixture of relief that, for now, she had it all to herself. Hospitality was all very well, but with all this going on, with Niccolò – she remembered, suddenly, that she had intended to telephone the Duncans about Beatrice this morning.

'Damn.' She walked down the corridor to Beatrice's room again, and found it still empty. She frowned, looking around the room at the habitual disorder, trying to discern any change, any sign that Beatrice had been back. It was possible; scarves, jewellery and make-up were strewn over the dressing-table Nicky had designed, jeans on the floor, drawers were open. The bed remained neatly made, however.

At the Villa Duncan the phone rang for several minutes before it was answered, by a terse, breathless Vivienne, Lady Duncan, whose voice, to Jane's irritation, gained a sly, insinuating tone when she learnt the caller's identity.

'Darling! You mean she hasn't been home? No, she wasn't here last night. She went out with Ned in the afternoon – late afternoon, actually, I think it was getting dark. I'd assumed she was going back to you, I must say.' Vivienne lowered her voice, with ill-disguised excitement. 'Why, has something happened? Have you – had trouble with her? Is it this business with her father?'

Jane ignored her. 'Is Ned there?'

'Sorry, darling, he's not here,' Vivienne said airily. 'I think he might have gone down to the sea for a day or two, before the weather breaks. He mentioned something about it, and he's taken his car, so he must be out of town. I could give you his mobile number?'

'Mmm,' said Jane, distractedly, thinking about Niccolò,

about what she should tell him. *Still, damn him, he hasn't phoned, has he.* 'Yes, all right, I'll take it.'

Twitching with suppressed fury at Lady Duncan's tone, Jane replaced the receiver with deliberate care before slamming her fist down on the carved Moghul side-table with such force that the telephone jumped and clattered. Almost immediately, it rang.

'Jane.'

Her heart pounded, suddenly, unexpectedly, at the sound of his voice, and her head spun. Her mind seemed to be working on a time-lag, still trying to work out the puzzle of Beatrice's whereabouts. She put some steel into her voice, infuriated that he should phone now, wrong-footing her.

'Niccolò. You got my message.' With Nicky, you could never afford to lose it; after thirteen years of marriage Jane had learnt that much and so, even though what she wanted to do was howl, she held her fire.

'Yes. Is Beatrice there?'

This incensed Jane almost beyond reason. Why did she never come first? Why always the girls?

'No. She's out.' Her voice shook, and she made an effort to steady it.

'Not with Ned Duncan?'

She lost it.

'I don't know. She's your daughter, you look after her. Or are you only interested when she's got a pretty best friend for you to play with? What were you doing with her, Niccolò? What were you thinking of?'

The line was silent. Jane felt like crying with frustration. This was how he did it; he switched off. 'Niccolò? You'd better talk to me this time, I warn you. The police want to question me, too, did you know that? What am I supposed to tell them? That you were having an affair with her, but it's nothing serious, it was all fine with me? Let me tell you, Nicky, it's not

235

fine with me. Not Natasha Julius, not the whores, none of it is fine with me. It never was.'

For a moment or two she thought he'd hung up on her, but then she heard him breathe. When he spoke, his voice was soft and even.

'Jane. Darling. You're deluding yourself. We didn't have that kind of a relationship, did we? We work together, we complement each other, we agree on so many important things. You always knew it wasn't going to be a – a physical thing. Not a sex thing.'

Niccolò's voice was soothing and persuasive, and Jane almost allowed herself to be lulled by it into agreeing; after all, she yearned for it to ring true, his story of their spiritual intimacy. But those last words brought her round as though she'd been slapped. She steadied herself; she would be a match for him.

'Perhaps for you it wasn't, Niccolò. But you obviously don't understand me as well as you like to think. Do you think I've spent our marriage like you, finding the . . . the . . . *sex thing* somewhere else? I assumed – well, I was stupid – I assumed you loved me.' The words sounded ridiculous, ringing in her ears like some trite piece of romantic melodrama, and Jane knew she had had enough. She put down the phone, and walked away.

Mila sat on a dark leather sofa in a white room, staring at the huge, blank television screen that all but covered one wall, just where a fireplace should be, perhaps once had been. She had eaten and eaten until she couldn't get anything else down; her shrunken stomach felt as tight as a drum and her chin was shiny with grease. She had eaten bread and ham and cake and cheese, drunk a litre of water and three cups of sweet coffee. She didn't know what to make of her hostess – English, she thought, with her pale, anxious face – who had sat there, watching her as she ate. She, Gina, had already been much more trusting than any old *contadino*'s miserable wife, but it did occur to Mila that she might have been put in here while Gina worked out what to do with her – perhaps even she would wonder whether Mila would run off in the night with the silver. If there *was* any silver; Mila had looked around when she'd finally stopped eating and it wasn't furnished like a rich man's place, just very plain, dark, wooden country furniture and whitewashed walls.

This room was different, though; it didn't feel like the rest of the house. For a start the TV she was gaping at looked like it had cost a fortune; not to mention the rest of the equipment, which all seemed to be set in the wall below the screen, a bank of dials in brushed steel flush with the plaster was all there was to see on the outside. Mila slid off the sleek leather and cautiously approached the wall. Wonderingly she placed her fingertips on the screen; it felt warm and yielding and was as flat as a painting, hanging there. She'd never seen anything like it; it certainly didn't have much in common with the ancient TV and video at the flat in Florence, festooned with tangled wires and every knob loose or broken. She lowered her hand, and tentatively prodded at a button, twisted a dial, but nothing happened. Then she saw a switch, and clicked it on; a row of lights blinked, the machine clicked and whirred softly and a tiny tray hissed out, on it a silver disc. The TV screen's static crackled minutely against her cheek, and carefully Mila pushed the little drawer and its slender burden back in, then stepped back and watched as the screen filled with colour.

In the kitchen Gina, who was thoughtfully washing the dishes in the red-marble sink while she considered what to do next, heard the smooth, expensive click of the machinery in the room next door and relaxed briefly. Mila was watching TV; that, at least, would buy Gina some time. Perhaps she

237

could give her a bit of money, and give her a lift to the bus stop. She looked out of the window at the dusty little car parked beneath the lean-to. Something to wear, maybe, and perhaps Jane would have some foundation to cover the bruises. Did she need to go to hospital? Gina thought not; she'd seemed alert enough, no sign of concussion, and, although she walked stiffly, as though she might have been bruised even beneath her clothes, she couldn't have run that fast if she'd had anything broken. Gina shook her head involuntarily, wondering at the life she must have led, to be so desperate to escape. She went upstairs, to sort out something for Mila to wear.

Mila stared at the screen, her mouth open. She was clutching at her sleeves, arms crossed across her chest and shoulders hunched as though to protect herself. At first it was hard to distinguish anything, the screen was so dark; a kind of swimming pool but the water was black, surrounded by hedges, a view out over the darkening hills beyond, the sound of splashing. Then the camera swung round and up at a house, this house, and a laughing face, illuminated by the light flooding out of the long windows, a girl with black hair cut like a boy's and slanting, almond eyes, her mouth wide open and laughing. Her arm was around another girl's shoulders; this was Evelina, and she looked sullen, and afraid. From off camera a sweet high voice called something, and the short-haired girl drew up her shoulders and giggled, her finger to her lips. Mila couldn't understand what they were saying – it was in English, she thought. The camera spun and lurched; they were running, the girl pulling Evelina behind her, then the camera changed hands, and she saw the man. Walking away with her. Evelina wasn't wearing her shoes.

As she watched the screen, Mila's eyes became opaque, glazed with tears that seemed to burn as they trickled down her cheeks, at the sight of Evelina, the little girl on a dark hillside. Mila was crying for herself, she knew it; she had been a girl once, although it seemed long ago now. She rubbed savagely at her eyes, but then she felt herself grow cold, and the tears dried on her face. The man's hand reached out for Evelina and cradled her breast, and Mila did not miss the tiny movement of Evelina's body as she flinched away from his greedy hand. The man looked up at the camera and for a moment his face distracted Mila from what he was doing; his eyes were dark and there was something in them that Mila recognized; a look of fathomless hatred born of disgust and longing and rage. It was the look she had seen in the jeering bloodshot eyes of the truck driver who'd kicked her down the hillside and left her for dead, but she'd seen it in a hundred other faces, too.

Mila watched the man on the screen and thought he could be a high-priced lawyer whose wife had been screwing his best friend for years, or an ashen-faced junkie who burnt out his moral sense along with most of his brains before he got to sixteen but still knew enough to realize he'd blown his future; he could have been an old peasant whose mother used to lock him in the outside privy in the Ukrainian winter seventy years ago while she serviced her clients, or a racist psychopath who thinks a black girl is dirt but wants her all the same. Hunched and shivering, Mila watched on.

Gina was coming slowly back down the stairs, the too-tight linen suit she'd tried to squeeze into on her first night in Florence draped across her arm, when she saw Mila come out of the screening room, her face very pale, one hand clutching at her dress, holding the torn sides together. Gina moved faster down the stairs and towards her, holding out the clothes. Hesitantly, the other woman took them, and tried to smile, but her face seemed stiff and wooden. Holding the linen bundle to her chest, she spoke, in Italian.

'I will go now.' She gestured towards the door, where the hazy, humid day was darkening, the sun already behind the hills to the west. 'With these,' and she held up the clothes, 'I can take the bus, to the city. I know where to go.'

Faintly perturbed by Mila's pallor, and the residual impression of something like shock in her frozen features, Gina frowned. This was probably the best way, a perfect solution to her dilemma, that Mila should leave, but she looked so frightened. 'I'll give you a lift,' she said, with faint reluctance. 'To the bus stop.' Mila nodded slowly, and Gina took her by the hand.

Jane was getting ready to go out, and she looked her best. She wore sharp black trousers, slit at the ankle, black leather sandals, a crisp white shirt unbuttoned at the neck to reveal the creamy skin of her *décolletage*. Her silver-blonde hair was demurely tied back with a velvet ribbon, her lips were subtly glossy and her wide, pale-blue eyes were fringed with black. She wore the huge chunk of blue-white diamond Niccolò had bought her for an eternity ring, all those years ago, her wedding ring, and eighteenth-century diamond drops in her ears. She had dabbed rosewater from the Farmacia di Santa Maria Novella behind her ears and was dusting mother-of-pearl powder on to the perfect arch of her browbone when she heard her taxi pulling up outside. She straightened her back, put on her suede jacket, which she had chosen because it was exactly the colour of honey, and left for the police station.

'Signora Manzini.'

The *carabiniere* who had so unnerved her on her doorstep was, to Jane's considerable satisfaction, looking at her rather nervously under the hostile glare of the overhead lighting. '*Avvocato*.' He bowed slightly towards her lawyer, their lawyer, who, when informed of the summons to give a statement, had insisted she accompany Jane and was now sitting to her left and a little behind her.

'Thank you for your co-operation.' Jane inclined her head graciously. She was not prepared for what came next.

'You were aware that your husband had enjoyed a sexual relationship with the murder victim, Signorina Julius, when she was below the legal age of consent?' A flare of her delicate nostrils was the only indication that Jane's equilibrium had been disturbed by the implication behind what sounded barely a question, more a statement.

'Indeed I was not aware of any such relationship. Are you suggesting that I would condone a criminal act *and* my husband's adultery?'

The lieutenant shrugged in a parody of apology. 'Can you tell us where your husband was on the night of Natasha Julius's murder? Between the hours of midnight and two o'clock in the morning?'

'I'm afraid I can't. I didn't see my husband until the following morning, when I got up. He told me that he had arrived after I had gone to bed, and didn't want to disturb me so had slept in his dressing room. So I wasn't aware of the exact time of his return from Rome, no. I have only his word for it.'

The policeman leant forward. 'You mean you don't believe him? Why should he lie?'

'I mean I do not have any independent corroboration of his whereabouts, nor did I witness his return with my own eyes. Isn't that merely the accurate answer to your question?'

This seemed to infuriate the policeman. 'And you, Signora Manzini. Do you have any "independent corroboration" of your own whereabouts during this period?'

Jane frowned. 'What do you mean? I've just told you that I was asleep in bed. I went to bed at about eleven.'

'So the answer is no.'

'The answer is no. Unless Beatrice, my stepdaughter, was aware that I was in my bed asleep when she returned. Or,' she paused, 'my husband. If he arrived home at midnight then that was the time he saw me asleep in bed and he is therefore my alibi.'

'Your husband has stated that he could not tell us precisely when he returned to Borgo Tegolaio, unfortunately. And although we have urged him to return to make a further statement in the light of this new information, we are unable to contact him at this moment.'

Jane looked the policeman in the eye. 'I fail to understand, however, why you would consider me a suspect. What possible motive could I have for Natasha Julius's murder?'

The policeman sat back with an enigmatic smile on his face, his eyes narrowed as he observed Jane closely, monitoring her for her reaction. He shrugged, as though it would be the most natural thing in the world for her to strangle a nineteen-year-old girl. 'She had been your husband's lover. And she was pregnant.'

22

As the shadows between the grey mountains of Lazio deepened until only the highest of hill-towns still glowed pale gold in the last rays of the setting sun, Frank Sutton was sitting in the Piazza Navona at one of the Tre Scalini's tables; in front of him stood a beer and a plate of the tough, salty ham that was the bar's speciality. Perhaps because the journalist had lived in the city briefly, years before, or perhaps because of the relative anonymity it afforded, he looked at home in Rome, more relaxed than the Frank Sutton Gina had driven out of Florence with that morning. It was eight o'clock, and as he took an appreciative sip from the tall, cold glass Sutton scanned the crowd in front of him, looking for Niccolò Manzini's sharp, tanned profile and cropped head in the teeming mass of visitors.

In summer the Tre Scalini's interior was always empty of customers, and served only as the place where the waiter barked his orders to the barman. On the wall hung a photograph of the Piazza Navona in the 1950s, taken from high up on one of the buildings that overlooked it, reproduced in black and white. Frank had often thought how easy it was to tell, before any close examination of hairstyles or fashion, that the photograph was not contemporary, although it was not so easy to say why. The piazza was much emptier in the old photograph than it was now, for one thing, and there was a kind of restful uniformity about the figures walking through it; either many more of them were Italian – even today, Frank observed, the Italians *en masse* created a wonderfully comforting illusion of harmony and propriety in their manner of dress – or it was simply that, in those days, people didn't feel the need to assert their individuality so aggressively. They didn't mind looking alike, in their sharp light suits, their heads sleek with oil, the women in little heels and puffed skirts. Looking out now at all the garish variety of tourist uniforms, from baseball caps and low-slung jeans to the high-tech outdoor clothing of the type of traveller Frank classified as the 'thwarted explorer' and the yellowing seersucker suits of elderly cultural pilgrims, Frank experienced a weary nostalgia for an era in which he had never lived, and, feeling old, ordered another beer.

It was almost nine, and as night fell the noise and colour of the piazza were muted by darkness, the day's chaos receded and the atmosphere of the old square began to mellow and soften. Frank looked at life as it passed him by and decided that he would not think of Niccolò Manzini; he would not expect him. Frank knew what he was going to ask, after all this time, some thirty years, during which he had allowed the questions to simmer, sour and thwarted, where guilt, recrimination and the distortions of adolescence had hidden them from reasoned examination. He knew what he was going to ask, so he did not have to think about Niccolò Manzini. Instead Frank leant back in his little metal chair and watched the *passeggiata* unfold.

The mass of tourists in the piazza was tempered now by native Romans, coming out in the relative cool of the evening, and idly Frank looked on as an elderly couple made their way slowly around the square's perimeter, she impeccably dressed in white linen and leaning heavily on her husband's arm. They wandered among the café tables that lined the piazza on this side, and paused to look into the shop windows, at painted pottery or ceramic dolls, and Frank watched as mildly they passed judgement to each other. Frank thought of Frances, and how pleasant a place Italy seemed to be in which to grow old, even without an arm to lean on. He thought of his old friend's soft, paper-thin cheek as he had kissed her goodnight and Frank felt a chill as he realized that she was old enough to die. This winter, the next, perhaps even in five years' time but not in fifty, not any more, after a bout of flu that younger bodies might resist, or a bad cough turned to pneumonia, perhaps not through anything as terrifying as cancer or as violent as a car crash, she might not survive to see the following spring. What would he do without her? It seemed an outrage to Frank, suddenly, that someone as unassumingly life-affirming as Frances could die, a woman who threaded others' lives through with hope and pleasure, encouraging them, giving them something to look forward to with her parties, her dinners, her leisurely chats about life and love at the bar of the Medici.

Frank was thinking of himself, he realized with a shock, and suddenly he felt ashamed of his failure to come up with the goods for Frances, to make something of himself emotionally if not as a journalist. That, after all, was Frances's goal; she didn't care whether he was rich or famous, but over the years Frank had been well aware of her discreet efforts to find someone for him, her sadness on his behalf when, every year, he left her parties either alone or with someone quite clearly unsuitable, a smokescreen débutante or incurably serious academic. Frank had always bridled whenever anyone described Frances as a hostess; and now he thought that perhaps it was not so ignominious a characterization, to be the giver of hospitality. He was grateful, he finally realized, almost too late, for the way in which she continued to welcome him to her gatherings, her gentle persistence, her refusal to dismiss him as a lost cause. After all, were it not for Frances's perpetual hospitality, there would be little chance of Frank seeing Gina again after tomorrow; she would have flown back to her family and he would have gone on the same, in his circumscribed world, his bachelor flat, his interviews with architects and philosphers and Vatican bureaucrats, a *tramezzino* for lunch at the Medici. Frances was offering him another chance.

Gina. Frank remembered the feel of her against his chest when he had said goodbye at the Manzinis' country house; he thought of her slicing onions for a salad, her back to him, the soft hair at the nape of her neck. He thought of her serious, candid gaze as they had talked in what now seemed the perfect intimacy of his car's battered interior, and Frank frowned as if the memory were a painful one. Suddenly his dissatisfaction with his life became more urgent; he thought of the shambles of his flat, and saw it through her eyes. He saw himself, too: squeamish, hopelessly irresolute, the journalist who would rather write about the beatification of a long-dead minor mystic than the fourteen-year-old girls coerced into prostitution with whom he might find himself sharing the bar at the Medici. Frank raised his hand and the waiter came across to his table, poised to take his order. Would he stay, or would he go?

But Frank ordered a coffee; he was comfortable here. The evening was warm and the long oblong of the piazza was softly lit by white lights on the pastel façades of the stuccoed buildings around its edge. The fountain glowed turquoise at its centre like a magic pool and the crowd – couples hand in hand, girls from Spain or Sweden heading for the fountain to throw in their coins, groups of swaggering boys – wandered among the handcarts that were parked around the square selling souvenirs and sweets, nut-brittle and nougat, or perched on their *motorini* like extras from a Fellini film. Frank had stopped thinking about Niccolò Manzini; the thought of Gina had driven him away. But as a church bell somewhere rang a doleful peal to mark the hour, the architect emerged from the darkness of a narrow alley at the far end of the piazza and began to thread his way towards Frank through the idling lovers and lounging teenage boys; lazily good-tempered now, the crowd parted here to let him through as Frank watched.

Niccolò Manzini looked relaxed, one hand in his pocket, his white shirt open at the neck, a neutral smile on his lips when his eyes locked with Frank's, when the distance between them made such a smile the only alternative to open hostility. He arrived at the table at the same time as Frank's coffee, and smoothly, cleverly, he caught the waiter's eye before he left, ordering himself a grappa before dismissing the man with a small inclination of his head. Niccolò pulled out a chair to sit in parallel with Frank, both men facing not each other but outwards into the square. Niccolò placed his keys, on a silver key-ring, on the table between them and ran a hand over his close-cropped hair. Next to him Frank looked solid, implacable, his broad face stern beneath unruly hair; for a moment or two neither man spoke.

As Manzini looked into the square, softly radiant and mellow in the evening light, and took in the spectacle of architecture and humanity in civilized harmony, his face seemed visibly to relax. Then Frank spoke, and it was as though he had thrown a stone into still water.

'How's Jane?'

Manzini stiffened and turned his head a fraction towards Sutton. 'Jane?'

'Jane. Your wife. How's she taking all this?'

Manzini took a deep, angry breath, and turned away. 'Jane's all right. She can deal with most things. Although of course this is . . . distressing. For Beatrice particularly, but for all of us. Don't you think so?' He glared at Sutton, who nodded mildly.

'I'm interested, though,' Frank went on. 'How much does Jane know? About you?'

At the next table sat two men of a similar age to Frank and Niccolò; they were Italian, elegantly dressed and also both facing the piazza. Their stance, however, somehow indicated something different, an easy companionship quite lacking between Manzini and Sutton. They talked lazily, their conversation punctuated by nods and smiles, and each had a tanned, manicured hand resting on the table between them. Already the nearest of them, no more than six inches from Frank's elbow, had cast a curious glance across at the journalist and the architect.

'Jane's not a fool. She doesn't need you looking out for her.' Niccolò's voice effectively blocked Frank. 'I had assumed you wanted to talk to me about my work,' he went on, more calmly. 'That was Claudia's impression.'

Sutton shook his head slowly, his eyes fixed on a couple and their daughter passing in front of the Tre Scalini. Plump, pale and in early middle-age, the wife wore a headscarf from which faded red hair frizzed; her husband wore shorts and sandals on stocky legs. Their daughter was perhaps the age of Beatrice Manzini, dressed unflatteringly in a loose T-shirt and a dirndl skirt, but the round, white face she turned back to her fondly smiling parents was glowing with animation.

'I suppose, in a roundabout way, we might get on to your work. But no, not really. It was family, I suppose.' He gestured now at the round retreating backs of the parents and their daughter, so comically unlike Manzini's own sleek family. 'And a bit of ancient history. Don't you think?'

The journalist's mild tone seemed to prompt something in Niccolò Manzini, a kind of cold rage. 'My family has nothing to do with you, Sutton,' he hissed. 'Do we have to go on with this? It's almost thirty years.'

Frank shook his head. 'But it hasn't gone away, even after all this time, your nasty little secret. Although I can see why you wish it had.'

'No. No.' Manzini's voice was savage, and the two men at the next table glanced over at them sharply. There seemed to be a sudden lull in the conversation, and even the waiter, poised with a trayful of drinks at the bar's open door, turned his head to left and right in an attempt to trace the owner of the voice, tuned as he was to the sound of fomenting aggression on his shift. A Sri Lankan pedlar, narrow-shouldered in a shirt too big for him, his arms full of single red hothouse roses wrapped in cellophane, stopped his meandering passage between the tables and watched. Manzini took a breath, and when he spoke again his voice was calm.

'We were young, Sutton. Adolescent boys, in an environment where rules were not adequately applied. We have to . . . forgive ourselves. Move on. Isn't that what they say?' The architect seemed quite controlled again, looking at Frank with an expression that seemed to contain no more than mild impatience. The waiter appeared at Manzini's shoulder with his grappa, and set it down, hesitating just fractionally before leaving the table, a frown briefly passing across his blandly smiling face as he warily examined these customers for signs of impending trouble. Manzini looked at the waiter sharply and he left, his back suggesting eloquently that he had his doubts about the pair.

Frank, watching the man depart, shook his head slowly. His voice was measured and even. 'What's that girl doing now? Do you think she's forgiven us? Yes, we were drunk, she was drunk, we were all teenagers, but didn't you look at her? She looked like she'd been hit by a bus after – after you'd finished with her. She couldn't stand up.'

Frank Sutton looked at Manzini directly now, but still his body language was relaxed, in sharp contrast to his words, and at the neighbouring tables, perhaps convinced by the men's outward calm, the buzz of evening conversation resumed. A small girl, dark-eyed and in a grubby gypsy costume, cheap bangles on her thin wrist, approached them along the row of tables. She paused at each table with her hand out and her eyes fixed beseechingly on the evening drinkers, and eventually she stopped in front of the two men, murmuring her barely audible litany of need in a wheedling monotone. Niccolò Manzini looked through the girl as though she didn't exist; Sutton pushed a note across the table to her and jerked his head along the row, moving her on.

Gazing into the distance, Manzini shook his head regretfully, his face blandly unresponsive.

'Sutton, that girl, wherever she is now, she's probably got on with her life. She's got a good job, or a family. You're indulging yourself, imagining that she's on the street some-where, taking drugs, or in therapy, or dead. I think you'll find that most people don't have your need to relive the past constantly. It's not productive.' The architect paused, eyeing Frank thoughtfully, then went on. 'And besides, there was no control in that place. Children – adolescents – need discipline. It was inevitable, that something like that should have happened, that's what all the papers said, wasn't it? We were victims, too.' Beneath the table a ragged pigeon pecked at the crumbs of a fallen canapé, and Manzini's foot jerked reflexively to kick it away.

Frank shook his head, and when he spoke there was an edge to his voice at last. 'Since when did you believe what you read in the papers? We didn't need someone else to tell us that what we were doing was wrong. It *was* wrong. You – we – were acting on our worst impulses, and we knew it.'

Niccolò shrugged. 'Who's to say that when that girl got drunk with us in the pub, when she decided she wanted to come back with us, that she wasn't making her own decision? Perhaps she had something else in mind, but then, that's life. Grow up, Sutton.'

Frank's face was white, but when he spoke his voice was level.

'I wasn't the one who raped her, Niccolò. That was you. That was your decision.'

Niccolò's eyes were hard and flat as they held Frank's, and his shrug was dismissive. 'You don't understand sex, do you, Frank? It's not supposed to be pretty. And if you thought she didn't want me to do what I was doing, why didn't you stop me, instead of just standing there crying?' His voice was full of contempt. 'That's why this thing is still going on, isn't it? That's why you can't let it drop.'

Frank's head was in his hands now, but he was looking fixedly at Niccolò Manzini from between them. 'Do you know what happened to her really, Manzini? She killed herself; took an overdose of paracetamol and took three days to die of liver failure. Fifteen years old. It wasn't reported, she was protected that far, just like we were protected, too young to be named. I found out, though, someone made sure I found out.'

Niccolò said nothing; he just stared at Frank, his green eyes luminous in the uncertain light. Looking down at his hands, turning them over as though they might tell him something, Frank went on talking.

'You knew, didn't you? If they made sure I knew, her parents, or whoever it was, they'd have made sure you knew, wouldn't they? You knew she hadn't lived happily ever after.'

Niccolò spread his hands, and his voice was quiet and soothing, like a doctor giving bad news. 'Nobody made her take an overdose. She should have been tougher; it's a lesson you learn, isn't it? You make your own decisions.'

'She was fifteen. She shouldn't have even been in the pub, Manzini. You don't feel sorry even now, do you? You just understand punishment as the price you pay for doing what you want. At least I know what I did was wrong.'

'Good. You've learnt something,' said Niccolò dismissively. 'So perhaps we can stop this now? Is this the end of all this – this infantile stand-off you've kept up all this time? Or perhaps I could give you a run-down on my architectural achievements, just so you have something to put in your notebook? Something to show for your life.'

And the architect stood up from the café table, his chair grating harshly against the stone. Several heads turned to watch his slender, refined figure, some even leaning forward as though eager to see what might happen next.

'No thanks,' said Frank brusquely, still sitting at the table. 'I'd like to ask you about Natasha Julius.' Niccolò half-turned towards him, and Frank went on. 'She had, a relationship – is that the right term? – with you.'

Abruptly Manzini sat down again, but he did not pull up his chair, which seemed suddenly too flimsy to hold him. 'Is that what it's all about?' he said, savagely. 'Get yourself a girl of your own, Frank. This interest in my sex life is starting to look prurient.'

'Were you just a father figure, then?' Frank's tone was even, but it concealed the barest note of triumph.

'Look,' said Niccolò, 'I know what you're getting at. I didn't have anything to do with it. I wasn't there, I didn't see her, and I didn't kill her.' His expression was guarded, impassive. Behind them a shocked English whisper was clearly audible, but neither man turned his head to trace the sound; perhaps it was too late for that.

'I know you saw her. I know you were there, in the piazza, looking for Beatrice, or for her. You were seen.'

Manzini's olive skin seemed sallow now, unhealthy, a pallor beneath the tan. 'I didn't touch her, Sutton. Not that night. You won't give up, will you? By persecuting me, you won't make it all better, you know, won't absolve yourself. Do you think I don't know how interested you were in Natasha Julius? All that Grand Tour stuff, the gilded-youth story you were supposed to be writing, that was just an excuse to sniff around, see if you could dig any dirt up on me, wasn't it? And then she died; I suppose that must have been annoying. Were you starting to get somewhere with her?'

Frank was pale too, whiter than Manzini, his eyes dark. He went on, his voice cracking, 'And what dirt might she have had on you? Do you still like hurting girls?'

A harsh sound, of inarticulate fury, rising in his throat, Manzini stood up again, and this time he did not pause, nor did he look back. He walked from the table and into the crowd, leaving behind him his full glass of grappa, on the metal table, and Frank Sutton, who watched intently until the architect's back, taut and jerky with suppressed rage, disappeared from view.

Up at Il Rondinaio, in the fading light, Gina had been unable to start the car; the little Fiat had coughed once or twice, then died. Perhaps it had no fuel; perhaps it had been left there for too long, long enough for its engine to rust solid, or fill with dust. She didn't know. So she'd walked with Mila to the top of the road, thrust a handful of notes into her hand – she didn't know how much – and waved awkwardly to her as she walked off down the track, its shadows lengthening and merging in the half-light of dusk, her legs streaked with white dust, stiff and slow as she walked away, into the darkness of the valley. She'd turned to look back once, and Gina had felt a twinge at the sight of the worried, pale oval of her face in the twilight.

Now darkness had fallen in earnest, and Gina lay in the white muslin-tented splendour of the guest bedroom, wide awake still after the disturbing events of the day, a lamp lit at her side as she tried to concentrate on the guidebook she was using as an aid to sleep, the house below her dark and shuttered for the night. Far off she could hear the hum of the road, and she pictured the bridge across the valley, with its burden of cars on their way back from the sea. She thought of the dark, vaulted space beneath it, the river running silently below the eerie echoing roar of traffic 300 feet overhead, and the women perhaps still by the roadside, their dark faces and bright clothes half hidden in the bushes, each one willing every car not to stop, willing themselves back home for the night in their own beds. Gina sighed heavily, unable to forget the sight of Mila's face on her way back towards that road, and turned over, her back to the light. Then she heard something.

It was a faint crunch, as of a light step on the gravel outside, and Gina's heart thudded, the pit of her stomach sour with apprehension. What was she doing here, alone? It had seemed such a good idea at the time, getting away from Jane, out from under her feet. Something to tell the children about, a chance to see the house that had featured in a thousand design magazines. She hadn't counted on all this. *Maybe it's Mila, coming back*, she thought. Or maybe Mila had told someone else that Gina was there, that there was a woman at the house all alone, undefended. Stoutly she reprimanded herself for her mounting panic, turned out the light and went to the window, narrowing her eyes to see out through the slats in the shutters. Below her at the kitchen door she could see a dark head, a slender figure with shoulders drooping as though with tiredness, a hand raised to the door holding a key out towards the lock. It was Beatrice.

Gina clicked the light back on and ran down the stairs, heedlessly taking them two at a time, and landing, out of breath, at the bottom just as the inner door opened and Beatrice came in, her lowered head jerking up in alarm at the sound of Gina's descent. Her dark hair straggled about her shoulders, unbrushed, unwashed, and her white face was tired and grubby above a loose, heavy woollen jersey and greasy jeans. Her shoulders dropped and she released an exhausted, hopeless sigh, looking up at Gina with a pleading look as she sank down on to a kitchen chair, a nylon rucksack at her feet.

'I didn't know you'd be here.' She didn't sound angry, just despairing. She looked to Gina as though she was about to burst into tears.

'I'm sorry,' said Gina, unable to resist the impulse to cross the room and put her arm around the exhausted-looking girl's shoulders. 'What's the matter, Beatrice? Is it . . . Natasha? Your friend? You look as if you've walked miles.'

Beatrice shook her head slowly. 'I . . . well, I missed the bus. And I got a lift, but he stopped in the lay-by, a couple of miles back, and I had to walk the rest of the way.'

'You hitched? In the dark?' Gina was aghast, thinking of the fast, lonely road and the sordid traffic through the lay-bys, of the girl walking inches away from the lorries that roared along it.

'Don't you get on my case too.' Beatrice's voice was high and thin. 'I couldn't stand it there, in the city. Dad's out of town, Ned's mum didn't want me at his place. I stayed with some guys in a squat in San Niccolò last night, friends of Ned's, but it was awful there. They were laughing about – about Natasha. Laughing.' Grief and incredulity mingled in her voice. She was clearly still traumatized, and Gina could not believe that she had been left alone to deal with the events of the past days. Where was this girl's mother? And Jane – how could she? Gina could not fathom the depth of Jane's callousness towards this girl. Was Beatrice being punished for being the connection with Natasha, the girl whose death Jane seemed to see as obscurely shameful, or for being Manzini's child with another woman, or was it for simply being in the way? Gina became aware suddenly of the lethal violence of the forces at play within the Manzini marriage, and she didn't want to know. She pulled the girl to her, the narrow shoulders vulnerable as Beatrice shivered uncontrollably beneath her hands.

'No, no, it's all right.' Gina was anxious to calm her. 'I hitched at your age, too, before I knew why you shouldn't, it's OK.' Although, she thought, with a spasm of affection, her parents would have been furious if they'd found out. 'You poor thing. I'll run you a bath, come on.' As they walked up the stairs, Beatrice dragging her feet in scuffed trainers, Gina was uncomfortably aware that, had she been a bit braver, she would probably have made the same offer to Mila. By now she would be miles away in the dark, maybe on the bus not knowing where she would sleep, wearing only a thin suit and her ragged cardigan, tired, bruised and alone.

In fact, Mila was standing at a bus stop less than a mile away, where she'd been for two hours – where she'd been, flinching as every car passed, when Beatrice trudged up the hill from the bridge towards her and crossed the road to turn up the unmade road towards the ridge where Il Rondinaio looked down on them both. Shivering as night fell and no bus came, her eyes filled with tears of anger and frustration, she sat on her haunches, all her worldly possessions in the carrier bag crushed in her lap, and put her face in her hands.

Up the hill, Gina was looking around the bathroom for soap and towels as the water trickled into the tub. The pressure seemed very low, up on the ridge; perhaps the reservoirs were empty at this time of year, after a hot spell. Far away Gina heard the crack and rumble of distant thunder, and looked out through the little porthole window. No stars were visible and the heavy dark sky seemed dense with moisture, then a fork of lightning, far away to the south, lit up the hills. She heard a gasp from Beatrice's room.

Hurrying across the little sitting room she stopped at the door. Beatrice was standing beside her bed in the impeccably tidy room, staring down at something on the smooth white bedcover. Her face was crumpled with misery and she pointed at it, a little Indian bracelet plumb in the middle of the bed like an offering. She looked up at Gina with bewilderment and fear.

'What – what – did you put it there? It's Tash's, her bracelet. I gave it to her.'

Gina shook her head. 'I don't know how it got there. Maybe someone was tidying up?'

Beatrice seized the bracelet and flung herself on to the bedcover, curled in her dirty clothes in a foetal position, her clenched fist pressed between her small breasts, and sobbed, on and on, until Gina felt her own eyes fill with tears. She sat down next to the girl and softly put her hand on Beatrice's rigid, trembling shoulder. At first Beatrice didn't move, tightly curled as she was, then, head down, she flung her arms around Gina's waist, repeating Natasha's name, over and over again, keening in a terrible, despairing monotone. At last she stopped, then sat up, slowly, her face swollen with crying.

'Sometimes she was afraid. She would wake up in the night, she couldn't breathe. I thought maybe it was – the drugs.' Gina nodded dumbly, thinking of the girl's death, the air forced out of her, her young body struggling vainly against the strength and malevolence of her attacker, of someone who hated her enough to desire her extinction.

Beatrice gazed into Gina's face and it was as though she saw Natasha's death reflected there again. 'Nobody knows what she was like, only me. She was so sweet. You don't understand, Ned doesn't understand, he thinks she had it coming. She was wild, she was – sometimes she did bad things, you know, just to tease, or for a dare. But she wasn't a bad person, she was so beautiful, and so funny, and I loved her –' Her head went down again and she cried once more, her sobbing now quieter, less strident.

Gina thought of her own painful adolescence, of the older girlfriends, the glamorous ones you were never quite sure of, but whom you worshipped all the same. The ones who liked to have a younger girl, as a mascot, to reflect back to them their own sophistication and ease, to giggle with and laugh at, to pick up and discard at will. She bent over Beatrice and pressed her face against the girl's hot, wet cheek. 'It's all right; I know,' she said, softly. 'I'm sure she loved you, too. It's –' She stopped, unable to find a form of words to offer comfort or explanation for the older girl's death. 'It's not fair.'

Although the doors along the Via Maggio had long since been locked, the security grilles fastened and the fancier items on display removed for safekeeping elsewhere, the window at the back of Pierluigi's shop was still unshuttered, although inside the shop was dark. The only illumination in the narrow Vicolo degli Innocenti came from inside the all-night garage, with its dirty concrete and rows of shiny, expensive machines brightly lit by overhead strip-lighting. The light was cast in a block out into the street, too, and extended across the narrow alley as far as the shop-front opposite, even illuminating the dusty chandelier and the carved oak chest beneath it in the window. You would have had to look very hard, though, beyond the window display, to realize that Pierluigi himself was still in there, sitting quite immobile in his wooden armchair, only the tips of his immaculately polished brogues visible in the light cast through the garage doors. He was gazing out through his window, but even had his shop been well lit, it would have been impossible to say exactly what he was looking at.

Pierluigi couldn't have said what he was looking at, either, so consumed were his thoughts by something he couldn't see, not any more. He was not himself. Pierluigi was a sentimental man, he would have been the first to admit it, but he was also practical. He found it difficult to justify, even to himself, why he was so upset by the dead girl pushed through his window, and perhaps that was why he was making such a fuss to his friends about moving out old stock, setting things in order in the shop. To disguise the fact that he couldn't get her out of his mind. She had been so young, with her hair as short as a boy's, her skin so pale and smooth, like milk. Just a little girl. Pierluigi leant forward and put his head in his hands.

As Pierluigi shook his head, as though to clear his thoughts, the unmistakable throaty purr of a Ferrari filled the narrow street outside, moving slowly down from the Via Santo Spirito towards him. Absently, Pierluigi craned his neck to watch for it, unable to shake the habit of a lifetime, and sure enough soon the sleek lines of a Ferrari Dino, twenty-five years old, maybe, so much prettier than the new one, slid into view and down the ramp into the garage.

A man's tanned, white-cuffed wrist appeared through the open driver's window, a gold-ringed hand inserted a plastic card into the squat machine beside the ramp, and the barrier in front of the elegantly curved scarlet bonnet rose jerkily to the vertical. As the restrained chrome trim at the rear of the car slid away from him down the ramp and on to the lower floor, carved out of the ancient building's foundations, which was reserved exclusively for such vehicles and was where

Pierluigi kept his own Fiat, something caught the antique dealer's eye high above the disappearing Ferrari. It was a movement up at ceiling level, not fast but deliberate, the whir and swivel of a small, square machine suspended from the roof and the flash of a lens as it caught the light. A security camera.

No more than half a mile away from Pierluigi, on the far side of the Piazza Santo Spirito, Frances stood in Roland's old silk dressing-gown at one of the long windows in her drawing room, the central one, with her hand on the cracked paint of its ancient glazing bars, looking at the street below, a couple wandering past leaning in to each other in the warm evening, on their way, perhaps, to the bright lights and bars of the piazza ahead. If she had been an Italian woman of seventy-five she would probably have long since closed her shutters against the dangerous cool of the night air, but as it was, being Frances, she cleaved to the world going on outside, unable to let it slip away quite yet.

The flowers were bought and standing in the flagstoned chill of the Casa Ferrali's cavernous ground floor, the lilies still creamy-white and waxy in the cool, the gardenias just coming into flower, the lemon trees upstairs on the balcony so that the warm spring air would encourage their fragrant flowering. Tomorrow would bring deliveries of linen, glass and silver, of fruit – pomegranates and peaches from Sicily and the first cherries from Vignola – the suckling pig from Umbria, with its personal attendant and wood oven; on Friday, paper packages of fresh tagliatelle tied with ribbon and prickly steel-blue baby artichokes flushed with purple. There were crates of champagne and Chianti, bundles of fat church candles and Chinese paper lanterns, tapers to go in the candelabra. There would be a little Neapolitan band to serenade those walking through the garden and after the meal, so that those of her friends still so disposed – a surprising number; perhaps she had a particularly romantic acquaintance – could dance under the trees at midnight.

Frances felt the rough surface of the shutters' flaking paint with faint regret, thinking that at last she was too old to contemplate the renovations her elderly apartment required, in the way that some cautious old people will not buy a new winter coat, superstitiously afraid that the winter coat will outlive them and thereby mysteriously hasten their death. She refused the thought, because if she accepted it, she felt she might as well be dead already. The only reason she didn't redecorate her flat, she chided herself, was that she had no interest in doing so; all the same, just a suspicion that she had begun to accept her mortality lingered in Frances's mind. Defiantly she decided that tomorrow she would buy herself something new, something beautiful, and she could live like a débutante again, with her life golden with possibilities ahead of her, ready for her party.

A long way to the south, Niccolò Manzini was approaching a police station, a run-down *carabiniere* post in a southern suburb of Rome.

He pulled up opposite the crumbling building, and turned his engine off. Except for the flat glare of strip-lighting shining from every window, the building looked more like an opera set than a police station, its plaster façade faded pink and peeling, the shutters of the long elegant windows cracked and sagging. As Manzini watched, a *carabiniere* in full dress uniform, his back straight, peaked cap at a jaunty angle, strolled out on to the first-floor balcony, smoking. The outline of the policeman's body was proud and upright, and the gesture with which he flicked his cigarette butt into the street below spoke of casual arrogance. He went back inside, and the sound of raised voices spilt out of the open window into the street.

For a moment it seemed as though Manzini was about to get out of the car. But instead he slumped back in the seat, lowered his head, and brought up his hands to cover his face. Then he sat up, turned the key in the ignition and the big car leapt away from the kerb. He drove away from the *carabiniere* post and skirted Rome to the southeast, apparently oblivious to the teenage prostitutes slouching beneath the sodium-lit industrial estates at the city's edge, his paled grim face staring straight ahead out of the dark interior of the expensive car. Then he headed out towards Grosseto by the *superstrada* that clung to the marshy coastline, where birds flew in from Africa, wheeling and swarming above him like locusts in the warm evening sky.

Ten miles or so south of Grosseto Manzini suddenly turned off the broad highway and into the gathering darkness of the plains that extended down to the sea. A five-mile crescent of utterly flat, empty land criss-crossed by drainage ditches, the plain was flanked on either side by looming, shadowy mountains that plunged into the Tyrrhenian Sea. Between these Manzini headed west on a long, straight road; a mile or so from the coast he entered a forest of thickly planted umbrella pines which met overhead to form the impenetrable roof of prickly, pine-coned green. This canopy was populated by a huge colony of *cicadas*, their shrill, pulsating buzz at this time in the evening almost deafening in its intensity. Manzini drove on and on until the expanse of trees ahead thinned and parted to reveal the last gleam of the dipping sun across the sea, and the gentle susurration of the waves on the beach became audible over the sawing of the insects. He parked his car on the cool, dry, compacted sand beneath the trees, and got out.

Niccolò walked out on to the sand of the beach, which, perhaps because it was so early in the season, was clean and smooth, littered only with the ghostly, silvered white of fallen trees, the pines that had fallen victim to the salt spray, the shifting sand and the soft, endless, prevailing wind. He looked along the coast, which curved gently away from him towards the mountains, and out to sea, where the dark outlines of the islands, Isola d'Elba or del Giglio, were just visible against the deepening blue of the sky. He unbuttoned his white shirt and took off his shoes, placing them side by side and the shirt on top, then his dark wool trousers, folded carefully along the crease. He walked away from the little pile and towards the sea and the setting sun. He waded in, a lean silhouette, pausing when the water reached his waist, as though reluctant to go further, the sea still holding the last of the winter's chill. But then he lowered his shoulders and swam, a leisurely graceful crawl, not out to sea but south along the coast, to where the great dark bulk of Monte Argentario shelved into the black water.

The traffic was a little lighter now on the road from Grosseto to Siena; it was too early in the year still for the day trippers of July and August, the Germans in their camper vans in search of nature not yet despoilt. The beaches were deserted and the few hardy spring bathers, mostly foreigners, back in their hotel beds. Stefano shuffled the gears to try to give the engine of the exhausted Opel a break as it strained on the incline approaching the bridge; the car, an old banger used for this run, would be a disgrace to a Neapolitan – its bumper was held on with string. He didn't want to use his real car, in case the police stopped him, in case he was seen, but mostly because he didn't want the women in his car, dirtying it with their cheap perfume and dusty shoes, filling it up with sweet wrappers and garbage.

They were all in the back now, chattering with relief at the end of the day, giggling and laughing, even Betty who was usually hard-faced as they come. Stefano wondered idly, as they passed Evelina's pitch, where Manzini had got to, and whether it was time to follow that one up. Stefano could hardly be bothered to waste the time thinking about Evelina any more; he was beginning to think sleeping dogs were best left to lie. All the same, as he passed the turn-off to Manzini's place, up somewhere on the ridge, he found himself looking up and there, sure enough, was a light on high overhead, an expensive pergola floodlit against the dark hillside.

Because Stefano's head was turned that way, he didn't see the bus stop to his left and the crumpled figure at its base, Mila crouched small with her head in her hands. As he drove past her across the bridge and into the tunnel that led its load of traffic out of the Maremma, Mila was willing a bus to arrive, any bus, to get her out of there. But it was almost midnight, and there would be no bus until tomorrow, and Mila was starting to think that she would never get out again.

Up on the ridge, at Il Rondinaio, the timed floodlighting switched itself off at midnight. Gina, having coaxed Beatrice into her warm bath and then clean pyjamas and bed, was herself fast asleep and dreaming. She dreamt of her children.

Gina dreamt that she had left her children, two boys, one girl, with someone she didn't know, someone she might merely have met queuing to pay in a supermarket, and now she had to find them, track them down and bring them home. So overweening was the fear this scenario engendered, so urgent and demanding were the chemicals it produced in her body that she stood up from her bed while still asleep and, quite unaware, walked to the staircase and down to the kitchen. There she stood in the dark, staring at the sacrificial wreath of bay that gleamed up at her in the moonlight, until at last she remembered where she was and, trembling, returned to her bed.

Thursday

23

In the misty grey outdoors beyond her window at the approach of dawn, Gina could hear the chattering of the magpies in the broad, sparse canopy of an umbrella pine right outside her shutters. A gang of them were generating an extraordinary clamour, a loud, bad-tempered, discordant scraping and clacking, like an irascible old couple arguing over the washing-up. Carefully Gina opened the window but they didn't pause at her sound and movement, only a yard or two away, and seemed quite unafraid of her. For all their bold colouring, she found magpies eminently dislikable creatures: carrion-feeding, noisy, aggressive. She could see their outline in the tree, six or seven of them, their tails bobbing and sawing as though joined like the flails and flanges of some sinister, broken Heath Robinson machine.

The sun was coming up across the far hills, beyond the road, and the sky took on colour at last, a milky pale blue high up that strengthened as the sun rose, streaks of lurid salmon pink striped with turquoise at the horizon. There was no sign of the previous night's storm; the only cloud was high and thin, and was burning off almost as Gina watched. Deafened and intimidated by the bullying birds in the tree, Gina gave in, put on, over her nightdress, a white-cotton dressing-gown she found on a hook on the door and went downstairs.

Gina put the kettle on the stove and opened the doors into the garden. As she stood waiting for the water to boil, she gazed at the jug of bay leaves, frowning; it reminded her of something, but she couldn't think what until an unsettling memory of her dream stirred. Barefoot she walked out into the garden and to her surprise the birds took off above her and headed towards the sunrise, trailing their long stiff tails, only to flap clumsily back down to earth just out of sight, where the hill pitched steeply down at the garden's boundary.

Beneath her feet the close-cropped grass, which from above had looked like velvet, was stiff, coarse, and drenched with dew, or possibly rain from the night's storm, and the cushions on the wooden loungers were soaked, too. Gina heard the kettle's hoarse shriek behind her and turned to see Beatrice standing in the doorway. She wore her pyjamas with an old blue blanket, worn and soft as a child's comforter, over her shoulders. She was pale but seemed to have lost some of the haunted weariness of the night before. Gina went to her, put her arm around her shoulders and rubbed her thin arm as though to warm her after a swim.

'You look better. Did you sleep all right?' Beatrice nodded drowsily and allowed herself to be led to the kitchen table where they sat in silence, warming their hands around cups of black tea, and looked out at the sunrise. Then Beatrice spoke.

'She was pregnant. Three months.' Her hands were trembling.

'Natasha was? Whose –' Gina recoiled at the thought of the murdered girl's body. 'She told you?'

'Mmm. She didn't tell me whose it was. I think she didn't know herself. There's a guy who sells – sold – her drugs. Stefano. But there were others. She . . . Look, it's not like she committed a crime. She liked it. Sex. She didn't do it to hurt anyone.'

Gina nodded sadly, not willing to say to Beatrice that life wasn't that simple. 'What was she going to do? About the baby?'

Beatrice laughed miserably at the question. 'That depended. On how stoned she was. Sometimes she ignored it, pretended it wasn't happening. Or maybe she just forgot, but anyway she'd talk about going back to London, getting a job in a gallery, modelling and stuff. Sometimes she seemed to have whole plans that included it, how cool it would be, she'd get a flat of her own, take the baby everywhere with her, paint its room purple with stars on the ceiling. That kind of stuff.'

Gina smiled ruefully, remembering the shock of a baby, the first baby, and how little it had to do with the colour the nursery was painted. 'And when she wasn't stoned?'

'She cried a lot. Maybe the father wasn't going along with it all, I don't know. She'd get angry and say she was going to get rid of it. She was scared she'd damaged it with the drugs, but she had to keep taking the drugs to deal with all the mess she was in. She didn't have any money, you know. She just – drifted around. There was always someone she could stay with. Us. Ned. I thought she was brave, but I don't think she knew what to do at all.'

Beatrice's face was downcast, and Gina could see her grappling with the memory of her friend's flawed and hopeless courage, trying to find a meaning in her short, screwed-up life. 'Beatrice. Do you take stuff? Drugs I mean?'

Gina knew nothing about drugs, and she didn't know how you had this conversation with your children, but she tried to keep any hint of criticism or even oppressive anxiety out of her voice. Beatrice looked shamefaced.

'No, not really. I smoke a bit of dope now and then. It makes me feel sick, though. Don't tell Dad, will you?' She looked at Gina pleadingly. 'I've never taken the other stuff. I don't like even seeing them do it.'

'What stuff? What did they take?'

'Mostly coke. Cocaine. You know, for parties. I hate that stuff; you can always tell when they've taken it, they never stop talking and laughing, like monkeys. But just lately I think they were doing heroin. I don't know, I never saw them, but

Natasha, she had marks on her arms. They laughed at me a bit, for being such a chicken, but they never made me do anything. Take anything.'

'They?' Gina asked softly.

'All that lot, the stupid junkie losers that hang out in Florence. The squat I was in yesterday. But mostly Tash and Ned.' She stopped, looking pensive and miserable.

'But it's not like it sounds. We have – we had –' She faltered. 'It was just us three, mostly, and we just hung out, drank coffee, drank wine, I cooked stuff, we came out here and swam and went for walks on the little hill paths, it was great, it was . . .' Beatrice looked puzzled, lost, as though she was trying to put something back together and it wouldn't work.

Looking at Beatrice's sad, fallen face, its freckles dark against the pale skin, Gina felt a painful throb of sympathy. There was something about the dynamic between the three, the older girl with all the confidence and the looks, the naive, adoring younger one, the surly, manipulative boy, that was poignant, familiar and disturbing. The classic *ménage à trois*, with one always left out, left in the dark. And that one was Beatrice.

With Beatrice upstairs getting dressed, Gina thought maybe she'd phone home; it was early, still, not much after seven in England, and perhaps the foot-stamping, shrieking, abuse-hurling frenzy that marked the later stages of dressing for school would not yet have been reached. The faint and imperfect memory of her dream had left her with a disquieting sense that she had been taking this too lightly, her abandonment of her children.

The line crackled and hummed as though the phone was in a Congolese missionary station instead of a hilltop only a mile or two from the tourist epicentre of Europe. Gina felt oddly shy waiting on the echoing line for Stephen to pick up, as though she had been away for weeks rather than days; she could only distantly summon up the picture of the phone by the bed, the cluttered, steamy house, the children racing around the stairs trailing school sweatshirts and screaming for breakfast. And when at last her husband answered the phone, the house seemed oddly silent, and he sounded sleepy.

'Where are they all?' she asked. 'It's so quiet.'

'They're asleep,' hissed Stephen. 'That is, if the phone didn't wake them up.'

'Asleep? But they – it is seven, isn't it? They never sleep this late.'

'Ten past,' he said, wearily. 'They've been sleeping rather well, actually, staying in their own beds.' Gina detected a hint of smugness with an undertone of reproach, but she couldn't be bothered to defend herself. She felt a tug at the thought of their sleeping faces, their mouths always half open as though they'd fallen asleep in the middle of a conversation, smooth-skinned, long-lashed and sweet-breathed. But in fact, she realized, she was relieved that they seemed so settled, so far from the lost children she had dreamt of.

'Well, as long as they're not staying up too late at night.'

'Mmm.' Stephen sounded a little shifty. 'Actually, they were up till nine last night. I opened some wine and – well, Stella fell asleep on the sofa and I let the others watch television. Sorry.'

'No, no, doesn't matter.' Gina reflected that soon enough they would have to get used to the children staying up later than them.

'I'm in the country now,' she said, 'but I'll be going back tonight, and I'll see you on Saturday afternoon. I won't phone again, if everything's all right.'

'Yes. I – we miss you. It'll be nice to see you.' Gina's heart softened at the half-disguised endearment, so typical of Stephen.

'Me too. Lots of love.' Softly she replaced the ancient receiver. It was only after they had been disconnected that she thought to wonder at how little curiosity she felt about what Stephen was doing in her absence. He could be taking advantage of it in all sorts of ways. But somehow giving in to the tranquillizing appeal of a bottle of wine and then falling asleep on the sofa next to Stella seemed by far the most plausible. She smiled and turned back from the gloom to the bright rectangle of light at the door.

Frances was in the Piazza della Signoria, walking slowly home from the newsstand, under her arm a copy of an old-fashioned literary magazine she bought, very occasionally and for old times' sake, because it was still edited by a friend of Roland's. As she crossed the square in the crenellated shadow of the massive Palazzo Vecchio, Frances noticed Jane at a table outside Rivoire, dressed beautifully as usual but sitting stiffly, as though her body contained a tension she could not subdue, as though she was afraid she might spring away from herself if she relaxed. She did not look as though she would welcome a visitor to her table.

Frances felt quite sorry for Jane, sometimes; she could tell, although she imagined the younger woman had no idea how transparent her life could be, precisely what Jane's marriage was like, and she knew, too, how difficult Jane's chosen method of dealing with it was to maintain. Keeping up appearances could be very destructive.

When she had first become aware of Roland's attitude to fidelity, that is, when the wife of one of his friends – one whose husband treated her as Roland treated Frances, and who had had enough of Frances's innocence – had maliciously taken it upon herself to explain to Frances how it was, with men, or at least with men like Roland, and, in that context, to point out the French barmaid in the Soho pub in which they were, at that moment, drinking, as one of his lovers, Frances had thought she would die of shame.

They had been living in London at that time, not long after the war, and it had been a wonderful place. Roland had been demobbed from the navy, at last, and they were waiting for him to take up his first posting with the diplomatic service, and were making the most of it. They were out every night, roaring around Soho and Chelsea, roaming from pub to pub; the French House, the Museum Tavern, the Antelope; they never seemed to eat, in those days, they only drank, and smoked, and talked. Nobody really drank, here, she reflected; perhaps that was why they stayed on the rails, more or less, the Italians.

After her solitary childhood, and then the war spent doing war work in a Whitehall basement, half mad with fear that she would never see Roland again, it was exhilarating, at first, to find that she could be with him all the time. She had so loved pubs then, she thought ruefully, on Roland's arm, in a great gang of them talking, reciting poetry and laughing just because they were alive and the war was over. It was only gradually that she had begun to feel out of her depth, when Roland drank too much every night and she couldn't keep up. Then she became pregnant and miscarried. Then Roland would stay out, now and again, and although he'd be full of laughter and affection on his return Frances would feel sick at the thought of the night he had spent without her, a blank in their history together, a black hole.

Frances had begun by pretending, as Jane did, that it wasn't happening, never admitting for a moment what she had discovered to any of their friends. But the strain had almost killed her; more and more she had felt cut off from them, less and less willing to go out, to talk freely, in case something slipped out, in case someone made a joke about a barmaid, or the pretty girl who played the cello in the house next door to their little basement in Kensington, or if an old flame of Roland's turned up again minus a husband. Frances began to think she might have to go back to her parents, to her mother, who had warned her about Roland and his poor prospects as a husband.

So Frances gave in; she waited for Roland to come home one morning, and she shouted at him, she tried, ineffectually, to hit him. She had cried until her face was swollen and her chest ached, but it had been better than keeping silent. Thinking about that now, as she passed Jane, trapped in her bubble of impotent and unexpressed rage, Frances felt a great relief that she no longer had to tolerate love, not that kind of love, anyway. And of course, in time, Roland had calmed her, and, somehow, she had believed him when he said that none of them mattered compared with her.

Frances had undertaken her own miserable infidelity out of desperation, or revenge, or just daring Roland to find out, willing him to understand what it was like to be betrayed. She had met her lover during a brief spell working at an art gallery, replacing a déb who'd upped and married without warning. It was just a part-time job while she and Roland were in London. He'd just walked in off the street, good-looking enough, a big, confident fair-haired patrician type, and when she'd seen the look in his eyes when they alighted not on the paintings, which were rather indifferent, but on Frances, she had decided that he would do. He'd pursued her enthusiastically, too, even passionately, once his primitive radar had detected that all was not quite well in her marriage. But he hadn't been Roland; the thing that bound her irrevocably to Roland, Roland's wicked, renegade charm, the feeling she had of being needed absolutely by him, whatever happened, that was entirely lacking.

Roland never found out, but perhaps he had a conscience, after all, because after that there seemed to be fewer unexplained nights away, and the pitying glances from the other women dried up, too, once she let them know she knew, once she no longer irritated them with her innocence. And then she and Roland had been sent abroad, to Paris, for a little while, where Frances had seen a lot of Lucienne. Paris had been like heaven, luminously beautiful, the evenings full of long, labyrinthine conversations with a whole new set of friends Roland managed, as he always did, to pick up. With these people – unshaven men in shabby suits, women with dark lipstick and wild hair – they would embark on debates about philosophy, existentialism and war that wound around and around themselves into the early hours, only terminated by someone leaping up and leading them to an Algerian bar in the Marais, or a dancehall on the edge of town. And how clearly she remembered Lucienne putting her head on one side, like a little bird, and telling her in her blithe, practical French way not to worry about Roland; Roland would always belong to Frances.

Frances walked on, towards the Ponte Vecchio as the heat of the morning began to build towards noon, back to the south of the city. She thought perhaps she would walk up to the rose garden at the very top of the Boboli Gardens, where you could look out over the olive groves and where there was generally a fresh wind; this early, it should still be quite empty.

She rested, on a sandstone bench beneath an old creamy-yellow rambling rose, after her long, slow, deliberate climb all the way up the cypress avenue to the little rose garden. It perched over the city wall, looking away from Florence with its heat haze and endless roofs, and towards the perfect illusion of countryside. Frances gazed out over the dark-green hills to the southeast, across a few terraces of olives to gardens with lemon trees, turreted villas and the little striped church of San Miniato, its perfect Romanesque arches and the soft gleam of gold mosaic shining back at her as it nestled in the hill's deep shade and dusty green trees. She surveyed the parterre in front of her, enclosed with a miniature maze of box, brilliant peonies and dark-red roses spilling over their boundaries.

Perhaps, Frances reflected idly as she looked at the flowers, and observed their faint, English incongruity against the incontrovertibly Tuscan backdrop, she should have been a peaceful old lady, pottering about her garden and tending to her roses and delphiniums. But Frances was too restless; she hadn't the patience, nor the skill; she would have had to give in, helplessly, and sit back and let someone else do her gardening for her. And Florence sometimes seemed half old England, anyway; the roses in front of her were shipped from an English nursery, and behind San Miniato lay a cemetery full of English poets. Frances had no desire to be shipped home to die, when the time came; she had no need.

Unable to stand the inhospitable dazzle of her own drawing room at eight in the morning, Jane sat at her lace-covered table outside Rivoire, the most outrageously overpriced bar in Florence but the only one that provided the atmosphere of inviolable privilege she needed this morning. She did not notice Frances passing through the piazza; she was barely aware of where she was, so intent was she on other matters. In front of her on the dainty little table stood a small glass of French brandy, her slim, silver mobile phone and an espresso. In the cool sharp light of the early morning, Jane was, for once, looking her age.

She had been pacing the apartment since six, taut with misery and frustration, everything that surrounded her, from the velvet sofas to the pewter light-fittings, reminding her of her compromised life. The walk across the Ponte Vecchio had calmed her a little, and the sight of the great palaces lining the river invigorated her; they afforded her the long view, a revelation of the passage of time, and offered a reminder of the wealth and cunning of Renaissance princes that she took as an instruction to go on, not to surrender.

What she needed, Jane felt, was a strategy to keep images of Niccolò and his betrayal out her thoughts. Memories she had suppressed from year to year, finding explanations, excuses, at every step, diligently disposing of every inconvenient reminder of his other life, now refused to evaporate, marched up and down inside her head, declaring themselves. She remembered the times their supposed friends had mentioned seeing him, barely able to conceal their prurience, with this or that dressed-up schoolgirl, models, budding artists in high heels and slash-fronted satin, at private views or in the kind of old-fashioned, expensive restaurant where you could rely on the management's discretion. She remembered the cool look he would give her, if ever she even hinted at his infidelity and her humiliation; she remembered the ritual gifts – the diamonds, the exquisitely plain clothes – for the trophy wife. To keep her quiet, and to remind her of her position. She was, however, beyond the stage of rehearsing what she would like to say to him, supposing he deigned to telephone her again. It was too late for that.

In England it would be just after nine. Jane dialled the number of her parents' lawyer in Holborn, a smooth-talking elderly predator who wore pearl-grey suits and was as discreet and professionally charming as the waiters at Rivoire. She was put through immediately.

'Charles. It's Jane Stamp. Jane Manzini. I want a divorce.'

24

They came early, before most of the staff had arrived, sounding the buzzer as though they were trying to wake the dead and startling Claudia out of her carefully maintained composure. Not that it was much of a veneer today, anyway; the last thirty-six hours had brought calls from creditors, the revenue and two or three nameless, menacing types with southern accents, and not a word from her employer, and Claudia was feeling jittery, to say the least. The stamp of their neatly shod feet as they marched up the marble staircase and pushed their way into her foyer, crowding it out with their aftershave and dark uniforms, sounded to her like an army on the march. And they were armed.

'I – can I help you?'

Their leader, a man not much older than Claudia but with an air of easy authority, smiled, not very pleasantly, and held out a piece of paper ornamented with half a dozen official stamps and signatures.

'We have come to remove certain items from Signore Manzini's offices. Computers, to begin with. How many computers do you have on the premises?'

Claudia's pretty jaw dropped. 'Signore Manzini is not here –'

'We know that.' The policeman laughed. 'I don't think you will be seeing him again very soon, either. This warrant provides us with the necessary authority; we don't require his presence. Now. The computers?'

Claudia directed them up the stairs and watched in dismay as the ten *carabinieri* removed every computer from the building, along with several drawerfuls of files from Manzini's private office, where they seemed to have no difficulty with his locked cabinet. Claudia felt like crying, quite unable to imagine what she would say to the staff when they arrived for work. As she watched the last machine disappear down the stairs and the policeman stood in her doorway informing her when they would return, she remembered.

'Wait. One moment. Signore Manzini thought you might need these. To provide some evidence to support his account?' She reached into a drawer and pulled out the tapes, and handed them to him. 'They cover the period he was in the building working, on Sunday night. Between eight and midnight? Or so?'

A shadow passed briefly across the policeman's face, but he put out his hand to take the tapes.

'That's not going to help him much. She wasn't killed until one or two in the morning, at least.' And he turned on his heel and left Claudia staring helplessly after him.

Once decided, it took Gina a map and a little over half an hour to walk down the winding, dusty road to the place where she had swum with Frank, where the scalding spring poured out of the hillside and filled the ghost-white, sulphur-encrusted basins like troglodyte baths. She hadn't felt like swimming in the dark water of the Manzinis' pool; the morning air was too fresh or the setting too secluded for her mood, and she had found herself thinking instead with longing of the stimulating, soothing heat of the sulphurous water. Beatrice had told her she should go, assured her that she would be happy to be left behind, and so she had set off alone.

It was quite empty at nine or so, when she arrived; there was no sign of the vendor of ethnic clothing, and, although she could see a thin plume of smoke near a grubby teepee some way off in the bushes, she couldn't see any other human being, either. The sun hadn't yet reached the valley floor, and the air was deliciously cool. Gina stripped and lay down in the water to soak. After half an hour or so, hearing sounds of movement from the direction of the teepee, she climbed down to the river and set off swimming in a new direction, away from the echoing chamber beneath the bridge, upriver. The deep water of the bathing pool didn't extend very far in that direction, but she swam far enough to see a track that led up through the cork trees in the direction of Il Rondinaio, and she resolved to walk back across country. After all, for the moment she had no other demands on her time, and the ex-hilaration of the climb down had reminded her of the particular pleasures of walking unhindered by complaining children, looking around without interruption, pausing at will without fear of losing a wandering dependant. As she set off, looking back through the trees she glimpsed the wigwam dwellers, or one of them, emerge from their encampment, a large, semi-naked, pale-skinned German hippy picking her way heavily down the hill, fat lying thick and firm as rubber on her hips, her bare breasts small and conical. Her hair was snaked in frowsty, mouse-coloured dreadlocks around her head and she stared sullenly up at Gina from beneath a frowning mono-brow. Gina wondered at the girl's casually proprietorial air; she felt glad that she hadn't lingered to outstay her welcome and sorry, not for the first time, for the local population who had to tolerate the presence of so many squatters on their land. Herself included, she realized with a guilty twinge.

The path through the scrub wound and jerked up the hill, which became progressively steeper until Gina found herself having to look for hand-holds to help her up, and paused for breath. The view was quite lovely; the river rippling quietly over mossy stones between the green banks, even the crossed poles of the teepee, just visible through the trees, looked picturesque, and, although she could still hear the road, from here it was invisible. She turned to look up, towards Il Rondi-naio, and she could see that soon the slope would flatten a bit, though it wasn't at all clear from this angle that this route would lead her in the right direction. She went on.

After 500 yards more of steep climb, the path swung to the left, away from Il Rondinaio, and appeared to turn downhill. Gina's heart sank. Above her, in the right direction, was a little plantation of cork, and the ground beneath the stunted trees was relatively clear. *It can't be that far*, she thought to herself, *and what's the worst that can happen? A scraped knee, a few scratches*. She tried not to think of vipers and wild boar, and set off through the trees.

It was a much more pleasant walk, away from the prickly

juniper and myrtle that had clawed at her on the early stretch, the light filtering softly through the trees. The firm, cool, dusty ground beneath her feet had a light, slippery covering of fallen leaves, and all was peaceful and silent. But before long the trees stopped and the hope they had promised of an easy climb faded when she saw the thick tangle of wild vines and overgrown olive trees that followed. High above her she could see the roofline of Il Rondinaio towering from the ridge, and so she fought her way on and up, itchy in the increasing heat, burrs clinging to her skirt and sweat stinging in the scratches on her arms and legs until she saw what she thought should be the light at the end of the tunnel. Two great slabs of rock that marked the foot of a steep, raw slope. At the top of the slope, Gina could see the pergola at the edge of Il Rondinaio's lower terrace.

When she was almost there, almost close enough to touch the smooth golden sandstone, Gina stopped, and as she gasped for breath in the moment of silence that followed, she saw a magpie hop up out of the cleft to perch, swaggering like a frock-coated beadle on top of the nearest rock, just above her head. It looked insolently down at her, then flapped slowly off up the hill. She heard her breath wheeze and whistle in her ears with the effort of the climb and felt the thud of her heart behind her chest wall. She put a hand on the rock where the magpie had so recently perched, and pulled herself up, her eyes level with the rock wall's top, then higher, then she could see down into the cleft from which the bird had emerged. A noise came from her mouth and her heart seemed to slow, its boom echoing in the cavern of her ribs after a long interval. She stared.

Her first thought was how uncomfortable the girl must be, her position so sharply bent, her head twisted. She willed herself to understand what she was looking at; the unnatural angles of the arm, the neck, the purple bruises obvious even on the dark, dark skin, not glossy but dull, the skin, dull and dead as rubber. Beneath the sheaf of hair – but she averted her gaze, the mutilated eye socket too horrible to look at. *It must have been the magpie*, she told herself, although it seemed no less terrifying for that. She looked again, her breathing shallow, her lungs working against the panic, slowing her down.

She thought of the girl she had seen standing in the field of maize like a totem, her terrible, frozen face staring out at the road. This girl was one of those, her clothes, her purple halter top, her little shorts, small enough for a child, the glitter polish on her toes. A little girl's idea of glamour, and this is where they ended up. Gina felt sick. Her poor shoeless feet, the soles paler than the rest of her and crusted with blood, the torn earlobe. Slowly, automatically, Gina looked to the other ear and registered the golden hoop. Then something moved at the top of her field of vision, a flicker, and she looked up to see Mila standing there at the top of the slope, half sliding and trying to steady herself on the steep bare earth, her mouth open.

Gina blinked to dispel the hallucination which must, she thought, be of a piece with the spots that danced in front of her eyes, a product of temporary delirium. But Mila was coming closer, stumbling down the hill, and she was sobbing; this was the response that Gina wanted to have to the battered body she could no longer look at now, but her eyes remained dry. She pulled herself around the rocks and up on to the earth beyond them, and climbed with difficulty up towards Mila, her palms up to face her, to stop her coming any closer.

'It's Evelina,' Mila sobbed noisily. 'I knew it. She's dead, isn't she?'

Gina took in the ragged, gasping Italian, and she nodded, helplessly. 'You know her?'

Mila pointed towards the road. 'She – like me, she worked

on the road. I saw her shoes –' She sank to her knees, slumped against the hillside.

'She was here, she was here.' Mila looked fearfully up at the stone of Il Rondinaio looming over them.

'Here?' Gina couldn't understand what Mila was saying. 'Here?' Then she heard a voice above them, the sound of Beatrice calling nervously from the garden. She must have heard them. 'Come on. We'd better phone the police.' Gina pulled Mila by the arm and pointed up the hill, and reluctantly Mila followed. If there was one thing Gina was sure of now, it was that she must prevent Beatrice from seeing what they had seen.

25

As Jane smiled cheerfully at the white-coated students filing into her kitchen to take up their places around the table, it occurred to her that she could get used to drinking brandy for breakfast, and she had better be careful. It wasn't just the spirits, though; her conversation with her lawyer had given her a warm feeling in the pit of her stomach, too, the sensation, she thought, that comes with taking control. Charles's soothing, mellifluous voice, his command of all the legal niceties of her particular situation, his perfect confidence in a satisfactory outcome, summoned up for her in its entirety the oak-panelled, velvet-curtained solidity of empire and justice, obediently awaiting her instruction. Jane could feel order reassert itself, enabling her, once again, to take charge of her life.

Perhaps it was the restlessness that often came after the halfway mark in her courses, but the students seemed particularly fidgety this morning, whispering and darting meaningful glances at each other across the huge table, which today was laid out with balloon whisks, copper bowls, organic free-range eggs from the Mugello, Madagascar vanilla pods, Sicilian marsala and sugar. Jane drew herself up almost imperceptibly, just enough to focus the group's attention on her, and began to speak.

Today was puddings, and Jane always began this part of her instruction with a discourse on the reputed paucity of elaborate dessert dishes in Italian cuisine. She laid out for her students the historical, sociological and geographical reasons for the country's lack of refined patisserie skills (these boiled down, as far as Jane was concerned, to the twin facts that the heat curdled cream and the Italian peasant couldn't afford sugar) and went on to emphasize the very modern benefits of the traditional Italian sweet course, consisting largely of fruit, sweet cheese, custards and dry biscuits. Her gist was that, if these were arranged prettily enough on the plate, the absence of any actual cooking would go unnoticed and the cook could garner praise all the same. So, a gilded and scalloped plate of figs with a dollop of mascarpone, topped perhaps with toasted hazelnuts, or a pretty heap of almond biscuits and vin santo in a Bohemian crystal goblet, would at this point be presented to the students, themselves unaware that the very same deception was being perpetrated upon them, namely they were paying to be shown a plate of fruit in the guise of a lesson in cookery. Jane enjoyed this innocently ironic little *jeu d'esprit*; she evaded any possibility of criticism by following it up with a real lesson in cookery: zabaglione.

Jane was not a great cook. She wasn't a versatile cook. Sometimes she could barely remember, when asked, how she had turned herself into a professional cook; in fact, it had been a spin-off from the highly orchestrated dinner parties she had been talked into giving for Niccolò's clients when she first married him. Quite a number turned out to be in the media, and Jane had been asked to make the odd contribution to features pages, magazines; it was all lifestyle stuff, really, and Jane knew the score. She would write up a few recipes, but the pieces mainly comprised photographs of the various houses and of Jane reclining in a pretty outfit and an exotic setting, one arm proprietorially on the arm of her handsome and talented husband. Jane was not under any illusion that she was sought after merely because she could cook. She was more concerned with what food looked like than what it tasted like, and in her cookery classes she relied very heavily on the quality of her fresh ingredients, her connections with suppliers and, perhaps most importantly, her presentation skills.

But she knew how to make zabaglione; she had forced herself to learn because she sensed that it was one of those showpiece dishes with which you could earn yourself a reputation. She did not actually like the taste of it at all; the richness, the egginess, the sickliness of the marsala. But she liked the fact that, like making pasta, and unlike, say, making tiramisu, it was tricky and it was a skill that commanded the respect of her students, so whenever she felt the see-saw tipping back down on their side, she did puddings.

Although she would have laughed off any such suggestion, Jane also liked the fact that her students almost always failed on their first try at zabaglione. So it was proving today; perhaps it was the thundery heat, she suggested kindly, that was curdling all their attempts. But as she walked slowly behind the row of women sweating over their whisks at the bank of heavy-duty Viking hobs ranged along one wall of the kitchen, she saw, to her annoyance, that one woman was doing very well with it; the square-jawed, Trollope-reading one from Wiltshire.

'Very good,' she said graciously. 'You seem to have been paying attention, Mrs Grice.' She dipped a little finger elegantly into the pale, creamy custard and tipped it with her tongue, suppressing her distaste. 'Lovely. A little more marsala, perhaps?'

'Oh no, Mrs Stamp – or do you prefer Manzini? I find the trick is not to be too heavy-handed with the marsala.' Jane looked at her sharply, but found herself quite unable to decipher the woman's expression of innocent friendliness.

'Do call me Jane,' was all she managed by way of reply, and was turning away when the woman spoke again. Jane turned back to look at her; greying hair, solid around the middle, plump shoulders, skin going a little papery under the eyes. Smug. With revulsion Jane eyed the great heft of her hips, shifting like some monstrous, hidden sea-creature beneath the coarse weave of her gathered skirt.

'. . . so looking forward to it,' the woman was saying. Jane looked at her blankly. 'They're quite celebrated, your end-of-course gatherings, quite the highlight. Not, of course, that we aren't loving the course, too!' She laughed merrily. *Shit*, thought Jane, who had managed to skip over the loathed half an hour of graduation drinks in her mind, perhaps because she had been focusing on Frances's party afterwards.

'And I can't wait to meet your husband. I've been raving about that little gallery he did in Seville.' Jane's jaw tensed. One of those. Architecture groupie, though she didn't look like it, and they didn't usually come from Wiltshire. Clerkenwell, generally. Unless the husband had a place in Clerkenwell and she was safely stowed away in the country, practising her zabaglione.

'My husband's an architect, of course; the practice is in Shoreditch, we've got a little place there, it's very up-and-coming. Though I'm mostly in the country, with the children.'

Jane smiled at her grimly. *Should feel a little sisterly, under the circumstances. Not bloody likely.*

'Well, I do hope we won't disappoint you. Niccolò's in

Rome just at the moment, but he does love our Friday evenings, and I'm sure he'll be able to make it.' And with that, she glided away to administer sympathetic advice to the woman's woebegone neighbour with her failed zabaglione, the sense of triumphant possibility with which she had begun the day's lesson dented but intact.

Approaching Il Rondinaio in the midday heat, her heart still racing, Gina didn't know how to explain Mila to Beatrice, anxious as she was not to alarm her, and so she made no explanation at all, only bringing Mila up the hill with her arm around her, as though she had been in an accident. And indeed that was how it looked, the bruises still fresh on Mila's face and her pallor testimony to recent trauma.

'She's had a shock. Can you make a cup of tea, Beatrice, with sugar in it?' Beatrice nodded dumbly, looking more than a little bewildered, but she got on with it. Mila smiled cautiously at her; Gina was reasonably confident that she'd made herself understood, that Mila knew to keep quiet. It was obvious, after all, that Beatrice was young and vulnerable herself, and in need of both their protection.

Gina scrabbled in her cluttered bag for the paper Frank had given her with his mobile number. She didn't feel quite up to doing all this alone, keeping Beatrice from hysteria and her eye on Mila, who, she suspected, would run for it again given half a chance, let alone dealing with the police. She didn't even know what number you dialled for the police in Italy, and she wasn't about to ask Beatrice, not yet. He answered on the third ring, sounding sleepy.

'Frank, it's Gina. Donovan. I hope I didn't wake you?'

'What? No, no. Are you all right?'

'Yes. Yes, sort of. It's just that there's –' She looked at Beatrice, in the kitchen, and swivelled, casually turning her back on the girl to block her voice. 'I went down to the river this morning, along the road, and I was walking back up here – I thought it would be a short cut, across country – and I came across a . . . a girl. Her body. A dead body. Just below here, just now, maybe ten minutes ago. I – I –' She stopped, feeling a sob rise in her throat, pressed her lips together. Then she breathed carefully, and began again.

'Beatrice is here, she arrived last night in a bit of a state. She doesn't know yet. I've got to phone the police. There's someone else around, too, a girl I found hanging about last night, she recognized the body. It's rather complicated –'

'Stop. I'll come right away. Calm down, then phone the police, in half an hour. I'll probably arrive before them, I'm only an hour away.' He hung up.

Gina put the phone down carefully, took a deep breath and turned back. Mila and Beatrice sat together at the table, each with their hands around a cup of tea, but neither was drinking. They both looked up at her wordlessly for an explanation. She sat down next to them, and took Beatrice's hand.

'Beatrice,' she began. 'There's something I've got to tell you.'

Beatrice's eyes grew large and dark as Gina explained what she had found, and her hand gripped Gina's ever more tightly, but she said nothing. When Gina had finished, she nodded towards Mila and asked, 'Was she there too? Is that why you brought her here?'

The thought that this was as accurate an explanation as any made up Gina's mind. 'Yes,' she said. 'I think Mila knows her. Knew her. The dead girl. She'd been looking for her.'

Beatrice looked at Mila, then hesitantly put out a hand. 'I'm sorry,' she said.

Gina phoned the police. She needed Beatrice's help in explaining where the house was, about the unmade road, and some detail of what had happened, but Beatrice didn't seem fazed by it. She was pale, but careful in her explanations, and polite. Gina wondered at her self-possession, at her gentle friendliness with Mila. They sat down to wait.

As he had predicted, Frank arrived before the police, and immediately asked Gina to point out to him where the body lay. He walked down there alone, leaving the women at the top of the slope looking anxiously after him.

There was a smell, of putrefaction in the heat, but not an overpowering one, just a sweet, rotten tang overlying the clean, dry smell of grass and thyme. And some animals had found the body – birds and perhaps a wild boar – and had pulled and torn at it in places. She looked very young. Frank Sutton stood within arm's length of the girl, but for some time he didn't move. Then he raised his hand as if to touch her dull, bruised skin, but he let it drop before he made contact, and just stood there, and looked. After a while he turned and looked up the hill to the prettily overgrown pergola above, wild roses winding and trailing around it, then back at the girl's body.

At the top of the hill Gina and Mila stood and waited for him, out of line of sight, unable to advance, unwilling to look down. Around them the birds were silent now, as the heat built towards midday. From out of the trees the sound of the *cicadas* filled the air, a sound like static, deafening and oppressive.

The police took nearly an hour to arrive, and when they did they treated the foreigners brusquely, establishing only who owned the property, taking their names and addresses and instructing the four of them to wait in the house. A *carabiniere* stood at the door, smoking, ostensibly standing guard over them but in fact paying them no attention at all as they sat around the table. They watched as first a small group of *carabinieri* sauntered past the kitchen door and headed down the hill, apparently nonchalant but grim-faced, followed soon after by a succession of masked, white-coated figures carrying tripods and shovels and the folding parts of some kind of tented structure.

It was perhaps two o'clock, and lunch had come and gone in the form only of innumerable tiny cups of coffee, none of them having any appetite, before Gina thought to phone Jane. She quailed at the thought, and when the phone rang on and on unanswered in the flat in Florence it was with considerable relief that she decided she would call when they were closer. At last the officials showed signs of packing up to go, and they were given permission to leave. Frank had agreed to take them all back to Florence, and to give his flat as the address at which they could be found. Each of them had by this time been taken aside and questioned in what Gina felt was a rather perfunctory way, and instructed to leave details of their whereabouts for the following few days. Gina was alarmed at the thought that she might be prevented from returning to England, but the policeman questioning her only smiled and shrugged.

'I'm sure it will not be a problem, *signora*. We do not consider you to be a suspect; in fact I imagine you had not even arrived in this country when the death occurred. However we may need to contact you again if any details of your statement come under question or have a significance we do not at present understand. So . . .' He shrugged again, as though to indicate the impossibility of providing any kind of conclusive answer to her concerns.

Gina was not reassured but at least, she thought, she wasn't being forced to remain here; the idea of spending another night in the tasteful, gloomy interior of the old farmhouse, with the black pool concealed behind it, filled her with apprehension. The policeman leant towards her and nodded in the direction of the door, where Beatrice stood looking out.

'Signorina Manzini. Do you think she knows where her father is to be found? Is she aware that the authorities are looking for him?' Gina shook her head, slowly, considering Beatrice's fragile state of mind. 'I am sure she has no idea. Or, rather, she thinks he is in Rome, at his place of work. Isn't he?'

The man nodded absently, leaning back in the chair thoughtfully and showing no sign of having heard her question. 'And the other one, your friend,' at this he looked dubious, 'Mila Grigori. Her papers are not very convincing. I need some reassurance from you, *signora*, that should we need to contact her she will be available.'

Gina's heart sank, but she said stoutly, 'Certainly. At Signore Sutton's address in Florence.' She had no idea of how Frank would respond to this. Though he had already offered his hospitality to them, she told herself, albeit a little hesitantly and assuming, she was sure, that he would be committing himself for no more than an evening. *Still*, she thought, *it'll probably be all right. Probably.*

Jane stood under the shower and let it run until the water turned cold. The afternoon hadn't been too bad: roasting and braising methods, with a *bollito misto* to round the whole thing off, boiled calf's head and tongue, *cotechino* sausage, a nice piece of beef, garnished with mustard fruits from Cremona; it always left them dumb with mingled horror and awe. Jane liked to think of it as a little time bomb, a dish quite utterly authentic, beyond reproach, and so very unlikely ever to be reproduced in their suburban dining rooms. But if it was! A reputation for *haute cuisine*, built up over a lifetime, could be destroyed at a stroke when Mrs Grice brought out that plate of grey boiled meats and unmistakably awful animal parts.

So that just left some pasta sauces and vegetable dishes to cover tomorrow, and the drinks, of course. As for next week . . . It wasn't sensible, Jane thought, to think about next week's course just now. Tomorrow she could expect to hear some more good news from Charles, and then she would be ready for anything. But as she stood dripping in her dove-grey bathroom, surveying Niccolò's expensively specified fittings with a jaundiced eye – tiny glass mosaic tiles, antique French basins, hand-made nickel plumbing – Jane heard the phone. It was the police. Could they come and see her now, with a few more questions?

While she waited for them to arrive, Jane carefully dried her hair, applied her make-up, just a little lipstick and mascara, and dressed. Prada, she thought, for this kind of thing; a dark, soft dress with tiny pleats beneath the empire-line bodice, and grey cashmere slung over her shoulders. No jewellery.

Jane was sitting beneath the window, a glass of mineral water with a squeeze of lemon juice on the table in front of her, when the buzzer sounded. She let them in, two of them, dark-chinned and with knife-edge creases to their trousers, the one she'd met twice before and another, younger one whom she hadn't. They removed their stiff-peaked caps and sat on the sofa opposite her with them balanced on their knees. Jane thought they seemed apprehensive.

'So. What can I do for you?'

'Signora Manzini. There have been some developments. Firstly, could you tell us when your husband was last at your house in the country? Il Rondinaio?'

Jane shook her head. 'I'm afraid I have no idea. A couple of weeks ago, perhaps? Unless he called in there on the way back from Rome the last time he was there, at the weekend. You really should ask him.' She sat back in her chair and sipped her mineral water, and waited. The policemen exchanged glances.

'*Signora*, the problem we have is that we cannot speak to your husband. Since we spoke to him on Tuesday, two days ago, we have been attempting to contact him, and he has persistently evaded our inquiries. And now we have reason to believe . . .' the policeman, the familiar one, paused, as if contemplating how to proceed.

'Signora Manzini, what was your husband's mood when you last communicated with him? Was he under stress of some kind?'

Jane leant forward, fierce suddenly. 'What do you mean? Of course he was under stress; he was very concerned about your investigation. What are you suggesting? That he might have – might have done something? Killed himself? No.'

'*Signora*, are you sure? Are you aware that an investigation into his tax affairs was under way also?' She shook her head, defiantly. 'I know that the *guardia di finanza* was pestering him, yes, he spoke about it to me. He didn't seem worried about it, not particularly. After all, they're always pestering people, aren't they? My husband is not capable of taking his own life, he is too –' She couldn't think of a way to describe Niccolò that would show these people. 'His life is too important, *he* is too important.'

The policeman looked at her with cautious sympathy. The other one, the stranger, said, carefully, 'We have reason to believe that he may in fact have taken his own life. He was seen entering the sea. We have found his clothes; not his car, but it's possible that may have been stolen.'

Quite suddenly Jane was furious; she felt herself consumed with rage at their suggestion. She kept very still. 'No. That's not enough. He would not kill himself. Show me his body, then I'll believe you, but I suggest very strongly that in the meantime you continue to look for my husband. He must be given the opportunity to explain himself.'

They nodded in agreement. Jane didn't understand – did they think he was dead, or not?

'As you say, *signora*, the evidence is by no means conclusive; however, you must understand that what you have told us as to your husband's state of mind is not inconsistent with the possibility of . . . of suicide. And there may be another reason for your husband's – let us call it his *disappearance*. A body has

293

been discovered in the vicinity of your country property; the body of a young woman.'

Jane felt the colour drain from her face; her lips felt numb. She thought of Beatrice, and a terrible, silent convulsion of guilt and fear seized her; suddenly she wanted to tear at her smart costume. 'What – who? I mean – have you identified the . . . the body? How long –' Jane broke off, quite unable to find coherence in her thoughts; she felt her expression slip, her hair grow wild as she ran her hands through it fiercely. The policemen watched, then the younger one spoke.

'The body had been there for some days. Possibly longer. She has been unofficially identified as – one of the –' The policeman paused, as though searching for the appropriate term. 'The immigrant sex workers we know to be active in that area. She was underage – fourteen or fifteen years old, perhaps.' Dumbly Jane nodded, and the policeman leant closer.

'You are aware of them, *signora*? These women?' Jane heard something in his tone, realized he had seen complicity in her nod, and she drew herself up.

'Of course.' She forced herself to remain calm, made an attempt at a contemptuous snort. 'One can't drive 500 yards without seeing a – a prostitute on that road. It's a disgrace. And now – this!' With a boldness Jane did not feel, she held the policeman's gaze, and she could hear the question falter as he pronounced it.

'But you – your husband – you have never had any contact –' His voice tailed off. Jane stared at him, her expression genuinely incredulous, the suspicions she had about her husband's habits insignificant beside the overwhelming rage and misery this man's insinuations provoked in her.

'Contact? With a prostitute? No. Never. As for my husband – of course not. As he will tell you himself. When you find him.'

At this the policemen looked at her oddly; she thought for

a moment that they pitied her, but she said nothing. With faint reluctance the two men replaced their caps and stood; in a daze Jane saw them to the door and closed it carefully behind them. As she turned back from the door suddenly the flat seemed horribly empty, then she felt as though her legs would not support her any longer and she sank to the floor. On her knees in the middle of her drawing room Jane put her face in her hands and, to her astonishment, she wept.

26

For the first half an hour or so, the mood in Frank's little car was muted, and no one spoke. Mila was in the front seat next to Frank, bolt upright and looking ahead, and Beatrice and Gina in the back. To begin with Beatrice had leant against the door and away from Gina, looking out of the window in the lowering light, dusk falling early considering it was approaching midsummer, but after they had jolted down the narrow track for half a mile or so, the two of them, the older and the younger, had been shaken together and they sat with their shoulders touching. Then, once they were on the main road, Frank half turned to the rear of the car.

'So. Where to?'

Beatrice and Gina began to speak at once.

'Do you think –' They looked at each other, and laughed sheepishly. Beatrice began again.

'I really don't want to go back home, not if Dad's not there. If . . . Could I doss down at yours, just for the night? If Mila's going to be there, maybe –' she hesitated. Frank looked back at her quickly.

'OK, if you don't mind sleeping on the floor. The more the

merrier.' He looked at Gina, but didn't say anything, then looked back at the road ahead.

Gina said, 'But you'd better call Jane, let her know where you are.'

Beatrice laughed scornfully, and Gina felt the girl's hunched shoulders relax next to her. At the same time, in the front Mila seemed to settle into her seat, leaning her head back and sideways, turned to face Frank.

'So, you're not married, then?' The women all laughed at once. Frank smiled.

'No, not me. What about you?'

'I was married once,' said Mila, her face suddenly serious. 'No more.'

The atmosphere in the car changed; it felt warm, relaxed, friendly, Gina thought. There was a palpable sense of relief, approaching euphoria, as they drove out of the dark mountains and there, on the horizon, was the red sprawl of Siena across a series of soft hills, topped with the pretty, festive striped tower of the cathedral, bright as a birthday candle in the dying light of early evening.

They talked about Mila, and the immigration centre in Florence where Frank would take her. Hesitantly, Mila mentioned a man she knew – the cousin, or maybe the brother-in-law, of a girl she'd worked with – who had a job in a restaurant in the city, who might help her. Frank said he thought there was a cultural centre for Albanians somewhere, too. Gina looked at her; Mila was laughing at something Frank said and her face was as animated and happy as though the previous three days, or even three years, might have been just a bad dream, the only reminder the bruises on her face, now fading to yellow.

The little car wound up the valleys south of Florence, heading towards the city, the fresh green of the woods a welcome contrast to the black scrub of the Maremma. Then the thick stone walls of the Certosa appeared above them, the hilltop monastery that marked the end of the *superstrada*, the last hill was topped and the great city laid out before them. They coasted down between ancient cypresses towards the massive stone gate, the Porta Romana itself, and it welcomed them back to Florence just as night fell.

Frank stood with the three women at the door to his flat, which smelt stale and stuffy, looking in at the piles of books and the unmade bed, the single electric ring and the tray still waiting to be returned to the Caffè Medici. He watched as they frowned, an unvoiced reproof; Mila silently went to open his windows, and the cheerful noise of the street came in. There was another room off the little hall, apparently unused and still full of unpacked boxes and more books; a couple of inflatable mattresses stood in their boxes in the corner. Frank showed the women their decidedly unappealing bedroom, and they fell silent. In here the mood seemed different, suddenly; the dingy, neglected flat, the gloom, the stifling atmosphere. Frank closed the door to the inner room again.

'Let's get something to eat first,' he said, and Beatrice, Gina and Mila all agreed enthusiastically, united in relief that they weren't going to be spending a long evening here, squeezed between piles of papers while Frank improvised supper out of a three-year-old packet of spaghetti on his single ring. Frank showed them the bathroom, and when they all emerged, having washed their hands and brushed their hair together at the little sink, he seemed to have found a clean shirt and was sheepishly standing by the door carrying the Medici's tray.

Leaning across the bar, Massi took the tray from Frank without a word, but when he saw the three women waiting in the street, he went so far as to raise both eyebrows at once. Before Massi could open his mouth to make the inevitable comment, Sutton had disappeared out of the door and the barman watched as they all walked down towards the piazza.

They ended up in the Casalinga, a modest, half-empty *trattoria* tucked away behind the square, which turned out to suit them very well; none of them felt like a smart evening out, and weren't dressed for one anyway; Beatrice was in her jeans, Mila in Gina's crumpled cast-offs and Gina wearing the skirt and T-shirt she had stepped into that morning, still faintly smelling of sulphur from the hot springs. The Casalinga was a scruffy, shambolic and old-fashioned family restaurant, with an assortment of eccentric ornaments – a gong, a brass platter, straw-covered wine bottles and a whole collection of dolls in traditional dress – ranged around the walls. It had a fixed menu, so they didn't even have to order. To Gina it felt like being in someone's home, like being a child or a guest, waiting obediently to be brought whatever they happened to have in the kitchen, and she relaxed.

All the way back in the car it was as though they had made an agreement not to talk about the events of the day, as though the car was too confined a space to begin any such conversation, and they wanted just to be an ordinary group of friends, coming back from the country. But now they were seated here, in the homely surroundings of the little restaurant, for the next hour or so at least no further decisions had to be made by any of them, and subtly the atmosphere seemed to shift. Mila was the first to speak.

'I saw her, on Sunday. She was still there, when I went home, it was late. I remember looking at her, thinking I was glad it wasn't me still out there waiting. But you know, Sunday ... It's a busy night, often you don't get collected until late. A lot of people going home from the sea. Then I went looking for her on Tuesday, when I saw her shoes.' She looked down at her plate, her eyes glittering with unspilt tears.

Beatrice put her hand on Mila's shoulder, and rubbed it softly. 'At least you went to look for her.' Mila looked up at her, a question forming behind her dark eyes, but she said nothing. Gina could see Frank watching the two of them, looking faintly confused.

'You were there on Sunday, all of you? Did you – see anything?' she asked Beatrice softly, lapsing into English, although uncomfortably aware of Mila frowning in an effort to understand.

Beatrice shook her head unhappily. 'I tried not to look at those girls. I thought they were frightening. They always looked like they didn't care, about anything. Tash and Ned used to laugh at them, out of the window of the car. She used to tease him, asking him if they were his type.' She glanced over at Mila, shamefaced and miserable.

'But –' Gina tried again. 'When you were at Il Rondinaio, did you hear anything, down the hill? Did you see anyone, you know, hanging about, walking in the woods?'

Beatrice shook her head slowly. 'We were at the sea all day. We came back, around, oh, I don't know, seven or eight? I think – I think Dad had been there. Maybe on his way back from Rome. Their bathroom was all steamed up, I remember, like someone had had a shower.'

Then Frank spoke, his voice hoarse and hesitant. 'He wasn't there when you arrived, though? He'd gone?'

'Oh yes.' Beatrice seemed quite sure. 'We wouldn't have stayed if he'd been there. He doesn't like Ned, you know, well, I know he doesn't. And he – I don't know, he never stays there with us, we just don't do it. It ended up being just where we all went separately, to do our own thing. When they first got it, Dad and Jane, they used to have these big weekend parties there, but she just stopped going after a while. Don't know why, especially. She's not really the outdoor type. She doesn't go for barbecues in a big way, and she always used to complain they never had any decent food in the village shops.'

'So, what did you do, usually?' Gina prompted her. 'When you went out there?'

'Well, swimming in the river, at the hot springs. Sometimes there were some cool people down there, and it's just lovely. Isn't it?' She looked at Gina, who nodded absently, but the truth was she was now barely able to remember that first rapturous bathe in the pungent waters; it had been eclipsed by what had followed – the prickle and sting of the undergrowth and the terrible discovery, the broken body.

Beatrice went on, oblivious.

'Cooking. I like cooking. Don't tell Jane, though, I can't bear the thought of her taking an interest. I like looking in the cupboards and seeing what I can make; sometimes we buy fish by the sea or bring stuff from Florence, and we all sit down outside under the pergola and eat.' She fell silent, biting her lip. *Not any more*, thought Gina.

'So that's what you did at the weekend? On Sunday?' Frank seemed intent; Gina thought of the three of them, Beatrice and Ned and Natasha, sitting under the pergola, which had been visible up above from where she had stood, by the rocks below, by the body.

'Mmm.' Beatrice looked as though she was trying to remember, but not happily, not willingly. 'I cooked and they went off. They said they were going to get something for pudding. I didn't know what they were going to get, this time of year, but I think they must have gone to the bar, they came back with ice-creams, but they were all melted. I heard them come back, but they didn't come into the kitchen straight away. They went upstairs, maybe they got their swimming things, because then I heard them out there in the pool, making a lot of noise. I made some sauce, tomato and capers and anchovies – that was what there was in the cupboard – and we had it with spaghetti.'

Gina found the scene thus evoked unaccountably disturbing, the image of Beatrice busying herself in the kitchen, playing house for the older ones. She could imagine, even unworldly Gina could imagine, the relationship between Natasha and Ned Duncan, laughing just out of sight beyond the kitchen window. She saw Mila leaning forward, trying to understand what was being said.

Gina persisted. 'But they – Natasha and Ned – they didn't say they'd seen anything strange? If they walked down that way, to the bar?'

Beatrice looked distressed. 'No, no, I don't think – no. They didn't say anything. They were just being . . . Well, sometimes they could be, like they had a little secret. They thought I didn't know, but they used to go off to smoke, you know, dope and stuff, then come back and laugh at me for being such a goody-two-shoes. That's what they were like, on Sunday, at least Tash was. She kept laughing.'

Beatrice hesitated for a moment, then she went on, quite calmly. 'I sometimes wondered whether – well, it's all too late now – maybe they were sleeping together. That's what you think, isn't it? I'm not stupid. But it doesn't matter, not now, don't you see?'

Gina stared at her, at the girl's small, pale face, wondering whether there was anything left she could be protected from. Beatrice looked back at her.

The food arrived. Their waitress, a homely woman in a flowered apron with a shiny red face and black hair lank from exposure to grease and steam, looked at their serious faces uncertainly before setting down a big dish of risotto with zucchini in front of the foreigners. They all sat back with relief, absolved for the moment of the need to say any more, and she smiled at them. 'Buon appetito, signori!'

Frances leant back on her rose-red velvet sofa in the soft glow of her drawing room, a cloth-bound photograph album open in her lap, her feet in Moroccan slippers and resting on a worn leather footstool. She was waiting for Lucienne and Nino, for their last evening together before the party.

On Saturday morning Lucienne and Nino would, as always, be returning to Cortona for the summer, and she wouldn't see them again for some time. At the party, although she was always glad of her old friends' comforting presence, she rarely had time to sit down with them to talk, but tonight they could go over the last-minute details. While Nino looked on with mild amusement, occasionally interjecting with a piece of sober sartorial advice; they would plan what they would wear and make sure nothing had been overlooked. Frances was beginning to wonder whether, in fact, she didn't enjoy the anticipation of her birthday party almost as much as the thing itself.

Hanging from the frame of her bedroom doorway was the embroidered Indian shift she'd bought today. It was long and loose, of very fine, pale, almond-green silk, tiny mirrors at the hem and delicate embroidery around the neck. She had a pale-green fringed wool shawl, too, that she could fasten around her shoulders with the diamond star Roland had given her for her thirtieth birthday. She thought of that day, and found herself trembling; despite her bravado, she was beginning to feel a chill in the evenings. Frances gazed at the garments, comforted by their prettiness. *Odd*, she thought; *what is it they say about the potency of cheap music?* Perhaps it was because she was fundamentally superficial, Frances thought idly, without distress, but she could always remember clothes. For Frances they were repositories of memory and emotion. She could remember the dress she wore to be presented at court as a débutante, white duchesse satin with tight-fitting sleeves; the colour of the skirt she wore when she broke her arm climbing a tree at the age of nine; almost every one of her mother's evening dresses, scarlet velvet, black satin, scoop-necked, strapless, chiffon, all fragrant with tuberose and her mother's perspiration.

Frances could remember what she was wearing when Roland first kissed her: a dark-red wool suit with glass buttons, a nipped-in waist and reversed cuffs, a flared, ballet-length skirt. She had bought it from a bombed-out shop on Shaftesbury Avenue with three months' War Office pay, unable to resist its hauteur as it stood on the wooden mannequin in the shattered window. She had admired its defiance, a symbol of better things beside the cheap war-manufactured clothes scattered around it, and it had served her well, after all. They had been walking back to Kensington at midnight after a terrible party in a basement in Mayfair, all thin beer and too many cheap cigarettes, and Roland had stopped in a doorway without warning and pulled her against him, burying his head in her neck as the sirens went off behind them, his cheek rough but his mouth very soft, one of her glass buttons flying off into the street. Frances felt a warmth behind her eyes and she closed them and leant her head back in the chair for a moment, longing for it all to come back. She felt the weight in her lap and looked back down at the photographs.

She couldn't think what had prompted her to pull down the album, unless it was a residual desire to settle her emotions with regard to Gina, to remind herself of her marriage, to reassure herself of Roland. She had taken one at random, and this turned out to be from the mid-sixties. She was looking at a big black-and-white photograph of an evening she could still remember, a Chelsea Arts Ball with a classical theme. She and Roland, hands entwined, shoulders touching and heads leaning in towards each other, laughed up at the camera, the photograph taken from slightly above them.

Frances remembered Roland's friend Ted, dressed as a gladiator and clambering up on a velvet seat at the Albert Hall, telling them to smile, before he toppled off, holding his precious camera up to stop it falling. In the photograph Frances was wearing a long toga of white satin, her feet in laced gold-leather sandals, her long dark hair wound up on her head and tied around with cord. Frances realized, to her surprise, that she had been almost beautiful then. Not much older than Gina was now. She was taken aback by the thought; Gina had seemed so tired, worn out and quiet, that evening, when she and Olympia had turned up at the flat. And yet – Frances suspected she had it in her to let go, to enjoy herself. She wondered about the husband, whether he was good enough for her. In Frances's experience, they often weren't.

In the photograph Frances was laughing helplessly, reluctantly, beneath the extravagant Egyptian eye-make-up, and Roland's cheek was pressed to hers, his eyes half closed in an expression of dreamy, pantomime submission. Typically, he had not dressed up. He was wearing his ancient dinner jacket, the grosgrain lapels dull and worn even then; she would still, from time to time, reach into the back of her wardrobe to find it and hold it to her cheek, inhaling the dusty fragrance of Roland and old parties.

Frances turned the page and frowned; there was Vivienne Duncan coyly smiling at the camera. Frances had quite forgotten Vivienne had been there, if indeed she'd ever known. She looked about thirty but couldn't have been more than eighteen, long, smooth, slim legs revealed by some draped white velvet that barely covered her bottom, fluttering false eyelashes, pale lips and an elaborate blonde beehive. She looked back at the photograph of the girl, hanging on for dear life to the arm of some horse-faced son of the aristocracy, fifty if he was a day and dressed as Caligula complete with golden laurels. Vivienne Duncan had become such a monster. *Poor Ned*, thought Frances, *alone up there*, as she allowed the book to fall shut, and closed her eyes so that she might think of happier things.

In her self-imposed dark Frances listened to the comforting sounds of her flat, the bump and scrape of chairs from the apartment above, the creak and shuffle of the old building's timbers, the muffled hum of traffic from outside, and imprinted on her closed eyelids she saw Roland's face. Strange that she always chose to remember him looking as he did when they had first met, dark-haired and strong-boned, rather than as she had last seen him, beaky and yellow in death; then again, perhaps not so strange. She remembered how he had seemed to become transparent, once dead, his body lying in their bed as she waited for the undertakers; in her memory she could almost see through him to the rumpled sheet beneath. It had been as if he had already gone, and all that remained was as thin and light as a shed skin, as if the body was the ghost, not the soul.

Frances sat for some moments like that, with her eyes closed, and very still. Then, taken with the idea that from the outside she might look as though she was already dead herself, she began to laugh and sat up straight, dismissing ghosts from her thoughts. Turning her mind to her newest friend instead, Frances wondered how she might go about persuading Gina to enjoy the party; she wouldn't know many people to begin with, of course, but there were Olympia and James, Jane and Niccolò, and of course Frank. Lucienne and Nino had loved her, and then there was a very handsome radical councillor, Giovanni Neri, Gina might find him interesting, and a fierce painter who lived in an attic in San Niccolò and was always saying how uninteresting young women were to paint and what he wouldn't do for a model with a history . . . That would do very nicely, to begin with, thought Frances, and happily she began to plan the introductions she would make, until she heard the door and stiffly she rose to her feet to greet her old friends.

When they got back to Frank's, drowsy with food and wine, to Gina's eyes the place looked almost like home, and was certainly a lot more like her actual home, with its lopsided lampshades, grubby blanket over the sofa and piles of books, than the polished perfection of the Manzinis' apartment. Gina thought gloomily of the prospect of returning to Jane, the burden of explaining the day's events to her and listening to her ranting about Beatrice's decision to stay away. Perhaps she didn't have to.

Frank inflated the two mattresses in his spare room, but Beatrice had already fallen asleep, fully clothed, on his bed. They all stood and looked at her for a moment, then Mila shook her head and gently removed the girl's grubby trainers and pulled Frank's bedcover over her. She mumbled a little, but barely stirred in her sleep, just pulling her knees up a little. Mila disappeared into the bathroom, leaving Frank and Gina together. They stood in silence for a moment, then Frank cleared his throat nervously.

'Do you want a drink? I think I've got some – some – ' Frank turned and rummaged in a cupboard by the bed, coming out with a crusty bottle containing an inch of Amaretto and another, fuller one of grappa. 'Or tea?' He looked around doubtfully, as though trying to work out where the tea would be, if he had any. 'I don't think I've got any tea.'

Gina looked at him. She felt as though she was eighteen again, wondering whether the offer of a drink meant something or not, and, if it did, whether she should accept. But she didn't feel half as nervous as Frank looked. She pointed at the sweet liqueur. 'Amaretto, that's fine.'

Frank pulled another chair up to his table for her, pushing his laptop back to make room; Mila looked around the door at them, wrapped in a towel, looking pale and young and clean. Frank held up the bottle towards her, but she smiled and shook her head, pointing back towards the inflatable mattress.

'I want to sleep,' she said. 'Last night, the night before, too,

I was sleeping on the ground. This bed looks very good to me.'

Gina sipped her sweet thimbleful of alcohol; it tasted like marzipan. Frank had a glass of grappa, but he didn't drink from it. They sat quietly, and Gina felt as though she was on some surreal camping holiday, the two of them parents to the sleeping Mila and Beatrice, winding down after a day out.

'What do you think?' she asked Frank. 'About the dead girl? Do you think she just ended up there at random, someone killed her and dragged her there because it seemed like it was the middle of nowhere?'

'It wasn't, though, was it?' said Frank. 'In the middle of nowhere, I mean. You can see the house, it's right there, over your head.' He shook his head. 'No. I think she was there, at the house, or on the way there. But I don't know – Manzini, he does have a reputation for dabbling. With prostitutes. But Mila said Evelina was still alive at nine, and he'd gone by then, back to Florence. Isn't that what Beatrice said?' Gina watched as he looked at the small, peaceful head on his pillow, his eyes dark as he contemplated the possibility perhaps, that her father had killed a girl younger than her. 'That he'd been and gone.'

Gina nodded slowly, thinking of what Mila had said, trying to make it fit together. *Evelina was here*, meaning, she had been at Il Rondinaio. Hadn't there been something about the way she'd said it, not like she was speculating, like she was sure? Gina looked across at the darkened doorway to where Mila lay. She could ask her in the morning. Gina didn't want to go yet; she felt as though she had discovered a different life in this room, the air full of possibilities, Frank leaning across the table towards her as though he wanted to ask her something. But she finished the last, sticky drops of her drink, and they stood up together, suddenly very close in the dim room.

Gina looked down and saw Frank's hand, resting gently on

her breast; he looked too, helplessly, but didn't take it away. The room around them seemed suddenly to grow darker, to spin, leaving just the two of them at its still centre. Gina could feel the heat of his hand, something foreign; she had grown so used to the same thing, the same way of doing this, she didn't know what to do next. It was as though the heat created at this point, where their bodies met, carried the burden of an urgent communication she couldn't interpret. She was almost overwhelmed by an impulse to lean her head on his shoulder and breathe him in, but instead she turned very slightly towards the door and his hand dropped back to his side.

They both sighed, together; then, as though nothing had happened – nothing *had* happened – Gina leant over and picked up her little case, the one she'd been carrying when she first saw Frank, and pressed her cheek against his, her eyes closed tight.

'See you tomorrow. Shall I?'

'Yes,' he said. 'Yes.'

Mila lay with her eyes wide open in the darkness of the stifling inner room. As her eyes adjusted to the almost complete lack of light, no window on the street, not even a gleam of moonlight, only a crack under the door from the next room, she could see the stacks of books, a box with saucepans, some kind of broken machine under a film of ancient grease, a coffee machine, perhaps. There was a tall box, the kind you used when you moved house, for your clothes, a couple of dusty suits just visible in it. She wondered about him; there was no sign of a woman here, no kitchen, no stuff for cooking.

Someone had packed up those saucepans for him somewhere; maybe his mother. *If only I had somewhere like this,* she thought, *I would make it beautiful, I could buy a lamp, a tablecloth . . .*

Mila turned over, trying to get comfortable on the mattress; she couldn't get used to the way it gave way beneath her as she moved. She reached out a hand for her carrier bag, now ripped, but knotted to keep its contents from falling out. Her dress – really she should have thrown that away. Her photographs, her money; she couldn't believe she still had all of it, her immoral earnings. Mila pulled the bag towards her slowly and, careful not to let it rustle in the silence that now reigned in the flat, tugged at the knotted ends. She felt around inside, but it wasn't the money she wanted, nor the photographs, this time. She pulled something else out and put it down quickly, as though it might burn her. A silver disc with a film on it. She hadn't wanted to show the others straight away; she had not been sure enough of their connection with the house where Evelina had died. She didn't know whose side they were on, did she? But she was beginning to wonder.

Reluctantly Mila held the CD up to the dim, filtered light from the door, at arm's length like something dangerous, a poisoned talisman. Against her will the images came into her mind, the pictures she had seen on the giant plasma screen: Evelina's sullen, frightened face, the pretty white girl laughing as though it was all a game, the pool of black water. Mila's stomach churned, sour with apprehension, as the other face swam unbidden into view, good looks turned ugly with disgust, a pretty boy intending nothing but concentrated harm, his greedy hand reaching out to hurt and punish Evelina. It came to Mila that he didn't just exist on the screen; he was out there still, somewhere, and if he knew . . . In a sudden access of panic she pushed the thing back into her bag, out of sight. She'd get rid of it tomorrow, Mila thought, ditch it, hand it over to Gina, anything. She heard the door shut as someone left, then the flat fell silent.

Outside the air was hot and damp, the stones of the street slick with moisture. There must have been a shower while they were inside but, although the air felt saturated with humidity, it was no longer raining. The silvered pavement gleamed in the moonlight; it was late, after midnight, and here the city felt quite silent. Gina shivered in the dark, despite the heat, but her mind turned over and over, and she didn't feel ready to go back to Jane quite yet. She walked slowly towards the Piazza Santo Spirito, where she detected light and noise and life.

Despite the weather, the four or five restaurants around the square were busy, late diners eating and talking, some of them damp from the rain. On one corner, at the foot of a huge *palazzo*, the Palazzo Guadagni, sat a line-up of assorted dere-licts and misfits on a stone bench. There was a girl in a wheelchair talking wearily to an emaciated hippy with shaggy hair and crusted nostrils, and a small, dark-skinned man with wild black curls and a bomber jacket was propped on the corner, his legs nonchalantly crossed at the ankles as he tried to sell something to the teenage-girl backpacker sitting next to him. She was blonde-haired and ruddy cheeked, and was looking back at him wide-eyed, shaking her head slowly, a nervous hand on the rucksack at her feet.

On the far end of the bench, half in the shadow of a massive doorway, stood the distinctive figure of the man she had seen, it seemed so long ago, talking to Manzini in the orangery. A man with long white hair and a hawk-like profile, talking to a striking young foreigner, whose murmured Italian was, she thought, accented with English. The younger man had long dark hair, he was attractive, and, by comparison with the rest of them, he looked clean. *He could be Ned*, Gina thought, *Beatrice's Ned, Natasha's Ned, out here again, getting his drugs*.

Gina walked past, looking straight ahead, but she could imagine how she looked, a foreign woman carrying a suitcase, she could feel their eyes on her, nods passing between them that were neither innocent nor flirtatious, and she thought they whispered then fell silent as she passed. She was getting paranoid. She kept walking, through the square, past the church and out the other side, unwilling suddenly to stop or even to slow down until she reached the sepulchral silence of the Via Santo Spirito, and she was alone.

Gina turned towards the Ponte Vecchio, feeling sure that from there she would find a busy route back to Jane's, a road full of strolling honeymooners or college kids, a road where she could feel safe. Disorientated, her bag feeling heavier by the moment, she crossed the Via Maggio, then turned back again, thinking that Jane's street was somewhere to the left, but she found neither the turning nor the busy thoroughfare she was looking for. She stopped. The narrow street seemed quite empty, the towering silent palaces on either side showing no sign of life, the reflections in the wet stone of the pavement undisturbed by movement. Then she heard something, the barely perceptible click and shuffle of feet behind her, and she turned, but there was no one there whom she could see. Each one of the colossal buildings had a great arched entrance, some with huge wooden doors that stood closed, but some open to the street, each offering a dark vaulted space as a hiding place.

Gina turned back again and went on towards the light of a road far ahead that crossed this one, walking faster this time, her case swinging awkwardly as she quickened her pace. She could still hear tiny noises behind her as she walked, the city breathing, the echo of a laugh or a whispered conversation, and she tried to suppress the panic she felt rising in her chest. She passed the darkened portico of an ancient, crumbling church on her right, a rough-sleeper stirring under his blankets, and then she was there, back in the light. She took a deep, delirious breath and waited for her heart to slow.

Jane stood, dry-eyed and motionless, at her window, looking down into the street. She was waiting for Gina to come back – surely she must come back, after what had happened –

and, for the first time since Gina's arrival, Jane found herself wanting, needing, to see her. She would have some kind thing to say, some comforting thing. And then there was Beatrice. Jane quailed at the thought of speaking to her about this, telling her she believed her father might be dead. She couldn't say it yet, not even to herself. *Wait until tomorrow*, she told herself; *let her get a night's sleep, things will look better in the morning*, surprised by her need to spare the girl for a little while longer, or perhaps by her own weakness. Jane felt quite unlike herself, light-headed, unsteady, as though something solid and dynamic inside her had folded and collapsed. She looked down, but the street was still empty, and she turned and went to bed.

Gina ran. She ran and ran until her chest burnt, ran to the Via Maggio to find her bearings, ran down the broad street while the last stragglers stared at her, and found herself, at last, back at Jane's. She slipped silently in through the front door, holding her breath as she listened for any clue that Jane was in, and still up. She didn't want to see Jane, not now. But the drawing room was dark, the shutters closed against the street, and the curving brick staircase in the corner she'd walked down only yesterday morning was dark too.

Slowly Gina walked into her room. It was still and calm, everything as she had left it. She walked out on to the balcony and looked up towards the dark hillside and the brilliant deep blue of the night sky above it, her head back and breathing in the warm evening air. She looked down and in the cone of light cast by the street lamp beneath her she detected the movement of bats in the air, each one just a tiny diaphanous blur as it flittered into the light. *This is a complicated place*, she thought; *this is not a safe place*. And suddenly she felt very tired.

Gina turned back, climbed out of her dirty, crumpled clothes and into the cool, clean sheets, and the last thing she saw before she fell abruptly, deeply asleep was her dress, her new dress for the party like a ghostly alter ego enrobed for romance, shimmering silver in the moonlight.

Friday

27

Had the gatekeeper at the Villa Duncan awoken from the night shift at six, as he should have done, and looked up the hill towards the big house, he would have seen that while he slept Signore Ned had returned; certainly his big American car was back, parked up on the gravel. But the man's head still rested on the copy of *La Pulce*, the local paper he'd been studying vainly the night before in search of a job with more sociable hours.

Up at the house, there was no sign that anyone was awake yet; the shutters were closed, inside and out. In the expensive fitted kitchen everything was neatly tidied away from the previous evening's dinner – just an informal supper, Lady Duncan and an old friend – and now Lady Duncan was in bed, her hair in a net and rollers, her face carefully painted with night-cream, the faint lines around her eyes and mouth ironed out by sleep. In the *mansarda*, the attic room, the maid, Giuseppina, lay on a narrow bed, her features even in repose fixed in an expression of stern disapproval.

The windows to Ned Duncan's room were the only ones left open, and he was the only member of the household already up – or perhaps he hadn't been to bed. Ned lay on his bed and thought about money. Maybe, he wondered, that was what he needed to solve all his problems just now; maybe it was just a question of money. He could pay what he owed, he could get away, he could start a proper life. He could take Beatrice with him – poor little Bea, she'd had such a bad time; and he was old enough, they weren't children any more, after all. At this thought his mouth turned down, as though he were about to cry. They could get married.

Ned had never really thought much about it before, he had just assumed there would always be money there for him. He'd had a job once, after all, although he'd only been paid a kind of token salary; that hadn't mattered then, of course. But if he wanted to get married, if his parents decided, finally, as he supposed they might, that he was turning into a bad lot, then they might stop funding him altogether. This was a thought that Ned found disturbing.

When Cat Morley had died, they'd threatened him – they'd said he would end up like Cat if he wasn't careful – and they'd stopped his allowance for a month or so. But even they, even his stupid, insensitive parents, could see how it had nearly killed him already, when he found out Cat was dead. He had spent a night waiting in the emergency room of a terrible New York hospital, filled with sick people, poor people, people who would soon be dead, too; it had been like an awful cold-turkey nightmare. He hadn't been able to work, he hadn't been able to go out, not for months after that, after he'd come home from New York to stay in the country with them, holed up in the terrible, dreary English countryside, too frightened to go out. So his parents had relented, and the payments into his account were resumed.

Ned sighed wearily. He had to get away. He had to stop being their child. If only his grandfather had not been so obstinate in his determination to prevent Ned gaining access to his trust fund until his twenty-fifth birthday, if only his father didn't try to tie him to the estate, wanting him to go to agricultural college before making him a decent allowance. If only he'd had money, his own money, maybe none of this would have happened, he wouldn't have ended up here, in Florence, at the mercy of people like Stefano. In a mess. He wanted to see Beatrice. Stiffly Ned sat up and swung his legs off the bed.

*

At around eight the phone shrilled in Jane's ear, and she flailed about blindly trying to locate it. She felt leaden with tiredness.

'Yes?' she croaked, when finally she managed to bring the receiver to her ear.

'Sorry, Jane,' said Ned Duncan. 'Did I wake you?' She could hear hostility in his voice, but felt no desire to rise to it. 'I thought you'd be up by now. Hard at work.'

Jane ripped off her eye mask and squinted at the alarm by her bed. Eight. Thank God for that.

'Ned. What can I do for you?' she asked, resignedly.

'Is Beatrice there? I need to see her.'

'I really don't know how you have the gall to ask, Ned. Weren't you the one who dumped her and ran off to the seaside? She's not here. She hasn't been here. I haven't seen her in days. But, if she does turn up, naturally I will tell her you've been asking for her. Where did you leave her, as a matter of interest?'

'Oh, with some guys I know,' said Ned, vaguely. 'She said she didn't want – she wanted to be with friends, after . . . after what happened. But now, well, I just want to be sure she's all right.'

'I see,' said Jane, who did, for once. 'She's not still there, then?'

'No, I checked. Woke them up, too.' He laughed uneasily.

'Well, when she comes back, I'll tell her you phoned. But Ned –' Jane bit her lip, uncertain of how to proceed. 'Could you, why don't you look for her? She won't come back if I ask her, but, I need to talk to her. It's . . . there's –' She stopped, an unfamiliar sensation overwhelming her, of fear, or despair, a stinging at the back of her eyes.

'All right,' said Ned, after a pause, and Jane thought she detected something careful, guarded in his reply. *I must sound mad*, she thought, and pulled herself together, as much as she could.

'I've got to go now, I *am* sorry, Ned, carrots to chop, you know.' Jane put the receiver back down beside the bed with deliberate care and lay down again, staring at the ceiling.

Upstairs Gina lay with her eyes closed, listening to the sounds of the city. It was nothing like the bass rumble of London's rush-hour, a difference which was something to do with the acoustics, the sound bouncing up the canyons created by the tall, narrow, sunless streets, perhaps even something to do with the light blazing through her window, left open last night in the thundery heat. Gina understood that her holiday – the word seemed surreally inappropriate – was nearly over, but she couldn't make it stick; home didn't seem real from this distance and after all that had happened. She felt like she was embroiled in something here, embedded in the terrifying complications of the Manzinis' life, and a few complications of her own, and she didn't feel quite ready to think about any of it.

Gina tried not to think about Frank, either. She wondered instead how Beatrice was feeling this morning, after a night on Frank's bed. What got into teenagers? They seemed to float through death and disaster, drifting from one unsuitable resting place to another, hitch-hiking to Turkey, working in bars in Greece or Israel or Portugal, never phoning their parents. Would that happen to hers? To her beautiful, sleepy Jim, with his long eyelashes. Would he want to trek around India without calling her from one week to the next? Had Beatrice phoned to tell Jane where she was? Gina could hardly blame her for choosing to forget that particular obligation; she'd been grateful enough, after all, not to find Jane waiting up last night. And to be fair, the blame should lie more squarely on Niccolò's shoulders; he was effectively the one who'd cut Beatrice loose.

Gina heard sounds of movement downstairs, but she stayed where she was. She'd heard the phone ring earlier, but hadn't moved; she was in no hurry to greet Jane, and besides, there was a train of thought that was nagging her to follow it to its natural conclusion. What if Manzini had had that girl back at his place, Il Rondinaio, on Sunday, before the kids turned up? And something had happened, something had gone wrong, he'd panicked and got rid of the body as quickly as he could. Perhaps Mila had got the timing wrong – it was possible, after all – or maybe he hadn't come back to Florence when they thought he had. Maybe he'd been down there with her all the time. She thought of what Olympia had said, about Manzini liking young girls, liking to control them, and of what Frank had said, about a man's private tastes sometimes being at odds with his public persona. The beautiful, pure, clean architecture, the perfect couple, impeccably tasteful, with their lives so carefully controlled. Perhaps she was just jealous; Gina thought of home, and, for once, didn't think that she'd want her life perfectly under control.

She felt queasy at the thought of the architect, with his handsome, slender face, his charm, the way he'd held Olympia's hand between his so tenderly. She wondered where he was, whether he'd be back for the party. And then there was Natasha, dead the same night, at the other end of the road from the Maremma, a line stretching between two dead girls. And then last night. But she wasn't going to think about that, was she? It wasn't as if it was connected. If anything could have turned her mind away from the obstinate, ridiculous longing the thought of Frank's hand on her breast provoked in her, it was this train of thought.

Reluctantly Gina got out of bed, and washed her face, startled by the murky water she left in the sink until she realized that she hadn't been near a bath in days and probably still smelt of river water. She stood under the shower and scrubbed, washed her hair, lathered herself from every delicious-smelling bottle in the bathroom and then, beatifically cleansed in every pore, sat on her bed to contemplate what might remain in her suitcase clean and uncrumpled. A white shirt, worn soft and thin from washing, and cotton trousers.

Gina knew exactly why she was suddenly thinking so hard about what to wear, but she wasn't going to admit it to herself. And, if she was honest, if she allowed herself to admit it, there was something dangerous in Frank's appeal, though she wasn't sure whether it was the mere idea of infidelity, or that she barely knew him. After all, the fact that he was still unattached could be seen as suspicious; there was something unhealthy about the musty miasma of a bachelor's shuttered flat.

She rolled up the shirtsleeves carefully, looking absently at her smooth forearm, golden from her few days in the sun. She brushed her hair, and rubbed Vaseline into her lips. If I was listening to another woman tell me about this, she thought before she could stop herself, I'd tell her to sleep with him. She went downstairs to face Jane, her chest tight with anticipation.

Gina couldn't have said exactly what it was about her, but Jane seemed distinctly changed. She was pale and distracted and less groomed than Gina had ever seen her, if not actually dishevelled; a stray hair springing up from her head's smooth profile, her eyes pouchy and tired, no lipstick. Gina apologized for having crept in without waking her, but Jane waved her away.

'Darling, you were right. I needed my sleep last night. Christ, I don't know what's going on, do you?'

Gina was taken aback. 'You mean – the –'

'The dead body of a Nigerian prostitute a hundred yards from Il Rondinaio, is what I mean. No, that sounds . . . I mean, you found her, didn't you? What a nightmare.' Gina looked sharply at Jane, trying to determine whether or not it was sympathy she'd heard in her voice.

Jane went on. 'Sorry. You must have tried to let me know, I was teaching all day. The police told me, and they enjoyed it, too, if you ask me. The thing is, Niccolò – Niccolò's disappeared. Hasn't been seen since . . . Well, Giuseppe, that's his site manager, said he last saw him on Wednesday afternoon, and he thought something was up. He said he'd never seen Nicky like it. Rattled. The police think he's – done something stupid, that's the phrase. They think he's killed himself.'

'What!' Gina was incredulous. 'Do you believe it? Do you think he's – *done* something? To himself? Killed himself?'

Jane shrugged helplessly. 'I don't want to. Believe it. But Giuseppe told me the things they said – all sorts of things about what he's done, or they think he's done, some information the *guardia di finanza* have on him, a corruption charge.'

Gina frowned. 'Surely he wouldn't kill himself because of that? Not a man like Niccolò?' But even as she said it she realized she had hardly any idea of what kind of man he was, only that she didn't much like him, or trust him, and then she remembered the conversation she had overheard in the Boboli Gardens, in that beautiful, scented orangery, the conversation about buying and selling, and blackmail. About Niccolò Manzini's nasty habits. The man with the long white hair and the leather jacket, the man she had walked past last night, talking to an English boy.

Jane shook her head slowly, and looked down into her hands. 'There's the – the dead girl, at Il Rondinaio. I'm sure they think he did it. And they practically accused him of having something to do with Natasha's death before – before all this. Because . . . he had some kind of liaison with her.' She put her head in her hands, and Gina, her mind reeling, gingerly put her arm around Jane's shoulders.

Then Jane jerked upright suddenly, and said, with desperate bitterness, 'They're a real curse, those dreadful girls, you can't pull off the road without bumping into one. And of course they're always getting murdered.'

Gina was startled by Jane's savagery, but rather to her

surprise she found this version of Jane considerably easier to take than the earlier one, the bland, solicitous, concerned one.

'Not really their fault, that, though, is it?' she said softly, thinking of Evelina's glittery toenails and bleeding feet. Jane crumpled.

'No,' she said. 'I suppose it isn't.'

'Did Beatrice call?' asked Gina, knowing that she hadn't. 'To say she'd been with us?'

'What do you mean?' asked Jane sharply.

'She came to Il Rondinaio; she turned up late the night before last. Then yesterday, everything – everything happened, and we just came back. She's at Frank's at the moment.' Gina decided not to mention Mila.

Jane sighed. 'Oh, well. At least she's safe. I'd better . . . I think I'll wait a bit before I tell her, about Niccolò. Until they're sure. Her mother's coming out to collect her on Saturday. Nicky – Nicky called her on Monday night.' *At some point, at least*, thought Gina indignantly, *someone had concerned themselves with Beatrice's well-being. Shame no one's been thinking about her since.*

But Jane was lost in thought, shaking her head slowly and didn't catch Gina's expression. 'I think it's better if we do it together. Tell Beatrice.'

Jane made an effort to smile, but there was a desperate look to it, and the smile turned into a sigh. 'I've got to teach in half an hour, so I'd better get ready. Probably just as well. Make yourself at home.' And she disappeared into the corridor.

Gina looked around the tall white room, which now seemed to her strenuously to resist any attempt on the part of the visitor to make herself at home. It put her in mind, she decided, of nothing so much as an interior designer's idea of a place of Zen Buddhist retreat in which she – or any other human presence – would constitute an unwelcome reminder of the untidy world outside. She retreated into the kitchen, where she looked in vain among the gleaming chrome saucepans for anything resembling breakfast; the concealed cupboards were designed without handles to prevent the uninitiated from ever discovering what they contained, and when Inés bustled in with a frown and a crate of artichokes to prepare for the day she made it quite obvious that Gina was in her way. With a certain amount of relief, Gina went out.

Jane sat in Niccolò's study, the telephone in her hand, looking out of her window at the back of the house opposite, which was hung with washing; giant greying underclothes, a cheap tracksuit, a flowered overall. Its plaster was peeling away in places to reveal crumbling brick beneath, and a stout middle-aged woman was shaking her tablecloth out of the back window. Generally Niccolò kept his curtains drawn to protect himself from sights like this, but this morning she found them curiously soothing. She sat back at his desk. There was a photograph of Niccolò by the sea, at someone's beach house; she felt again that unfamiliar burning behind her eyes as she thought of him, his body in the water, bloated and white. And suddenly she knew he hadn't done it. Not like that. She stood up with a violent movement, and the chair fell backwards behind her.

If Niccolò had killed himself, then he was a much bigger coward than she would ever have imagined. But that wasn't why she didn't believe it. At that very beach house, she remembered him refusing to join a snorkelling party – he hated the idea of the sea swarming with tiny, gelid, slimy creatures, primitive forms of life with claws, or thousands of soft rubbery teeth. He would never do it. Jane had made herself believe the worst, because she had no time for denial, she couldn't be the grieving widow who would rather believe anything than that her perfect, all-powerful husband might kill himself. But now a germ of doubt began to form in her mind, and as she analysed the doubt and it grew into a certainty she felt the debilitating misery of the past twelve hours begin to lift.

She knew he wouldn't do it, whatever trouble he might be in; Niccolò simply didn't believe the world could continue to exist without him in it. Nor, if truth be told, did she believe he could murder a girl, or two girls, with his bare hands. Too messy. What he was capable of, however, was laying a clever false trail in order to buy himself some time. Niccolò loathed the thought of his privacy being intruded upon, and, she felt instinctively, was postponing the moment at which he would have to give in to the police's inquiries. He might – who knew? – even be contemplating beginning a new life somewhere else. But that, Jane decided, was not going to happen. *Over my dead body*. Jane heard the click of the front door as Gina left the flat, and she looked at her watch. Twenty-five minutes, then she would have to begin Roman stewed spring vegetables, and fifty-seven ways with *cavolo nero*.

Over the course of their thirteen-year marriage, Jane had had her fair share of practice at going through Niccolò's pockets – before sending his suits to the dry-cleaner's, naturally. She also kept his credit-card receipts in order, and managed his diary, not to mention making dental appointments and travel arrangements. Because she had always been discreet, and calm, never hysterical, careful never to nag, Niccolò had continued to leave all of these things to her, perhaps without thinking that he was giving her the opportunity to amass any amount of evidence as to his preferences.

Jane knew, for example, which restaurants in Rome Niccolò liked to visit with clients, and which he reserved for his own private entertainment; where he bought birthday and Christmas presents, for her, for his daughters, his ex-wife. There was a specialist lingerie shop she knew he frequented in a southern suburb of Rome, but she never saw anything he bought there. But the information she chose to retrieve under the present circumstances was the whereabouts of his pre-ferred bolt-holes. Some of them were very nice places; an expensive villa-hotel in the mountains near Switzerland, an apartment in Venice he borrowed very occasionally, a private residence in Sardinia. Such places as were shared out among the rich as favours, never lived in, casually offered for a weekend here or there. Niccolò had never taken her to any of these; he kept them for other women. But she didn't think she was looking for that kind of place. Somewhere more downmarket, she thought, this time. Decisively she opened a drawer in her desk, pulled out a folder, and began to go through its contents.

28

Frances was leaning out of her window, looking up at the sky. The sun fell on her face and above her all was clear pale blue, but far across to the west she could see a low, distant bank of cloud, the cumulative heat of the week building and gathering moisture from the sea, perhaps, or a massive front moving in from the Alps. *It only has to hold off for a few hours, now*, she thought, but without urgency. Really, she felt, this close to her party it didn't matter; its meaning was so diffuse, its success or failure wasn't just to do with the physical realities of the weather, how the food was laid out on tables, the temperature of the wine, the musicians, the Chinese lanterns. *All the same,* thought Frances, for whom the pleasure of anticipation was so precious she was reluctant to give up one moment of it, *a visit to the kitchens at the Casa Ferrali might be a good idea.*

Gina walked in the street below Frances and breathed the pungent, fruity foreign smell of drains and exhaust fumes and garbage without disgust, as though born to it. She was on her way to the Caffè Medici – not, she reminded herself, to see Frank. She found herself looking at a dimly familiar brass doorplate with its list of names, then, when she recognized Frances's, looked up at the decrepit, grubby building and its beautiful windows, catching a glimpse of what she thought was Frances's smiling, patrician profile in one of them.

The Medici was empty, except for the man with long white hair drinking beer in a corner, the one she'd seen last night in the piazza. He was reading a sports newspaper, but lowered it slowly when Gina entered in order to examine the new arrival, looking at her curiously. She felt uncomfortable at being inspected so blatantly, and turned quickly away from him to Massi, the barman, who shook his head slightly, the ghost of a frown on his serious, handsome face.

'Don't worry about him, *bella*. Nothing to do with you. Cappuccino?'

She nodded, smiling at being called beautiful so casually, and accepted a warm sweet pastry filled with ricotta, feeling as though she was making progress, now that it was almost too late, in her lessons in Italian ritual. A hefty black girl came in, and Gina stared; she was dressed in a tight catsuit of what looked like black rubber, and her hair was in a stiff, high ponytail. Ignoring Gina, she strode across the pink marble floor of the bar and planted herself next to Stefano, who looked at her without interest.

'They've found her, have they? Evelina? That's what I heard. And where were you?' She was shouting; Massi blithely polished glasses as if nothing was happening. Gina's mouth opened and closed when she heard Evelina's name and she struggled to understand what was being said.

'Evelina's nothing to do with me. I said I'd find out what I could.' Stefano sounded evasive; his voice, however, was more measured than the girl's, easier to follow.

'Yeah, yeah,' said the girl. 'I've been down there in the Hotel dei Bagni. I asked. They said you were in there drinking from seven till you came to get Mila, around ten. So ten other guys could have been with her after the big-shot, the architect you're so keen to screw money out of, while you were drinking with your buddies. *You* they treat like a human being, in the Hotel dei Bagni, huh? If Evelina had gone in there with her throat cut they wouldn't have helped her, would they?' Perhaps only half of what she said was decipherable to Gina, but the gist was very clear.

Stefano leant towards the girl. His voice was loaded with contempt. 'I said it was nothing to do with me, didn't I? If you want bodyguards for your girls, you pay for them. Anyway, there's plenty more where Evelina came from. Though I guess she hadn't earnt enough to pay you back yet, is that why you're mad?'

Betty drew back from him and hissed through her teeth, cursing him in some language neither he nor Gina could understand. She brandished a cheap mobile at him, her Italian becoming almost incoherent. 'She got a mother, though. You want to talk to her mother? Lost her little baby girl? She can make another, I suppose, that's it?'

Gina swallowed; she felt cold. She thought of the girl's dusty, battered blue-black body, her chipped nails and torn feet, and then she found she could not bear to imagine a mother for her. Betty slapped Stefano, beating at him with her flat hand, and Gina gripped the bar, flattening herself against it as though to stay out of their way, although they were on the other side of the room.

'Hey!' Massi called across to them sharply. He shook his head in warning and Betty turned furiously on her heel and left. Stefano flapped out his paper and disappeared from view behind it; shaken, Gina paid for her coffee and left.

*

329

Jane wasn't having fun, exactly, but she was warming to her task. She was nothing if not methodical. Laid out on the desk in front of her were a Rolodex, a pad, a sharpened pencil and Niccolò's laptop. Every few minutes she flipped through the cards, cross-checking names and dates; she made notes in a neat, small hand on the pad, telephone numbers, mostly, frowning with concentration, occasionally smiling, and nodding.

A number of receipts were smoothed out and centred in a small pile on the blotter in front of her; each one, she thought with irony, telling a romantic little story. *Prosecco*, spring lamb, courgette flowers stuffed with ricotta, a good vintage Barolo; strawberries (out of season, she noted, consumed in October in a hotel on Lake Maggiore). Charged to room number 14; perhaps it had a balcony looking over the lake and up to the Alps. Venice came up quite regularly; restaurant receipts, mostly, and she knew he generally stayed in Ferrucci's flat there, but once a bill, stamped 'Paid', from the Cipriani. She had put that one quickly down on the pile without scrutinizing it. They had spent their honeymoon at the Cipriani, although that was not the visit to which this receipt belonged.

By five to nine Jane had tracked Niccolò down to a back-street hotel in Trieste. She had calculated that the city would be a perfect starting point for her search, being both of architectural merit and famously full of whores. It was also handy for Venice, if you wanted to move upmarket, and the Croatian border, if you wanted to disappear altogether, which, in this case, was a strong possibility. In this city, as in every great city of the world that Niccolò visited, she knew there were only one or two hotels where he would be prepared to stay, and Jane suspected that, even in extremis, even when on the run from his wife and the authorities and in desperate need of anonymity, his architect's sensitivity to aesthetics would not permit him to stay in a Holiday Inn or a Best Western hotel, where his sensibilities might be offended by a trouser press or floral border to the wallpaper. In Trieste Jane even knew the hotel from memory, the Miramare, a decaying Belle Epoque boarding house near the port; she and Niccolò had stayed there once, playing at slumming it en route for a conference in Dubrovnik.

Jane asked for him by his own name, by Stamp, and then by his mother's maiden name, Elliott, which was when she struck lucky. She was also fortunate that Niccolò appeared to have already antagonized the management, to judge by the sour tone of the gruff male receptionist, who didn't seem to feel obliged to respect the privacy of this particular guest.

'Could you put me through, please? You could tell him it's his – tell him it's his daughter.' The answer was a grunt rich with contemptuous malice, but she was transferred.

'Niccolò.'

There was a long pause, then with a sigh Niccolò replied. 'Jane,' he said, his voice steely with bitter resignation.

'I haven't got time to talk to you. I haven't got time to tell you what you put me through. And what about your daughter? When were you planning to tell her you weren't dead after all?' There was an uncomfortable silence, and Jane went on.

'I've got a lesson in,' she looked at her watch, 'four minutes. As you already know, the *carabinieri* would like to speak to you; they've found a dead girl – one of yours – at Il Rondinaio.'

'What?' Perhaps it was her imagination, but Niccolò sounded genuinely flabbergasted.

'Jesus Christ, Jane, don't joke about this kind of thing. What do you mean, one of mine?'

'I mean, she's – she was – a whore, by the sound of it.'

'At Il Rondinaio? They found a – a dead prostitute in my house?'

Jane felt like laughing, just for a moment, at the sound of his outrage.

'Not in the house. In the garden. Just the right age for you, too. Fourteen, fifteen? Now, listen to this, and listen very carefully. I want you back here. I've had enough of taking this kind of shit all on my own – your shit. I want you back here. By tonight. If you're not back in Florence for my graduation drinks –'

'Christ, no, Jane, this is infantile,' Niccolò groaned.

'Shut up. All this week I've been humiliated, by the police, by these bloody women, that bitch Vivienne Duncan, even Inés is starting to get insulting. You come back now, I'll stand by you until it's all over, then, if that's what I decide I want, we'll get a quiet divorce. If you disappear, I warn you, your life is over. I'll go to the police, I'll go to the papers, I could even go on TV, couldn't I? I could even call the police in Trieste right now and have you picked up, notify the border police. I want you to go to the airport, or get in your car and drive, I want you to leave your mobile phone on so I can find out where you are every step of the way. Have you got that, Niccolò? Do you understand? Now, I've got to go and teach. Tell me you'll do it.'

'All right,' said Niccolò, quietly. 'All right.'

She slammed the phone down. Jane had never yet had reason to doubt her instincts, and it didn't occur to her that to blackmail a suspected double murderer could look like playing with fire. This was Niccolò, after all, and it was looking like Jane was pretty good at second-guessing him so far. She strode out of her bedroom and into the kitchen, where her students stood at their artichoke-laden chopping boards already looking at her, she thought, with a new respect.

As Gina stood on the threshold of the Caffè Medici, undecided as to which way to turn, three doors along Frank emerged from his front door, deep in thought, and her mind was made up.

'Frank,' she said. His face broke into a smile of pure pleasure, and she found herself smiling back. He kissed her quickly on the cheek, and jerked his thumb back over his shoulder at his front door.

'They slept like babies. They're still in bed. I was just coming out to get breakfast. Are you coming too?'

'Just had mine,' said Gina nodding back at the Medici. 'But –'

'Let's not go in there, eh? I've had enough of Massi's meaningful looks. Let's find somewhere else.' He took her hand, and they set off towards the edge of the city. They stopped outside the gates into the Boboli.

'There's a bar at the top,' he said. 'It's got a nice view.' Gina nodded. It seemed to her that he wasn't going to mention the previous evening, so she said nothing. But after about five minutes spent walking through the high-walled avenues, swallows shrieking and whistling exuberantly overhead, they reached a secluded copse, landscaped to imitate a natural arbour, and Frank stopped.

'Look,' he said, 'I'm sorry, about – last night. It was stupid of me. Insensitive. I didn't mean . . . I just couldn't stop myself somehow. Or is that what they all say?' He laughed, rather miserably.

Gina felt herself tremble suddenly, with the shock of his mentioning it, but she held as still as she could. *Idiot*, she thought, of herself.

'It's all right,' she said, then, thinking how lame that sounded. 'It wasn't – unwelcome. That's not the problem, you know.'

She gestured helplessly, wondering how to explain what she had only just realized for herself: it wasn't that, as perhaps he thought, she was such a devoted natural mother that she was horrified at the thought of being touched by a man who wasn't the father of her children. It was that she was overwhelmed by the possibility that she was in fact a natural bolter – offer her an opportunity and she'd be off like a hare, with not a backwards glance.

Gina took his arm and they set off again, in silence this time, and after a while it was as though the subject hadn't been raised. They walked past a crumbling bust of Nero, a handful of muses and fauns and a grotto dripping with moss, through a tunnel of bent and tangled oak branches and up to the top where, at last, they found the bar. It was just opening for a lazy day's work, and they sat down. The view across the city from the wood-panelled bay window of the little eighteenth-century coffee house was spread out before them across to Fiesole in the north and to the Apuan alps in the west, where just a hazy trace of cloud was beginning to build. They sat and looked down in silence.

'So, how was Jane this morning?'

Gina looked at him, confused. Did he know? Surely he couldn't. Then she realized it was a light-hearted question, just making conversation.

'Well, not good, actually.'

Frank frowned. She went on. 'It's Niccolò. The police think he had something to do with all this. They think he's in trouble at work and that he may have – may have tried to, to kill himself. Has killed himself.'

'What?' Frank looked genuinely horrified; Gina thought she also saw something else – calculation, or guilt.

'Do you think he could have done it? Killed that girl? Or even both of them? Jane said he'd had an affair with Natasha.'

Frank shook his head slowly. 'I'm not sure. Could have done – probably, yes. But that doesn't mean he did.'

'But if he didn't, why would he commit suicide? Not just over a corruption charge?' Gina thought of Niccolò Manzini, of what she knew of him; he possessed a kind of unshakable conviction of his own importance in the world. She couldn't imagine him giving that up.

'Well,' said Frank. 'I did go to see him, on Wednesday. I said things to him . . . If someone had said them to me, perhaps I might – well, it might have seemed the only option.' He frowned, and looked down at his hands. 'But not Niccolò, no. He wouldn't.'

'What did you say to him, Frank?'

'It was about – what happened. When we were boys at school.' He sighed.

'What happened at school? It can't be that terrible, can it?' She looked at him more closely. 'Can it?'

'You don't understand,' said Frank, and he sighed. 'You don't know what it was like. The school wasn't like any kind of school you would know.' Gina nodded slowly, and Frank continued, his expression inward, absorbed in some vision of the past. 'It was a big place, an old Victorian school in Somerset, red brick with turrets, acres of parkland around it. Beautiful, I suppose, from the outside. It had been empty for ages and the headmaster, well, he was called a visionary at the time; he was young, very charismatic. He had revolutionary ideas about children's innate creativity. About making one's own decisions, choosing whether or not to attend lessons. Student councils.'

Frank's expression was full of an obscure longing and Gina thought of her own school, a girls' high school in a suburb of London, staffed by fiercely intelligent and largely unmarried women, a school devoted to moral obligation and high academic achievement that she had struggled against as though it were a straitjacket before submitting. She was taken by surprise with a spasm of affection for it.

Frank sighed again, grimly this time. 'The teachers would take LSD on Saturday afternoons, our creative time; they'd be in the staff wing, all out of it, and we could express our creativity all we liked. All boys – I think there was something about the Spartan ideal mixed in with the school's ethos. We would go swimming in the river, paint the walls, go on drag hunts through the woods chasing whoever we'd decided we didn't like that day. Not pretty.' He paused, and frowned as though trying to remember something, then shrugged and went on.

'The older boys were the dangerous ones. I suppose it should be just blamed on the hormones, you know, adolescence.' Gina nodded, but her eyes were wide, and inside her head she registered the chemical changes under way in the growing bodies of her own children. Frank looked at her, in his eyes a mute plea for understanding.

'Then I turned into an older boy myself, fifteen, nearly sixteen, we went to the pub. We could pass for old enough by then. And one night there was a girl. She . . . We chatted her up. She was very pretty, dark-haired, funny, a bit wild. She wanted to impress us, I think, with how wild she was. So she came back with us to the school – to the grounds.'

Gina sat very still. He went on. 'We were walking through the trees, nearly back at the school. You could hear the noise of the other children; and there was smoke – they'd built a fire. Niccolò stopped, and took hold of her by the arms, he pushed her against a tree, and he –' Gina made a sound, and involuntarily Frank put his hand out towards her.

'She didn't know what was going on, to begin with. She didn't know – she couldn't believe what was happening. And I just stood there. I couldn't even shout, my voice kept cracking, I was just whispering, trying to ask him not to do it.'

Gina was shaking her head slowly, in silence. Frank spoke again.

'He didn't care. It's hard to explain what Niccolò was like – *is* like, but he hides it better now. He didn't understand right and wrong. In a way, of course, that makes me worse than

336

him, because I knew it was wrong, but I was too frightened.'

'Frightened?' said Gina, looking into Frank's face, which was as still as marble and dark with introspection.

'I'm not frightened of him any more,' said Frank. 'But then – I had no friends at school, and it was all about allegiances, that place. My mother was dead, and Niccolò knew she had killed herself – I don't know how; perhaps his parents told him.' He stopped. Gina thought she should comfort him, but she couldn't bring herself to stretch out her hand, and the space between them seemed unbridgeable, a dark, cold place.

'I don't know. I'm so sick of finding excuses for myself. The truth is, I didn't know what to do. I should have known what to do.'

Gina nodded slowly and looked at Frank's bowed head; she thought about Beatrice, and the life that stretched ahead of her, with a father like Niccolò. Gently she put a hand on his shoulder. 'Better get back. I think Jane might need some moral support, believe it or not.'

They stood up, both stiff and pale, and turned to look outward, towards the bright roofs, then turned to walk back down to the city. Neither of them spoke as they walked, and at the gate they stopped.

'OK, Frank,' said Gina, 'I'll see you later. It's OK. Thanks for telling me.' She made to leave.

'Wait a minute.' She turned to see Frank dredging in his pocket. He came up with a silver disc that looked to Gina like a CD, only smaller. 'Mila wanted me to give you this. She seemed quite serious about it. She said it's a film, of Il Rondinaio. I wasn't quite sure what she meant. God knows what she's doing with it.'

Gina looked perplexed, turning the thing over in her hand, holding it up to the light as if it might reveal something to her. Then she shrugged. 'A DVD? I don't know how these things work. Maybe Jane's got a machine that'll play it, back at the flat. It's got everything, that apartment.'

'See you later? At the party?' asked Frank. 'You still feel like going, after all this?'

'Oh yes,' said Gina, 'I want to go.'

29

By two o'clock it was obvious that a change in the weather was under way. From up on the hills, at Fiesole or the great fort above the Boboli, some blue sky was still visible, far off to the east, but it served only to point up the grey of the clouds thickening and swirling around the wide basin of the city. Looking along the Arno to the west, the trees of the Cascine, the park running alongside the river, looked almost black, and the distant view of the marble mountains of Carrara was dimming as the moisture rolled in ahead of them from the sea.

Down to the south, in the far distance, looking from the ancient look-out posts and fortresses of the Etruscans and the holiday villas of the Medici, perched on the pretty hills of Chianti, the sky was black with thunder over the Maremma. A ghostly, shining mist hung in the air over Siena, joining the cloud to the earth, a mirage of rain. It was still very hot, and even in the air-conditioned shops around the Ponte Vecchio the aproned shop-girls flapped at their blouses, fanning themselves and complaining they couldn't breathe for the humidity. In the fetid backstreets of the Oltrarno it was hard to say if it was better to stay indoors, panting in the heat, or to walk the streets in the faint hope of catching a breeze in the still, scalding afternoon.

Along the Via delle Caldaie most shutters had been flung open to allow some air to enter now that the sun had all but disappeared. The sky was like neon, a livid glaring white, the fierce heat of the sun unable to break through the layer of cloud but illuminating it all the same and inducing migraine and palpitations among the population below. Mila hung out of Frank's bedroom window, watching the street, quite unperturbed by the heat.

It had almost been worth it, she found herself thinking as she looked, all of this weird last week, all the terror and the sleeping rough, worth it just to be back in a real city again, to breathe in the smell of drains and cars and to listen to people talking in the streets, going to the market, complaining about the weather. No more poisonous looks from country people, or hours alone watching lorries roar past in the middle of nowhere. She felt like hugging Frank every time she saw him but she thought that might freak him out, so she just tried as hard as she could to be helpful. While he was out she had cleared up: dusted his books, cleaned his windows and his bathroom and mended his fridge (a loose connection at the back). She had taken out his empties and the rubbish, and gone to find the restaurant where Eva's cousin worked; it was a surprisingly nice place, for tourists mostly but very clean, good kitchens. He wasn't there, the cousin, but they'd said she could come back the next day. When she had got back to the flat, Frank was back, and he'd taken her out for a meal, so he must have been pleased with what she'd done. Not a fancy meal, of course, just a little place around the corner, but still, she thought, that was nice of him.

The only thing that wasn't looking good was Beatrice. Mila had tried to talk to her in the morning, when it was just them, but she'd clammed up. Mila could tell she was a nice girl, still young; something had gone badly wrong somewhere in her life, though. They started talking about her friend who had died, and she'd been upset, but she'd managed, just a bit tearful.

Then Mila had asked if she had a boyfriend, and that was when she'd stopped talking. Now she was still where Mila had left her, lying on Frank's bed with her head buried in the pillow. She wasn't crying any more but she was white and still, cheek flat on the pillow and staring out of the window at nothing, like she'd given up. Mila wondered whether she'd done the right thing, giving Frank the disc for Gina; perhaps she should have shown it to Beatrice, maybe that would have helped. But all she could feel was relief that it was off her hands, and besides, Beatrice didn't look like she was in much of a state to deal with stuff like that. After all, both the girls in the film were dead, now – Mila knew that, because Beatrice had shown her a picture of her friend Natasha, who'd been murdered, and she was the smiling one, with her arm round Evelina beside the black swimming pool. In fact the guy with the camera, the one you saw going off at the end with Evelina, he was the only one of the three of them still alive, if you thought about it.

Gina lay on the grey velvet of the sofa in the Manzinis' living room, her bare feet up, chin propped on her elbow as she looked at the darkening street outside. It seemed early to be getting dark, no later than five o'clock, but perhaps it was the weather; she'd barely seen the sun since this morning. Above her head the air-conditioning fan turned lazily in the heavy air, but still Gina's white shirt clung to her, and she felt slightly feverish, as though she could not move without breaking out in a sweat.

There was something corrupt about the intense humidity of the city as the storm approached; she could imagine adultery breaking out like cholera in this kind of tropical heat, as though languid half-clothed expatriates stretched out on their verandas might well consider it to be the only possible activity for the endless, debilitating afternoons. Was that why Niccolò Manzini was unfaithful? She thought of what Frank had told her about Niccolò, and doubted it was anything so obvious. She heard the door behind her, the kitchen door, and Jane came in.

Jane looked tired, as she slowly removed her white apron, and Gina noticed that her hands, untying a troublesome knot, looked soft and worn, the nails unvarnished. Gina had never imagined she could look this – human – and her first thought was that perhaps it was getting to her, the uncertainty about Niccolò. But when she looked up at Jane's face she saw that in fact she seemed quite calm, and, more than that, she looked happy. She smiled at Gina.

'Thank God that's over for another week. Just the graduation drinks to get through, but I expect Nicky will be here by that time. Don't look so worried.'

'But –' Gina was astonished. 'What? Have you heard from the police? Have they found him?'

Jane laughed delightedly. 'No, they haven't found him. I've found him. He's coming back. To face the music. Now, darling, while I'm in the shower, why don't you get us a drink? Do you know how to mix a martini? Bring them into my dressing room, and we can get ready together.'

Dumbly Gina nodded, trying to work out this latest transformation. As Jane disappeared down the corridor to her room, she found herself shaking her head. She wondered if what Jane had said could possibly be true. It seemed more likely that she was having a breakdown.

The clothes hanging from a steel rail and covering an entire wall of Jane's dressing room were arranged by colour, although as they were all in tastefully neutral shades they appeared to merge seamlessly from black to charcoal to chocolate to taupe. Another wall was covered with shelving on which were stacked plump cashmere sweaters, and shirts in cotton and linen, crisply ironed and neatly folded and almost all a brilliant and unmuddied white. Despite the conclusions she had reached about Jane and Niccolò's household, Gina felt her heart lift in yearning for such order in her own life, although perhaps instead of the black leather Le Corbusier *chaise longue* resting along a third wall she would have chosen something rather more inviting.

Gingerly Gina sat down, with very much the same mixture of feelings she experienced at the dentist's; perhaps it was the leather *chaise*. She rested the brimming, frosted cocktail glasses on a little glass table that she assumed to be there for the purpose. She was considering the idea of Jane thoughtfully sipping at a martini while contemplating her wardrobe, and had decided that the image made Jane seem considerably more normal, when Jane herself appeared in the door, wrapped in a large white towel.

Jane's shoulders were lightly freckled and her face stripped of make-up looked its age and really quite ordinary, although at the pretty end of the scale. She sat beside Gina on the divan and leant over for her martini, draining half of it in one thirsty draught.

'Darling!' she said with mock surprise. 'A hidden talent! Delicious.' She rubbed at her hair and pulled off the towel that had been twisted around it like a turban.

'What will you be wearing tonight?' she asked. 'No, don't tell me, surprise me. If you bought it with Olympia I'm sure it'll be very striking. Striking is her thing. Anything you need to borrow? Jewellery? No? What about a little evening bag, I've got a lovely little silvery thing, goes with everything –' she broke off and carelessly pulled out a drawer. It glided open silently, smooth as silk, to reveal ranked evening bags: pouches and clutches, beads and velvet and brocade. Jane pulled out a little silk sack, and tossed it to Gina, who took it obediently.

'There,' Jane said. 'Now, I think I shall be indulging myself tonight, too; what do you think of these?'

She reached into the back of her wardrobe and pulled out a pair of shoes Gina would never in a thousand years have thought her capable of buying. They were red satin, with slender five-inch heels and a spaghetti-thin ankle strap set with tiny rhinestones. Jane put one on and turned her foot this way and that, admiring her slender calf and pretty ankle.

'Oh, they're – lovely,' stammered Gina. 'Gorgeous. Ah . . . what will you be wearing with them?' And she scanned the row of muted greys and browns across the wall.

With a sly smile Jane pulled open a concealed drawer in the wall behind them, and took out a silver box that rustled with tissue paper. Purple tissue paper.

'Niccolò would – will – have a heart attack when he sees me in this.' And she shook out a red-satin sheath dress, and stepped into it. It plunged at the front to just above her navel, draped so that it concealed her white breasts but offered the possibility that an unguarded movement would expose them completely. At the back it fastened with tiny crystal buttons which ran down from between her shoulderblades to the base of her spine. The transformation was dramatic; the impeccably tasteful trophy wife had become a kind of gorgeous, glittering Cruella de Vil, and Gina almost applauded. She was dumbfounded by the change in Jane. She was reckless, expansive, jubilant.

'Niccolò absolutely loathes this kind of thing. On me. But do you know, I am sick to death of grey. He's always saying how flattering it is to the older skin,' she curled her lip disdainfully, 'and how serious and dignified I look. For God's sake, I'm only thirty-eight! And not only that, when he started saying that kind of thing I was only *twenty*-eight.' She drained what remained of her martini and bellowed, 'Inés!'

She turned to Gina. 'He only likes girls. Of course, he

doesn't make it obvious, but I know, all the same. I think he knows if I had proof even I would have to go to the police. And –' she hesitated.

Inés appeared in the doorway, looking rather startled, possibly at the sight that met her eyes. 'Could you bring us two more martinis, please, Inés?'

'Yes, *signora*,' said Inés, then, hesitantly, 'I am laying out next door, the canapés and drinks. Will Signore Niccolò be here for the drinks?' Gina looked at Jane nervously, but she seemed quite calm and smiled sweetly at the question.

'He should be here in about twenty minutes, Inés. Although I don't know why you need to know.'

'It is the ladies, *signora*. The students. They have been asking.' Jane frowned, but said nothing, only flapped her hand at Inés to hurry her along. She walked thoughtfully across the room, up and down in front of her tasteful wardrobe, as if considering something. She seemed to make up her mind and stopped.

'You know why Melissa wouldn't let the girls come out here, for all those years? She suspected him of messing about with them. Abusing them. She didn't have any proof either, but she knew what he liked. Of course he wouldn't have any of that, got on his high horse and sued her, took her to court for access rights. She couldn't say what she suspected, because he'd have sued her for slander too. And then –' She stopped, but only to take a breath. 'Then he starts screwing their best friend. Darling little Natasha.' Gina felt as though she had been hit with a sledgehammer.

'But – did he? Abuse his own daughters? Surely not?' She felt herself pleading, unable to rid herself of the image of the fifteen-year-old Niccolò Manzini torturing a girl. Did Jane know about that?

Jane looked at her, then looked down, with uncharacteristic reticence. 'God, I don't know. I used to think absolutely not.

You tend not to believe that kind of thing, particularly if you have a good reason for wanting it not to be true. But now – who knows? The girls, I suppose, but they give nothing away. Not to me.' She looked up. 'I don't think it's true, Gina. It is the kind of thing Melissa would say, she hated him enough; after all, it must have seemed the perfect way of getting revenge.'

Gina nodded, slowly, and looked up at Jane, wondering whether she was trying to justify her inaction. Jane looked straight back at her.

'If I had really believed it, darling, I would have done something about it. I'm not such a coward, you know, and unlike a lot of people I'm not actually afraid of Nicky. Now Natasha, yes, he did have an affair with her. I have it from the horse's mouth. One of the horses, anyway. He admitted it.'

'But, does Beatrice know? You know how she feels – felt – about Natasha. She's in a delicate enough state as it is.' Gina stopped, overcome with horror at the thought of such heedless cruelty. She couldn't imagine how a father could feel those things about his daughters, or even about girls young enough to be his daughters. She thought of Stephen with a rush of affection, his slow, careful way with the children, his kindness, and patience, and about his tenderness with her. Then she thought of Niccolò, and shuddered.

'Do you think he cares? He doesn't give a damn. He thinks he's God, thinks these girls are put on earth for his pleasure, maybe he even thinks they like it. Maybe they do, for a bit. To be honest I don't care about the girls, I hate him for the way he humiliates me with them. I've had enough of it now, though.'

Thoughtfully, Gina sipped her drink and watched Jane. For a moment she thought she saw a sag in her posture, a defeatedness about the mouth, but it was swiftly corrected, and she stood straight, admiring the curve of her red-satin hip in the mirror.

'Jane –' she began, hesitantly, then took courage. 'Did you and Stephen – did you have a . . . a thing, once?'

Jane grimaced. 'Mmm, well, yes. Sorry, darling. But it was an awfully long time ago, you know.' She paused as if reflecting on something.

'But do you know, I think things haven't turned out too badly for you, have they, darling? I mean, of course, Stephen's a tiny bit – staid –' *No he's not*, thought Gina, defensively. 'But the children, I mean, all things considered it's probably just as well Niccolò and I didn't – but they are rather lovely, aren't they, children? If they're your own?'

Gina looked at her hard, unable to decipher Jane's expression, which seemed to contain a trace of regret, something she wouldn't have hitherto thought likely. She was considering how she should respond when she felt something at her shoulder in the doorway, a breath of cool air, a faint fragrance of lime and basil, and she half turned, and looked up, then felt winded with shock. It was Niccolò. He wore a close-fitting dark suit and a pale-silk shirt, lilac, and she found herself looking into his face, his narrow, saturnine face, which smiled down at her with a confident, boyish charm that was beginning, she saw suddenly, to look wolfish. She felt profoundly repelled by him, his scent, his smile, the feeling that he might at any moment lean down and take her hand lingeringly between his, and abruptly she leapt up from the *chaise*.

'I – I – I'd better get dressed,' she stammered, and backed out of the room clumsily.

'Darling,' called Jane breezily after her, 'would you mind just shutting the door after you? And could you pop along to the kitchen and tell Inés we'll be there in ten minutes?'

As Gina shut the door, she heard Jane say in a husky, mocking parody of seductiveness, 'So, darling. What do you think of the dress?'

In a daze, Gina walked down to the kitchen, trying to digest

Jane's new mood and the information she had so carelessly imparted. As she walked down the corridor she passed an open door which revealed a viewing room rather like that at Il Rondinaio, a giant plasma screen presented like a portrait on the facing wall; she barely registered it, but the sight triggered something in her memory, something she needed to do. As she stood in the gleaming kitchen and repeated Jane's instructions to Inés, it came to her: the disc. Mila's disc.

The film ran for no more than ten minutes. It was a home video, with a considerable amount of camera shake and occasionally wild movement, but the sound was clear as a bell. The first frame showed a pale, beautiful, laughing face, framed by short dark hair, eyes made up like a sixties starlet's, and a teasing, curved mouth. Swaying slightly, the girl drew another face close to hers, the face of a young black girl, and as Gina looked she felt a taste as bitter as bile come into her mouth.

The first stab of recognition came subliminally, as she saw that the girl was missing an earring; she had only one big gold hoop shining against her glossy dark cheek in the left ear, and the other was empty. Gina thought of the torn earlobe of the girl bent at the waist like a child's Barbie and left mutilated on the hillside, then, as she gazed wonderingly at the dark background and the camera swung around to the spotlit façade of Il Rondinaio, she realized where they were and she remembered what she'd glimpsed at the bottom of the black water of the pool: the golden hoop. Suddenly she knew, without needing to look at the date and time across the bottom of the screen; she knew what she was watching.

The face of the girl who would soon be dead, Evelina's face, was a mask of sullen misery, overlaid with determination; she gave the impression that she was stubbornly, desperately sitting something out, waiting for it to be over so that she could go.

'Just a little kiss, come on, give her a kiss. The camera's rolling, this is your big chance, darling. Turn you into a star,' crooned the other girl's voice. There was something slack about her diction, it was lazy and drawling, and it dawned on Gina that she was drunk, or high. She realized she must be looking at Natasha.

'God, you public schoolboys, you're so scared of it, aren't you. Go on, let your hair down. Do it for me. I know what it is, you're scared of what Mummy would say if she found out, aren't you?' Gina felt the hairs on the nape of her neck prickle and rise; her face felt stiff and immobile. She thought of the schoolboy Frank, and looked at Evelina's patient, frightened face. *The girl wanted to go home*, thought Gina. *Just wanted to go home.*

The camera skewed and lurched, and Gina caught a glimpse of suppressed laughter, a scuffle, then the camera seemed to have changed hands. Gina could see a man, a young man she did not immediately recognize, although there was something familiar about his pale, handsome features. The boy she'd seen in the piazza, talking to the man with white hair. He half turned his back to the camera, lifted his hand, slowly and deliberately, and placed it on Evelina's breast, squeezing until she winced, but she didn't pull away, held herself stiff. He began to pull her halter top over her head, jerking at her. There was nothing erotic in his touch; the rough, peremptory movements spoke only of latent violence, to Gina, and hatred, although she couldn't have said whether he hated Evelina or the girl behind the camera more.

The camera shook slightly, and then proceedings were interrupted by the sound of a clear, high voice calling from off-screen. 'What are you doing out there, guys? It's getting cold. Come on!'

'Quick. Get rid of her. Take her down to the track, she can find her own way back.' It was the girl's voice. The camera lost focus and tipped drunkenly, whirled round to show Beatrice's silhouette against a window, inside the house, cupping her hands around her head against the glass, trying to see out.

Then the camera righted itself to show the girl, Evelina, hunched and miserable from the rear, limping across the stiff coarse grass of the lawn at Il Rondinaio and next to her, stiffly keeping his distance, the tall boy – man. Evelina's hand was out, pulling on his jacket as though pleading for something; perhaps she wanted her money. But as he turned to gesture to Natasha with the camera to stop filming, to go, Gina caught an unforgettable expression of furious disgust on his face and she felt a premonition about him that raised the hairs on the back of her neck. Then white light flooded the screen and it went blank.

30

Slowly Frank Sutton was moving around his apartment, tracking down something to wear for the evening, a tie here, a clean shirt there, even a pair of trousers still in their dry-cleaning film. The presence of the two women seemed to be making him slightly uneasy.

Mila smiled at him cheerfully, upbeat after a more promising day than she'd had for some time. But Beatrice was listless, lying face-down on his bed, her face expressionless, turned sideways to stare blankly out of the window. Her hand was curled around her little silver mobile phone protectively.

'Has she called anybody?' Frank spoke in a whisper. Mila shrugged.

'Not as far as I know. Funny, isn't it? Hasn't she got any friends? The boyfriend?' She curled her lip a little as she said it.

He frowned in concentration, absently buttoning his shirt, an old silk shirt, nice heavy silk, Mila noticed, but fraying at the seams here and there. He tied his tie, then turned to Beatrice.

'Are you sure you don't feel like coming out to Frances's later? It might make you feel better. It can feel a bit claustrophobic in here, when the weather's like this.'

Beatrice shook her head, her face buried in the pillow.

'No thanks.' Her voice was muffled. 'Maybe I'll go for a walk later. I just don't feel like talking to anyone.'

Frank shrugged. Mila wondered why he was being so kind. Maybe he was a kind man.

'OK. I'll leave my mobile number; if you feel like getting out I'll come back for you, just give me a ring.' She nodded into the pillow.

Frank sat at the window for a while, looking at the street below, evening shoppers frowning up at the sky and hurrying to get home before the inevitable downpour. The atmosphere in the flat was making him uncomfortable, Mila could tell, and it did feel like a sickroom. She wasn't surprised when he said he was going out for some air, rain or no rain.

'Keep an eye on her, will you?' he asked Mila, jerking his head backwards towards the bedroom. Mila nodded incuriously. 'Sure,' she said, smiling. 'You have a nice time, huh? Say hi to Gina from me.' Frank nodded without giving anything away, and left.

Outside, Frank seemed uncertain about where to go, and finally he came to a halt in the Piazza Santo Spirito, beside the statue of Verdi. No drunks tonight; they were sheltering from the heavy glare of the grey sky. Although it wasn't yet actually raining, a few figures were visible huddled in the cavernous hallway to the Palazzo Guadagni, passing a joint and drinking beer. Frank looked up at the faded yellow façade of the church.

As he stood looking at the church and the little alleyway

down to its right, where Natasha Julius had met her death, Cinzia whistled at him from the stone bench below the Guadagni. When he turned she blew him a kiss from her wheelchair.

'Where you going then, beautiful? Gonna take me with you?'

Frank walked over and sat down on the bench beside her.

For a moment, as he smiled at Cinzia, she looked as though she thought he might be going to ask her to come with him. 'Not going anywhere, just yet.' She sighed.

'So what do you do then, when it rains?' he asked her.

She shrugged. 'There's a couple of bars we go to. Sometimes we go to someone's place, whoever's feeling generous. We used to go to Stefano's now and then, when he lived down here.' Cinzia gestured along the street, then fell silent. She looked like she was considering something. They sat together in silence.

'Get us a beer, will you?'

Frank went and got her a beer from the bar, the Cabiria, where he'd sat waiting for Stefano. The outside tables were empty tonight, the waitress wandering between them skimming them with a desultory wipe. Cinzia took a swig, then scrutinized the piazza as though looking for someone.

'She was pregnant, you know, that dead girl.' She nodded towards the Vicolo degli Innocenti. 'Everyone knew that, she would get stoned and walk around the square telling anyone who even looked at her. I think it was Stefano's. Last few weeks, she was hanging around him like she needed something from him he wasn't giving her, like a dog hanging around to be fed. It wasn't the smack – she was getting that. And he was screwing her, all right, we all as good as saw them at it, going off into his bedroom round at his place.'

She followed Frank's gaze, across the square to the façade of the church; on his face was an expression of unhappy longing, as though if he stared long enough at its noble proportions he could ignore the squalor and the wrecked lives it over-looked. Cinzia was looking down the alleyway beside it.

'He's not here, is he?' she said, looking around, nervously. Then in a rush: 'Down there, just a couple of doors down from the shop window where she – you know – there's a *fondo*, a garage, we go to sometimes, and a cellar. Used to be a wine cellar, owned by some old smackhead, and when he's feeling generous he lets us in to drink, or shoot up. When the police are about. I saw her go down that alley, with Stefano, the night she died, and I thought that's where they must be going, to the *fondo*, for some privacy. Then later on, I saw the young guy go down there too, her friend's boyfriend. Ned Duncan. Didn't see any of them come back. But you know, what I can't stop thinking about is, if there was a – like a party going on that night in the cellars, when they all came out, usual time, three or four in the morning, all those stupid hop-head junkie bastards, they'd have all walked right past her body, lying there. They didn't do nothing. Just left her there.'

Cinzia shivered, her face drawn and serious and frightened, no trace of her seductive, heartbreaking smile. Frank put his arm around her shoulders and squeezed them.

'You're not like them, though, are you Cinzia? You're telling me the truth. That's what's different about you. I'll come and find you later, OK? I've got a few things to get done first.'

He left her there, holding on tightly to her beer bottle and staring up at the church, and disappeared down the alley, still looking for something.

Frances stood on the balcony at the Casa Ferrali and looked out over the garden, her face held high, tilted up to the sun-set and smiling with every appearance of satisfaction. She was flanked by Nino and Lucienne, her old friends, he impec-cable in a satin-lapelled tuxedo and she in an embroidered purple velvet Moroccan kaftan. Lucienne had her arm around

Frances's waist, her little cropped head reaching only as far as Frances's shoulder, where it rested. As usual Nino was fussing about the weather.

'You know, Frances my darling, it isn't too late to have them lay the tables in the house. We could eat very comfortably in the large drawing room, we could even have the windows open to the balcony if you insist.'

Frances shook her head and smiled at him gently. She could not explain to Nino that she relished the idea of a storm, of a wild, Bacchanalian evening at the mercy of the elements. It made her feel young and brave and reckless, reminded her of England, where no party was ever safe from the prospect of rain, of drinking champagne as a débutante in a dripping, muddy-hemmed crinoline in the sodden countryside at coming-out ball after coming-out ball, of swimming in the Serpentine in winter. The Italians' insistence on taking every possible measure to protect themselves from the weather, particularly when their weather was, by and large, so very hospitable, was mysterious to her. They were quite unable to comprehend the sensuous thrill of running out into the rain bare-headed and shoeless, nor the glorious, exultant release of letting the elements have the upper hand, now and then. It was her last act of defiance, an Englishwoman announcing to the rest of the world that she was not afraid of anything.

At the top of the garden, beneath the high stone wall and its sentry post, tables were laid along the wide green avenue and between the fig and almond trees were stretched white canvas awnings, lifting already in the breeze. Gleaming candelabra were set along the tables, silver bowls filled with gardenias, camellias and rose petals scented the air. The coloured lanterns strung between the gnarled trees of the copse had yet to be lit; Lucienne had insisted that it should be done at the last minute, otherwise they would all burn out and the effect would be spoilt. In the formal garden the waistcoated waiters were already setting out ranks of shallow champagne glasses and filling vast ice-buckets. And they all laughed. Below them they heard the sound of voices, the first arrivals at the great oak door that opened on to the street.

Olympia and James emerged beneath the balcony and turned to look back up at the three of them. On their faces Frances saw the glow of happy expectation, and carefully she made her way down the little iron staircase to greet them. Olympia flung her arms around Frances, embracing her in a warm, scented cloud, and Frances smiled at James's handsome, lined face over Olympia's shoulder. He smiled back at her with an expression of relaxed indulgence.

'Isn't she something?' he said, indicating the laced curve of Olympia's back in her new dress. Olympia posed for them, a hand on her round hip; her lips were very red, and her hair, shining black as liquorice, was twisted up in a knot. Frances nodded in grave agreement. 'I think you've been neglecting your art, Olympia,' she said, 'For the Via Tornabuoni.'

Olympia laughed delightedly. 'This is my latest piece of work, Frances, my dearest one,' she said, spreading her arms. 'Have to make an effort, for your party, don't I? And besides,' she leant down with mock solemnity, 'you look rather lovely yourself.' She stroked the pale-green embroidered silk of Frances's sleeve, and Frances, smiling at the compliment, held out her hands, palms upwards in surrender.

Then she stretched out an arm and beckoned, smiling, to a waiter, standing attentively with his silver tray at the entrance to the kitchens. She gave her first guests each a glass of champagne as pale as straw, and for herself took a tumbler of cold water. She would wait, she thought, for her first glass. Frances wanted to preserve the feeling she had of calm and poise for a little while longer before that delicious first moment of letting go that marked the party's proper beginning, when the balloon would slip its moorings and begin to rise and the crowd would hum and spin and glitter around her. There was someone she wanted to see, something she had to say. But she watched as Nino, Lucienne, Olympia and James raised their glasses to the last of the sun, and raised hers too.

'*A bas les Boches!*' And they all laughed.

Gina was standing stiffly in a corner of the drawing room in Borgo Tegolaio holding a glass of sparkling wine (never champagne, not for the students, Jane had told her in a stage whisper, but it was delicious, all the same; whatever you thought of her, Jane did seem to have very good taste) and wondering when she could reasonably slip away to change. She had been leaving the screening room in low-grade shock, her mind working to unravel the disturbing scene she had just seen played out on the DVD, when Jane, coyly leading a subdued Niccolò by the hand down the corridor into the drawing room, had roped her in.

'Not changed yet, darling? What *have* you been doing? Never mind, you can do that later. This'll only last half an hour or so. No, no, you look fine.'

Uncomfortably aware of the outline of the disc – the DVD – in her pocket, and dimly remembering from university Jane's preference for friends whose dress sense would not outshine hers, Gina had acquiesced, silently determined to extract herself as soon as possible from what promised to be a fairly deadly social occasion.

It was better than she had expected, or at least more lively. The students gathered noisily in the Manzinis' *salone* were exclusively female, and from a narrow age band; no one much under fifty or over sixty. They also seemed well endowed with self-confidence, and were talking loudly, without pause and often, as Gina observed of the group standing closest to her, over each other. She was surprised to see that there was a broad range of physical types; she had somehow expected them all to be solidly built, in the farmer's-wife or Victorian-cook mould, and although that type was represented there were also several stringy, badminton-playing types, mostly with short, carefully tinted hair. *Children grown up and gone*, Gina thought, *and this is how we're supposed to reward ourselves after however many years it turns out to be, twenty at least*. All the same, she was vaguely encouraged by the amount of energy and animation the women generated, filling the room with noise and colour. And, after all, perhaps some of them had no children.

With the exception of Gina, they had all dressed up for the occasion. The room was a sea of pastel linen resurrected from summer weddings past, dotted here and there with something more sophisticated, the odd black cocktail frock, but all the same there had been a muted but audible collective gasp, of shock mingled with envy, Gina thought, as Jane had entered in her red satin and diamante. Now Jane was moving among her students very graciously, nodding and smiling at them, but with the faint air of one with a mission, and Niccolò did not stray from her side.

In the far corner a robust, sandy-haired woman with an expressively powerful jaw stood, taller than most of the others, in unsmiling conversation with a severe-looking blonde in a Japanese kimono, and they seemed to be Jane's destination. Taking a deep breath, Gina followed, dodging and weaving through the noisy groups of women, and caught up with them just in time to hear Jane's introductions.

'Mrs Grice, my husband. Darling, Mrs Grice has been quite desperate' – at this the unfortunate woman coloured a little – 'to meet you. It seems she's rather an admirer of the Galleria Nova in Seville. And her husband's an architect in Shoreditch. Has he built anything we would have seen, Mrs Grice?'

From behind Gina could see Manzini's jaw clench as he gritted his teeth. She plucked at Jane's sleeve. 'Is it all right if I –?' She pointed up the stairs.

Jane nodded conspiratorially. 'See you at the party, darling.' She made little waving motions with her hand before turning back to Mrs Grice, who now seemed as uncomfortable as Niccolò Manzini.

'No, he's not – mostly just domestic work.' She sounded flustered.

'Extensions? Conservatories?' Gina heard Jane inquiring sweetly as she left, and when she turned at the foot of the stairs she saw that Jane's face was glowing with triumph.

Frank Sutton was leaning carefully against Pierluigi's window; it was still shuttered, which was a little surprising, Friday evening being peak shopping time, but knowing Pierluigi he was upstairs preening himself before Frances's party. Frank was looking up and down the narrow street, quiet now and empty. It wasn't well kept, the Vicolo degli Innocenti, it was dirty and shabby and the brass of the door plates was tarnished.

Opposite Frank a light sprang on at the all-night garage, and with a creak the barrier began to lift. The gleaming shark smile of an old Aston Martin's radiator grille appeared in front of him and Frank straightened as the car's ravishing gun-metal curves breasted the ramp and glided past him. Then he saw what Pierluigi had seen: the robotic swivel of a camera, the bulging eye of its lens glinting as it turned, and at the same moment something turned and clicked in Frank Sutton's head. He walked down the ramp, the air of the underground parking lot blue with petrol fumes, and followed the signs reading 'Direzione'.

At first the thick-set, stubbled guy in the back office in his greasy overalls denied the existence of any camera. When Frank slapped down a 50,000-lire note he shrugged slightly, but when Frank put down another he sighed.

'Well, he said he'd take it to the police. You know, we never look at those tapes, unless there's a break-in, and we forget they're there most of the time. He was lucky there was one in there, tell the truth, half the time it's empty. Just for show.'

'He?'

The mechanic nodded across the road. 'Pierluigi.'

'The police hadn't asked to see it?'

He shrugged again. 'Don't think they knew it was there. Not my job to tell them, though if I'd thought about it I probably would have. Anyway, he said he'd show it to them. Said he needed it for something else first.'

'Have you seen it?'

Reluctantly the guy nodded. 'We watched it together. It's kind of fuzzy. I wouldn't have recognized my own mother on it. But he – Pierluigi – seemed to know what he was looking at.'

'Thanks,' said Frank, thoughtfully.

If he was at home, Pierluigi wasn't answering. Frank stood with his finger down on the buzzer, but nothing happened. He looked at his watch. Ten to eight. He was probably on his way to the party by now. Frank smoothed his hair and set off across the Via Maggio towards the Via de' Bardi.

31

Alone at last, Gina stood beneath the cool water and allowed it to pour over her bowed head in the brilliant, swimming-pool blue of her tiny shower room. The silver disc lay hidden among her clothes, slipped between the pages of a book at the bottom of her storm-tossed suitcase, but the images stayed in her head. She tried to make sense of them, then to get rid of them, and failed on both counts.

Rubbing at her hair with a towel, droplets drying on her

shoulders in the warmth, Gina crossed to the wardrobe. Her dress still hung there, not a dream after all, and quickly she slipped it over her head before it could disappear. The silk slithered to her ankles, as soft and slippery as she had remembered, and it still fitted as perfectly beneath her modest breasts, just where her body was narrowest. She slid her feet into the sandals, and wrapped the linen shawl around her pale shoulders; unused to exposure, she felt the need to cover herself. She crossed to the mirror. Her hair stood thick and wiry around her head, not sleek but then it never was; her skin looked clear and glowed pleasingly with the effects of a day or two of sun and the silk of her dress gleamed like mother-of-pearl. The silvery sheath made her feel less solid than usual, more like something ethereal, a mermaid, but she was glad, all the same, of the dark shawl to mute the effect. She hesitated, then retrieved the disc from the suitcase. Looking about, she saw the little silver pouch Jane had thrown her in her dressing room, and dropped the disc inside, adding her only lipstick, five years old and worn to a nub, as an afterthought. She'd have to give the disc to Frank; she'd be gone by tomorrow. This was a fact she didn't yet feel able to trust, the inevitable fact of her departure.

At the foot of the stairs Gina looked cautiously into the *salone*, its perfection ruffled now by the traces of Jane's graduation drinks, half-empty glasses here and there, the side-tables marked with wet rings and crumbs. Only a few students were still hanging on and Jane held sway over them in the far corner with Niccolò at her side, a resigned look about his narrow shoulders. Gina tiptoed across the room, waiting until she had her hand on the door latch before signalling her presence to Jane and Niccolò. Niccolò looked thunderous. She waved across the room at them to indicate her intention to leave, then, before any protest could be made, slipped out. As she closed the pretty arched door behind her, Gina paused for a moment and took a deep breath of the ripe air of the street, savouring the exhilaration of her escape.

Jane had told Gina where she would find the Casa Ferrali. It was a part of the city she hadn't seen before, and as she walked up the gentle curve of the Via de' Bardi, in the deep, damp chill that hung between the towering, shuttered buildings, it struck her as more silent and empty than anywhere she'd ever seen. It was like a ghost city; leaving the crowded thoroughfare of the Ponte Vecchio it was as though she'd walked through an invisible wall into another, uninhabited Florence, and she saw no other person from one end of the Via de' Bardi to the other. It was almost completely dark, although between the jutting eaves overhead a dark marbling of cloud could still be made out in the dusky sky, and away from the traffic noise a distant growl of thunder was just audible, coming from the south.

The Casa Ferrali alone among its sombre neighbours was showing signs of life. As the Via de' Bardi turned into the Via San Niccolò and widened briefly, there the massive studded doors to the entrance of the house had been flung open, and two lemon trees, just coming into flower, had been set on the pavement. Gina looked up at the house; it was tall, three windows wide, with not much adornment, and the shutters looked like they'd seen better days. But there was a kind of stone escutcheon, a shield with a crumbling, noseless gryphon carved on it, and the windows had arched stone surrounds with the distinctive Florentine teardrop shape. She went in.

Inside the gates a kind of wide vaulted tunnel led beneath the house. It was quite dark, lit only at the far end by two braziers, and immediately Gina felt the cool. There was a faint smell of damp stone. Momentarily she felt as though she was being swallowed up in the dark, but then, smiling at her from the shadows, she saw a waiter carrying a silver tray loaded with glasses, one of which she took. Firmly she told herself, as she came out at the other side of the Casa Ferrali, that once she had handed the film over to Frank she would forget all about it. It wasn't anything to do with her, really; Beatrice's mother would come and collect her daughter, the police, and maybe even Frank, would continue their investigations, and she would go home to south London.

Then she looked up, and saw the garden filled with people she didn't know, all chatting and nodding and smiling, and she suddenly remembered why she never went to parties any more, and wondered why she'd thought this one would be any different. But then she heard Olympia's sultry smoker's voice exclaim her name and turned. Olympia looked terrifyingly seductive in her corseted black velvet, with her hair rolled at the nape of her neck like a flamenco dancer's, her lips a rich, dark red, and she wafted clouds of scent whenever she moved. James stood at her side gazing at her with fond pride.

'Darling! Just the girl we've been waiting for. What have you done to poor Frank? He's not himself at all. He's been asking for you all evening.'

Gina blushed, rubbing at the imprint of Olympia's lips on her cheek and feeling ridiculously pleased. 'Ah – oh – has he? Is he still here? Am I late?' She tried to sound casual, without much success. Amused, Olympia nodded up at the balcony above them, where a dozen or so guests were congregated. Gina looked up and saw Frank, half turned away from her, frowning as he listened seriously to Frances, who was saying something to him. She turned back to Olympia.

'This is wonderful.' She gestured up at the garden. It was an extraordinarily pretty scene; at the foot of the hill, overhung by the dark trees of a little wood above it, was a box parterre crowded with stocks and roses and delphiniums and peonies, all in full bloom and loading the evening air with scent. Higher up, the lights hanging among the trees cast a soft coloured light on the few guests wandering slowly up through them to the top of the garden, and beyond that, at the foot of the massive mediaeval city wall, she could see the glow of candles along a tunnel of fresh green foliage.

From somewhere Gina could hear the sound of music, something like a little country band, a tinny, quaintly rustic sound, an accordion and a banjo and perhaps a violin. She looked back up at the house; in contrast to the plain grey street frontage, it was painted a warm, vivid ochre on this side, with a great wisteria softening its architecture as it wound up through a series of balconies to the roof. The windows were lit with a soft glow, and she could see more guests inside. She felt like closing her eyes and listening to the sound, storing it up; the hum of relaxed conversation, the top notes of excitement and flirtation, lazy, seductive laughter. But Olympia was asking her something else.

'So, is it true? You're at the thick of it, after all. I mean, what a time to be the Manzinis' house guest!'

'Is what true?' Gina asked.

'Niccolò's disappeared, buggered off, left Jane, dumped the business in it.' Olympia was leaning so close in that Gina could smell her warm skin, and she found herself laughing into her wide bright eyes.

'As far as I know, they're on their way here now, so you can ask them yourself. But he hadn't disappeared by the time I left to come here, no.' Gina couldn't help but feel pleased at the effect this new information had on Olympia, whose eyes opened as wide and dark as an old-fashioned cartoon vamp's. But she didn't feel like going into what else had happened, not with Olympia; she didn't even want to think about it. She could feel the champagne lifting her, and she didn't want to come back down.

At the top of the garden, only just visible to those below, the long trestles glittered with silver and glass, their surfaces reflecting the light that flickered from the candles along their length and some of the coloured light cast up from the trees below. There were plenty of people up here, too, and Pierluigi leant against the wall, absorbing its warmth. The sky was ominous; heavy, dark cloud was rolling in from the sea to the east, and from the hills to the south, but here and there the low, late-evening sun broke through and cast its light down, like the radiance of a Renaissance painting, heavy with symbolism: a spotlight on humanity wherever it fell. At Pierluigi's side Giulietta, his white-skinned, pomegranate-haired, sharp-tongued girlfriend number one, was scanning the throng.

'I like these – what are they?' She gestured to the globes of coloured light swinging in the trees below them. Pierluigi nodded absently.

'What's the matter with you, *caro*?' Giulietta said crossly. 'You aren't usually like this at parties. Come on, pay attention.'

'Sorry, angel,' said Pierluigi. 'I'm waiting for someone to arrive. I can't see so well from up here. Yes, they are pretty. Are they Chinese? Japanese?'

Giulietta nodded. 'Chinese, I think. Who are you waiting for, then? I think everyone's here already. Look, there's that English girl, staying with the Manzinis, the one we saw when we were closing up the other night. With the sculptress.' Pierluigi craned his neck, out of habit, but it didn't look as though Gina was the guest he was watching for.

Giulietta went on. 'Now *she* looks good, doesn't she? La Olympia. The other one, not so chic, but she doesn't look too bad. They can look OK when they make an effort, the English, even if they do look like the effort is killing them. And Frances, for an Englishwoman she really knows how to throw a party.'

Giulietta looked around admiringly, and popped a ripe, dark cherry from the table into her mouth. Against her creamy cheek nestled the pale-green velvety fruit of the almond tree, nodding on a branch and for a moment Pierluigi was almost distracted by the spectacle of the colour of the unripe almonds against her dark-red hair.

Then Giulietta leant forward, squinting through the trees to see what was happening far below them. 'Now, isn't that the architect, Manzini? And will you just look at her! She's usually such an icy creature, isn't she? Never makes the most of her colouring. But that red! She's put him in the shade all right.' And together they looked down the garden.

Frank was still talking to Frances on the balcony. Behind them Frances could hear the rising noise of conversation in the *salone* and she could feel the warmth generated by her guests inside the house emanating in waves through the open French doors. Something delicious was cooking in the kitchen, a smell of wine and herbs mingling with the richly artificial scent of her guests and the heady perfume of the gardens, orange blossom, gardenia and lilies.

'Cheer up, darling boy.' She put her arm around him, her old friend. 'Is it love or death that's putting that look on your face?'

Frank looked startled, then guilty. 'A bit of both.'

Frances frowned at him. 'I don't think I want any thoughts of death at my party,' she said. 'Couldn't you just make it love?'

Frank sighed. 'I want to find out about this murder. These murders. I feel – responsible. I was there, in the piazza that night, you see, I'd talked to her. I was trying to get her to talk to me about her relationship with Niccolò Manzini. Then she died. I left too early, I should have been there.'

'Frank. I didn't know that was the kind of thing you – you know, it just doesn't seem your kind of journalism.' Frances squeezed his arm again in an attempt to soften her words, but he didn't seem to pay any attention.

'No. I should never – no. It was just to get to him. Somehow.

But that's all over now. No. I just – I think I can find out who killed Natasha Julius. I just need to talk to Pierluigi.'

'Pierluigi? Oh, he's here, somewhere, with Giulietta. The redhead. Up at the top, under the almond trees?'

Together they turned to look up at the top of the garden, and the towering wall that dwarfed them, but just then they heard a note of laughter from below that turned Frank's profile in search of its author. Frances looked at him with fond exasperation. He scanned the sea of people that filled the formal garden below him, some of them spilling over the box hedging, others laughing as they leant out and practically embraced the statuary that punctuated the hedges. The new arrivals were still stuck in the bottleneck at the mouth of the vaulted tunnel below him, and Frances saw Frank catch sight of Gina's thick, wiry black hair among them, a dark, plum-coloured shawl slipping off her shoulders. Frances saw him stand in oblivious contemplation of her delicate shoulder-blades, just barely revealed by the linen, and the line of her neck as she leant to catch what Olympia was saying to her. She sighed, because she knew that Gina was going home to her family the next day; but perhaps, she reflected, Frank knew that, too. Perhaps he knew what he was doing.

Frances could tell Gina was still a little ill at ease from the way she held her shawl, but her face was animated in conversation, and she was smiling. Again she sighed. *She'll be gone tomorrow. He'll get over it*, Frances told herself, but when Frank began to make his way towards the old iron staircase that would lead him off the balcony and nearer to Gina, she thought, *Yes. Go on.*

Frances looked down at the crowded garden and up at the threatening sky; it was almost time to serve dinner. The wind was getting up and the torches illuminating the lower garden were flickering a little, but, in the lee of the wall further up, the candles were still alight on the trestles laid for supper. She could see the top of Frank's head as he descended the rickety staircase; she could see the Manzinis – he looking furious, she quite uncharacteristically radiant – and then Gina. She did look lovely, Frances thought, her thick wild hair framing the composed, thoughtful face and emphasizing the silver gleam of her shoulders. *I will talk to her, before she goes*, thought Frances, *but not yet. Not quite yet.*

Then, out of nowhere, before Frances could gather her wits and escape, Vivienne Duncan bore down on her, swathed regally in dark-blue velvet and diamonds, her hair a stiff coppery *pompadour* that gleamed like spun sugar in the lights.

'Darling Frances, it is a triumph. I'm sure the weather will hold off, never mind. And those little lanterns, are you sure they're quite safe? Has Ned got here yet with that sweet girl-friend of his? I'm so glad he felt up to coming; he has been rather down in the mouth since all this happened.' Frances sighed.

As Frank was making his way towards her, Gina was taking advantage of Olympia's momentary inattention (a suave-looking elderly man was running his finger down her spine under cover of a compliment on her dress) to slip away, and found herself moving towards the balcony.

They met at the foot of the stairs and in the crush Gina found herself pressed close up to Frank. Gently he moved her to the side, so that they were no longer blocking the stairway, and kissed her in the shadow beneath the balcony, his hand soft on the back of her neck, holding her face up to his. They moved apart again. 'I wish I'd met you before,' he said. Gina smiled, in an attempt to disguise what she was feeling.

'We've met now. Before – we would have been too young, maybe. There never was a before, not really.'

But standing here with Frank, holding hands as if they were at the beginning of a life together, it suddenly seemed to Gina as though he might be offering her a chance to go back, to pretend none of it had happened. Stephen's careful, unemotional courtship, the wedding in the registry office with Stephen's placid, unexcitable relatives, slipping beneath the waters of motherhood without a breath of protest. Gina looked down at their interlaced hands, and for a moment she thought she was going to cry. Then with a rush the dream of her lost children came back to her and she knew she couldn't go back and start again.

At that moment Frances's bright, curious face appeared at the foot of the stairs. She looked at them with amusement, and something else, something more serious.

'May I borrow Gina for a moment or two, Frank? There's something I need to talk to her about.'

Frances took Gina's hand in hers, and led her away, out of the throng and up through the trees, where other guests were threading their way up and down and little bright encampments had formed here, and there, a man lounging on the grass, a pretty bare-shouldered woman in yellow silk laughing down at his head in her lap. They waved and called to their hostess as she passed, and Frances waved happily back, but she didn't pause. The two women kept going until they reached the highest point of the garden, the hum and chatter of the guests rising, a rich warm sound, from just below them, and Frances stopped under a great overhanging thicket of philadelphus, its dense foliage heavy with white blossom and its shade heady with intoxicating perfume. The scented flower-laden branches almost concealing them, the two women looked down.

'What do you think?' Frances asked.

'It's lovely,' Gina said, honestly. 'I've never seen anything like it.' Side by side they stared in silence at the light and colour playing through the trees.

'Frank,' said Frances, gravely. Startled, Gina turned to face her.

'He's one of my favourites, Frank,' Frances went on. 'Do you know, I think, now that I'm old, that we have an obligation to be happy. To take what we're offered. It was a gift my husband had; he was very gracious about accepting what was offered to him. Of course, sometimes it didn't make our marriage run smoothly, and I think that perhaps sometimes he could have been more discriminating, but all the same, it made him what he was. I never doubted him.'

Gina nodded slowly. 'You don't approve of self-denial?'

'Of course, self-denial has its place. Particularly when there are others involved, those who need our sacrifice. Children. Just don't take it too far. Allow yourself some leeway. When something is offered to you, don't assume you aren't allowed to accept.'

'Frances,' said Gina, longing for her to say yes, 'can I come back one day, with my children, to visit? I don't want to never see you again.' Suddenly she knew that life was about this, about not letting things slip through your fingers.

'I can't think of anything that would make me happier,' said Frances. 'Really, I can't.' And she pressed her soft old cheek against Gina's for a long moment, smiling as though she had been rewarded for her patience. She straightened.

'Now,' she said, 'it's time for supper. I have to bang a gong.' And they both laughed.

Gina stood hidden among the trees above the little fountain, breathing in the scent of the jasmine and surprising herself by her feeling of unnatural calm. She watched Frances make her way down towards the gong, which awaited her at the foot of the steps. Absently Gina pulled at the drawstring of the little bag that hung from her wrist, and watched the thin fabric grow taut, revealing the circular shape beneath. She frowned as she looked at it; her conversation with Frances had so distracted her that for a moment she couldn't think what it was. Then her face cleared as she remembered and she almost laughed that she could have forgotten. Once again she looked around for Frank; she had to give it to him, then none of it was her business any more. She stared back down at the disc, and despite herself her mind returned inexorably to its closing frame. It had to be the man, she knew suddenly, it had to be the man. And the man, he must be . . . She looked up, and there he was, Ned Duncan, no more than ten feet away from her, bringing a glass of champagne to his lips as he came through the archway into the garden.

32

Mila was beginning to panic. She shouldn't have let them go. Such a coward, hiding there in the darkness. But what could she have done, got herself killed? Because she knew that was what it was all about, he would have killed her, just like he killed Evelina, she didn't doubt that any more. You could see it in his eyes up on that screen as he walked away with her into the darkness.

He'd buzzed the door, and that had been enough to frighten Mila, straight off, that was why she'd hidden in her room. No one should have known they were there, and he was the last person Mila ever wanted to see again on this earth. But Beatrice had gone over and answered the door, cool as a cucumber, like she'd been expecting him. She must have called him on her mobile; Jesus, the stupid little kid. Mila had looked through a crack in the door and there he was, all smiles. 'I've got you a present.' Giving her the box, a dress in it, and Beatrice was falling for it. He was all dressed up in a dinner suit, but there was something not right about his eyes, they were too dark, all pupil, and shifting about all over the place as if there was something he didn't want to see.

'You look gorgeous.'

He'd put his arm around her awkwardly, like he'd forgotten how to do it. She didn't look gorgeous at all, skinny little thing in a dress meant for someone older, a black-satin slip that fell off her narrow shoulders, but she smiled at him anyway. Mila knew that look in her eyes, like a fourteen-year-old street girl smiles at her pimp just before he clouts her, wanting to please him, pretending to herself he must really love her, but underneath it she's terrified. Then, before she knew it, they were off, the door was closing behind them, off to the ball. Beatrice hadn't wanted to go, Mila had heard her tell Frank earlier on, and she still didn't want to go by the sound of it, as the door shut behind them.

'Do we have to go? I don't mind if we don't.' But he had an agenda. He was planning something, or maybe he was just crazy. Wanted to show them all, Mila'd seen that before, too. She sat in the darkness, wondering what to do. Beginning to panic.

Gina stood quite still, staring at the man who stood next to Beatrice below the wisteria that climbed over the archway. It was the tall, beautiful young man from the video, from the piazza, smiling easily down at Beatrice from beneath a long, dark fringe, the man she had already begun to realize was Ned Duncan. Beatrice looked odd, her hair still unbrushed, hanging to her shoulders in a lank clump, her dark eyes enormous in her little pale face. She was wearing what looked like a crumpled black slip. Then Beatrice saw Gina and started towards her, reaching out a small hand. Ned Duncan followed.

'This is Ned, Gina,' she said, with a nervous smile, and Gina looked at him with a kind of fascination; she could feel her heart beat quickly, fluttering against her ribs. He took her hand in his, which was cool and light; and he kissed her softly on one cheek. Beatrice turned away from them and looked up the garden.

'Thanks for looking after Bea,' he said easily. 'I left her to it, a bit. I should have made sure she was all right. It's been – we've all been through it, in the last few days.'

Gina thought he looked genuinely troubled, and she nodded. 'She's been *amazing*.' And she believed it, suddenly: Beatrice had been much tougher than she'd thought possible. But here, now, with him, she seemed different.

'How is she now?' she asked, lowering her voice a little. 'She seems a bit – out of it.'

Ned nodded. 'She's very tired, I think. I should get her home soon. But this was too good to miss, don't you think?' At this Beatrice turned back towards them. There was something about her eyes, Gina thought; they were too big and dark, the pupils huge in the flickering half-light. Ned put his arm around her, and lifted his hand in farewell to Gina, and as they walked away Gina stared after them. *No*, she thought. *Don't take her.* But she couldn't move.

Then, as they threaded their way up the garden ahead of her, Ned Duncan looked back at Gina, and something covert in his glance, a kind of veiled warning, confirmed something to her, confirmed her every half-formed suspicion, and she started towards them. But then a shift in the crowd's dynamic stopped her, a change in the air. Something was about to happen.

A pocket of silence seemed to have fallen around them, and Gina could see some heads turning their way, and a few whispers started up. Then Gina saw Niccolò Manzini looking over at Beatrice and trying to smile, a lopsided, shamefaced smile. Then suddenly Beatrice started towards him and people moved aside to let her pass. She stopped right in front of her father, too close for comfort. Her face was white and rigid.

Then in a high, clear voice, she said, 'Thanks, Dad. For being there when I needed you. Have a good time, this time? Where was it, Bangkok? Amsterdam? Prague? I hear little girls are cheap over there, too. Ned told me all about you and Tash. You ruined her life, you know that?'

She turned her back on him and Ned Duncan took her by the hand.

White-faced, Niccolò Manzini tried to say something, but looked as though he couldn't get the words out. Jane looked on, smiling benevolently, as though she was at a family wedding. She took her husband firmly by the arm and turned him away from his daughter's retreating shoulders, which even now seemed to be shaking, and began to talk to him in a low voice. Slowly the noise level began to rise again.

Gina looked around wildly, to the staircase where she'd last seen Frank, but he wasn't there, then over her shoulder and she spotted him, up on the balcony. He was frowning, and she could see that he was staring at Ned Duncan. She waved her arm high over her head and she saw his eyes distracted by the movement. But then Frances, who was showing no sign of having witnessed the encounter between Beatrice Manzini and her father, struck the gong, and everyone fell silent. She climbed up on to the steps to raise herself above the crowd and held up her hand to silence their last murmurings. She stood very straight, beaming with pleasure.

'Everyone. Thank you for coming. I'm sorry to slow things down just briefly, but there was something I wanted to say.' A few hoots and gruff noises of encouragement came from the fringes of the party-goers.

'I think by now you all know how much these occasions mean to me. I often think that I enjoy my parties more than anyone. But I'm getting old and I think that this will be the last. So for me, I want you to make sure it is the best of all.' She raised her glass.

For a moment the scented, flickering, candlelit air of the garden fell quite still, and in the silence almost every glass was raised with Frances's. From out of the silence a cheer went up, but, just as Gina felt the tug of an undertow as the tightly packed crowd swayed and rose as one man towards Frances, a colossal peal of thunder broke overhead, like the crump of a mortar shell, rumbling around the amphitheatre of the garden. It was closely followed by a sheet of lightning that silhouetted the skyline and lit their upturned faces like a flare. The wave turned and Frances's guests rushed back, towards the house.

In the shuttered apartment, Mila sat shivering in the darkness as the thunder rolled outside, unable to imagine how she could prevent what she knew was going to happen. She was sitting at Frank's table, and as she gazed at the table's cluttered surface in despair she saw his number, the number he'd given Beatrice when he'd tried to talk her into coming with him. She grabbed the phone and dialled the number.

At the Casa Ferrali no one seemed to be dismayed by the weather. Laughing and exclaiming, Olympia and James, Nino and Lucienne, Pierluigi and Giulietta and a hundred or more others streamed into the house, up the internal stairs and the rickety metal stairway that led to the balcony. The passage was slow, as neither staircase was wide enough to accommodate more than two abreast, and every couple of minutes a long satin or tulle train would become entangled in the intricate metalwork and slow things down even further, but nonetheless the house soon filled up and the noise inside quickly became deafening. So when the little mobile began to ring in Frank's inside pocket, which he had taken off early on in the stifling heat and hung over the back of a little gold chair in the salone, only the few guests within a foot or two of it could hear it. And, as they were talking at the tops of their voices about the awning at the end of the garden that had just been lifted and torn away in the wind, even they didn't register the sound until it was too late. And Frank, making his way with painful slowness towards Pierluigi, who was gesturing urgently to him from across the crowded room, would have been the last person to hear it.

The garden was quite empty now, taken over by the wind and the fat drops of rain that were beginning to fall. A chair or two lay overturned, and glasses stood along the walls and ledges. In the tunnel beneath the house the waiters were chatting easily as they watched to see what would happen, and in the huge subterranean kitchen behind them the five cooks stood by their boiling water, awaiting instructions before dropping in enough pasta to feed a hundred.

Gina was halfway up the front stairs and waving wildly at Frank before she realized that she'd lost it. One moment – how long ago? – the little bag had been hanging from her wrist, and now it was gone. For a second or two she hesitated, then edged her way back down past the laughing faces and ran up the garden, one hand holding her shawl over her head against the rain, her long flimsy dress gathered up in the other to keep it out of the mud. She ran through the trees, as above her head the fringed paper lanterns were being buffeted violently by the wind and one by one extinguished, and up to where she and Frances had talked. The roses and gardenias that decorated the trestles were sodden already, the candles knocked over on to the white damask. Gina found the exact spot, the philadelphus swaying and spattering her with rain, its waxy flowers drenched and soggy, but no disc shone up at her from out of the grass. It wasn't there. Slowly she retraced her steps through the deep gloom over the knotted roots of the little trees, only the odd gleam now penetrating the darkness from the lighted house. She came to a little circular brick structure, something like an ornamental well, and leant over to peer down into it, then she heard voices, and instinctively she ducked down, her hand on the earth coming to rest on something small and hard. She grabbed at it. The shape of a lipstick wrapped in the slippery silk of Jane's evening bag, and something else, something round and flat. She closed her fingers around it, and then she heard Beatrice's voice coming from just above her, somewhere under the trees in the darkness.

'Do we have to go in there?' There was something faintly slurred about her voice, Gina thought. Was she drunk? Not drugs, she didn't take drugs, unless . . . Perhaps he'd given her something. To calm her down, or keep her quiet.

'You don't want to go in there, with all those people, do you? Don't you want to be alone with me?' His voice was gentle and persuasive, but Gina had never seen Ned's charming side before. In the darkness all she could think of was the glowering face of the Ned Duncan she'd last seen leading Evelina away down the hill, to where Gina had found her, three days later, and when she put that image together with the soft, insinuating voice she could hear whispering in Beatrice's ear, she shivered.

'Ned, Ned . . .' Beatrice sounded as though she was trying to concentrate, trying to gather her scattered senses to ask him something.

'Ned, did you, did you . . . You didn't do it, did you?' The words ran into each other: *You dint do it didjooo* . . . But his reply had an edge to it.

'Do what?' he asked her sharply.

'That girl, that girl, dead on the rocks. I know you were out there with Tash, up to something, I know and now she's dead too.' Beatrice's voice tailed off into a wail of uncontrolled misery. Gina stiffened. She knew.

'Oh, Bea, Bea, what are you talking about? Don't do this, you're just – well, if it helps, blame me.' Beatrice sobbed, trying to stifle the sound. He went on, his voice fuelled by something Gina didn't recognize, remote and cool, no longer listening. 'She'd have been dead soon anyway, this year, next year, that's what happens to those girls on the streets. What's the difference?'

Then came Beatrice's quavering voice, the last ounce of nerve she had drove her and she said, 'And Tash?'

But the thunder cracked again over their heads, obliterating his response, and a split second later the lightning lit the whole place up. Gina flinched and pressed herself against the brick, but they weren't looking her way. Ned was upright, looking back at the house, and Beatrice was trying to pull away. Someone shouted from the balcony, 'Hey, there's someone there, still out there!' There was a whoop of encouragement. Ned muttered something furiously and grabbed Beatrice, half dragging her back down, towards the house. Gina looked around desperately to be told what she should do but no one was there so she followed, skittering and stumbling down the slippery path, pausing only at the edge of the wood, reluctant to break cover. Below her Ned, his knuckles white around Beatrice's arm, was heading for the archway that would lead them back out to the street. On the balcony Frances stood, hair blown back from her frowning face, and watched as Gina followed them and disappeared through the archway below her.

Frank frowned at Pierluigi in an attempt to understand what he had just been told through the din of a hundred voices jabbering and exclaiming all around him. Suddenly turning he saw his mobile pulled out of his jacket, held up and reflected in the hundred tarnished mirrors that lined the salone, and he heard someone calling his name. He gripped Pierluigi's shoulder. '*Dopo!*' he mouthed at the antique dealer. 'Later.' And the antique dealer threw up his hands in exasperation as Frank turned his back and made his way towards his phone.

Then, smiling stiffly and apologizing all the way across

the room, he pushed through until he reached the shrilling mobile, held up to him by a man he vaguely recognized, a tall beanpole of an American academic who smiled and nodded in the din of voices, shrugging apologetically as Frank mouthed his weary thanks. The voice Frank heard as he put the mobile to his ear was Mila's, but he couldn't work out what she was saying in her fractured mixture of English and Italian, the relentless shrieking party talk almost drowning her out. He moved out on to the balcony and suddenly he could hear.

'It's him. He took Beatrice. He said he was taking her there to the party. It was him, it was the one who took Evelina. Do you understand me? Evelina is dead, the other girl, she is dead now, she saw him take Evelina. And now he has Beatrice. Her boyfriend.'

'Ned?' Frank wanted to be sure what he was hearing, this time, although it was a horrible echo of what Pierluigi had whispered, reluctantly, fearfully, to him in the salone. Only the girl's name was different; not Natasha Julius, this time, but Evelina. 'Ned Duncan killed Evelina?' For a moment he didn't know who she meant. 'Evelina?' Then he remembered. The girl whose skin he had reached out to touch just a day earlier, as she lay on the rocks among the scrub below Manzini's country house, the air around her full of the deafening, inhuman song of the cicadas.

Beside him Frances turned slowly towards Frank. She opened her mouth as though to speak, and held up her hand. He wasn't looking.

'I think. I am sure. Is he there with her? She's just a girl, don't let him hurt her, Frank.'

'It's OK, Mila. She's here, they're here. She's all right.' He could hear her sobbing hysterically, and he went on talking until she stopped. 'I'll get her, then I'll come back,' he said. But as he clicked the phone shut, Frances came across the balcony towards him, and from her expression he could tell that it wasn't going to be as simple as that.

33

When Gina reached the street it was quiet and empty, with no trace of either Beatrice or Ned. She looked left and right; if they had turned right she should still be able to see them, as the Via San Niccolò ran straight and uninterrupted to the Porta San Niccolò, the three-storey crenellated tower that blocked the street almost half a mile away. So she turned in the opposite direction, back towards the bright lights of the Ponte Vecchio, and almost the minute she rounded the corner she saw them, framed by the homely little arch of the Porta San Miniato, on their way out through the city walls to the dark lanes and olive groves beyond.

Gina followed, keeping as close as she dared, through the gate and then a sharp left, up a steep and narrow road that ran at the foot of the huge wall, on the other side a dark, silent hillside terraced with olive trees. It was still raining, though the storm had passed over and the lightning was now illuminating the far hills of Fiesole, and Gina's thin dress was wet through. She could smell the earth as it soaked up the rain, damp and cool and clean. At first there were a couple of street lamps and Gina could see the little trees' silver leaves gleaming in the rain, but after a hundred yards or so it was quite dark and she became acutely aware of the slap of her own footsteps, loud and unmistakable in the absolute quiet. She took off her sandals, and went on, barefoot.

Ahead of her the two of them climbed, not quickly but steadily, skirting the back of the giant fortress of Belvedere that marked the summit then along a narrow lane, old stone walls on either side, that led along the ridge, heading round the city to the southwest. Gina didn't know it, but Ned was going home, to Bellosguardo.

Frances stood on the balcony, the wind whipping at her hair, oblivious to the happy uproar inside the house. Frank would catch up with them; it couldn't have been more than five minutes between their disappearing into the street and his phonecall. She had barely been able to grasp what he had blurted out to her about Ned Duncan as she stood on the balcony, Frank holding her by her elbows and talking urgently into her uncomprehending face. Frances bit her lip. If only she had known, perhaps if she had been more perceptive; she had watched Ned and Beatrice emerge, after all, drenched and pale from the storm, or so she'd thought, and she'd seen Ned lead her down to the tunnel that led to the street. She couldn't remember how he'd looked; could you see it in someone's face, she wondered, the capacity for murder? But at least she'd seen them go. At least she'd been able to tell Frank . . . She grimaced at her stupidity, for the hundredth time since Frank had turned and taken the steps, three at a time, and hurtled out to the Via San Niccolò in pursuit. Then Frances thought of something. She went inside, and hurried upstairs, cursing her old legs for refusing to move as quickly as she wanted them to, to Nino's study. She riffled through his ancient Rolodex, found the number for the Villa Duncan, and dialled, bracing herself for the maid's condescension.

But the Villa Bellosguardo was in darkness, and in the great hall the telephone rang on and on unanswered. *Of course*, she thought. *Vivienne's still here*. And she registered that, sooner or later, she would have to find Vivienne Duncan and think of something to tell her. Slowly Frances replaced the receiver, before picking it up again to dial 113 and ask, her voice breaking with the terrible unfamiliarity of the words, for the police.

The three of them, two in front, Ned Duncan leading Beatrice as though she was a child unwilling to go to school, and the third, Gina, hanging back at every bend, had turned off the Via San Leonardo, which was almost a country lane, narrow and unlit between dry-stone walls. Now they were on a bigger road, its walls new and clean and topped with broken glass rather than rusty wire, and every hundred yards or so a gravel drive swept up to an expensively secluded villa. At each gate a security light illuminated the patch of road around it, but there was no one else to be seen. Although the rain had stopped in the twenty minutes or so since they slipped through the Porta San Miniato, just one solitary couple had passed them, walking the other way in the darkness. They'd turned to look back at Gina and shaken their heads, at the wet dress that clung to her, at her bare feet, and the curious way she kept stopping, as though she didn't want to be seen.

Suddenly, Ned and Beatrice had stopped, at the one gate that wasn't illuminated. Gina paused to watch as their dark silhouettes slipped inside, past a darkened gatehouse and up the drive. Considering for a moment, Gina carefully placed the disc she still carried just inside the fence. She paused in the lee of the little building, suddenly seized with doubt, now that she was about to trespass; why hadn't she called the police, or waited for Frank, or taken any one of a number of sensible precautions? *No time*, she thought, and nor was there any time now. She followed them in, not thinking to look inside the gatehouse and rouse the sleeping gatekeeper; she had no idea he was there.

She walked on the grass so as to make no sound, and the roses, heavy and sweet with moisture, showered her as she brushed against them. As Gina skirted the flowerbeds she realized with relief that they would provide her with cover right up to the house, where Ned and Beatrice now stood, next to a big, battered American car. The house seemed to have no exterior light but a low-wattage emergency bulb over the porch, and the car showed black in its dull glow, the faces of the couple standing next to it sallow and serious. Gina could hear what they were saying.

'Let's just go. We could get in the car and drive down to Rome. We could go to Morocco, get a boat from Brindisi!' Ned sounded as excited as a child at the thought. But when she answered, Beatrice sounded bleary with exhaustion perhaps, or alcohol, or drugs.

'Can't, Ned. Mm-Mum's coming to get me tomorrow. Got to go back home.' And she laughed, as though with disbelief. *She's still a child*, thought Gina, *with a home to go to*. But Gina was barely able to believe it herself.

'I suppose not.' Ned's voice was flat now, with resignation. 'We'd better go in. You'd better lie down; you're very tired, aren't you?' He sounded regretful. Beatrice nodded dumbly, and he took her by the hand and led her into the dark hallway.

Frank's lungs burnt and briefly he wished he was fitter as he pounded down the Via de' Bardi and back into town, no sight of anyone ahead of him until he reached the river, where a steady stream of tourists still poured off the Ponte Vecchio even in the rain. He turned left past the Pitti Palace and ran towards the Borgo Tegolaio. There was no answer at the Manzini apartment, so he went on, up towards Bellosguardo and the Villa Duncan.

Gina couldn't understand why there were no lights. By the time she dared to tiptoe across the threshold she could hear Ned upstairs, speaking in a low, soothing monotone; somewhere she could hear the sonorous tick of a big clock, but otherwise the house was silent. It smelt of wax polish, no cooking smells, just clean and empty, like a museum. Under her bare feet there was parquet, then a Persian rug. Slowly she approached the staircase, and looked up; massive, centred in the great hall, it loomed ahead of her, endlessly. Cautiously she tested it with a foot; solid mahogany and oak, thick with Wilton carpet, the staircase bore her weight without complaint, and before she could stop, and think, and be afraid, Gina ran up to the first floor.

At first-floor level a balustraded gallery ran around the hall, doors opening off it. If Ned were to emerge from any one of the doors Gina would immediately be discovered, and she felt acutely vulnerable. She dropped to her knees and began to crawl, following the sound of Ned's voice until she reached a door. As she got closer she could make out what he was saying. He was muttering fast to himself, fuelled by some manic, poisoned energy, his voice thick with resentment and disgust.

'I had to. Tash would have said anything. What if she'd been there when you and that woman found the body? She'd have blurted it out, she'd got nothing left up top, she'd got no sense. And she just wouldn't fucking shut up, about her little baby, her fucking baby, even after the things she'd done to get my drugs. My head was hurting. It's still hurting.'

Like a child whose tantrum has gone past the point of no return, a sob rose in Ned's throat, a sob of self-pity, of shame and disgust and misery.

So he killed Evelina, then he killed Natasha. Gina felt as though her head was humming with sound, as though she had walked out of a cinema into the darkness and couldn't shake her head clear of what she had heard and seen. And now what? Now Beatrice?

On her knees in the gallery, Gina looked around the door and there, no more than a metre away, a big, mahogany bed loomed, and on it two figures silhouetted against the window. There was something unnatural about their position. On the floor a heavy tumbler rolled back and forward gently in a puddle of water and drooping from the bed above it hung a long, bare, slender arm. Beatrice's arm.

Ned was kneeling astride her, his hands on either side of a pillow that he was pressing down on her face, his long hair shielding his profile from Gina. It was the hair that saved Beatrice, that prevented him from seeing Gina as in one swift unthinking movement she crossed the space between them, lifted the sandals in her hand and cracked him with them across his head, bringing them down just above the ear, bringing to the blow all the force she had saved as if for this moment, all the strength her arms had accumulated from ten years or more of carrying children, of saving children from falling, snatching them out of danger. She hit him as hard as she could have ever hit anyone and he fell off the bed like a stunned animal.

Gina grabbed the pillow with her other hand, snatched it away from Beatrice's face. She lay immobile beneath it, her face tinged with blue in the half-light. Gina slapped her hard on the cheek, leant over and blew into her mouth, all the while desperately afraid of hearing a sound from the far side of the bed. 'Beatrice,' she whispered urgently.

There was no response, but from the darkness where Ned lay she heard a groan. He began to mumble, a string of gibberish. Gina blew again into Beatrice's mouth. Slowly his hand on the coverlet began to grope around, no more than an inch from Gina's leg, and at that moment a shocking, hoarse gargle came from Beatrice's mouth. Gina leapt back as though stung, and Ned lifted his face up to her, wet with tears and blood from a cut over his eye. *They bleed a lot*, thought Gina in a moment of inappropriate lucidity, remembering some long-ago doctor's reassurances over a child's matted head. *Scalp lacerations bleed a lot*.

Gina stared at him and shook her head. 'No,' she said. 'Not

Beatrice, too. Stop it now.' She spoke gently, as though to a child, and eased herself backwards off the bed, standing on the far side from Ned, Beatrice between them as though paralysed, her mouth just twitching, almost imperceptibly. Gina stood by the bed, her knees braced, and waited for Ned to move. Below her a door slammed. She heard Frank call and she opened her mouth to respond, but it seemed as though nothing would come.

His breath coming in ragged gasps after his run across the *viale* and up the dark avenue, Frank heard nothing at first when he entered the house through the wide-open door. He shouted. And from upstairs he heard a voice calling his name, and he took the stairs three at a time.

Gina could hear the sound of footsteps, and she knew it must be Frank, but still she gazed at Ned. 'How could you have done it?' she asked, wonderingly. 'They were just girls.'

'I didn't want to,' Ned said brokenly, and put his face in his hands. 'She made me do it. Tash did.'

'No, Ned.' Gina's voice was quiet; she had to try very hard to stop it shaking. 'She didn't make you do it.' She looked at the boy opposite her and wondered how he could have so lost control of his life. He was barely a man, narrow in the shoulders still, smooth-skinned, but his life, which should have been so full of possibilities, had shrunk down to a small point. He sighed, a shuddering sigh. 'I couldn't stand her touching me any more.' Gina looked at him, and said nothing. This wasn't enough.

Ned looked away from her, but he went on, his voice high with indignation.

'She just kept pulling at me, my arm, all she was interested in was the money. I couldn't stand her touching me. Tash wanted me to screw her – me, screw a dirty little tart; maybe that's something Bea's dad taught her. I could see her, Tash, getting ready to laugh if I didn't. I couldn't stand the way it felt, her hanging off me like that, she was so heavy, sweating . . . I just gave her a shove. I didn't push her hard.'

He looked up at Gina, wheedling, and she knew it was a lie. She thought of the girl's head, caved in by the force of the fall. Or the blow. Gina stared back at Ned and his voice became quieter, as though he was musing to himself, only a faint but indelible undertone of disgust giving him away.

'They're not really human, though, are they? Way they stand there, chewing their gum by the side of the road, and stare through you, like you're the one, you're the one worth shit. Don't you think?' And he turned to look at Gina. She concentrated on remaining calm, and after looking at her curiously for a moment Ned continued.

'I told Tash I'd given her some money and left her on the path. But she looked at me like . . . Anyway, doesn't matter now. After that – Jesus, I couldn't – I couldn't keep it together. And when we got back here Tash did all that cuddling-up-to-Bea bit, giggling and looking at me, like she had a secret. Talking to me about getting married. Christ!' He was suddenly savage and furious as he turned his face towards her, and Gina caught a glimpse of something unfeigned for the first time, all the terrible disillusion of Ned's wasted life exposed.

'Getting married? She talked about marrying you, in front of Beatrice? In front of your girlfriend.' Gina couldn't understand. 'Were you the father of Natasha's baby? Did Beatrice know, then?'

Ned stared at Gina, head slightly tilted to examine her for a long moment as if she was stupid. 'Did she know? Of course she didn't know. Why do you think I had to do it?' He looked down, unseeing, and there she was, lying between them on his bed. Gina tried not to follow his gaze, to distract him from her. But he wasn't looking at Beatrice.

'Marry a pregnant fucking junkie. Happily ever after with princess Tash and Christ knows whose kid, living in some shithole, my mother screaming down my neck and my dad – *Jesus!*'

'Ned,' said Gina, 'couldn't you have done something – something else? Couldn't you have done what other people do? Got a job, left home?' Gina knew she sounded like every parent who had ever despaired of a child, the words ringing hollow in the darkness. But she needed to understand.

'A job?' The look Ned gave Gina was composed of contempt and boredom. 'You sound like my mother. What would I do with a job?'

'So you killed her?' It was Gina's turn to show contempt, and Ned lowered his head, his defiance ebbing away.

'I watched her go off with Stefano. Stinking bloodsucker. I didn't plan it, I was just walking, trying to get it out of my head, then when – she was just there in the dark, waiting. For him, or me, I don't know. I just wanted to get rid of her. Make her disappear. And now it's too late.'

On his knees Ned stared up at Gina, pleading, and it was as though he thought she might have the power to forgive him. Behind her in the door she felt someone appear, felt the air displace, but she didn't turn her back on Ned, whose begging eyes seemed quite empty. She went on looking at him. 'Yes,' said Frank, behind her. 'It's too late.'

Because it had taken Frances more than ten minutes to complete their procedural inquiries and convince the police to pay a visit to the Villa Duncan, by the time their sirens wailed up the hill this was what remained for them to discover. Oxygen was being administered to Beatrice in an ambulance in the drive while Gina held her hand and waited a long time for the colour to return to her pale lips. Upstairs Frank sat with Ned Duncan in his ruined bedroom, both men as motionless as statues, staring out through the long, rain-spattered net curtains at the darkness outside, waiting for the police, and for Vivienne Duncan.

On the other side of town, Pierluigi stood at the booking desk of the principal police station trying to justify his delay in handing the garage's security video over to the police, while in a windowless room at the end of a long grey corridor two police officers sat and watched the last moments of Natasha Julius's short life played out, a succession of blurred and grainy images on a small television screen.

Even jagged with distortion her outline was beautiful, flat-hipped in a short loose dress, with long, slender arms and a velvet nap of short black hair, her face a perfect oval although her features were indistinct. She was dancing, spinning and swaying, just keeping her balance. Next to her walked Stefano, looking ahead, his hands in his pockets, ignoring her.

Then they stopped. Stefano pointed to a door two houses along, and said something. Her shoulders dropped. She sidled up to him in an attitude of pleading, her face turned up to him. He stared, then turned and walked away; she ran after him, pulling at him, but he prised her fingers off his leather jacket and shoved her off the pavement into the gutter. He entered the door he'd pointed at earlier, and left her in the street, her face in her hands.

A car drove up and the camera turned to monitor its entrance into the garage; when it returned to the street, Ned Duncan was standing beside Pierluigi's shop, his hands in his pockets, staring down at the girl.

Ned bent over her, his body in outline not much more substantial than hers, as though perhaps he was offering to help her up. But then he placed his hands around her neck from behind, and his weight bore down on her from above. Natasha stiffened, then writhed, her legs flailing out in front of her. It seemed as though she must be able to fight him off;

but he twisted her around and drew her up to face him; there seemed no emotion in it, he just went on and on, neither of them making a sound. Like an automaton he frogmarched her, her swollen face looking up at him from between his hands, back across the pavement towards the shopfront and suddenly, savagely, thrust her away from him and through the glass. There must have been a monumental crash, followed by the shrill clang of the alarm, immediately braking the silence, and Ned Duncan turned and ran, off the screen and into the darkness. The alarm rang on and on in the empty street; no girl, no boy.

Saturday

34

On Saturday morning Gina woke up in Frank's bed, her cheek against his bare chest in the darkened flat, and for the first time during her week away she remembered immediately where she was and why. It was nine o'clock by Frank's battered alarm, and less than five hours since the police had finally completed their paperwork and allowed Gina and Frank to leave, just as light was beginning to leak across the eastern horizon.

The police station had come as a surprise to her; after a brief interrogation in Vivienne Duncan's chilly study one of the police cars had driven them through the silent streets from Bellosguardo to a wisteria-covered courtyard in the shadow of the Duomo. Warm, dusty and untidy, with shelves loaded with toppling box-files, the ancient building was manned by a single, dishevelled young desk officer, his tie loosened and his hair long enough to brush his collar. It had felt curiously comforting, like home. Gina must have looked surprised, though, because the round-faced young policeman had felt it necessary to explain to her that this was the tourist police station; it had skeleton staff for the night, but it had no cells. Ned Duncan was being held elsewhere; the man had waved a hand out to the northeast.

'On the *viale*. Porta al Prato.' Gina had nodded without knowing where he meant. She had thought of Ned Duncan in a police cell, and wondered whether he would survive it. Perhaps it would be better if he didn't. Perhaps his mother – Gina had seen Vivienne Duncan, her hair askew, her face old and sunken with shock, arriving at the villa – perhaps she was there, waiting for him. Although, of course, he wouldn't be coming home.

Gina had been given a blanket when they noticed her shivering, and the police had asked her questions gently, smiling and agreeing with her often, even when agreement was not called for. One of the questions on their form inquired after Gina's marital status, and when she had given it the young policeman had asked her if Frank, who was giving his statement somewhere else in the building, was her husband.

'No,' she said, smiling. 'No. My husband is at home in England. With the children.' The young man looked at her, perplexed.

Gina went on. 'I'm on holiday, until tomorrow. Tomorrow I return to England. To my family.' The man nodded slowly, but it was obvious that he thought this a strange kind of arrangement. Then he shrugged, as though acknowledging that Gina was a foreigner, and therefore he was not obliged to make sense of her personal life.

Soon afterwards, Gina had been allowed to leave, with the injunction that she would certainly be required to return to give evidence if – when – Ned Duncan was brought to trial. Frank was waiting for her on a hard chair outside in the hall and Gina realized she had nowhere to go. She had not brought a key to the Manzini flat to the party, she had no idea where Jane and Niccolò were now, nor what had become of any of it – all the guests and flowers and candles and music, the open bottles of champagne and the plates of food; in her mind they had all folded into dust, or been blown away like smoke by the storm. But even if she had had somewhere else to go, she would still have gone home with Frank.

Gina drew her head back to look up at him, and Frank's eyes opened at the movement. He looked down at her, unsmiling, a dazed look on his face, but his arms tightened around her. In the hall the erratic wail of the flat's entrance buzzer broke the silence, and next door Gina heard Mila stir in her bed.

Out in the street the air was clean and cool after the storm, and the stones were still damp from the night's rain. As she walked the few yards from her front door to the Medici Frances herself felt as though she had been tumbled around in some kind of strenuous cleansing process during the night; she felt old and worn and softened up, a few layers of skin gone, her fragile bones rearranged.

As she walked into the Medici, Frances caught Massi's smile. *So reliable*, she thought with some relief; his good nature, his welcome. She smiled back, gratefully taking in the familiar details of Massi's appearance that this morning contained something of epiphanic perfection in her eyes; his clean shirt, his perfect shave, the faint sweetness of his aftershave and the tiny hint of concern in his greeting. Frances registered the coffee he placed in front of her precisely as she reached the bar and put out her hands to touch the pink marble, part support, part lucky charm. Sometimes, Frances thought as she looked down at her old hands, the relationship she enjoyed with Massi seemed the happiest of her life, and the thought made her laugh. All at once it made her appear to herself, as perhaps she appeared to others, the very epitome of class-conscious, aristocratic English repressiveness, Massi gracefully playing the part of servant to her Lady Richardson.

Beside Frances at the bar a well-dressed woman, perhaps on her way to work in her dark suit and high heels, set down her empty cup and carefully wiped the traces of lipstick from the rim; Massi nodded to her as she left and returned her good morning – not a servant, but an equal, naturally. And as Frances observed the propriety inherent in the exchange, the woman's instinctive neatness and composure, all the terrible disorder of the previous night's events came back to her, and

Frances felt herself surprised by an emotion close to despair. Perhaps, she thought, along with Frank and Jane and Niccolò Manzini, along with Ned Duncan, perhaps she didn't belong here after all, among a people who knew so precisely how to behave. Frances thought of Manzini and his daughter Beatrice, and their ugly confrontation the night before; then, unwillingly, her thoughts turned to Ned Duncan, his life degenerated to the point at which it was worth less than nothing, and none of them, who should have acted as his family, able to see it. *We believe ourselves to be so civilized*, thought Frances, *but we're no better than the rest of them; at least the beggars from Albania and the Africans selling handbags know what they're doing here.* Frances shook her head slightly at the thought, the tiny movement concealing a great burden of doubt. Massi, seeing her crestfallen face, paused in the act of polishing a glass and leant towards her. 'Signora Frances?'

She looked up at him, and made an effort to smile. 'Sorry, Massi. Just a bit tired, maybe. Feeling my age.' The barman nodded gravely.

'I think perhaps you got up too early, after your party. It was . . . eventful. So I hear.'

Frances nodded ruefully and took a sip of her coffee, cooling now. She had assumed Massi would know all about it by now. Perhaps he was right, too; it had been four o'clock before she had finally got to bed, and even then had only been able to sleep with Lucienne beside her, her old friend's reassuring murmur lulling her to sleep. Dear Lucienne, still the voice of continental pragmatism, taking mayhem in her stride and reassuring Frances that madness and murder were only temporary, just as she had assured her about Roland's infidelity, nearly fifty years earlier. Frances sighed, weary suddenly.

'We don't belong here, do we, Massi? Don't you get sick of us, all the mess we make?'

Frances gestured tiredly around her, attempting to indicate

not just the tourist flotsam, the broken bottles, the graffiti and take-away wrappers left by the foreigners who wandered, day and night, through Massi's exquisite city, but also the general blundering hopelessness of their emotional lives. For a moment she thought that, if she were to allow it, her eyes might fill up with tears.

Massi looked at her narrowly, and went on polishing the glass.

'Signora Frances,' he spoke lightly, but Frances could tell that he was choosing his words with care, 'we are capable of making a mess just as well as anyone. And as for belonging; who is to say who belongs here? Myself, my mother was from Pisa.' And he shrugged, as though there was nothing more to be said, and carefully slid the glass into its place on the marble shelf.

Frances rested an elbow on the bar and gazed at Massi, tempted to reach across it and kiss him, but he was looking down, stretching for another glass to polish. When he straightened up, he was focusing on something behind her, almost beaming, and Frances turned to see what he was looking at. Gina stood in the doorway, dressed in a black linen shift that Frances could have sworn she'd last seen on Jane.

'Hello, Frances,' she said, and she smiled, a wide, happy smile. Frances held out her arms.

It had been Jane at Frank's front door when he had opened it, looking quite unlike herself; practically dishevelled, with unwashed hair and no make-up, and cheerful. Jane, naturally enough, had realized even before Gina herself that she would have nothing in which to leave the house other than a flimsy and very crumpled evening dress; Frank's shirts, obviously, were beneath consideration. She stood at the door and pushed a smart carrier into Frank's hands.

'It's an old thing of mine. She can keep it. But she'll have to come and say goodbye, because her case is still in Borgo Tegolaio.' And then Jane had smiled, turned and gone.

So, an hour later, Gina had said goodbye to Mila, and to Frank. She didn't know what to say to him, but he seemed to prefer it that way. He had just nodded, and kissed her dryly on the cheek, keeping his head beside hers just a fraction of a second longer than a casual acquaintance would have done, but it was long enough. Then Gina passed through the door, and it closed behind her.

At Borgo Tegolaio Jane greeted her warmly; Gina gazed at her dumbly. Her fringe was standing on end, and she was wearing a sweatshirt.

The flat in Borgo Tegolaio was hardly recognizable, either. Two large suitcases lay open on the silver-green sofas, disgorging suitbags and shirts on to the cushions, and the contents of a sponge-bag – a half-squeezed toothpaste tube, nail scissors and most of a shaving kit – were strewn across the little Indian teak table. Through the kitchen door Gina could see a dirty coffee cup sitting on the counter, a cupboard stood open, and there was no sign of Inés.

'Come in, darling,' said Jane. 'Sit down.' She shoved a suitcase aside, and half a dozen ties fell on to the floor in a heap.

Looking at the sofas, taking in the silence of the flat around them, suddenly Gina remembered Beatrice, the girl's limp, cold hand as she had sat holding it no more than a few hours earlier, in the ambulance up at Bellosguardo. 'Where's Beatrice?' she asked quickly, trying to subdue the rising panic. Jane sighed. 'They've kept her in for observation, just overnight. But I think she's fine. She wanted to say thank you, to you, but I told her, she'd get another chance.' Gina let out a breath of relief.

Jane leant back on the sofa and a pair of loafers slid to the floor. 'Sorry about the mess,' she said brightly. 'We're sorting a few things out for Nicky; he's going to Rome. Or perhaps England. It depends on the police; they want to talk to him again. Such a bore.' She grimaced cheerfully, obviously unmoved by the police's further involvement with Niccolò, and showing no trace of concern about his future whereabouts, either. Gina nodded dazedly, trying to take it all in.

'I think I managed to track everything of yours down,' Jane went on, and she pushed Gina's little suitcase towards her. 'I could have brought it with me to Frank's, but I wanted to say goodbye.' And with an impulsiveness Gina did not remember ever having seen in her before, Jane put an arm around her and pressed her cheek gently against Gina's.

'Come back, won't you,' she said softly. Then she shouted over her shoulder.

'Nicky? Darling? Come and say goodbye. Gina's going.' From down at the end of the corridor Gina heard a nervous cough, and Niccolò appeared in the doorway. He was keeping very quiet, thought Gina, who had assumed Jane to be alone in the flat. Suddenly a picture, of Niccolò sitting silently on his bed waiting to be summoned, like a child sent to bed without his supper, came unbidden into her head.

'Ah, goodbye,' Niccolò said, awkwardly, without moving towards her. He was dressed in a suit, but was unshaven and wore socks but no shoes.

Gina nodded back, guardedly. Then she thought of something. 'Will Beatrice's mother be coming today?' she asked. 'To get her?'

Something like alarm flickered across Niccolò's face. 'Mmm. Yes,' he said, and it was as though he was trying, not very successfully, to sound as though he was the one in control. 'We've got a lot to sort out.'

Jane snorted. 'I should think so.' She looked at Gina as though they were mothers standing over a recalcitrant child. 'All right, darling, you'd better get on with your packing.

Gina's going to miss her flight if she's not careful.' And Niccolò turned away, dismissed.

Gina had refused the offer of a lift to the airport from Frank; suddenly she was quite sure that she needed to leave the city on her own, as she had arrived, and to leave them all behind her. Now, as she walked along the cracked concrete of the railway platform at Pisa *aeroporto*, approaching the great glass doors that would admit her into the concourse, back where she had begun, Gina felt things shift; the previous week took a lurch backwards, the first step away from her into history.

Slowly Gina walked through the airport, the place of transition; she walked past the little tourist shops selling handbags and soft toys and mosaic photograph frames, paused at the café, where a plane-load of new arrivals were chattering noisily at the bar in front of a jaded-looking barman, and then drifted into a check-out queue which, as always, turned out to be the longer of the two available for her flight. At the desk far ahead of Gina an elderly couple were emptying out the contents of belt pouches and handbag in search of passports that had, they were sure, been there when they had joined the queue. She stood patiently and waited while excess baggage and vegetarians and smokers were laboriously processed and dispatched ahead of her, not yet eager to be anywhere in a hurry.

Gina's flight was not delayed, and the journey passed without incident; a plastic tray was placed in front of her and removed, then purchasable items were brought round and, on auto-pilot herself, she bought a Barbie watch, a plastic aeroplane on a stand, and a pencil case. And, as she sat in her window seat and gazed across the bed of cloud that separated her from the earth, Gina allowed the memory of her week in Florence, and most particularly of her last night, to drift like fog, like an unsettling dream, into the secret recesses of her subconscious mind. Then, when the plane landed and Gina walked out into the mild, damp, green of an English May, she breathed in the bouquet of mown grass and aviation fuel and left the memory where it lay.

As she walked through the interminable maze of carpeted, neon-lit airport corridors in England, pushing herself on through transit, baggage, customs, Gina accelerated towards her destination on legs suddenly weak with anticipation and longing until, finally, she was there, blinking in the noise and light and open space of arrivals, and there they were, too. Although it was late and they were tired, there they were; and, as she looked into their eyes, Stella and Dan and Jim and Stephen, their faces split with smiles that answered hers, she knew she was home.

Epilogue

On his arrest, Ned Duncan confessed straight away to the murders of Evelina Mwange and Natasha Julius, a confession that found corroboration on the security video handed to the police by Pierluigi; the evidence on the DVD handed to the police by Gina, although shocking, was found to be inconclusive. Duncan was found guilty and sentenced to be confined for an indefinite period at a psychiatric institution outside Naples. An appeal has been launched by his lawyers by his mother on the grounds that the conditions in which he is held are in breach of the European Convention on Human Rights, but Ned Duncan himself has shown no interest in being released.

Despite Ned Duncan's confession and subsequent conviction, the Italian police interviewed Niccolò Manzini eleven times in connection with the murders of Evelina and Natasha Julius, kerb-crawling and under-age sex offences, but were unable to find sufficient evidence to charge him with any crime. Commissions for Manzini's work dried up completely within six months of the murders and his company went into receivership shortly afterwards. Niccolò Manzini now runs an architectural practice in Malaysia, but, since a recent attempt by the Italian government to extradite him to face charges of the distribution of obscene images, his business has not been thriving.

Jane closed her cookery school one year after her separation from Niccolò Manzini, and returned to London, where her divorce settlement paid for an elegant mews house off Walton Street from which she runs an exclusive interior-design service much disapproved of by the minimalist architects whose careful lack of detail she disguises with swags and pelmets. She lives with a wealthy American lawyer seven years her junior, and she never cooks.

Mila stayed with Frank as his housekeeper for two years, until he had managed to legitimize her position in the eyes of the authorities. Equipped with a work permit and a temporary visa she found herself a job as a seamstress and a bedsit in one of the more humble suburbs of Florence, and on his eleventh birthday her son arrived from Tirana to live with her. Frank's piece exposing the traffic in women from Africa and Eastern Europe to work in the sex industry in Italy was picked up by an American cable network and Frank's editor doubled his salary. Frank is still single, but whenever Gina visits Florence she spends at least one night staying at his apartment.

Gina kept her promise, and exactly six months after she left Florence she returned with her children to visit Frances, whom they soon came to consider their surrogate grandmother. The trip became an annual tradition until, three days after her eighty-second birthday, Frances died in her sleep. In her will she left Gina her flat in the Via delle Caldaie. Gina had a fourth child at the age of forty-five, a girl she named Frances.